About Tricia Stringer

Tricia Stringer is the bestselling author of the rural romances *Queen of the Road*, *Right as Rain*, *Riverboat Point* and *Between the Vines*, and the historical saga *Heart of the Country*, the first book in the Flinders Ranges series.

Queen of the Road won the Romance Writers of Australia Romantic Book of the Year award in 2013 and *Riverboat Point* was shortlisted for the same award in 2015.

Tricia grew up on a farm in country South Australia and has spent most of her life in rural communities, as owner of a post office and bookshop, as a teacher and librarian, and now as a full-time writer. She now lives in the beautiful Copper Coast region with her husband Daryl. From here she travels and explores Australia's diverse communities and landscapes, and shares this passion for the country and its people through her stories.

For further information go to triciastringer.com or connect with Tricia on Facebook or Twitter @tricia_stringer

Also by Tricia Stringer

TRICIA STRINGER

Dust *on the* HORIZON

First Published 2016
First Australian Paperback Edition 2016
ISBN 978 1 489 22829 1

DUST ON THE HORIZON
© 2016 by Tricia Stringer
Australian Copyright 2016
New Zealand Copyright 2016

Published by
Harlequin Mira
An imprint of Harlequin Enterprises (Australia) Pty Ltd.
Level 19, 201 Elizabeth St
SYDNEY NSW 2000
AUSTRALIA

® and TM are trademarks of Harlequin Enterprises Limited or its corporate affiliates. Trademarks indicated with ® are registered in Australia, New Zealand and in other countries.

Cataloguing-in-Publication details are available from the National Library of Australia www.librariesaustralia.nla.gov.au

Printed and bound in Australia by McPherson's Printing Group

MIX
Paper | Supporting
responsible forestry
FSC® C001695

For Steven

Prologue

1868

In the bottom of the dry creek bed, the heat pressed like a weight on the motionless figure sprawled beneath the branches of the massive red gum. The sun had burned his pale skin to red and sucked the moisture from his body but the boy was still alive. He had crawled to the shade to gain some respite from the relentless rays and to conserve his energy for one last look. There was a mouthful of precious water in the bag on his hip and he was taking a gamble. At stake was his life.

He had been following the meandering creeks through the hills for three days. Each time he thought he'd found a way through, he had been confronted by steeper, more impassable hills and he had been forced to retrace his steps and take another course. The land that stretched out behind him was parched. There was little water for the few sheep that had managed to survive the blistering hot winds and evade the wild dogs.

The remaining hardy stock had become impossible to shepherd and he had given up all hope of saving any of them when, somehow, they'd ended up higher into the ranges than he'd been before. He'd been about to turn back and leave the sheep altogether when he'd found a small waterhole that hadn't dried up and his spirits had lifted.

Then, in the late afternoon, he had seen several kangaroos and a flock of screeching birds. They had to be getting water nearby. He'd left his horse to try to climb a rocky outcrop for a better view of his surroundings. A startled kangaroo had bounded away and scared his untethered horse off, with his swag, food and extra water tied to its saddle. All he had was his water flask. He'd fallen to the ground in despair, thinking it was the end. Just in front of him something sparkled. His hand curled around the rock and his eyes closed.

The sun lowered in the sky as he gathered his strength for one last attempt. He would probably never be found anyway. If he was going to die he wanted to do it looking out over this ruthless land he'd been born in and loved. He staggered to his feet and drained the last precious drop of water into his parched mouth.

Ahead of him the tall sides of the narrow gorge glowed red. The creek bed in front of him was choked with old gums, young saplings and an assortment of timber debris, washed there in some previous time of flowing water. Above him a flock of screeching birds flew in and disappeared inside the gorge.

The boy stumbled on towards the impeding bush. He clasped the rock in one hand and rubbed at his eyes with the other. Black dots swirled in front of him. He peered closer. There was a gap, a path though the saplings. He pushed on through the overhanging leaves and his tattered boots sunk into the ground. Cold registered in his seared brain. He looked down. Damp grit encased his boots. Several sets of animal tracks indented the sand.

Up ahead he glimpsed a glint but he didn't dare hope. He sucked in a feeble breath and, with a final push, surged forward.

Beneath his feet the soft sand gave way and he fell headfirst into the pool. The flock of large white birds rose from the surrounding trees screaming their protest.

On the ridge above, a shadow moved and took the shape of a man. Binda had been motionless for some time. And even though he no longer feared the figure sprawled below him, the young Aborigine had thought it best to be cautious.

Hunting alone, Binda had been terrified the day before when a huge four-legged animal had crashed through the trees like a wild monster. Once the bush around him had settled, Binda had resumed his hunt for kangaroo, only to be startled again by strange footsteps crunching on the ridge above him. Binda had followed the young white boy ever since, watching him become more and more helpless. Stories were told around the campfire about the pale-skinned men who trampled the bush and spoiled food and water with their animals and the large loads they carried but Binda had never seen one until now.

He took small silent steps down the ridge. Now that life had finally left the intruder, Binda couldn't walk away. He was curious to get a better look and he knew if he didn't move the body the rotting flesh would spoil the waterhole.

The setting sun glowed on his glossy skin as he made his way down the ridge. Once he was in the creek bed he knew he could blend with ease into the shadows if he needed to but he was no longer afraid. Binda was thinking about the elaborate story he would have to tell around the campfire. He would be able to describe in great detail what a white man looked like. He pushed through the last clinging branches at the side of the waterhole and froze. His eyes opened wide in surprise and then fear surged once again through his veins. At the edge of the pool, the sand showed the signs of the intruder but the body was gone.

One

1881

Jack Aldridge's feet left the ground and his head tilted sideways. He flew out the door with the help of strong hands on his back, and landed sprawled face first in the mud.

"Don't come back again, you black trash," Smedley's voice boomed behind him. "Unless you've got more money to lose, Jackie Boy."

Raucous laughter echoed in his ears then the door slammed shut and he was in darkness. Jack dragged himself to his feet and leaned against the slimy wooden board wall of a storage shed. He looked down at his last set of half-decent clothes. They were coated in mud and whatever other filth trickled along the lane between the storage sheds at the port. He put one dirty hand to his jaw and moved it from side to side, then he ran his tongue over his teeth. Nothing broken. He slammed his fist into the wooden wall. The pain of it barely registered.

Smedley had fleeced him. Jack could have beaten the cheating bastard to a pulp on his own but the other card players had rallied around, all whites, and one of them had a knife. Jack stood up to his full six feet and looked back at the door. He'd get Smedley another time when the man didn't have helpers. They'd cheated him of his money, beaten him up and tossed him in the street like rubbish. Hatred burned deep in his chest. It rose to the surface easily after years of being treated like something people stepped on.

Jack made his way along the lane and turned into the dark road. A fine sea mist hung in the air, enveloping Port Augusta in its salty tendrils. The shadows of the huge wool stores loomed above him, black against an even blacker sky. No moon tonight, but further down the street there was a lamp outside the Flinders Hotel. He made his way in that direction and went round the back to the stables, found a trough with some water and scrubbed his face and hands. There was nothing he could do about his clothes but at this hour of the night he doubted anyone would notice. He removed his boot and pulled out his last stash of coins; enough to buy some liquor and help him forget his useless state for a while.

When he left the hotel several hours later, the only thing he felt was the anger still smouldering in his chest. In spite of the liquor he'd swallowed his strides were steady as he made his way along the back streets to the house he hadn't seen for several years.

He stopped when he reached it. The two-storey building was made of wooden boards and had a picket fence at the front which leaned at a precarious angle. It was hard to see much about the state of the building in the darkness and no welcome light shone from the windows but he suspected nothing much would have been done to it in the four years since Ned had died.

Briefly his thoughts softened at the memory of the man who'd been the only father he'd known. He gripped the wobbly fence post and pushed the image of Ned away. In Jack's world there had never been any place for sentimentality. Ned was gone, but Jack hoped Ethel still lived here. The old woman was the reason he'd come back to the port. There had been several jobs taking him to various parts of Victoria and then back to South Australia but they hadn't lasted. Someone always found fault with his work. Now he was in desperate need of money and a place to stay. He doubted Ethel would have much cash but he was sure she could provide the information he needed to unlock another source of income for him. He stumbled on the verandah step, crouched down and felt for the rock. It was still there. He lifted it and retrieved the front door key.

It took him a moment to get the key in the lock and a jiggle to get it to turn but finally he was inside.

"Stay where you are." A bulky figure loomed from the door to his left.

"Mam, it's me."

There was a gasp. "Gawd sakes, is that you Jackie Boy?" She reached a hand towards him but he pushed past her in the narrow hallway and made for the tiny kitchen at the back of the house where he hoped there'd be a fire.

She followed him, lit a candle and held it up close to him. "What have you done to your face and what's that smell? You been rolling in cow shit, Jackie Boy?"

Anger filled Jack's brain. How he despised the name Jackie Boy. It had been used as a taunt so many times it stirred instant rage when he heard it.

"Jack," he yelled in her face. "My name is Jack."

"Settle down. I've got tenants upstairs you know. Paying customers." Ethel poked a finger in the air towards the ceiling then she poked him. "Anyway don't get yourself in a twist. It's only a term of endearment from your old mam who hasn't seen you for four years."

"You're not my mother."

Ethel pursed her lips. A small frown turned her wrinkled brow to furrows. "No, but I did my best to be one for ya and you always called me Mam. I guess you're too old for that now. Ethel will do." She turned her bulky figure and shuffled to the fire. She was even bigger than she'd been the last time he'd seen her and her movements weren't as sure. She poked at the fire and added more wood. "Would you like a cup of tea?"

He slumped into a chair at the battered table that wobbled unevenly as he placed his elbows on it. "I'd rather some of your whiskey."

Ethel straightened and put her hands to her hips. She wore a loose gown over her nightdress and a cap on her head. She looked like a ship under full sail. "Would ya now?" She studied him closely in the dim light. Then she grinned. "Well I wouldn't be past having one myself. A bit of a nightcap to ease me aching bones."

She put two mugs on the table and went to the cupboard built into the corner of the room. He watched as she extracted an earthenware pot and poured some pale liquid from it into the mugs. Ethel and Ned had made their own brew for as long as Jack could remember. They'd run a pub in the hills behind Port Augusta when he'd first gone to live with them as a boy of nine. When that closed they'd moved to the Port but they'd never had much success there. Ned had died a poor man.

Ethel sat opposite him and took a swig from her mug. He did the same. The liquid was smooth as silk and warmed him all the way to his stomach.

"You haven't lost your touch." Jack wiped the back of his hand across his mouth. The smell of something rotten lingered in his nostrils. He'd need to wash, clothes and all. He'd learned early that people were quick to judge an ill-dressed unkempt half-caste, as they called him. Jack liked to keep himself tidy.

"Ned was better at brewing beer. I've always been able to turn my hand to a good drop of the stronger stuff."

Jack glowered at her across the table and drained his mug. He put it back on the table in front of her. "I think I need to test it further."

She eyed him a moment then poured him some more. "What's brought you back here after all this time with never a word?"

"I'm a bit down on my luck."

Ethel hissed through her teeth. "If you've come here looking for money you can forget it. You can see this place is falling down around my ears. My lodgers barely pay enough to keep me clothed and fed without having any to give away to the likes of you."

"You owe me."

She snorted. "What for?"

"All the years I worked for you for nothing."

"Nothing." Ethel's beady eyes bulged. "Ned and me put a roof over your head, fed ya and clothed ya. That's not nothing."

Jack felt the fire from the whiskey spread to his arms. He clenched his fists as her words continued to pour out.

"You always did have ideas above your station. We only took ya in 'cause we felt sorry for ya. Your poor mother came to us begging for help to look after you and your little brother. When they took sick and the little one died and she knew she was going too, your mother implored us to look after ya. We only did it for her. Dulcie was a good sort. Her downfall was taking up with that scoundrel of a man. His poor wife never knew he had a black family hidden in his hut in the hills behind the pub. Didn't think we knew about it, Ned and me, but we did." She leaned across the table and smirked. "Not only are you a bastard, Jackie Boy, but you're a black bastard."

Jack leapt up from his chair, knocking it to the floor. He leaned across and slapped Ethel's smug face. The shock of it silenced her. She put a pudgy hand to her cheek. Jack glowered at her. How many times had the reverse happened? She never let Ned see how she treated the boy they'd taken in but she was always quick to dish out a slap or a backhander if she was displeased with Jack about something. That had been a regular occurrence.

"I always knew you'd turn on us one day." Ethel hissed at him. "I'm just glad me poor Ned isn't here to see it after all we've done for—"

"Shut your flapping mouth." He raised his hand again.

She kept her piggy gaze on him but she remained silent.

"I need a bath and somewhere to sleep." He reached across the table and felt some small satisfaction as she jerked back. He picked up the pot of whiskey and poured himself a mug full then he sat down. "But first I want to know about my father."

"He's dead."

Jack had always been told that but he'd held a hope that somehow it wasn't true. "How can you be sure?"

"He wasn't in much of a state when they found his body but my dear Ned recognised his clothes and his hair. There's no doubt it was him. He was a nasty piece of work, Jackie … Jack." Ethel drained the last of her liquor and plonked her mug on the table. "Better for everyone he was dead."

Jack wasn't so sure. He had vague happy memories of his mother, his baby brother and the white man who used to visit them at the hut in the hills. They were all dead now but there was still another side of the family he knew nothing about.

"What was his name?"

"What does it matter? You have a name."

Jack did. He'd been given the name Aldridge, same as Ned and Ethel, but he needed a name if he was to track down his father's family.

"He had a wife. Not my mother, a white wife. She was the woman he implored to help him when my uncles dragged him away."

Ethel's eyes widened. "Were'd ya hear that? You were too young to remember what happened."

"I was nine when my father died. Before that I grew up in two places, I lived in the bush with my mother's black family and a wooden hut when my white father visited." He drew himself up and looked across the table but he was looking through Ethel rather than at her. "I remember my uncles being angry with my mother and coming to take my father away. I thought they were just going to beat him. Teach him a lesson."

"Oh, they did that all right. Both his legs were broken. He was probably still alive when they finished with him but he had no way to get out of the creek where he was found."

Jack's eyes refocused on Ethel. "What was his name?"

"What does it matter?" She slapped the table. "I told ya he's dead."

"But he had a wife, perhaps other children."

"His wife didn't want to know about you. She was a lady and he kept your mother and his bastard offspring a secret from her."

Once more Jack leapt up. Ethel cowered back but he was around the table with one hand over her mouth and the other at her neck before she could get up.

"What was his name?" he hissed in her ear.

Ethel's eyes bulged. He lifted his fingers away from her mouth and leaned in closer.

"Wiltshire," she gasped. "His name was Septimus Wiltshire."

Two

Henry Wiltshire stepped off the verandah and smiled up at the newly painted sign, *Hawker General Trader & Forwarding Agent*. He had wanted his name on the shop front but his mother had insisted on Hawker, the name of the town which in turn had been named after well-known grazier and member of parliament George Charles Hawker. The shop name had been a sticking point but Harriet had a large share of money invested in the enterprise so he'd let her have her way on this.

Over two hundred and fifty miles from Adelaide, Hawker had been proclaimed on the first of July the previous year and was surveyed on a pronounced bend in the railway line which was to extend north-west. The original intention had been to build only a railway station but Henry had great expectations for Hawker already. The town would become a major service centre for both the railway and the pastoralists and farmers who took up land all around it and his shop and services would be in great demand.

The sun beat down on his hatless head as he looked left and then right. There was no-one in sight. Nothing but dust moved along the road. None of the wagons that usually rolled past to and from the train station, and even the constant sawing and hammering from the building across the road had ceased.

It was a surprising lull in a town where constant movement of wagons, teamsters and camel trains was the norm. The distant stations Henry had only heard of, with names such as Wilpena, Holowiliena and Arkaba, made use of the rail that extended to Hawker and was to continue further. The town itself was being constructed on a flat dusty plain but in the distance to the north a huge mountain range rose into the sky. It had been named Flinders Ranges. Today its grey heights shimmered in the heat haze, a huge barrier to the nothingness beyond. A trickle of sweat slithered down Henry's back. It really did seem like he was at the end of the world but it was here he would make his mark.

He took a crisp white handkerchief from his pocket, patted the back of his neck then went back to the shade of the verandah roof. From there he slid a sideways glance across the empty space next to his shop, to the wooden structure that housed his opposition. Not a soul stirred there either. Henry's stone establishment was a much better building than Garrat's. People would flock in for his superior goods when things picked up. He tucked the handkerchief back in his pocket and brushed down his dark suit, determined to keep up an appearance in spite of the late summer heat

He opened the door to his shop. A bell tinkled but otherwise there was no sound. Henry frowned, pulled out his fob watch and checked the time, then he shut the door firmly which produced another sharper tingle from the bell. There was a movement from behind the heavy velvet curtain separating the shop from the living quarters at the back.

His pretty young wife walked unhurriedly to the counter. "Oh, it's only you, Henry," she said.

"I hope you will be more prompt when we have customers, Catherine." He looked pointedly at his watch.

"Of course, Henry." She smiled at him and fanned herself with her hand. "But in this heat no-one wants to go shopping."

Henry put away his watch. Her smile always charmed him. She was right, but he needed her to help him if they were to build a strong business in this new community.

"If you're staying in now, I'll go back to my sewing."

Henry watched as she stepped back behind the curtain. Catherine came from a wealthy family of strong religious faith. She was an appropriate partner for someone of Henry's standing and he had been both pleased and surprised when she had consented to be his wife.

Soon after their marriage they had made the journey from Adelaide, by train, to the new township of Hawker. Henry smiled at the thought of the large sum of money the father of a fourth daughter had been prepared to pay to get her off his hands. His new father-in-law had been very generous but there had been quite a to-do when Henry had announced where they would be living.

Town was a grand word for the straggle of makeshift premises people lived in and did business from but Hawker was just starting out and Henry's was only one of the new permanent buildings recently erected or in the process of being built.

He had come to the town last year with money to bid for land. He'd had to go as high as £100. His mother had been worried but he had convinced her he'd secured the best site. It was in a prime position facing the railway, and close to the station. Henry had conducted his business from a temporary dwelling while overseeing the building of his premises.

Hawker was the town of the future. Henry knew all the farmers and pastoralists would need quality goods and someone to sell wool and grain on their behalf and who knew what else in a town that was just starting out. Times could be fickle on the land and when they couldn't pay with money he was prepared to give them credit. He looked out the window across the dusty road to the flat brown terrain that stretched to the distant ranges. There was barely any bush let alone trees like those that had dotted the creeks they'd crossed on the journey from Adelaide.

Henry gave a brief thought to the capital of the state of South Australia. The original plan had been to build a business then sell it, using the profits to start a shop in Adelaide. This was what his mother and Catherine's parents believed but since moving to Hawker and discovering the potential here, he was full of optimism. Not only was he going to build a shopping empire, but he was planning to acquire land, lots of land. Their parents would all be happy once they saw how well he would provide for his wife and their future family.

Catherine sat back in the chair and undid the top button of her high-necked blouse. She picked up her handiwork but instead of stitching she used it to fan herself. She hated the heat. The heat was why she'd been slow to respond to the bell. She had heard the first tinkle but had been fumbling to do up her buttons. Henry was very particular that they should present a decorous picture to their customers.

When they'd first moved in to the tiny accommodation behind the shop she hadn't liked it at all. Not that she dared say anything to Henry. Then last night he had surprised her with a promise to build her a grand home once their business was established, a place that would befit their status and acknowledge their prosperity. She'd wondered at that. It made their life here sound more per-manent and yet Henry had said they would only be in Hawker for a few years until they had enough money to set up a fine business in Adelaide like his mother's.

She sighed and looked around her little parlour. It was the room that led directly to the shop and was the only place Henry had to conduct his business. She had to have it prepared at all times in case he needed to use it.

Their two comfortable chairs were squeezed into one corner where she was sitting now. Under the window was their small dining table. There was room for the two of them but if they had guests they would have to rearrange the room and move the table to accommodate them. Not that it was likely they would entertain in the near future. Henry did not feel there were many people of their social standing in the district and few women came to the shop.

A large dresser filled one wall. It contained all the beautiful china and glass they had been given for wedding presents. A chiming clock, all the way from Germany, sat on top. It had belonged to his mother. Beside it was a small picture of Harriet. She glared out at Catherine. Harriet was not an easy woman to like. Catherine was sure she didn't live up to her mother-in-law's expectations of a suitable wife for Henry. She turned away from the prying eyes.

On the wall opposite the window was Henry's desk where he did his paperwork and conducted his forwarding business and next to it was a small cabinet where he kept an assortment of ointments and pills in little bottles and jars. His mother hadn't wanted him to sell them. Catherine had overheard the conversation between mother and son. It had surprised Catherine to learn her mother-in-law had once travelled the land in a wagon selling goods. There was nothing about Harriet's manner that suggested she'd ever lived such a basic existence. Evidently Henry's father had run into a bit of trouble with some of the pills he'd sold and Harriet hadn't wanted her son to jeopardise his new business. Henry thought people in the isolated town would welcome some basic medicinal assistance. They had compromised by keeping the pills and ointments in the living room and not having them on show in the shop. Henry sold them discreetly.

Above his desk hung a beautifully framed portrait of them on their wedding day. Henry was not usually extravagant but he had thought it fitting they should have the photograph to mark the occasion.

Beside that was the door into their bedroom. Catherine felt the heat rise in her cheeks. They had been married for five months now but she still could not get used to having to share her bed with Henry. Her mother had explained to her the relations he would expect of his wife but Catherine had still found his attentions vulgar.

Some nights once the lamp was out Henry would cover her mouth with a long sloppy kiss until she thought she would not be able to breathe. At the same time he would squeeze her breasts tightly and press his body hard against her. Then he would pull up her nightgown and plunge into her recklessly for a few minutes, moaning loudly. Just as suddenly as he had begun, he would stop, flop onto his back and go to sleep. It was the only time Catherine ever saw him look untidy. The heat and dust of their new home only added to her distaste. Thankfully Henry did not approach her in this way very often.

On the back wall was the door through to the tiny kitchen and washroom. Catherine could not tolerate going out there until she had to. The wood stove raised the temperature unbearably during the day. She rarely felt like eating at midday but Henry always wanted his meals on time. He was happy with cold meat and pickles for his lunch but liked a hot meal at night. Catherine dreaded the thought of cooking the fatty meat hanging in the kitchen safe. Just lately even the smell of it made her nauseous. The sudden tune from the clock made her jump. Henry would be expecting his luncheon in fifteen minutes.

A loaded wagon rolled past outside, drawing Henry's gaze to the window. He was about to put out his *Closed for Midday Meal* sign but he would remain open if he had customers. He crossed to the window and peered out at the wagon, which had pulled up further along the road in front of the railway station. A man jumped down and brushed at his clothes sending up a cloud of dust. Probably making a delivery.

Henry dismissed the man as of no consequence then remained fixed to the spot as he saw bundles moving in the back of the wagon, taking the shape of children. Suddenly a black man appeared from the other side of the wagon. He was wearing a battered hat like the other man but the clothes on the Aborigine were much too loose and hung from his lean frame. Henry watched in astonishment as together the two men lifted down five children, three white and two black. The oldest Aboriginal child was a girl by the look of her clothes and she hefted the smallest white child to her hip.

"Well I never," Henry muttered.

The group huddled together listening to something the white man was saying. Henry scanned the wagon again expecting a woman to appear from the load as the children had but there was no sign of an adult female. Just as well, the kind of woman who would produce these children should be kept out of sight of polite society.

He glanced behind him in case Catherine should suddenly appear. He had hoped there would be a few more women in the town by now but after another dry season, trade was slow and the town hadn't boomed quite as quickly as he had expected.

The tall man in charge of the group outside bent and brushed a hand over the fair curls of the young boy beside him. Maybe this man was one of the farmers still clinging to the land. When Henry had made his first trip to Hawker, he'd crossed the Willochra Plains where he'd heard about farmers raising bumper wheat crops in magnificent chocolate soil. All he'd seen were downcast men with ragtag families barely hanging onto land that was dust as far as the eye could see. That was over a year ago and things had only got worse for the farmers since then. He read the defeat in their eyes when they came to his shop and he'd been astute enough to acquire any goods and chattels they'd wanted to sell that were still worth anything. Just last week he'd acquired a piece of land at what he believed was a mere pittance of what it would be worth again in the future. Times would improve again, he was sure of it.

The group in the street split up. The tall white man strode towards the railway station and the Aborigine was leading the children towards Henry's shop.

Henry let out a low growl. "Oh no you don't."

He opened the door a crack, slid his arm out to attach the *Closed* sign then firmly shut the door and drew the bolt. He wasn't fussed about whose money he took but from the look of this lot they had little and he wasn't giving credit to a black man. Mr Garrat could serve them in his little general store. There was some custom Henry wasn't prepared to accept.

The clock in the parlour chimed and he took out his watch again, twelve midday exactly. He replaced the watch, brushed his hand down his lapels and made his way to the parlour. All thoughts of the rabble outside were dismissed as he anticipated the meal ahead and the appointments with pastoralists he had booked for later in the afternoon.

Catherine had run out of jobs to do in the shop and had welcomed the tinkle of the bell signalling customers. Now, from her position behind the counter, she tried to keep the smile from her lips as she watched the young native girl stick out her hip and heft the small child higher. The little girl in her arms was obviously heavy but she wouldn't put the child down and, to add to her load, on her other side she clasped the hand of another little girl. The neatly clothed dark man had removed his hat and stood just inside the door. He didn't make eye contact with Catherine but murmured the occasional instruction to the two older boys who were also part of the group but only looked to be about five or six.

What a collection they were. The two boys were about the same height but one was fair and the other as black as the night. The native girl was the tallest and obviously the oldest of all the children. She kept her eyes lowered but Catherine couldn't help but stare at her glossy black hair that fell in tight curls to her shoulders. Her skin was also very dark; a striking contrast to the two little girls in her charge.

Catherine glanced behind her where she could hear the murmur of voices coming from the parlour. Thank goodness Henry hadn't long started his meeting with his last appointment for the day. She knew he wouldn't approve of the customers that had just filed into their shop but what he didn't know wouldn't hurt.

Unsure if the natives would understand her, Catherine addressed the white boy. "Can I help you?" she said.

He snapped his clear blue eyes towards her and opened his mouth then closed it again.

"They need hats."

The native girl spoke so softly Catherine barely heard her.

"What kind?" Catherine turned to the girl.

"Father said I could choose my own, Mary." The white boy finally found his voice.

"They all need hats." Mary's English was stilted, a little louder this time. "And William has to pick something broad and sturdy." She sent a hard look in the young boy's direction then looked back at the floor.

William opened his mouth. There was a shuffle of feet from the man at the door and once again the boy closed his mouth without speaking.

Catherine really didn't know what to make of this strange little family. She wondered if the man at the door could be father to them all and if so, did he have two wives? She felt heat flush her cheeks at the thought.

"We can pay." Mary lifted her dark gaze to Catherine as if daring her to say otherwise.

Catherine clasped her hands together tightly, then released them. It was none of her business how this family came to be, but the shop was hers to run. Henry had made it quite clear he wanted her to take charge when he was not available and she was very keen to do so. It was pleasing to have something to do other than manage their tiny house and good to have people in here after a very quiet week. And one thing she did have was an assortment of hats. Certainly some for the older children although she wasn't sure about the youngest. Maybe they could improvise.

"They're over here." Catherine stepped purposefully around the counter and made for the wooden shelves that lined the side wall.

Henry had been aware of the sound of chattering voices as he'd finalised his business with the man sitting opposite him. He was pleased there were customers in his shop and hoped they were spending up big, although the commissions he'd made this afternoon more than made up for lack of sales in his shop.

He stood and shook the hand of the tall pastoralist who'd just sold a large consignment of wool. Henry had inspected the samples Joseph Baker had brought in and if the rest was as good they both stood to make a lot of money. Wool prices were on the rise again and while wheat farmers were doing it hard, those pastoralists who'd managed to survive the droughts, wild dogs and grasshopper plagues of the last few years could look forward to some better times.

"Your wife hasn't travelled with you today, Mr Baker?"

"It's a long journey. She stayed at home with our youngest child."

"You are most fortunate. I hope that my wife and I will be so blessed in the near future."

"Clara is not up to the travel." Baker began to pack his samples into his calico bag. "She's been a little poorly of late. Suffers from headaches in this heat."

Henry glanced at the cupboard beside his desk. This was his chance to ingratiate himself further with this welcome customer. "Perhaps I can offer some assistance." He pulled a key on a chain from his pocket, unlocked the cabinet and withdrew a small glass bottle. "I have a remedy that I keep for special customers. This tonic is a certain cure for headache, loss of appetite and low spirits. It's quite safe to take."

Baker looked at the bottle Henry offered with interest.

Henry jiggled the brown vial. "Please take it, Joseph. My gift for your wife."

Joseph accepted the bottle. "There's not a lot of female company in our part of the world. Perhaps my wife will accompany me one day."

"I'm sure Catherine would make her most welcome and be glad of the company. As you say, there are not a lot of ... suitable companions here."

Baker gave him an appraising look then pushed the small bottle into his pocket.

Henry studied Baker as he packed away the last of his samples. Joseph was obviously a hard worker with good prospects; a fine fellow to have on-side. He was tall like Henry and despite his work clothes he had a fine air about him, belying an inner strength. A small battered leather pouch that had been in the wool bag still sat to one side of the table. As Joseph picked it up, it fell apart in his hand and a rock landed on the table. The stone had many sides and looked rough and dirty but where the sunlight reached it from the window it sparkled.

"That looks unusual." Henry reached for the stone but Joseph snatched it up.

"It needs a new bag."

"Maybe we have something suitable in the shop."

Henry turned to lead the way out. What he saw when he pulled back the curtain made him forget his manners completely, along with any thought of the fine leather pouches he'd recently stocked. He let the heavy fabric drop behind him to shield Baker as he hurried forward.

"What are you doing, Catherine?" he snapped. The scene before him was scandalous and his wife appeared happy to be a part of it. Henry clenched his fists as he strode around the counter.

Catherine lowered the little girl she'd been holding to the floor. The child looked ridiculous in a straw hat that was too big and had been tied down with a length of ribbon. There were more children scattered around the room and he thought they looked a lot like the collection he'd seen pour out of the wagon earlier today. They all wore a hat from his shop except for the oldest native girl who was holding a roll of ribbon and they all had something in their mouths. Sweets, he presumed. There were several jars on the counter with their lids off.

"What are these vagabonds doing here?" Henry's voice was a low growl and he whipped the ribbon from the black girl's hands and the hat from the head of the black boy beside her.

Catherine crossed quickly to his side. "Their father wants them to have hats, dearest, and a few other items."

A movement across the room drew Henry's look from his wife's worried smile. He gasped. There by the door stood the native, surrounded by neatly stacked items from the shop. So he was the father. What would Harriet say, or even Catherine's parents, if they knew he was allowing her to mix with natives?

Henry could feel throbbing in his temple. He pulled a handkerchief from his pocket and mopped his brow. Outside the late-afternoon sun beat down on a clear still day, but inside the heat was oppressive. "Who's paying for all this?" he growled.

"I am."

They all turned to look at Joseph Baker. He had come from the other room and was now standing tall behind the counter as if he owned the place.

"I believe the business we've done today will more than cover any items my family needs, Mr Wiltshire."

Henry noted the formal use of his name. When he'd shaken hands with Joseph Baker ten minutes ago they'd been on first name terms.

"Your family?" Henry looked from the other man's unreadable expression to the children scattered around the shop then back at the tall man he'd just done business with. "I don't understand ..." He couldn't equate the tidy-looking man with the dusty ruffian he'd seen by the wagon earlier today but now that he thought about it they were both extremely tall and, if he looked closely, Joseph Baker's clothes did have a well-worn appearance.

"There's nothing for you to understand, Mr Wiltshire ... other than you have customers." Joseph looked past Henry. "Did you pick a hat for me, son?"

"Yes, Father." The young fair-haired boy stepped carefully past Henry and offered up a hat he'd been holding behind his back.

Joseph pressed one of Henry's best broad-brimmed felt hats onto his head.

"Perfect," he said and moved around the counter to the shop side which was suddenly getting very full.

Henry cleared his throat to speak but Joseph cut him off.

"I am sure your wife has made a note of our purchases." He lifted his hat and smiled widely at Catherine.

Henry felt the throb again in his temple as he saw the return smile and flush of his wife's cheeks.

"I have, Mr Baker," she said.

Once again Baker turned to Henry. His lips were curved up in a smile but his blue eyes showed no amusement. "Then you can deduct them from what you owe me." He turned his back on Henry. "Come on everyone, we have to get this loaded. There's a long journey ahead of us."

Henry stepped forward then stepped back. He wasn't sure whether to offer his assistance or not. In the end he took up a position by the door so he could be sure of what they took from his shop. He had thought the mild-mannered Joseph Baker to be someone he could perhaps include one day as a friend. During their business discussions he'd learned only a little about the man who didn't have as much front and swagger as the previous two pastoralists he'd dealt with. They'd been only too happy to tell Henry how well they were doing. Baker, on the other hand, had been much more circumspect. He and his father ran sheep properties two days' wagon ride from Hawker and sounded as if they had adapted their methods to survive the harsh conditions of the Flinders Ranges.

Now, as Henry watched the disparate group of men and children load their wagon with food and goods, he realised that he must have mistaken Baker's aloofness for shame. After all, no decent man would include the natives and bring them in to town as if they were his family. Henry was appalled to think he'd entertained the notion of having Catherine befriend Baker's wife. Now he was thankful that Mrs Baker had remained on the property with their youngest child. Was it black or white he wondered?

The last of the items were loaded and Baker called from the wagon.

"I'll be back in a few months for the rest of my money."

Henry scowled as the man gave him barely a nod then urged his horses forward. A lot could happen in a few months. Henry watched the wagon rumble away, loaded with the ragtag rabble of humanity perched amongst his goods. He doubted Baker was the astute businessman Henry had first thought him to be. And there was no way Henry would allow him to bring those black people into his shop again. Deduct it from what he was owed indeed. By the time Joseph Baker came back he would find dealings would be very different.

The bell gave a harsh jingle over his head as Henry shut the door. He turned to find no sign of Catherine. The curtain to the parlour remained perfectly still.

Three

William Baker creased his young face into a frown and peered back along the street from under the brim of his new hat. He was perched on the back of the load as the wagon rolled and lurched away from the shop with the strange man. It was a warm day and he was thankful for his new hat. He only wished he could have had the new leather belt to replace the rope that held up his trousers. He'd seen it hanging in the shop, a deep rich brown with a fine buckle, but his father had been in such a rush to get away William hadn't been able to show him.

Gradually the buildings grew smaller and were finally lost from his sight amongst the trees. This was only the third time William could remember coming to town and the excitement he had felt was replaced by a niggling disquiet. That man at the shop had been angry about something. He'd treated them as if they were thieves but William knew his father had money to pay for what they'd taken.

William didn't know what to make of it but he had the distinct impression it was something to do with Mary. It couldn't be her brother, Joe. He was so quiet and never did a thing wrong but William had seen the dislike on the man's face when he'd snatched the roll of ribbon from Mary's hands. Not that it bothered William that much. He wasn't fond of Mary either. She was six years his senior and often given the task of looking after the children. William was the oldest of his family and didn't like being bossed by Mary, but what could she have done to make the man at the Hawker shop dislike her and then spread his disdain to all of them?

William turned to look at her, tucked in behind the seat with his little sisters, Violet and Esther, one under each of her arms. She cared for them as if they were her own children which he knew was a big help to his mother who had his baby brother to look after as well as all the cooking and cleaning and sewing and sometimes even helping his father with the sheep. At that moment Mary lifted her eyes from the children to him. She held his gaze for an instant then lowered her head as Violet babbled something. William continued to watch her. Something had happened in Hawker that he didn't understand but he was determined to work it out.

Joseph raised his head from the bag he'd folded into a pillow as the smell of smoke wafted over him. Binda was at the fire and something was cooking. The sun was a golden glow along the edge of the ranges and the early morning sky a soft blue. Not a breath of wind to ruffle the leaves of the tall gums or the smaller blue bush they'd camped amongst. Joseph climbed out of his swag and stretched. He'd obviously fallen into a deep sleep and remained in the same position. He felt stiff and sore as if he'd been a week on a horse. There was no movement from the wagon where the children were sleeping under canvas, the girls amongst the supplies on the tray and the boys on the ground below. He joined Binda at the campfire.

"You getting old." Binda passed him a mug of black tea. "Sleeping in."

"I was tired."

"That's what you get, sitting up late, thinking too much."

Joseph glanced at the man beside him. Binda poked at the fire. He rarely stared anyone in the face but there was little the native didn't see. Joseph took a sip of the warm tea and wrapped his fingers around the tin cup. He'd sat up well after the children had been tucked under their blankets and he'd heard Binda's snores from beyond the wagon. Yesterday's events had given him much to think about.

After they'd left Hawker they'd made good time to the first creek. Their second wagon, the one with the bullocks they'd used to cart the wool to the railway station, waited where they'd left it the day before. Then the two men had taken a wagon each like they had on the way in to town. Binda drove the smaller wagon loaded with goods and children, pulled by the horses. He didn't like horses but he liked bullocks even less. They'd made it to the next creek just before dark and had set up their makeshift camp. The two little girls had been full of excitement at all they'd seen on their first trip to town but the rest of them, children and men, had gone about their jobs with little conversation, so different from their excitement on the night before they got to Hawker.

"Maybe my family should stay home next time you go to town."

Binda's words echoed the sadness Joseph was feeling. His friend was wearing trousers but his scarred chest was bare. Joseph knew he would have only just pulled the pants on. Binda would have been as good as naked when he hunted the small animal that was cooking over the fire.

Joseph stared into his cup hoping some wisdom would suddenly emerge from the murky liquid. "I'm sorry for what happened yesterday."

"It was not your doing."

Joseph looked up. "You should be able to go where you like without fear of persecution."

"Some people are like that. I keep away from them. I think it is best we don't come with you to town anymore."

"It's preposterous." Joseph tossed the remains of his tea at the fire sending out a short hiss and a small billow of smoke.

"Hey you silly whitefella. Don't go messing with my fire. Didn't I teach you that lesson long ago?"

Joseph gave Binda a playful slap on the arm. "Yes, right after I scared your shiny black backside. You thought a white monster was going to eat you for dinner."

"Some monster. You collapsed at my feet, weak as newborn joey. It took this hunter a lot of work to save your sorry life."

"Hunter! The way you crashed through the trees you were never going to catch anything."

"Except one crazy white boy."

A small branch rolled from the fire sending up a crackle of sparks. Joseph leaned forward to push it back and his small leather pouch slipped from his pocket.

Binda nodded towards the tattered pouch. "You still carry the rock."

Joseph picked it up and pushed it deep down into his trouser pocket. "My lucky charm. First I found this funny rock, then I found water, then I found you."

Binda gave a soft snort. "Your memory's not so good nowadays either."

They both smiled at the recollection of their first meeting. Joseph had been only fifteen and almost lifeless by the water-hole he'd discovered in the gorge above Smith's Ridge. Binda had thought he was dead and had come to claim him as some kind of trophy. He'd made so much noise it had roused Joseph who had managed to hide himself in the bushes.

Joseph laughed. "That was one terrified face you had when I came out of the bush."

"Yes, you were so scary you fell at my feet." Binda's warm chuckle joined his.

Joseph stood and clapped a hand on his friend's shoulder. He was a good head taller than Binda, the sun-browned skin of his hand a stark contrast to the native's glossy black skin.

"I'm sorry our friendship has caused you pain."

"It is not only the white fellow who can't see change. My father would have killed you that day, finished you off."

Joseph remembered Yardu's simmering anger like it was yesterday. Binda had carried him over his shoulders back to their camp and Yardu had waved a spear at Joseph's half-alive form. Binda had defied his father, nursed Joseph back to life and taken him home to his grateful family at Wildu Creek a week later. Binda had been made so welcome he'd been a regular visitor until he'd eventually joined Joseph when he'd taken over neighbouring Smith's Ridge.

"After meeting that bigot of a man, Wiltshire, I can see why your father might have wanted to kill me." Joseph tapped the hard shell of the damper on the edge of the coals.

"You should make peace with that man."

"Wiltshire? You are jesting, aren't you? I'll be back to collect my money. After that he can rot in hell before I darken his door again."

"He is not a man to make an enemy of."

Joseph was going to ask Binda what he meant but they were interrupted by a piercing wail. Esther was awake. She sat up from her bed on the wagon rubbing at her eyes, her short tufts of hair sticking out every which way.

Joseph strode over to her and plucked her up into the air. "Good morning, sunshine."

Not to be deterred by her father's bright mood, she scrunched her little face up tight and let out another wail. Groans came from the boys underneath the wagon.

"Hush, little one." Joseph tried to soothe the child. He wrinkled his nose at the strong smell of urine.

Mary appeared at his side and reached for the little girl.

"Thank you, Mary." He was happy to relinquish his daughter to Mary's capable care. Esther was never a happy riser.

Violet stirred and sat up. Although similar in looks she was the exact opposite in temperament to her little sister. Immediately her face, pink from sleep, lit up at the sight of her father. He lifted her from the covers and she reached her arms around his neck. He kissed her cheek. Esther's wails could still be heard from the direction of the creek. While she was often full of complaints, Violet was the opposite: always smiling, happy with everyone and everything. The little girl cuddled her warm body against him.

At least her mother would be getting a break at home with only baby Robert to look after. He frowned at the thought of Clara. She hadn't appeared to be very well the last few weeks. She'd reassured him she was in perfect health but she looked tired. More so than usual. He thought of the bottle of tonic Wiltshire had pushed on him. Joseph would happily have tossed it away but maybe it was just what Clara needed.

"Food's ready."

At Binda's call the two young boys crawled out from under the wagon, jostling each other for first place. Mary came back with a cleaner, calmer Esther.

"Ladies first," Joseph said, ruffling each boy's head of hair as he passed. He noticed a scowl on William's face as he watched Mary take enough meat and damper for herself and the two little girls.

Joseph sat Violet beside her on the ground and turned in time to see William push young Joe aside to reach for some food. The boys were a similar height even though Joe was two years older than William.

"I should go before you," William growled.

"William." The boy looked up at his father's call. "Where are your manners? No need for pushing and shoving. There's enough for everyone. Now you can wait until we've all taken some before you help yourself."

William glared at his father but stepped back. Joe grinned and took a helping of the food. Joseph followed and insisted Binda do the same before William could take a share.

Joseph sat next to Binda. "Good food, thank you. We're all grateful for your cooking skills."

"Mary made the damper." Binda nodded to his daughter who kept her head down, encouraging Esther and Violet to eat.

Joseph glanced over at his son who was sitting slightly apart from the other children, his head bent low over his tin plate. "Looks like Esther's not the only one who woke up grumpy this morning."

"He's not a little boy anymore." Binda kept his gaze on his food.

"He's not so old he can be too big for his boots."

"Town is very different to the bush."

"If that's what he learns from a trip to town he can stay home next time."

"You know better than anyone, my friend, you cannot stop change and everyone deals with change in a different way."

Joseph took another mouthful of food and watched his unhappy son while he thought on Binda's words.

William's eyelids fluttered and he jolted awake. Once more he was sitting on the back of the wagon, dangling his legs over the end. They'd been on the move since breakfast and the sun was well past its zenith. His stomach rumbled. He'd only picked at his food after his father's telling off. He wished now he'd eaten it all. When the sun had been at its highest point Mary had offered him a piece of one of the oranges they'd bought in Hawker. He'd ignored her and turned his back on her but not before he'd seen the smile on her lips. When he'd glanced back she was gone, easily moving faster than the wagon to climb back into the smaller cart in front.

The sound of sheep bleating drew his attention forward. They were still half a day's travel from their own boundary so these were not Smith's Ridge stock. His father called the bullocks to stop and the wagon slowly rolled to a halt. William climbed higher on the pile of canvas-covered building materials that had replaced the wool in the wagon, for a better view. A small mob of sheep was being herded towards them by two men on horses. William's father moved his horse close to the front of the wagon where Joe was perched.

William could see his father's back was ramrod straight. The sheep fanned out around them and kept moving forward. Joseph studied them then lifted his head as the men passed Binda and the girls on the lead cart with barely a glance and stopped beside the bullocks.

"Hello, Joseph." The bigger man lifted his broad black hat slightly, to reveal his thatch of red hair. William recognised him. Ellis Prosser, the owner of Prosser's Run, the property they were crossing. He wore his trademark leather vest and the veins on his exposed arms that he crossed loosely over the saddle were knotted like thick rope.

"Ellis." Joseph inclined his head stiffly to the first man and then the other.

"Been to town?" Prosser looked from Joe seated at the front of the wagon up to William. His eyes were dark and his lips curled up in a tight grin under his pencil moustache. "I see you've got your tribe with you."

"My family and friends."

Prosser's lip curled up in a sneer. "That what you call them? No doubt there'll be brindle to go with the black and white soon enough."

William could see his father's hands grip the reins tightly but he didn't say a word. Prosser's piercing gaze swept over William and then back to Joe. William felt his cheeks burn. It was the second time in two days that he'd felt uncomfortable being seen with Binda and his children.

"I see you're shifting some sheep." Joseph jerked his head over his shoulder.

"We are."

"You've checked they're all yours?"

Prosser walked his horse closer to Joseph's so their faces were barely a yard apart. "Are you accusing me of something?"

"Not at all." Joseph met his look. "I found a fence down."

"That's the trouble with fences. They need constant upkeep. I prefer shepherds to keep an eye on my stock." Prosser glanced over his shoulder to where Binda sat on the stationary cart. "Ones I can trust. Maybe you need to think about the colour of the skin you employ."

"Fences save a lot of trouble," Joseph said. "I hear you've had a problem with some sheep from neighbouring properties getting mixed up with yours. Maybe you need to think about investing in fences."

"Waste of money. My shepherds keep my sheep together."

"As long as none of them are mine."

William could see Prosser's eyes glittering back at his father. The other rider, one of Prosser's shepherds, Mr Swan, brought his horse up on the other side of his boss.

"These sheep all bear the mark from Prosser's Run," Prosser snarled.

"I'm sure they do."

"Then what is your concern, Baker?"

"No concerns. Just a neighbourly chat." Joseph lifted his hat. "Good day to you." He urged his horse and his bullocks forward. Binda had already set the horse and cart in motion.

William let himself slide down the canvas as the cart lurched forward. He positioned himself so his legs dangled over the back again. His stomach grumbled but the sound was lost in the rumble of the wheels over the rough ground. He still couldn't quite put his finger on his discomfort. Nothing had been said exactly but an unspoken conversation had taken place between his father and Mr Prosser. One William didn't understand. He watched Prosser and his man until they were no longer visible and continued to watch the spot between the trees where they had disappeared until it dwindled from his sight. His stomach churned, empty except for the spreading unease.

Four

Henry looked out his shop window at the barren landscape with not a tree to soften the view. A camel train made its way steadily along the road, each animal loaded with large wooden sleepers tied either side for the journey to the railhead stretching north.

Across the road the new stone building that was to be a butcher shop was nearing completion and next to it a smaller wooden building housed Mr Black's grocery store. Further along past Henry's shop the saddler had recently opened for business and the railway goods shed, a fine structure equal to anything north of Adelaide, was nearing completion.

In spite of all these signs of the community growing, the poor water supply remained Hawker's biggest problem and Henry had been one of many to sign a petition to the government to assist with the building of a better reservoir.

A sniffle drew his attention back to the woman standing behind him. He had drawn out the pretence long enough. He turned, parted his lips in a conciliatory smile and gave a small nod.

"Of course you can have credit, Mrs Adams." He reached for the sad-looking woman's hand and gave it a pat. She wore no gloves and her hands were rough like a man's. "We have to stick together in the hard times so we can enjoy the good times."

Her gaze lifted to his and he saw the hope rekindle in her eyes.

"You've had a long journey." He drew up a long-legged wooden chair to the counter. "You give me your list. Sit here while you wait. My wife will make you a cup of tea."

"That's very kind, Mr Wiltshire. I've been that worried about how we would manage." Mrs Adams wriggled her wiry frame onto the seat. Her once pale green dress displayed several patches, the hem ragged and brown. She fanned her worry-lined face with her hand.

Henry turned and called to his wife. "Catherine."

"My husband's a proud man but we've had three bad years in a row and we've a family to feed," Mrs Adams continued.

"Of course." Henry looked towards the curtain. There was no movement. He called a little louder. "Catherine."

Finally the curtain twitched. Catherine peered around, dabbing at her red cheeks with a handkerchief. "Yes, Henry?"

"Can you make Mrs Adams a cup of tea?"

"Of course." She cast one of her sweet smiles in the direction of the older woman. "How do you take your tea, Mrs Adams? Sugar, milk?"

"Oh yes please, my dear. Both." The poor woman looked so grateful Henry thought she would slide off her chair.

"Now tell me what you need?" Henry moved around his shop collecting the items while Mrs Adams listed her requirements. Anything that was weighed out he erred on the lighter side of the scales. No point in giving away more goods than necessary to achieve his goal. He was already being generous and he hoped that generosity would come back to him through his eventual acquisition of the Adams property.

"Here you are, Mrs Adams." Catherine came into the shop carrying a tray set out with a teapot and the special china cups

Henry's mother had given them as a wedding present. Harriet had placed much importance on the gift. He was pleased to see Catherine appreciated them.

"Oh thank you, Mrs Wiltshire."

"Please call me Catherine, Mrs Adams. I am sure you will be one of our best customers."

The woman lowered her gaze. "I hope so. Times are very tight at the moment and your husband has been so kind."

Catherine handed over the delicate teacup she had just filled. "There, there, Mrs Adams. Things are bound to get better soon." She poured a cup for herself and continued to chat to the woman.

Henry smiled and put a bag of flour on the counter beside the rest of Mrs Adams's provisions. He could rely on Catherine to make the woman comfortable.

Suddenly the door burst open sending the little bell into a harsh jangle. They all looked at the ragged man filling the doorway. Mrs Adams slid from her seat. Catherine took her cup and saucer as it threatened to fall from her hands.

"There you are, woman," the man barked. "What are you doing in here?"

"Getting some provisions, dear."

Adams looked from his wife to the teacups with the items stacked behind. The look on his face softened. He stepped across the room and took his wife's elbow. "I'm sorry but we can't."

Henry stepped forward and held out his hand. "Good morning to you Mr Adams. I am Henry Wiltshire, owner of this establishment, and this is my wife Catherine."

Adams shook his hand. Henry felt the roughness of his skin against his own.

"I know you will be pleased to discover we've come to an arrangement regarding supplying you with goods. I will expect your payment when your next crop return comes in."

Adams pulled the hat from his head. "But that's not likely to be—"

"We understand, Mr Adams." Henry hastened to reassure the man. "My wife and I know what it's like to experience hard times." He put an arm around Catherine's shoulders and hugged her to him. "Don't we, my dear?"

A puzzled look crossed Catherine's face. He gave her arm an extra squeeze.

"We all have to help each other at times like this." Catherine's beautiful smile lit up her face. "Mrs Adams was having a cup of tea. You must be parched being out in this hot weather. Would you like a cup as well?"

Henry gave his wife a little pat and stepped back. His mother hadn't thought her up to the challenge but he knew Catherine would be an asset to him and she was certainly proving her worth.

"No thank you, Mrs Wiltshire."

"You must finish yours, Mrs Adams." Catherine handed the cup back.

"Why don't we load your wagon while the ladies finish their tea?" Henry lifted the large bag of flour.

Adams opened his mouth to protest.

"It's only a few items to get you by until times improve." Henry pressed the bag into Mr Adams's arms.

Outside there was barely a breeze, and the heat sucked the moisture from their eyes and mouths. Adams shoved his hat back on his head. Henry felt the full force of the late morning sun on his own hatless head.

Adams put a hand on Henry's arm as he turned to go back inside.

"This is very kind of you, Mr Wiltshire. It's reassuring to meet another honest hardworking man. I have to tell you that things are much worse than my wife knows. I don't think we'll be able to last another season." His voice faltered. He cleared his throat and brushed his hands down his grimy shirt. "I've barely enough seed from last year's crop to plant more than a few acres."

"Perhaps I could be of some help with that as well." Henry never missed an opportunity. He'd acquired one parcel of land and this could be a step towards another. "I have the capital to buy seed."

"No reason for it if we don't get rain."

They both looked up at the cloudless sky.

"It's not the time of year for rain," Henry said.

Adams flung his arm out to the south. "On those plains it hasn't been the time for three years." He put a hand on Henry's arm again. "We'll just take the flour, tea and sugar, Mr Wiltshire."

"But there are several other items your wife needed."

Adams face was downcast. "You've been most kind but I already owe at the Wilson store. I don't know how I'm going to pay any of my debts."

To Henry's horror, tears formed in the man's eyes. Adams would be a gibbering mess before much longer.

"As you wish, Mr Adams." Henry stood tall and clasped the lapels of his jacket in his hands. "But please don't forget my wife and I would be happy to help you out in the future."

Adams composed himself and gave a brief nod. Henry led the way back inside. The two women had finished their tea and were chatting happily, gathering up the rest of the provisions. Adams faltered beside him. Henry took in the look of despair that swept over his face. Good grief, the man was going to cry again.

"Please take the rest, Mr Adams." Henry kept his voice low. "Your wife looks like a capable woman. I am sure she will make the most of this opportunity."

Adams let out a sigh. He reached out and gripped Henry's hand. "Thank you Mr Wiltshire. You are a kind gentleman."

Henry smiled and turned to Mrs Adams. He took the calico bags laden with food staples from her arms and waved his hand to the door with a slight bow.

Mrs Adams gave him a wobbly smile, took the arm her husband offered and they made their way to the wagon. Henry and Catherine followed behind carrying their goods.

Once everything was stowed and covered with the canvas they stepped back and waved as Mr Adams urged his tired horse forward. The cart rolled away leaving a small trail of dust in its wake.

Henry put an arm around Catherine. Even though he'd just waved goodbye to a selection of his goods without receiving payment, he had the urge to celebrate. He felt it wouldn't be too much longer and the Adams' land would be his.

Catherine stretched up and brushed her lips across his cheek. He looked around and gave a little cough. The Adams' wagon was all but gone from sight and there were no other people in the street. Catherine kissed him again. He looked down into the sparkling eyes of his wife.

"What was that for, my dear?"

She gave a coy giggle. The sound of it sent an excited stirring through his loins.

"You're such a good kind man, Henry Wiltshire. You know they will have trouble paying for all those things but you let them take them anyway. I'm lucky to have such a caring man as my husband."

Henry was mesmerised by the tip of her pink tongue as it slipped over her lips. Catherine was only replacing the moisture sucked out by the heat but the gesture sent blood pounding through his veins.

He looked up and down the street again. The Adams' wagon was out of sight and there was no other movement bar a dog scratching at fleas in the shade of a wagon across the road. He pulled out his watch. It was almost midday.

Catherine had moved to the shade of the verandah roof. Her top button had come undone and her face was flushed a pretty pink.

He took her arm, guided her through the door and locked it behind them.

"Time for luncheon?" She smiled up at him.

He took her in his arms and pressed his lips against hers.

"Oh, Henry." She gave a squeaky giggle.

He lifted her into his arms.

Her eyes widened in surprise and the pounding inside him became almost unbearable.

"What are you doing?" Her voice came out in a squeak.

He pressed his lips to hers again and carried her through to the bedroom. He halted at the door. A vague memory stirred of his father carrying his mother into their bedroom and slamming the door. A sudden feeling of terror coursed through him.

"Henry?" Catherine's voice was shaky like his mother's had been.

He frowned down at his wife. The skin of her neck was pink and he could see the pulse throbbing just under her skin. His terror was replaced by another rush of blood. He laid Catherine gently on the bed and caressed her cheek. "It's all right, my dear." He began to undo the rest of the buttons on her shirt.

"Henry. It's the middle of the day." Her hand closed over his, a worried look on her face.

"We'll eat later." He paused at the sight of her plump pale flesh bulging from the top of her undergarments. He pressed his lips to one soft breast and then the other. Desire coursed through him and he began tugging at her clothes. Henry had a sudden urge to see his wife totally naked.

Catherine lay perfectly still listening to the soft breaths of her sleeping husband. His head was nestled onto her naked breast. It was the middle of the day and they were in their bed with not a stitch of clothing between them. Heat radiated from her cheeks. She put a hand to her mouth to suppress the giggle that threatened to escape. Her mother had never mentioned marital relations could be so … Catherine gave a little shudder … exquisite. Six months they'd been married and Henry had never done anything like this before.

After he'd laid her on their bed, he had stripped her naked. He'd done it so carefully, layer by layer, then gazed over every part of her with the eyes of a man who'd had too much to drink. She'd been so embarrassed she'd lowered her own lashes. Then he'd used his hands and his lips on her body until she'd been writhing with a new-found desire. He'd stopped then. She'd risked a peep through squinty eyes. He was stripping off his own clothes. She'd gasped at the sight of his manhood and he'd smiled, a funny lopsided grin.

He hadn't entered her then. Not like the dark nights of fumbling and quick thrusting that had left her uncomfortable and disappointed for something she hadn't known existed. Today he had used his lips, his fingers, until once more she'd been writhing beneath him and, shameless hussy that she'd become, begging him to enter her.

A wave of embarrassment swept over her. She tried to reach the sheet to cover herself. Henry's breath turned to a sharp snort and he woke. He lifted his head and looked around as if he didn't know where he was. His eyes met hers. He gave a self-satisfied smile then replaced the look with a frown.

"What time is it?"

He climbed from the bed to find his watch. She studied his naked back, the tight curve of his buttocks, as he bent to retrieve his clothes.

"It's nearly one o'clock, Catherine, and we haven't eaten. The shop has to be open again in five minutes." He pulled on his trousers.

"I'm not hungry." Catherine rolled over and curled into a ball. She had a funny full sensation in her stomach and she felt sleepy. She hadn't dozed when Henry did, too busy recalling every step of their lovemaking. Now she felt like she could sleep the afternoon away.

"Get dressed, Catherine." Henry's tone was sharp. "We've a business to conduct."

She sat up and slid her legs over the side of the bed. Her breasts felt heavy. She looked down. Her skin glowed with a rosy hue. She didn't study her own body very often but she was fascinated by her own large dark nipples. Henry's attention had made them bigger somehow. He paused in front of her. She glanced up and took in the hungry look in his eyes.

He turned away. "Hurry up, Catherine. Bring me some cheese and bread once you are dressed. I will have to eat it in the shop." He stepped out into the parlour and closed the door firmly behind him.

Catherine smiled. Henry could put on as much bluster as he liked but she knew something had changed between them and it made her feel deliciously wicked. She stood up. Black dots whirled in front of her. She gasped and sank to the floor. Vomit surged up her gullet, warm and burning. She tugged the chamber-pot from under the bed, thankful she'd already cleaned it as she emptied the contents of her stomach into it.

Five

William sat on the long bench that ran under the windows of the stone house his father had built at Smith's Ridge. There were three windows set in the front wall and another in the adjoining corner. Even though it was dinner time the sun still provided enough light for them to have no need of the lanterns yet.

On his left, closest to the head of the table, sat Joe. On William's other side were his little sisters. His father sat at the top end of the table and his Uncle Binda at the other. Not that Binda could ever be seen as William's real uncle but as his father's friend he had always had the title. William's mother Clara held nine-month-old Robert over her shoulder, pacing the floor and patting his back in a steady rhythm. William could see the baby's cheeks, pink and full from his feed, a small dribble of milk leaking from the corner of his plump lips. His eyelids fluttered with each pat. He would soon be asleep. Uncle Binda's wife Jundala could be heard chatting in her own language to Mary. They were out in the kitchen, dishing out the mutton stew.

The room that served both as a dining room and a living space was big. Even bigger than Grandpa and Grandma Baker's front room at their neighbouring property Wildu Creek. William had only recently heard his grandma mention the size of the house at Smith's Ridge as if it was a bad thing. But there were six of them living there now, ten if you counted Uncle Binda and his family. Not that they slept in the house, a thing his grandma was grateful for, but all ten of them ate their evening meal together when possible.

It was always a puzzle the things grown-ups said and didn't say. William had recently discovered there was often more to be learned. He was well practised at listening in when people didn't think he was paying attention. His eyes met Uncle Binda's across the table and William lowered his gaze; unless Uncle Binda was around of course. The native who was his father's best friend always knew if William was nearby and listening.

With the food handed out, his mother put baby Robert in his box crib in the corner and took a seat on the bench beside Esther. Mary and Jundala sat in the chairs on the other side of the table opposite the bench.

William had never given any thought to this arrangement of theirs but from what had transpired on their trip to town and Mr Prosser's remarks, he looked at his family and friends gathered around the table with fresh eyes.

Everyone bent their heads as his father said grace. No sooner had he finished than Esther began to wail. Her mother tried to put some of the stew in her mouth but the little girl pursed her lips together firmly.

"Don't press her, Clara." Joseph gave a little chuckle. "Eat your own dinner while it's hot. At least it means she's quiet."

Immediately Esther opened her mouth and let out another cry. Quick as a flash her mother shovelled a spoon of stew in and just as quickly had it spat back at her. She smacked Esther's fingers and the little girl bellowed.

Violet's lip trembled. William put an arm around her shoulders. Joseph pushed back his chair and stood, his empty tin cup clattering to the floor. Except for Esther's cry there was silence. William stared at his mother. Her cheeks were red but there were dark shadows under her eyes. He'd never seen his mother lash out like that. He'd had his father's hand across his backside a few times but never his mother's, and not when he was as young as Esther and Violet.

Mary stood. "Let me take her, missum," she said.

William thought about the funny word Mary called his mother. It was a cross between Mrs and mum. He was glad she didn't call his mother mum. Mary had her own mother, Jundala, and it didn't seem right. There was no way his fair-skinned mother could be considered Mary's mother.

"You haven't finished your own meal, Mary." Clara's voice was weary.

"Let her take the child, Clara. Mary can eat later. You look worn out."

"I am quite well, thank you Joseph."

William noticed his mother give his father an odd look but she handed Esther over into Mary's waiting arms, took her plate and sat in Mary's empty chair beside Jundala. Joseph gave his wife's shoulder a squeeze and sat back down. Once more William felt the air was heavy with things left unsaid.

"What news is there from town?" Clara asked her question looking from Joseph to Binda and back again.

"We are having an easy time of it compared to the farmers on the plains."

"Really?" Clara's voice had a ring of disbelief.

"At least we've had a little rain here in the hills to water stock and encourage some summer grass. They've had almost nothing on the plains for three years. We spoke with some desperate farmers, didn't we Binda?"

The native man nodded.

"Quite a few won't last until the new year," Joseph said.

"What will they do?" Once more Clara asked her question of both men.

Joseph shook his head. "Leave it and walk off."

"Surely not. What about their homes, their animals?"

William was anxious at this new topic. How could someone leave their land? Could it happen to them here at Smith's Ridge and to his grandparents over at Wildu Creek? His grandfather had taken up the first lease on Wildu Creek and the great uncles he'd never met had started this neighbouring property of Smith's Ridge. William had been born in this house. His father had built it for his mother when they had taken back the lease. The country here was more rugged than Wildu Creek and the waterway his grandfather had first called 'Wildu' wriggled its way down through the Wildu Creek property and across the bottom of Smith's Ridge. It still held pools of water and there were several natural springs in the hills behind the home yard. William couldn't imagine no water.

Joseph broke off a piece of bread and mopped up the juices on his plate. "Most of them have sold anything of any value to feed their families."

"How terrible," Clara said.

"Ran into Prosser on the way home."

"What did that uncouth man want?" Her tone was sharp.

"He was shifting sheep." Joseph glanced down the table at Binda. "I wonder if they were all his."

"Lots of tracks where the fence came down," Binda said. "Plenty going in his direction and horse prints with them."

Clara put down her spoon. "How can someone get away with such open thievery?"

Joseph shook his head. "We can't be sure he's taken our stock. We don't even know if there's any missing."

"His wife called here while you were away."

"What did she come for?"

"Who would know?"

"Eyes, looking." Jundala pointed to her own eyes.

"She didn't want to come in and take tea." Clara gave a nod of her head. "Jundala's right. A stickybeak is all that woman was here for, I'm sure."

"Odd." Once more Joseph looked along the table to Binda. "Perhaps we should be keeping a closer eye on the boundary between us and Prosser's Run."

Worry wormed inside William. Here was another thing to add to the list of things he didn't understand. He poked at the stew with his spoon. He'd been hungry for the delicious-smelling meat but now it was congealing on his plate.

"This is delicious, thank you Jundala." Joseph's plate was almost empty. Clearly he was having no worrying thoughts blocking his appetite.

"You are welcome."

William watched Jundala bend her head to the bowl and slurp up the last mouthfuls with her spoon. Uncle Binda and his family often didn't use a spoon at all but ate with their fingers. If he ate like that he would earn a reprimand from his father.

"I like the hat you chose, William. Did you enjoy your trip to Hawker?"

He looked up at his mother's question. Her face was composed with the hint of a smile. He shrugged his shoulders.

His father frowned. "Answer properly, son."

"We had sweets." Violet chipped in before William could respond, her face lit up in a smile.

"Did you? Your father spoils you." Clara gave her husband a brief glance.

"The lady gave them to us," Violet said.

"One for each of us." Joe's grin was wide.

"How nice of her." Clara looked back at her husband. "Where is this shop?"

"It's near the railway station."

"A proper shop?"

"It had four solid walls and windows."

"And a big wooden counter." Violet's voice was pitched high with excitement. "And shelves with lots of things. There was a doll. It was so pretty, Mama."

Clara clasped her hands together. "Perhaps I can go into town if there's a proper shop."

"I don't want to go there again." William put down his spoon. "The man in the shop didn't like us."

His mother chuckled, reached across and tickled his cheek. "How can someone not like you?"

"He called us a funny name," Violet said.

"Vagabonds." William frowned. "What is a vagabond, mother?"

Clara opened her mouth.

"It's of no consequence." Joseph's spoon hit his empty plate with a clang. "We won't go there again."

"I like the lady," Violet said.

"If we go there again we'll get more sweets." Joe folded his arms across his chest. "You can't stop me from going."

William was shocked. Joe rarely spoke in front of the adults and here he was being disrespectful to his … what was Joseph to him? Anger surged through William's body.

"It's your fault he didn't like us!" William's shout drew all eyes to him.

"Why is it my fault?" Joe's voice rose a notch.

Joseph put a gentle hand on Joe's shoulder. "It's nobody's fault, son."

"He's not your son." William clambered over the bench and around the end to stand between Joe and his father. He thrust out his arm and placed it alongside Joe's. "He's too black."

Clara gasped.

"Where did you learn something like that?" Joseph's voice was low but William knew the tone well enough to know he'd crossed some invisible line. He remembered their neighbour's words.

"Mr Prosser said we were black, white and brindle."

"Joseph," Clara gasped. "Where has our son been to learn such things? He's only six years old."

The shock in his mother's voice sucked the fury out of William. He saw the smouldering anger in his father's eyes and put his hands behind his back. He figured this was about to be another of those occasions when he would feel the slap of his father's hand on his backside. Joseph lifted his hand. William flinched but instead of hitting him his father pushed his plate back and rested his hands on the table. He closed his eyes and when he opened them he looked down the table at Uncle Binda and smiled. Uncle Binda nodded.

Once more William was puzzled by the hidden messages between adults that he wasn't privy to.

Joseph reached out and took both William's hands in his. "In this family we don't judge people by the colour of their skin." He flipped over his left hand taking William's hand with it. "You see that scar?"

William nodded with barely a glance. He knew his father had a small, jagged scar on his left wrist.

"Binda is my dearest friend. He saved my life twice. I love him like a brother. We cut our arms and our blood was the same colour. This mark is where our blood was mixed. Mr Wiltshire and Mr Prosser do not understand this. They are not charitable men."

William gave a quick glance in Uncle Binda's direction. How had his father been so weak that the smaller native man could save him from anything?

"You are a better person than them, William." Joseph let his hands go.

They fell limply to his sides and tears brimmed in his eyes.

"I think that's enough, Joseph," Clara said. "He's only a boy. He can't be blamed for the way you've chosen we should live."

"I've chosen?"

Clara held out her arms. "Come here, my young man."

William scampered past his father and into her arms. His tears flowed freely now.

"Shhh. Shhh." She patted his back gently.

Behind him William could hear the sound of the metal plates being gathered up.

"Leave them please Jundala. I will manage." His mother's voice rumbled in the ear he had pressed against her chest.

Chairs scraped. Binda said something in his own language to Jundala then he called to his son. "Come Joe."

Baby Robert began to cry from his crib in the corner of the room. Esther joined in. Joseph rose from his chair. "I will meet you at the yards in the morning, Binda?"

"Yes."

"Thank you my friend. I'm sorry for—"

"No," Binda said. "No sorrow."

William raised his head a little and looked over his mother's shoulder. Mary was standing in the doorway holding Esther. William's gaze met hers. He was shocked by the hostile glare on her face.

Clara let go of him and used her thumb to wipe the tears from his cheeks. The noise created by Robert and Esther was loud in everyone's ears. Clara sighed and stood up.

"You see to Robert," Joseph said. "I'll take Esther."

Robert's cries ceased instantly with Clara's cuddle. Esther's grew louder in her father's arms.

"Thank you, Mary." Joseph lifted Esther over his head and sat her on his shoulders. Immediately she began to laugh.

"There's no understanding that one," Clara said.

William looked down as Violet's little warm hand slipped inside his. She smiled up at him. Mary crossed the room to collect the plates.

"Please leave them, Mary." Clara cuddled Robert's chubby body to her. "Join your family. We can manage. It's about time William learned to dry dishes."

William opened his mouth but closed it again when he saw the sly smile on Mary's face.

"Okay, missum," she said and left the room.

Apart from the noise of the younger children, nothing was said once Mary had left.

William noticed the angry look his mother gave his father.

"We'll talk later." Joseph's voice was low.

William knew that meant there'd be an adult conversation the rest of them wouldn't hear but he badly wished he could listen. He still had an uneasy feeling about his family and their close cohabitation with a native family.

Six

The bulk of the large wood-and-iron shearing shed was still in shadow as Joseph walked up the slope from the house. The sun had not yet risen above the highest ridge to cast its heat over the yards filled with sheep. The shearing shed had been built on a small plateau and Joseph had extended and improved it since moving here after he and Clara were married. Clara had wanted a better house and he had been more than pleased to knock down the old place that only served to remind them of his uncles' past misfortunes at Smith's Ridge.

Now his thoughts were on his stock. The sounds of the lambs and their mothers filled the air. He was working on creating a strain of merino better suited to the rugged conditions of the Flinders. These lambs were the offspring of his first trial.

The early morning air was cool on the skin below his rolled up sleeves. With five hundred lambs to tail he knew he would soon be warm. Across the rails he could see the dark curly hair of Binda as he bobbed up and down, separating the ewes from their lambs. Jundala and Joe worked with him. Mary was down at the house with Clara and the younger children. William had been sent to feed the hens and collect the eggs and then he could join the men at the yards.

Joseph stopped at the wooden rail. He still worried over William's outburst at the dinner table. A week had passed since then and life had settled back to normal. Joseph had been too busy to find an opportunity to talk about it with William. The boy had always been a deep thinker and was often hard to read.

Clara had been distressed by her son's words and had given Joseph a tongue-lashing that night. He puzzled over that too. It wasn't like Clara to lose her temper like she had with Esther, even though he knew the little girl's tantrums were enough to test a saint. Then there had been Clara's accusation that including Binda's family with theirs was Joseph's choice not hers. He'd never realised she'd felt that way. Binda had been his friend to the detriment of the native's relationship with his own father and the rest of his family. He was like a brother to Joseph.

"You going to help or daydream all day?" Binda's words brought him back to the task at hand.

"I thought you had it all under control."

The first of the sun's rays reached them, giving everything a pink hue.

"We have but you keep scaring the sheep. You look like a great white ghost hanging over the rails like that."

"Just as well you've got pants covering that shiny black backside of yours or they'd be blinded by the sun reflecting off it."

Joseph climbed the rails and dropped to the other side, enjoying the sound of Binda's chuckle. Joseph only had one sister. Ellen was much younger than him and while they'd had lots of adventures together she wasn't a brother. He'd formed a strong friendship with Timothy who'd come to work for them at Wildu Creek but he was several years older than Joseph. Back then Joseph had also played with Tommie, the son of Gulda, who worked with Joseph's father. Once Tommie had reached initiation age his mother, Daisy, had taken him bush to be with her family. Joseph had missed him until he met Binda. He'd become the brother Joseph never had. They joked about things like the colour of their skin but now Joseph was second-guessing himself. A man like Prosser was a bigot and his words of no consequence but the new shopkeeper was a different proposition. He knew nothing about Joseph's family or Binda's and yet they'd been given such a hostile response.

Binda's call and the sound of hooves heading his way brought him back to the present. There was no more time to ponder, he had work to do.

Clara gripped her hands together. She was worried if she left them apart she would slap Esther again like she had the other evening at the dinner table. Violet was trying her best to placate her little sister but was having no success. Esther wanted to be outside watching the sheep and she was wailing her frustration. To top it off Robert hadn't been sleeping well and he was restless again now. Clara knew her milk was drying up and the baby was reluctant to take any form of alternate sustenance. She'd tried cow's milk, custard and runny porridge like she'd fed the others but Robert would have none of it. He lay on a blanket on the floor kicking his legs and chewing on his fists.

Esther gave an extra loud yell. Clara managed to reach her before she clouted her sister with the wooden doll Violet had been trying to amuse her with. Clara hugged Esther to her but the little girl kicked and screamed. Mary was in the kitchen. It would have been so easy to swap places with her. She could always distract and placate Esther but that was the reason Clara had insisted she do the inside housework while Mary prepared the morning tea for the workers. William's anger and confusion over their living arrangements with Binda's family was something Clara had thought might happen one day. She'd lived in Port Augusta before she married Joseph. She'd seen what white settlers thought of cohabiting with natives and how they were treated. Joseph had grown up with natives living close by. His parents had always had native workers at Wildu Creek and treated them with respect.

She accepted Joseph's close bond with Binda and she enjoyed Jundala's female company even though her English was basic, but she had often thought their arrangement unusual. They got away with it living so far from others but there were more and more settlers in the region now and towns growing on the plains. She knew there were plenty of people who would look down their noses at the close bond between Binda's family and theirs.

Esther struggled in her arms. One small bare foot connected with her shin. Clara yelped.

"Hello, what's going on here?"

"Grandpa!" Violet called.

"Gram pa! " Esther's response was much louder.

Clara looked at her father-in-law through watery eyes. Thomas Baker was tall like Joseph but with dark hair now peppered with grey and a face that Clara always thought of as gentle, in spite of his bushy eyebrows and weathered skin. "Hello Father Baker. What are you doing here?"

"Came to offer some help." He patted Violet's head as she clung to his leg. Esther slid from Clara's grip and raced across the room. Thomas hefted her up in his arms and stepped inside to allow his wife to follow.

"Hello, my darlings." Lizzie Baker carried a huge basket in two hands. She was a small woman but with enough energy for ten. Clara took a deep breath. She smoothed her dress with her hands. She had always felt inadequate in her mother-in-law's presence.

"I told you I'd bring that in for you, Lizzie." Thomas put Esther down and tried to take the basket.

"Nothing wrong with my two hands that I can't carry a little bit of food. There's plenty more to be brought in." She put the basket on the big table. "Hello, Clara dear." She turned back to the two little girls. "I think I might be able to find a small piece of toffee for anyone who can help Grandpa unload the cart."

Violet and Esther squealed with delight and raced ahead of their grandpa across the verandah and down the steps.

Robert's little grizzles grew louder. Clara plucked him from the floor.

"How are things here?"

Clara turned to find Lizzie right beside her. "Fine thank you, Mother Baker. Are you both well?"

"Fit as fiddles. Although I did find that last heat spell very tedious. Even the evening breeze along the creek deserted us there for a while. Thomas never complains of course. I suppose it was even worse for you here. Smith's Ridge never did seem to catch any breeze. I hope you don't mind me distracting the girls with toffee, Clara."

"Of course not." Clara jiggled Robert up and down. Lizzie's barrage of words always flustered her.

"Can I take him?" Lizzie reached out her arms for Robert. Clara handed the grizzly baby over.

"Hello my fine young man." Lizzie snuggled him into the crook of one arm and tickled his toes. "Haven't you grown since I saw you last."

"Grandma, Grandma." Esther raced through the door carrying a small calico bag.

"Yes, sweet Esther, I'm right here and I haven't lost my hearing. You'll be scaring your brother with all that shouting."

To Clara's surprise Esther steadied to a walk and carefully held out the bag.

"That's some soap for your mother." Lizzie patted the little girl's wayward hair.

"Thank you Mother Baker, you didn't need to bring me anything."

"It's a gift for your birthday."

Clara didn't want to be reminded of that horrible day. "Thank you." She took the bag from Esther and breathed in the delicious scent of roses. She'd been alone on her birthday. Joseph had taken the oldest children with him on the trip to Hawker along with Binda and his children. Jundala had gone to visit her family. Clara had been alone with Robert. She'd been feeling unwell for days but was worse on that day. After an awful morning of trying to placate the baby and stop herself from being sick she'd realised what the date was and that had led her to discover why she felt so unwell.

Violet and Thomas came inside with arm loads of bags and baskets. Clara shut the door behind them to keep out the heat and the little black flies that crawled over everything. She pulled her face into a smile. "Goodness, what's all this?"

Thomas put his load on the table then helped Violet with hers.

"We've come to help with the lambs. I thought I'd bring you some food. I've stitched some overalls for young Robert." Lizzie lifted the baby into the air and kissed his red cheeks. "He looks like he's teething. I've brought some of my mulberry jam, I've made a new nightdress each for the girls and there's a pocketknife for William."

"She didn't make that." Thomas chuckled as Lizzie drew breath.

"We've been into Hawker." Lizzie kissed Robert's fingers as he tried to grab the chain around her neck. "There's a new shop there."

"A proper shop," Violet said.

"Have you been there?"

"The lady gave us sweets." Violet's big eyes were round with delight.

"We're vagabongs," Esther added proudly.

"Vagabonds." Violet corrected softly which earned her a glare from Esther.

"Are you indeed?" Thomas lifted the two little girls, one in each arm. "I thought you were young ladies. How about we go and see what's happening with these sheep?"

"Yes." Esther's squeals of delight were as ear piercing as her cries of displeasure. "And toffee."

"I did promise." Lizzie chuckled and dug in the corner of the big basket.

"Thank you Grandma," Violet said ever so sweetly.

Esther echoed her in a louder voice.

"Shoes on, girls." Clara moved towards the kitchen door.

"It's all right, Clara." Thomas headed her off. "I can do it."

"And their hats," Lizzie called after him. "That sun is ferocious on fair skin."

The sound of the little girls' laughter echoed back at them.

Lizzie turned back to Clara. "Now, my dear. How are you really? You look exhausted. I love all these beautiful grandchildren but they must tire you out."

Clara felt her lip tremble. She put a hand to her mouth, sank onto a chair and burst into tears.

Joseph pulled off his boots and listened. The house was quiet. It was always a relief when all the children were in bed. His parents had retired to the hut that had been built for Binda and his family but it was rarely used. Binda and Jundala preferred the widlya, a dwelling they'd made for themselves further away from the main house. Mary sometimes slept in the hut but had gone with her parents and brother tonight.

Joseph pondered his mother's parting words. She'd urged him to take more care of his wife. His father had echoed her concern and added it might be Smith's Ridge that was wearing her down. Lizzie had laughed at that point saying it was much more likely that being the mother of several young children was what was ailing her.

Joseph always ignored his father's remarks about Smith's Ridge. It hadn't been a happy place for Joseph's uncles, his mother's brothers, and it had ended up in the hands of a terrible merchant, Septimus Wiltshire. It had come back to the family, bequeathed by Septimus's wife, after the odious man had died. Thomas had not been over-joyed by the prospect and had put a shepherd in the house.

When Joseph married Clara he'd been keen to take over Smith's Ridge and build a place of their own. His father had helped him, along with Binda, to knock down all the existing dwellings except the shearing shed and clean the place up, then they'd built this lovely stone house. Clara had been ecstatic with happiness at the sight of it. His mother was right; it was more likely the children that were wearing Clara down. And he'd hadn't brought Clara a gift for her birthday. He'd fully intended to buy her a bolt of fabric for a new dress at the shop in Hawker but after the bad experience with the owner, he'd forgotten. Joseph felt his anger surface just at the thought of the pompous man.

He pushed the shopkeeper from his mind. Joseph needed to find out what was bothering his wife. He entered the bedroom. Clara was standing in her nightdress. Her long fair hair hung lankly past her shoulders. The light from the lantern combined with the pale fabric of the well-worn nightdress gave her face a washed-out appearance. They had all been working so hard of late but he had wondered at the darker than normal shadows beneath her eyes and her short temper. "Is something wrong, my love? Mother thinks you're ailing."

"Does she?" Clara hung the dress she'd just taken off on the hanger behind the door. She turned back to him, hands on hips.

"And what do you think, Joseph Baker? Do you have an opinion of your own?"

Joseph hovered. He knew he was on dangerous ground here. Damned if he did, damned if he didn't. He reached for her, she slipped away. Joseph stayed put. "I think I married the most beautiful woman in the world."

"Ha." She spat the word at him. "All the flattery in the world will get you nowhere tonight." She went to step past him.

He grabbed her and pulled her close. "I can wait," he whispered in her ear. She shivered in his arms and he knew she'd come round. Tonight there was no child in their bed, at least for the moment.

She pulled away and pushed a hand against his chest when he started to lean forward. "No, Joseph." She glared at him. "Not tonight. In fact, not again."

"What?" He couldn't help the grin that spread across his face. "Not ever?" Clara had always been feisty, that was one of the things he loved about her, but he had always been able to cajole her with his kisses. She could usually be persuaded to make love, and often she would initiate their intimate moments, something that they both enjoyed. Now tears brimmed in her eyes.

"What is it, Clara? Have you tried the tonic I brought you?" Joseph had reluctantly handed over the only thing he'd brought her from his trip to Hawker. It rankled that it had come from the pompous shopkeeper but at least he'd had something to give her.

"I have. It eases my head but I still feel so tired."

"Are you truly ill?"

Clara looked up at him. His heart gave a thump as he saw the despair in her gaze.

"What is it, Clara?"

"I'm with child again." She brushed the tears from her cheeks with her fingers.

Relief washed over him. "But that's wonderful news."

"No it is not wonderful news." She sank to the bed. "How am I to fare?"

"We are very lucky." Joseph sat beside her and took her hand. "My parents had such trouble having children. They buried two babies. We're blessed, Clara."

"Is that what you call it?" Clara's eyes filled with tears again. "What am I to do Joseph? I can't manage the children we've got. My milk is drying up and Robert won't take anything else. Esther throws tantrums and poor sweet Violet doesn't get a word in. And then there's William. He gets none of my attention. He's such a deep thinker but he needs to express himself somehow."

"He did it quite well at dinner last week."

"And so he should but we shushed him and the topic has not been discussed since. How's he to know what to think?"

"Calm down, Clara." Joseph pressed her head to his shoulder. "It will work out. Mother would love to help more."

Clara pulled away from him and stood up. "She's no longer a young woman. She has more than enough to do at Wildu Creek and your sister will be in need of her help soon enough. Her baby is only a few months away."

Joseph rose and gently pulled Clara to him. "We'll get more help if we need to."

"More natives?'

"They don't have to be if you'd prefer not." Joseph knew Clara didn't share the same close affection for Binda and his family as he did but she was always considerate and thankful for their help.

"I worry for our own children. They have to be able to fit into normal society and not be treated like outcasts by people like that shopkeeper."

"He wasn't a nice man."

"Maybe not but he probably only said what others think about us, Joseph." She gazed up at him, her eyes worried.

He kissed her. "We'll work something out, Clara." He slid his hands down her nightdress and cupped her buttocks, pulling her close. Love and desire surged through him. He adored his beautiful wife as much now as the day he'd fallen in love with her. She always blossomed during pregnancy. He loved their children. One more would be wonderful.

"Don't worry, my sweet." He kissed her gently.

She pulled away a little. "I said we're not doing this anymore."

He kissed her again. More urgently and felt her soften in his arms.

"Where's the harm in it," he murmured. "If you're already with child?"

"Joseph, I'm so tired."

He slid her nightgown from her shoulder and kissed the skin beneath her hair. "I'll get up to the baby." He traced his lips across to the soft flesh of her breasts. "He can have water in the night."

"Joseph." Her tone was half complaint, half desire.

He rang his tongue around one nipple and then the other. She arched her back. "Tomorrow, my beautiful wife, you can sleep in."

She opened her eyes and raised one eyebrow.

"My late birthday gift to you."

She shook her head. "How?"

"You'll see." Before she could say more he covered her lips with his and gently lowered her to the bed.

Clara opened her eyes then squeezed them shut. The bedroom was warm and stuffy and full of light. She lay back on the pillow and listened. There were no sounds of children, no footsteps, no banging of pans. She felt heavy and lethargic. She must have slept all night. She couldn't remember the last time that had happened. After their lovemaking she had lain awake listening to the soft breaths of her husband. It frustrated her so, that he could fall asleep so easily and yet she who was so desperate for sleep could not. She'd taken a bigger draught of the tonic he'd brought her from the shop in Hawker. She didn't use it often but it did ease her headaches on the days when they were bad. It had obviously done the trick and Joseph had been true to his word. He must have got up to Robert. She felt her breasts. They were soft, not full of milk for her baby.

Then she remembered. Robert would no longer be her baby. She put a hand to her stomach. Already it was rounding. Soon enough there would be another baby. Nausea gnawed inside her and, in spite of her sleep, weariness overwhelmed her. How was she to manage?

She gave a brief thought to her own mother but there would be no help there. Her parents had not been happy that she had fallen in love with a sheep herder, as they'd described Joseph. Her father had been the harbourmaster at Port Augusta and had planned for his daughter to marry someone he thought more worthy. Her parents had never made the long journey to Smith's Ridge and now they were even further away at the port of Wallaroo.

"You've made your choice," her father had said. "It will be a hard life. You'll be sorry and there will be no turning back."

Now those words had come back to nest. She hadn't stopped loving Joseph. He was a wonderful father, an attentive lover and yet she was just so tired. Clara rolled over and curled herself into a ball. Moisture seeped from her eyes. She wrapped her arms around herself and let the tears flow.

Seven

Henry looked up at the tinkle of the bell over the door. A tall man entered, wearing a long-sleeved shirt and a soft leather vest in spite of the warm day. When he removed his hat he revealed a thick thatch of red hair.

"Good day to you, sir," Henry said. "How can I be of service?"

"I heard you buy wool?"

"I can do that on your behalf, Mr …?"

"Prosser, Ellis Prosser."

"Henry Wiltshire." He thrust out his hand. "Pleased to meet you, Mr Prosser."

Prosser clasped his hand in a vice-like grip then let it go. Henry tucked the hand behind his back and opened and closed his fingers. Prosser was too busy taking in his shop to notice.

"You have a property near here?"

"A day's ride, almost two with wagons." Prosser's gaze had been searching the shop, now he turned his dark brown eyes on Henry. "This new town with its train line is much closer than Port Augusta."

"And you have some wool you'd like me to sell for you?"

"Only off-cuts but I'll have a new clip soon enough. If you get me a good deal I'll bring my next bales of wool your way."

"Of course, Mr Prosser. I'm sure we can come to a mutually beneficial arrangement." Henry moved back behind his counter. "Would you like to take tea? We can discuss our business in the parlour."

Prosser glanced towards the door. "I don't have long."

"Of course. I will ask my wife to mind the shop while we conduct our business." Henry pulled back the curtain. "Catherine."

Catherine's reddened face looked round the door from the kitchen. "Yes dear."

"I have a guest. Make a pot of tea and then come through to mind the shop."

"Yes, Henry."

He let the curtain fall back. Prosser was examining the row of leather belts. Henry had recently installed some hooks to better display them.

"Are you in need of a belt, Mr Prosser?"

The man turned. "No," he said. "I've a man works for me who is more than capable of turning a hide into anything we need."

"You're most fortunate." Henry lowered his gaze, annoyed to miss out on a possible sale. Some of these bush folk were very clever at turning their hands to making all kinds of things. Still, once they made a bit more money he was sure they would prefer the finer items he could provide.

Catherine stepped from behind the curtain. "Your tea is ready, Henry."

She smiled sweetly as Prosser swept a surprised look over her.

"This is Mr Prosser, my dear."

"How do you do, Mr Prosser? I hope you like pikelets. I've just taken some from the pan."

"Very kind, Mrs Wiltshire."

Henry saw the appreciative look Prosser gave his wife. He was sure it wasn't just over the offer of pikelets. Prosser gripped

Catherine's hand a little longer then let it go, as his gaze travelled down her body.

The bell over the door tinkled and a woman entered.

"Hello, Mrs Harris." Catherine went to meet her.

"This way, Mr Prosser." Henry held back the curtain and ushered the huge man through to the parlour. Ah, yes, Henry thought to himself. His wife was proving useful in so many ways.

Catherine rolled up the last of the bolts of cloth she had laid out for Mrs Harris. It had been hard work convincing her to buy something other than brown serge for a new dress but she had finally persuaded the dour woman to buy a dark blue, still serge but at least a different colour.

Behind her, Henry pulled back the curtain and ushered Mr Prosser back into the shop. Catherine smiled at the ugly man. She hated the way his eyes ranged over her as if she were another item to be purchased from her husband's shop. She did her best not to show her feelings. Mr Prosser was one of Henry's clients and it was her job to make him feel welcome.

Prosser inclined his head to her. "A pleasure to meet you, Mrs Wiltshire."

"Good day to you, Mr Prosser."

The door opened and let in a blast of heat along with the distant whistle of the train.

Henry drew out his watch. "Right on time." He closed the door on Prosser and turned, a broad smile spread across his face. "That was a most fortuitous meeting."

"I'm glad."

"Mr Prosser knows a lot about this country."

"Does he?"

"He says the farmers on the plains are doomed. The only place to make a living is in the hills."

"But there are so many families farming on the plains."

"Yes, I'm not sure that Prosser is one hundred per cent right about that but he's been in the area longer than me." Henry's dark brown eyes widened. "And you'll never guess where he lives."

"I'm sure I wouldn't, Henry."

"Mr Prosser is a neighbour to that uncouth Baker fellow who was in the shop a few weeks back."

Catherine frowned. "Baker?"

"With the rabble of children and natives."

"Yes, I remember." Catherine had found them all rather pleasant but she wasn't about to tell her husband that.

"Prosser says Baker has the natives living with him and ... well I won't tell you some of the scandalous things he told me about their arrangements. Not suitable for your delicate ears, my dear."

Catherine was disappointed. There was little of interest that happened in Hawker; the idea of some gossip, and more than that, gossip that might be a little salacious, was quite delectable. She knew there would be no point in pressing Henry.

"I've made a good sale in your absence. Mrs Harris took a length of fabric for a new dress, two shirts for her husband and a bag of grocery items."

"Well done, my dear." Henry gave her a condescending smile and patted her on the hand. "You are quite the salesperson. Once we get some more money behind us I will build you a separate house and employ an assistant. Then you can be a lady of leisure." His grin deepened and there was a glint in his eye.

Catherine held in the sigh that wanted to escape her lips. She longed for a fine home, there was no denying that, but she didn't intend to be a slave to it. Her mother had a housekeeper but she also lived in Adelaide where there were plenty of other pursuits to keep her occupied. Catherine had no idea how she would pass her time all day if she didn't have the shop and Henry's occasional clients to attend to.

His hand slid down and patted her bottom. She pretended she hadn't felt it and moved on to unpack some new handkerchiefs that were amongst the goods that had arrived on yesterday's train. He needn't think that she would sit at home waiting to attend to his needs at any time of the day either. She enjoyed his attention in bed most times now but when he took her during the day she was always so tired afterwards. He would have a short doze then go back to work with a spring in his step. She would be left to drag herself from the bed and then have to spend a long time redressing and doing her hair. Then Henry often became impatient with her. She had to be careful to keep his ardour sated at night so that during the day her body was her own.

Besides, she had a suspicion she was with child. She put a hand to her stomach. Was there a slight bulge? She glanced in Henry's direction. His head was bent over the book of figures he kept. She wasn't sure how he was going to take that news. There had been no discussion about children. She wondered where they fitted into his schemes, or if they did at all. She needed the counsel of another woman, but so far she'd met few, and certainly none Henry wished her to keep company with.

Catherine decided she would write to her mother. She needed help to decide on the best way to tell him. The very thought of it gave her heart. She went back to her handkerchiefs. Her mother would advise her on the best way to manage a husband. Catherine lifted her head with a start as a hand slipped around her waist from behind.

"Henry," she gasped.

"It's been a very profitable morning, my dear." He bent forward, brushed his lips across her neck and nibbled her ear.

Normally Catherine loved the feel of his whiskers on her skin and the nipping of his teeth but they weren't in the privacy of their bedroom.

"It's not even midday yet." She stiffened in his arms and tried to keep her tone confident.

Henry wasn't to be put off. He spun her to face him. "I think we should celebrate." He kissed her lips. "In the daylight."

"But Henry …" Her words were lost as he scooped her up.

The shop door opened and the bell jangled.

"Well my word. What is going on here?"

Henry nearly dropped Catherine in his haste to put her back on her feet. She had trouble standing. Her knees had gone to jelly at the voice she recognised.

"Mother." Henry straightened his coat and hurried around the counter.

Short in stature and carrying more weight than when Catherine had last seen her, Harriet Wiltshire glared from Catherine to her son, then, as he wrapped his mother in his arms, Catherine saw Harriet's benevolent smile.

"Hello, Mrs Wiltshire." Catherine's cheeks radiated heat and yet a shiver wriggled down her back as her mother-in-law looked her way.

Henry held his mother at arm's length. "This is wonderful. How did you get here? Why?"

"On the train. To see you." Harriet cupped Henry's cheek in her gloved hand. "I must say I wasn't expecting to witness what I did when I arrived." Once more she glared in Catherine's direction.

"We were celebrating, Mother." Henry's tone was subservient. That was rare. Catherine had only ever heard him that way in his mother's presence.

"Indeed. This is a place to conduct business, not a hotel. Although I shudder to think what kind of people carry on in such a way, even in a hotel." Harriet drew up her small frame and for the first time Catherine noticed her walking stick.

"Are you injured, Mrs Wiltshire? Should we get a chair?"

"This?" Harriet looked down and waved the polished wooden stick back and forth. "It's just a precaution. When I've been sitting a while my hip locks up. I don't need a chair but I'd be grateful for a cup of tea."

"Of course." Catherine turned and fled into the house leaving her husband to deal with his mother.

"So this is what you've built with my money." Harriet sat at the dining table with her cup of tea and a slice of Catherine's fruit cake. She had inspected each part of the shop and the attached dwelling.

Catherine hovered in the kitchen doorway ready to fetch whatever else took Harriet's fancy. Henry sat at the head of the table. He leaned across and patted his mother's arm.

"Our money, Mother."

Harriet smiled. Henry was her pride and joy. Catherine put a hand to her stomach. Would she feel this same adoration for her own child?

"You certainly have no room for visitors." Harriet flicked a look around the small room crowded with furniture.

Catherine was relieved she had managed to get everything dusted and tidy this morning before Henry had needed her in the shop. She felt the heat rise up her neck and into her cheeks. Thank the good Lord Henry hadn't taken her into the bedroom before Harriet arrived.

"I'm sure we can come to some arrangement." Henry gave Catherine an enquiring look.

She took a step forward, not sure what to say.

Harriet laughed. "Look at your worried faces. Don't be concerned my dears. A gentleman met the train with a delightful horse and trap. He is building a hotel and has temporary lodgings which will do me quite well. I will stay two nights then return to Adelaide. I can't leave my own business for too long. Miss Wicksteed keeps a good eye on the shop and Mrs Simpson is an excellent overseer in the workroom but some of my girls are still learning the sewing trade and I must be there to instruct them."

"How is business, mother?"

"Very profitable. The shop I bought in O'Connell St has been a very fortunate experience. North Adelaide is proving to be the most wonderful address for all manner of shopping and ladies appreciate my dresses and my fine linen." She took a sip of tea then put the cup back in its pretty saucer and traced a finger around the rim. "I see you are using your tea set."

"Yes, thank you Mrs Wiltshire. It was a most generous gift and has been put to much use already. Henry has had several clients who have enjoyed their tea from it."

"I've brought you a new cloth for your table and a rather pretty milk jug. They're still in my trunk at the hotel."

"That's very kind of you, Mrs Wiltshire." Between her mother and her mother-in-law Catherine had a number of fine linens and pretty china and glassware. It was as if they competed to outdo each other. She hadn't had a lot of use for much of it as yet.

"Your business is going well, Henry?" Harriet turned back to her son.

"I've made several good deals already."

"Perhaps you will make your money quicker than expected. There's room close to my shop for another. Gentleman's fashion would complement my shop. We could truly be in business together."

"I'm not that far advanced yet, Mother, but I am pleased with the direction business is taking here."

With both the chairs at their dining table taken, Catherine stood where she was as her husband and his mother discussed business. It was another unbearably hot day and she longed to undo her buttons. She was tempted by the comfortable parlour chairs in the corner but in this heat she often felt drowsy when she settled there. Someone could come into the shop at any moment or Harriet may require something more. Catherine needed to remain alert but an odd feeling crept over her from her toes to her head. Her lips tingled and spots danced before her eyes. The voices in the room receded and she crumpled to the floor.

Henry saw his mother's worried look then heard the thud behind him. He rose from his chair to find his wife on the floor.

"Catherine." He knelt beside her and patted her hand. "Catherine?"

"Has she been unwell?" His mother was peering over his shoulder.

"No." Henry frowned. "Perhaps, just lately. A bit peaky in the mornings but she has never been an early riser."

"Put her on the bed."

Henry scooped Catherine up in his arms. Her face had lost colour. "Catherine?" He laid her gently on the bed and undid her tops buttons. Her eyelids fluttered.

"Here." His mother came in and stood at the end of the bed, a cloth in her outstretched hand.

The cloth was damp and cool. He patted Catherine's forehead and cheeks and wiped her neck.

"Catherine, my dear."

Her eyelids fluttered again and then opened. Her sweet lips made a round O of surprise. She tried to sit up but he put a restraining hand on her shoulder.

"You must rest, Catherine. You're not well."

"Please don't fuss Henry. I was overwhelmed by the heat, that's all."

He frowned. "We've had nothing but heat since we arrived here."

"I know. It's silly. I don't know what came over me." Catherine took the cloth from his hand and held it to her neck.

"Some water perhaps?"

Henry looked back at his mother. She must have gone from the room and come back again, this time carrying a teacup. He took it from her and put it to Catherine's lips.

"Thank you." Catherine glanced from Henry to his mother. "Both of you. I'm feeling much better."

"Are you with child?"

Henry snapped his head around in surprise at his mother's direct question. She had pulled herself up straight and was peering down her nose at Catherine.

"I believe I might be, yes." Catherine's voice was barely a whisper.

Henry gazed down at his wife. "My dear." He clasped her hand. "My dear."

"You've said that, Henry," Harriet snapped.

"This is the most wonderful news." He bent and kissed Catherine's lips, ignoring his mother's presence.

"You're pleased then?" Catherine's big round eyes brimmed with tears.

"Of course."

"This house won't be big enough for much longer then, will it?" Harriet's tone was brusque. "There's barely room for a crib in your bedroom let alone another bed."

"We will manage." Henry felt as if his chest would explode with pride. He stood tall and beamed at his mother. "I will be a father and you a grandmamma."

Harriet took a deep breath through her nose. She opened her mouth but the bell from the shop gave a sharp ring.

"Come, Mother." He cupped her elbow and steered her to the door. "We'll let Catherine rest and you can meet some of my customers."

"Very well." Harriet's voice softened. "That is one of the main reasons for my journey."

Henry guided his mother out then paused in the bedroom doorway and gave his wife a broad smile. "Rest, my dear. I'll be back soon."

She waved her fingers at him and rolled over onto her side in a fluid movement that was rather sensual. Another surge of pride filled his chest. He had a growing business, a beautiful wife and now he was to be a father. Life was treating him very well.

"Henry!"

The sound of his mother's horrified call broke the mood. He stepped beyond the curtain into the shop and nearly ran into his mother. She stood ramrod straight. In front of her on the other side of the counter were two natives, a man and a woman. Henry glanced around. There was no-one else in the shop. He looked back at the natives. For a moment he thought they were the two who had accompanied that fool Baker a few weeks ago. Now that he looked closer he could see the woman in an ill-fitting dress was older than the girl who'd been with Baker, and the man in trousers, shirt and waistcoat more solid than the previous native.

"What do you want?" Henry stepped around his mother.

The woman lifted an empty calico bag.

"Surely you're not going to serve these ... creatures." Harriet's words came out in a low hiss.

"Of course not."

Harriet had instilled in Henry a dislike for native Australians from an early age. Her reactions to the sight of their black skin had deepened over the years from avoidance to animosity. Henry had never questioned it. He glared at the black man. "Out."

The man took the bag from the woman and waved it at Henry. "Flour."

"I don't have any for the likes of you." Henry pulled back his shoulders. He was a good head taller than the native. "Mr Garrat next door may serve you. His standards are lower than mine."

The natives spoke in their own language, first to each other then at Henry.

"Flour," the native man said again.

Henry ignored the sharp hiss from his mother. He strode around the counter to the door and opened it wide. A blast of heat accompanied the dust that met him. "Out," he commanded. "I have no flour for you."

The natives hesitated, then turned on shoeless feet and shuffled out the door. Henry ignored the baleful look in their big round eyes that didn't quite meet his gaze. He shut the door on them as soon as they were through.

Silence settled in the shop with the dust. Henry turned. His mother was still rooted to the spot. She put a hand to the locket that hung around her neck and grasped it with her fingers.

"I do wish you would reconsider my suggestion of returning to Adelaide, Henry."

"There are natives everywhere, mother."

"But out here … Your father." It was unlike Harriet to stumble over her words. She took a breath. "I worked hard to make our lives comfortable so that you didn't have to experience this." She flicked her hand in the direction of the door.

"Everything is going well for me here. I can choose who I serve in my own shop."

Harriet pursed her lips and reached for her locket again. "Very well. In some ways it is appropriate your first shop should be in a town named Hawker. Your father and I built a good living as hawkers in our early days."

Harriet looked across the shop but Henry had the feeling she was picturing something else in her mind. "You never speak of my father."

Harriet's back stiffened. She pulled at the waist of her dress and brushed her hands down the folds of fabric. "He died a long time ago. Nothing can bring back the past. We must look to the future." She turned her shrewd look on him "Make your way here so that you can build a fine home in Adelaide. You have more responsibility now with a child on the way. You will find it's much better to raise your son in Adelaide."

"My son?" Henry's lips twitched into a smile.

"I knew you were a boy from the start. Catherine will give you a son. I know it. You will want to bring him up properly."

"Of course, mother."

Henry's smile widened. He had a longing to own land, lots of land and this region was full of opportunity. He had no desire to move back to Adelaide. A few natives wouldn't frighten him off. He was happy to allow his mother to believe he would return. After all she had a lot of money invested in his business. Until he could pay her back he would keep his future plans to himself.

Eight

Thomas Baker took his wife's arm and helped her down from the train. They moved closer to the wooden walls of the new Hawker railway station building and stopped to take in the scene. Around them on the platform other passengers stepped down and greeted friends and family. Porters rolled trolleys loaded with bags. Steam belched from beneath the engine and blew around their feet.

"Thank you." Lizzie brushed the front of her deep blue cloak. "Well, wasn't that something?"

"I suppose you plan to take the train rather than the cart to visit our daughter from now on?"

"Wouldn't you? I won't miss bouncing along on top of a wooden seat for over half the journey. The train was much more comfortable. Besides it's so much quicker. I'll be able to make more regular visits to Ellen and the baby."

"We were with them a week. I don't think they need us interfering again for a while."

"Thomas Baker." Lizzie's cornflower blue eyes flashed. The blue wasn't as vivid as it used to be but his Lizzie was still a fine-looking woman and not a hint of grey hair. "It's hardly interfering. Our daughter has just given birth to the most beautiful baby."

"Ellen has certainly taken to motherhood."

Lizzie tipped her head to look up at him. "Didn't you think she would?"

"Well, let's say she's been …" Thomas wasn't sure how to describe his wilful daughter.

Lizzie laughed. "If you say a handful, Thomas Baker, I'll disown you. You're the one who always let her have her own way."

Thomas smiled. They'd buried two baby girls before Ellen came along. Joseph and Ellen were their only children. His son had grown into a fine man but Thomas's heart was captured by Ellen. After Lizzie she was the light of his life. "At least that husband of hers appears to have tamed her a little."

Once more Lizzie laughed. "We'll see. Ellen has him wrapped around her little finger as well."

A chilly wind blew along the platform. It was mid-afternoon and the sun didn't have as much heat as earlier in the day. Autumn was well advanced but it had not brought any longed-for rain to the dry plains. There was a grey smudge on the horizon. Perhaps it held some promise. One could always be hopeful.

Thomas gripped his hat and took Lizzie's arm. "This way."

They wove between people and boxes and luggage. Thomas arranged for the suitcase Lizzie had convinced him to buy in Port Augusta to be delivered to the hotel along with their old trunk. Outside the road was busy with carts and wagons loaded with wool. Dust hung in the air, blown from the plains and stirred up by the movement of hooves and wheels.

"I'm thankful that terrible summer heat has gone but the dust is still as bad." Lizzie held her gloved hand over her nose and mouth.

"We've been lucky with the rain we've had at Wildu Creek." Thomas looked along the street to the shops and buildings already erected or still in progress. Not a tree to be seen and dust coated everything. Hawker was so dry. "The plains need water badly. They say the reservoir here is nearly empty."

"Grandma! Grandpa!"

"Oh look, Thomas. It's Joseph and the children." There was no mistaking the delight in Lizzie's voice. Her grandchildren were precious.

William reached them first. He came to a sudden stop in front of them, kicking up more dust. Thomas ruffled the boy's hair. "Hello, young man." He looked over at his son who was carrying Violet and a few feet behind them was Mary carrying Esther.

"What are you all doing here?" Thomas tickled Violet's chin. "We've got the cart and horse in the stables."

"I had need of the blacksmith and I have wool money to collect." Joseph kissed his mother on the cheek. "We thought we'd meet the train but we're a bit late."

"Esther wouldn't get out of the wagon," William grumbled. "I wanted to see the train arrive." He scuffed a rock with his boot, stirring up more dust.

"We'll go and look now before we go to the shop." His father reassured him. "Clara has given me a list as long as your arm."

"How is Clara?" Lizzie's question brought a frown to Joseph's face.

"She's not very well." Violet stared up at them, her young face set in a serious expression. She reached out and climbed into Lizzie's arms.

"Mothers get tired just before they have a new baby." Lizzie swept the little girl's roughly brushed hair from her eyes. She could do with a ribbon and her pinafore was ripped.

A burst of steam hissed from the train beyond the station building.

"Is the train leaving?" William asked.

"Soon," Thomas said.

"I'll take the children to look at it." Joseph held his hands out to Violet. The little girl clung to Lizzie.

"I want to stay with Grandma."

"She can." Lizzie kissed Violet's cheek. "You take the others. Why don't we meet for a cup of tea at the new hotel? Your father and I are staying the night there before we travel back to Wildu Creek tomorrow."

Joseph raised his eyebrows.

"Your mother's idea," Thomas said. "It should be quiet enough. Evidently they don't sell liquor yet as the main building isn't finished."

Joseph moved off. Lizzie kissed Violet again and set her on the ground. Thomas took one of his granddaughter's little hands in his. It felt so fragile against his rough skin.

They watched as Joseph and William hurried into the station closely followed by Mary and Esther.

"I wonder if it's wise for him to bring Mary." Lizzie's voice was lower than her usual vibrant tone.

"Binda's family are friends, just like Gulda and Daisy have been for us."

"But it's not quite the same for us. We're friends, yes, but Gulda and especially Daisy have kept their own ways. They've helped us but I think Gulda only comes back out of a sense of loyalty to you."

"And what I pay him."

"Grandpa." Violet tugged at his arm. "I'm hungry."

"Goodness, we can't have that. Let us go and find this cup of tea your grandma has promised and perhaps there will even be cake."

Lizzie chuckled. "You and your sweet tooth, Thomas Baker." She thrust her arm through his and together the three of them made their way to the hotel.

★

By the time Joseph joined them they'd finished their tea and cake.

"There's cloud moving in from the west." Joseph pulled his hat from his head and sat in front of the cup of tea Lizzie poured.

"Anything in it?" Thomas cast a look towards the window. The day had darkened while he'd been inside sipping tea.

"I know they're desperate for rain here," Joseph said. "It certainly looks promising."

Thomas wished he hadn't agreed to stay overnight at the hotel. He was anxious to get back to Wildu Creek. Rain was welcome but would impede their journey.

"Stop fretting, Thomas." Lizzie brushed imaginary crumbs from her skirt. "We'll be home soon enough."

"We must set off soon." Joseph stood and waved to Mary and the children who were playing on the wooden verandah. "I am going to collect my money from the odious little man who is acting as a forwarding agent and then we will be on our way. I want to make camp at the first creek by nightfall."

"Did you say the agent's name was Wiltshire?" Thomas asked. "Yes."

"There must be several people by that name." Lizzie reached across and patted Thomas's hand. "No need to jump to conclusions."

"Wiltshire, of course." Joseph clicked his fingers. "That was the name of the man who swindled Uncle Zac and Uncle Jacob out of Smith's Ridge."

"And tried to take Wildu Creek from us," Thomas growled

"But his name was Septimus," Joseph said. "And this Henry Wiltshire is close to my age."

"Could be his son," Thomas said. "Especially if he is as offensive as you say."

"Or he may be no relation at all." Lizzie got to her feet. "He might be odious but his young wife is lovely and they have delightful items in their shop. Some of it better than I could find in Port Augusta. I'll come with you."

"We'll all go." Thomas stood, plucked his hat from the rack and handed Joseph his. "I'm curious to meet this fellow."

Lizzie stopped in front of them and held up her hand. "Let me go first. I'd like to have a look around before you two go causing trouble. Besides, I can have his family history out of him in two shakes of a lamb's tail."

"Lizzie," Thomas warned. His wife was adept at unearthing the facts but he didn't want her in harm's way if this Wiltshire fellow was indeed related to his old adversary Septimus.

Thomas knew he should turn the other cheek but he'd had trouble forgiving and forgetting Septimus Wiltshire. The man was dead now but not before he'd caused a lot of grief for both Thomas and Lizzie's families. He'd swindled Thomas in his early days in the colony and been a thorn in his side during their first years at Wildu Creek.

Thomas believed Lizzie's brothers, Zac and Jacob Smith, would both be alive now if they hadn't lost their lease on Smith's Ridge through Wiltshire's trickery. Even though Septimus's wife, Harriet, had tried to make things right after her husband's death by giving back the lease, none of the Smiths had wanted it. The brothers had ended up dying far too young. Jacob lost his life on the goldfields in Victoria and Zac drowned in the hills beyond Adelaide, trying to cross a swollen creek after one too many drinks. Joseph had been the one eager to maintain the lease, which had been done with the help of an overseer. Thomas would have eventually let it go but Joseph had badly wanted to keep it in the family.

Now as Thomas watched his wife disappear inside the shop, his sense of unease strengthened.

"Let's go," Joseph said.

He made to step from the hotel verandah but Thomas put out a restraining hand. He wanted to rush in like his son but he'd allow Lizzie her chance to meddle. If anyone could get to the bottom of things quickly it was his Lizzie.

"You know your mother is a capable woman," he said. "We'll give her a few minutes' head start."

Henry looked up at the jangle of the bell over his door. He'd had a busy morning. In spite of the continuing dry weather, the cooler conditions had brought customers to his door. His general produce was similarly priced to his opposition, Mr Garrat, but Garrat didn't stock quality goods such as the finer haberdashery and the fabric with pretty patterns that Harriet was adept at sourcing. Neither did he have the heavier-duty trousers, the soft felt hats and the superior axe heads that Henry had on his shelves. Some of Henry's customers had money and sales had picked up a little during autumn.

He smiled at the attractive older woman who came through his door.

"Good afternoon madam, how can I be of service?"

"Hello." The woman beamed at him and studied him with her pretty blue eyes. She was well dressed and wore gloves, something few women seemed to be bothered with out here. He wondered where she'd come from. Perhaps she was someone Catherine could befriend. There was an age difference but the woman may have daughters. Before he could ask, she had advanced across the shop and thrust her hand at him.

"You must be Mr Wiltshire?"

"That's right."

"Henry, is it?"

"Yes, and you are?"

"You have such wonderful stock here. Such exquisite table-cloths." She ran a finger over the display of his mother's fine needlework. "Much better than Port Augusta. I've just returned from there." The woman spoke quickly as she glanced around the shelves, taking it all in with her bright eyes. "I've only been in once before and a delightful young woman served me." She turned back and fixed him with a piercing gaze. "Your wife perhaps?"

"Catherine."

"Such a pretty name. Is she well?"

Henry felt his chest swell with pride. "She is very well, thank you, Mrs—"

"Oh that's good. She was most helpful finding a special gift last time I was here. It was for my daughter-in-law. We settled on some of your perfumed soap."

"Catherine is resting. She is with child."

"That's wonderful. Is this your first?"

"Yes."

"Congratulations, Henry." The woman beamed at him. "I do hope it's all right to call you Henry? How long have you been in these parts? I seem to recall there used to be another Mr Wiltshire who travelled the area selling goods from his wagon. He used to have such good quality items like you. I remember his wife was very adept at needlework." She tapped a finger to her cheek. "Now what was his name?"

Unease prickled at the back of Henry's neck. He watched the woman ponder. He still didn't know her name. His mother had suggested he not mention his father's name in these parts. That's why it wasn't displayed on the front sign. She said there'd been a few business deals that had gone awry and some people held grudges even though she assured Henry it was not his father's fault. That was a long time ago and this woman didn't appear to hold any resentment.

"Septimus." He said the name of the father he hardly knew and of whom he held his own vague, difficult memories. "He died when I was young. I hardly remember him."

"I'm sorry. And your mother? I do recall taking tea with her when we were both much younger."

Henry felt his confidence return. "Harriet. She is quite well thank you and living in Adelaide. She has a business of her own there. Those cloths you admired are hers. Or at least the women who work for her. Mother's eyesight is not the best for close work anymore."

"Oh. I'm sorry to hear that but I do understand. I have to get someone else to thread the needle for me these days."

The bell above the door jangled. Henry frowned as his eyes adjusted to take in the face of the man framed by the light from the open door.

"Mr Baker." Henry kept his tone civil for the sake of the lady at the counter. To his surprise she reached out her hand to Baker.

"This is my son," she said with pride in her voice. "Joseph was born not long after you, Henry."

Henry pursed his lips. So this woman was a Baker. Another man followed Joseph into the shop. They were a similar height. The older man had a darker head of hair, greying at the temples but there was no denying the likeness to Joseph.

"And this is my husband, Thomas Baker. He knew your father."

Henry saw the older man stiffen. Beyond him on the verandah, the native girl stood holding the hands of Joseph's two little girls. A boy swung on the hitching rail. Baker had brought his ragtag tribe with him again. Henry wondered where the sullen black man who had been with them last time was hiding. A chilly wind blew through the open door. The afternoon sky had darkened. He would need to light the lamps earlier than usual.

"I believe my son has business to conduct with you, Henry."

Henry turned back to the sweetly smiling Mrs Baker. What had been the true purpose of all her questions?

"The last time we will do business," Joseph growled.

"That's as may be, son. You go ahead." Mrs Baker turned and beckoned to the children. "Mary, bring the girls in please."

The man at the door, his jaw clenched, still had not spoken. He shifted aside to let the children in. Henry opened his mouth to protest at the native girl being in his shop but Mrs Baker stopped him with her sharp sparkling gaze.

"I wish to buy some ribbons for the girls. I'll pick them out while you and Joseph conduct your business."

Joseph made a move towards the end of the counter but Henry found his voice at last.

"You can wait here," he said sharply. "I have everything prepared." Henry turned away briefly to put his head around the curtain behind him. Catherine was sitting in one of the comfortable chairs reading a book. He sucked in a breath. The remains of their lunch still sat upon the table. "Catherine, my dear," he said through clenched teeth.

She sat up abruptly, the book slid from her fingers to the floor. "Henry, you startled me."

"Come and serve." There was no way he would give the Bakers free range in his shop while he collected the papers and money. He held the curtain for his wife. She made her way slowly. Even though the baby was still some months away Catherine had filled out all over and now wore a loose smock over her skirt. "My wife will see to your needs, Mrs Baker."

As he went behind the curtain he heard Mrs Baker exclaiming in delight over Catherine's condition. Neither of the men spoke.

By the time he had checked his figures and recounted the money, Catherine had measured out several lengths of brightly coloured ribbon. Henry moved to the end of the counter where

Joseph Baker waited. His father still stood, arms folded, just inside the door which was now closed.

Henry handed the papers and the money to Joseph who stayed where he was and studied it carefully. Henry glanced back at the little girls and their native shadow, Mary, who were at the counter with Mrs Baker. He still wanted to protest at the native's presence in his shop but something about Mrs Baker's manner prevented him. The boy had not come inside.

"This is not the amount we agreed on." Joseph's voice was low and unwavering.

"It was." Henry drew himself up. He flicked one hand towards the papers. "Less what you owed for the goods you took last time you were in my shop."

Joseph fixed him with such a hateful stare it was as if his look burned right through Henry but he stood his ground. Behind him there was silence except for the movement of Catherine, cutting the ribbons.

Joseph shuffled through the papers until he reached the itemised list. He looked back at Henry. "These are the most expensive hats I've ever seen."

"You didn't ask the price at the time."

Joseph flicked the paper with his fingers. "Everything on this list is overpriced."

"I run a fine establishment." Henry had been so angry after Baker's last visit he'd added extra to each item on the account. He clasped the lapels of his jacket in his hands and drew himself up straighter. "Other people are happy with my prices."

"I can't see how you could have any customers." Joseph spat the words at him.

"Time to go I think." Baker senior spoke up. They were the only words he'd uttered since entering the shop. Now he reached for the handle. "There's nothing more to be gained here."

"Thank you, Mrs Wiltshire." Mrs Baker's voice was still light and cheerful in comparison to the two Baker men. "I'm not sure when we will be back again."

"We won't be." Once again Baker senior spoke. He was obviously siding with his son.

"In the meantime," Mrs Baker continued without a glance at either of the men. "I do wish you well with your confinement."

The smallest girl tugged at the ribbons in her grandmother's hands.

"Yes, yes, Esther." Mrs Baker lifted the child to her hip. "We'll share the ribbons back at the hotel. Good day to you, Mrs Wiltshire, Mr Wiltshire." She took the other child by the hand and walked out of the shop, closely followed by Mary.

The Baker men, one on either side of the door, glowered back at him, pressed their hats to their heads and stepped outside. The bell jangled overhead as they shut the door firmly behind them.

A smattering of rain began to fall as Lizzie led the group back to the hotel. That had certainly been a most uncomfortable experience. She was glad to get Thomas and Joseph away before they exploded. She gave the ribbons to Mary to put in the girls' hair. William went to the end of the partly completed verandah and watched the rain drop. He had become quite sullen. Perhaps she should have bought him something. She'd forgotten all about sweets in the tense moments they'd just had.

"William," she called him to her and dug in her purse for a penny. "Take this to Mr Garrat's shop and buy some sweets."

His face lit up as he reached for the coin. "Thank you Grandma."

"Make sure you bring one each back for the girls."

The smile dropped from his face. "And Mary?"

"Of course, Mary." Joseph cut in. "Don't be long. We have to leave soon."

Lizzie bent down and whispered in her grandson's ear. "The girls won't know if you were to eat one extra before you return."

William dashed down the step with the penny firmly clutched in his palm. Lizzie watched him as he paused to wait for a team of bullocks pulling a wagon loaded with wool. The rain got heavier. There were cheers along the street. William hurried between two horses to the rough path that would lead him to the shop. Sometimes he appeared to carry the weight of the world on his young shoulders. She worried he was no longer the happy little boy he'd been as a toddler.

"Well, you were right, son." Thomas gave back the papers Joseph had handed him. "These prices are highly inflated."

"Let me see that." Lizzie forgot William a moment and cast a look down the list of items and the neatly printed amounts next to them. She stopped at the ribbon and pointed to the price. "This is certainly much more than I just paid."

"Not only was he downright rude to Binda and his children but he treated us like dirt at his feet." Joseph scrunched the papers in his fist. "Now this. I certainly won't be doing business with him again."

"If he is Septimus's son you wouldn't want to." Thomas looked across the verandah in the direction they'd just come.

"He said he was." Lizzie felt that was enough. She didn't want to think back on the horrible times Septimus had inflicted on her family. "There's no need to get your hackles up any longer. We will shop with Mr Garrat from now on. Pity though, Mr Wiltshire's shop certainly stocked some quality items but we've no need for them." She linked her arms with those of her husband and her son and jiggled them up and down. "Enough sour faces. We don't ever have to deal with Mr Wiltshire again."

Thomas frowned. "I hope you're right Lizzie, but if he's anything like his father he'll keep turning up like a bad penny."

Lizzie clicked her tongue. "Enough, Thomas. Now let's go inside. Perhaps another cup of tea before you go?"

"No thank you, Mother." Joseph extricated his arm from hers. "We must make a start. The rain has cleared for now but there's no telling how much we'll get. If the creeks come down I could get held up and I don't like to leave Clara alone for too long."

Lizzie's heart melted at the worry lines on his face. "Clara's a good strong woman and a wonderful mother. Let me know if you'd like me to come and help."

"You've enough to do." Joseph patted her hand.

"We can manage without your mother if we have to." Thomas put an arm around Lizzie's shoulders.

Joseph gave them a weak smile. "Thank you. Perhaps when the new baby arrives. Clara's own mother won't come."

Lizzie placed her hand over her son's and smiled up at him. "Send word and I'll be there in two shakes of a lamb's tail."

Nine

"Have you finished giving your final instructions to Mr Hemming, my dear?" Henry smiled benevolently at his wife who was pointing out the recently received delicate lace collars to their new employee. "I have your trunk in the cart."

Catherine turned in his direction. Her cheeks were flushed a delicate pink from her exertion. "I think Mr Hemming has a good understanding of our stock."

"I do." The thin-faced young man held his hands behind his back and gave Catherine a slight bow. "You are an excellent teacher Mrs Wiltshire, but I don't want to make you late for your train."

"Oh, we're not late, are we Henry?"

"No. If we leave now we will be right on time. Mr Hemming can have his first experience at minding the shop alone while I take you to the station."

Malachi Hemming gave a self-satisfied nod. Henry was very happy with their new employee. He'd arrived in town only two weeks ago, looking for work. There were plenty of shepherding and building jobs going but Malachi was not an outdoors type of person. He had walked into Henry's shop just at the time when

Catherine had made up her mind to go to her family in Adelaide to have the baby. They had been deliberating on the fact that her absence would mean they would need a shop assistant and Malachi appeared on their doorstep that very day. He was of neat appearance, quick with addition and very good with customers.

The new house Henry was having built would be finished by the time Catherine returned with their new baby. They would live in the house and Malachi could have the bedroom at the back of the shop. Henry was happy. Business was going well, he was building a fine stone house for his wife and he was about to become a father. His decision to build a business at Hawker had been the right one.

Catherine came around the counter, her steps reduced to a waddle and her swollen body hidden beneath her maroon travelling cloak. Harriet had sent it for her along with a matching hat. The rich red was the perfect colour for Catherine's rosy complexion and dark brown hair. The thick cord fabric would be warm against the cold July day outside and yet was soft enough to fall in a graceful drape around her.

Henry offered her his arm. "Your carriage awaits."

"Oh, Henry." She gave a soft giggle. "I could walk the short journey to the station."

"Not in your condition. I won't allow it and we need to get your trunk there too. I am sure it must be packed with half your wardrobe it's so heavy."

Catherine pouted. "You want me to look my best when I get to Adelaide and I have the layette for the baby and gifts for my family."

"It's all right, Catherine." He patted her hand indulgently.

Henry opened the door then stepped back quickly, bumping against Catherine as he moved. Outside the shop stood a bedraggled-looking woman with a thin shawl pulled tight around her shoulders. By the look of her blue lips it was doing little to protect her from the cold.

"Mrs Adams." Catherine peered around his shoulder.

Henry looked again. He hadn't recognised the farmer's wife who they'd given credit to on several occasions. No doubt she was here for more.

"Come in from the cold." Catherine opened her arms to usher the woman inside.

Henry stood back and cast an eye along the street. There was plenty of activity but no sign of Mr Adams.

"You look half frozen." Catherine turned to Mr Hemming who stood at attention behind the counter. "Please make Mrs Adams a cup of tea."

"I haven't come for any more of your charity." Finally Mrs Adams spoke and her tone was harsh. "I've simply come to give you this." She pulled a battered piece of paper out from under her shawl and thrust it at Henry.

"What is this, Mrs Adams?" Henry accepted the paper but kept his gaze on the poor downtrodden woman.

"The lease to our farm."

Catherine gasped.

"It should cover the supplies and the interest you charged." Once more the woman's tone was angry.

"There's no need of this, Mrs Adams. After the great rain we had back in May the season is looking very promising."

"It was too late for us," she snapped.

"Where is Mr Adams?" Henry looked over her shoulder. "Perhaps I should discuss this with him."

Mrs Adam's pursed her lips, pulling the lines on her pale face tight. "He's dead."

Catherine put a hand to her heart. "Oh, Mrs Adams. How?"

"No doubt you'll hear about it soon enough." The woman tugged her shawl tighter. "My husband took his own life. Your extraordinary demands for interest were the final straw."

Catherine gasped.

"Have a care, Mrs Adams." Henry put a protective arm around Catherine. "My wife is with child."

"My children are starving and now they have no father." All of a sudden Mrs Adam's anger left her and she crumpled to the floor.

"Mrs Adams!" Catherine cried and tried to help her but Mr Hemming appeared beside the fallen woman. He raised her to her feet and then onto the chair they provided for customers.

"Oh, poor Mrs Adams. Henry, we must help."

Henry thrust the paper into his coat pocket and propelled his wife to the door. "We must get you to the station or you will miss your train. Mr Hemming will look after Mrs Adams until my return and then I will see what's to be done."

At the cart Henry helped Catherine up on to the seat then he climbed up beside her. The day was fiercely cold. They'd had well over an inch of rain back in May but little since. Even so, most of the farmers were optimistic. Adams was a fool to take his life over a bad season or two.

Catherine turned her worried gaze to him. "What did Mrs Adams mean about the interest, Henry?"

"I will sort it out, my dear."

"But surely she doesn't think Mr Adams killed himself because of something we'd done. We only offered charity to people in need."

"Of course we did. Mrs Adams doesn't know what she's saying, she's in such a state. Please don't upset yourself, Catherine. You have the baby to think of and a long train journey ahead of you."

"Promise me you will help poor Mrs Adams and her children, Henry. We can bear the loss of a few supplies but they have lost their provider. We can't take their land as well."

Henry pulled up the horse and cart in front of the railway station. He noticed a few people give a second look at his fine bay horse and new sprung cart. He turned to Catherine.

"You must trust me on this, my dear. All will be well. All you have to worry about is you and the baby."

She gave him a feeble smile. "Of course, Henry."

He leaned forward and pecked her on the cheek. "I look forward to the day the train brings you back to me with our son."

"What if it's a daughter? Am I not to return?" She lifted her lips in a coy smile.

"You have my preferred names." He gave her thigh a squeeze. "I can't wait for your return, whatever you bring me." Catherine had been less inclined to enjoy their matrimonial pleasures of late and it would be at least a month, perhaps two, before she returned. Henry longed for the night she would share his bed again properly as his wife.

Catherine's eyelashes fluttered. "Henry, you'll make me blush."

He diverted his frustration to loading his wife and her luggage on the train. With little time to spare the train departed. He gave a final wave then retraced his steps to his cart and turned his thoughts to Mrs Adams.

He had recently sent her husband an updated itemised account with interest added. The land and improvements, provided there was anything of value left, would more than cover what the Adamses owed him. Now he had two properties on the plains but the first one had shown him very little return. He needed a better manager than the man he had; someone with a broader knowledge of the country who could improve both properties and provide Henry with extra income. Perhaps Mr Prosser would be of some help. He seemed to be doing well and even though his property was in the hills rather than on the plains he appeared to have some knowledge of the country in general.

Henry was quite convinced diversifying was his best way of making money. He'd set up a shop and a forwarding agency. He was having talks regarding adding the post office to his shop until a permanent office could be built and he'd recently heard the new telegraph would need to be housed somewhere. Once again his shop was the perfect place.

Now that Catherine was gone he planned to move into the little wooden cottage beside the new house he was building. It was for rent and he could keep a closer eye on construction if he lived right next door. Mr Hemming could move into the house at the back of the shop and the telegraph could be set up in the parlour.

Henry was full of enthusiasm as he hitched his horse and cart at the back of his building and made his way inside. Everything was working out well. There was just the problem of Mrs Adams.

When he entered the shop Malachi was serving customers, a man and his wife, but there was no sign of Mrs Adams. Henry kept himself busy, quietly observing his new assistant. The young man was more than competent. Henry was sure he would be a good asset to his business.

He smiled benevolently as the couple left, loaded with stores and the lady with some of his better quality soap and handkerchiefs.

"Well done, Mr Hemming. A good sale."

"Thank you, sir."

"And now what have you done with Mrs Adams?"

Malachi frowned. "Did you want me to keep her here? Only I didn't think you'd want her in the shop looking as she did and crying and saying terrible things about you. I suggested she take her children back to Adelaide. She has family there."

"She's gone?"

"She was persuaded it was for the best." Malachi met his gaze. The younger man's jaw was clenched and his dark brown eyes narrowed. "She left not long after you."

Henry smiled. "Very good, Mr Hemming, very good."

The bell jangled over the door. Malachi's lips lifted in a neat smile.

Henry turned to the lady who'd just come in, the stationmaster's wife. She was an older woman, short of stature but always smartly dressed and a very good customer.

"Mrs Taylor. How lovely to see you on this cold day. I don't believe you've met my new assistant, Mr Hemming."

"Hello, Mr Hemming. I assume you are taking over from Mrs Wiltshire."

"I am, Mrs Taylor."

"I saw you put your wife on the train, Mr Wiltshire."

"Yes. She is going to Adelaide to be with her mother for the delivery of our baby."

"Very sensible. Now I am hoping you still have some of that Hathaway Oil. Mr Taylor says it's helping relieve his leg pains and we've nearly emptied the bottle."

Henry went towards the cabinet behind the counter which housed all manner of oils, ointments and pills. They had proven so popular he had moved them into the shop, but Malachi was a step ahead of him.

"Let me help you with that, Mrs Taylor. We have the oil in stock and Mrs Wiltshire instructed me before I left to be sure to show you the delicate lace collars that have recently arrived."

"How very kind of her to think of me when she has so much else on her mind, I'm sure. She knows I like to dress well. Just because we live hundreds of miles from decent civilisation there's no need to lower one's standards."

"Indeed, Mrs Taylor. They were Mrs Wiltshire's very words."

Henry smiled. He was sure Catherine wouldn't have said that but Malachi had the right idea. Henry patted the paper in his pocket. He could leave his customers in Malachi's capable hands while he worked on a plan for his farming properties.

Ten

"Good night, Mrs Wiltshire."

Harriet smiled as the last of her staff left the shop. "Have a pleasant evening, Miss Wicksteed."

Harriet went to close the door then changed her mind, opened it instead and stepped out onto the path. It had been a warm day for autumn and now the Adelaide evening had a golden glow. The air outside was still and balmy, and there was no need for her jacket. Several people passed by and O'Connell Street itself was still busy with horses, carts and wagons.

She looked up and down the wide stretch of road and inhaled deeply, thankful again that she had found such a wonderful premises to set up her blooming business. The ladies of Adelaide travelled to her door not just for her embroidered linens but for her beautifully tailored outfits suited for every occasion, from undergarments to bridal trousseaus. This bigger shop was much better than the small place she'd rented in Hindley Street when she had returned from Port Augusta and it had the benefit of living quarters at the back which suited her very well. There was a milliner next door, then tea rooms, and beyond that a grocer who grew much of what he sold on the nearby fertile plains.

Adelaide had changed so much since Harriet's mother had brought her here as a young girl after her once happy childhood had been destroyed. The father Harriet loved had been forced to abandon them and her mother had become ill and died, leaving twelve-year-old Harriet in the care of a whorehouse madam. Septimus had saved her from a certain future as a lady of the night. She had loved him so much back then. They had travelled around the bush selling their wares to farmers, pastoralists and people in small towns. Once Henry had come along Septimus had installed her in a hut on his remote hills property. She suspected that's when things had started to go wrong with their relationship. Harriet shuddered. Thankfully by the time Septimus died she had established her reputation as a fine seamstress in Port Augusta. With his money and what she'd saved she'd been able to turn her back on their early existence and make a fresh start with Henry in Adelaide. She'd told her son little about her difficult early life and he certainly had no idea of his father's indiscretions. Harriet had worked hard to build a new respectable life in Adelaide. She would stop at nothing to keep her fine reputation and that of her son.

"Good evening, Mrs Wiltshire."

Harriet's thoughts returned to the present. She smiled and nodded at the well-dressed couple as they drew level with her. The young woman was the daughter of the retired sea captain whose arm she was on and she was wearing one of Harriet's dresses. "Good evening, Captain Chigwidden, Miss Chigwidden."

She watched them walk by, and admired how agreeably the tall captain in his dark blue suit and his much shorter daughter in the paisley patterned dress in a paler shade of blue complemented each other. Harriet watched the way the skirt moved as Miss Chigwidden walked. The cut was excellent. Harriet would have to remember to acknowledge her cutters and seamstresses again; perhaps an end-of-year bonus. They were doing fine work.

What a long way she'd come from those early hawking days with Septimus when everything they owned was in their wagon. They had been happy days for her but they hadn't lasted. Septimus had sought his fortune and his love elsewhere as it had turned out, but he had given her a fine son. Henry was the shining light in her life. She was also thankful for the contacts she'd made because of Septimus. She was often able to source exquisite fabrics and unusual prints through her direct links with importers Septimus had had business dealings with. A couple of less scrupulous fellows she was well aware but they gave her access to materials that no-one else in Adelaide could source.

With a self-satisfied feeling she turned, went back inside and swung the shop door shut. It stopped abruptly. She looked down to see a boot wedged at the bottom. A man's hand slipped around the frame.

Harriet gasped and pushed the door harder.

"Mrs Wiltshire?"

She paused at the sound of her name. The door opened wider to reveal a native. Well, he was part native from the pale-brown colour of his skin, the colour of toffee. She put a hand to her chest where she could feel her heart thumping.

"What do you want?"

"Only to speak with you, Mrs Wiltshire."

"I cannot imagine there is anything we need to speak about."

He smiled at her and a shiver ran down her spine. His lips were turned up but the look he swept over her with his dark brown eyes was appraising.

"We have something in common, Mrs Wiltshire."

"I think not, Mr …?"

"Aldridge, Jack Aldridge." He took off his hat to reveal gleaming curly hair. He wore clothes that had seen better days but appeared clean and well-cared for. The name sounded vaguely familiar.

"Do I know your parents?"

He chuckled. "My mother hardly at all I think, but my father very well as it turns out."

"Aldridge." Harriet's brow creased as she tried to recall the name. "Ned and Ethel Aldridge. I knew them both. I sold them the inn."

"Yes, but as you can tell by looking at me they are not my parents."

Harriet remained tight lipped. Nothing would have surprised her after discovering her own husband had taken a black mistress. Her eyes widened and she looked closely at the young man who blocked her door.

Once more he smiled a malevolent smile. "Will you let me in, Mrs Wiltshire, or am I to declare on the street that I am your husband's bastard son?"

Harriet felt the blood drain from her face and her vision narrowed. She staggered back from the door. Aldridge pushed right into the shop and closed the door carefully behind him.

He took her arm. "Can I get you a drink, Mrs Wiltshire? You look as if you've had a shock." This time the smile reached his eyes. He was laughing at her.

She drew herself up but she was still more than a head shorter than the man. "I am quite well, thank you Mr Aldridge." Now that she had her breath back she had to give herself time to think. What game did the fellow suppose he was playing at pretending a connection with Septimus?

He kept his grip on her arm. "Now that we've been introduced, you should call me Jack, don't you think, Harriet?" He began to steer her across the shop towards the door that led to the rooms beyond.

Harriet's head was spinning. Clearly he meant to do her some kind of harm. There was some slight chance someone might hear her cry out from the shop, none at all if he took her into the rooms at the back. She shook her arm from his grip and rounded on him.

"Why are you here, Mr Aldridge? My husband has been dead for many years and I have been living in Adelaide ever since. I cannot see any possible reason for your visit." She looked him up and down. "Unless you wish me to sew something for you."

He met her gaze and held it. His dark eyes smouldered and then he chuckled. "Well, I can see you're a lady who has made her own way in the world without the need for a husband. Just as well then that you let the natives drag him off and kill him."

Once more Harriet's strength left her. Who was this man who seemed to know so much about her? Then she realised. Her eyes opened wide. "You were one of the children."

"Jack Aldridge." He inclined his head to her. "Although perhaps I should take the name Wiltshire now."

"Your mother ..."

"Is dead along with my little brother. We all caught a cold; I was the only one to survive it."

Harriet felt a brief pang of sadness for Dulcie, the woman who had helped Harriet bring her own son into the world. She looked at Jack and her compassion evaporated. There was too much at stake.

"How can you be sure my husband is your father?"

"I remember him. My mother may have known his name but she never used it in my presence. We only ever called him Papa. I was in Port Augusta some months back and I visited my other mother, Ethel Aldridge." His eyes narrowed. "Ethel was able to tell me the name of the man who lived in the hills beyond her inn."

"Ethel?" Harriet's thoughts were whirling in her head. "How would Ethel know?"

"Evidently she and Ned were aware of your husband's supposed secret family. They took my mother, brother and me in when he died."

Harriet was mortified. How many other people knew about Septimus's indiscretions? And when it came to that, who else knew she had walked away when the natives took him?

"You could have tried to save him, you know." Jack stared into her eyes as if he could read her thoughts. "You had his firearm. A warning shot fired in the air would probably have frightened them off."

Harriet opened her mouth and closed it again. She felt suddenly cold, chilled to the bone.

"You look like you've seen a ghost, Harriet. I'm sure a nice place like this must have a good kitchen. Take me there and I'll make you a pot of tea. We have a lot more to discuss."

Harriet's strength deserted her. There was nothing for it but to hear what Jack wanted although she already had a good idea of what that might be. Money. She turned and led the way through the workrooms, past her sitting room and into the kitchen, aware of the man walking closely behind her and taking in the details of her business and home.

In her neat little kitchen she went straight to the fire. "Sit down, Jack." She indicated one of the chairs at her small kitchen table. "I will make the tea."

"I don't suppose you have any liquor?" He cast a look around the room.

"I do not partake of strong drink. I can offer you tea or lemonade."

"Tea will do." He sat in the chair on the side opposite the fire and watched her while she set the kettle to boil and prepared the tea.

"You live alone? I thought a fine-looking woman like you might have taken another husband."

"Since my husband died I have never felt the need for male company. My business keeps me occupied."

"No children of your own?"

Thankfully she had her back to him at that point. "Your father seemed to be busy elsewhere. Would you like a biscuit with your tea?"

"I am rather hungry. I was hoping you would have more than a biscuit to offer."

Harriet inhaled deeply and crossed to her larder cupboard. She took out some bread and cheese and a pot of pickles.

"I live very simply, Mr Aldridge. This is all I have to offer."

"It will do." He hacked off a slice of the bread and a lump of cheese and started to eat.

Harriet went back to the tea. She poured a cup for herself and a mug for him and sat down opposite him. He watched her while he took a mouthful of tea then he placed the mug back on the table and rested his clasped fingers beside it.

"Now, Mr Aldridge." Harriet felt stronger after a few sips of tea. "The purpose of your visit, if you please."

He smirked. "I'd have thought a smart business woman like you would have worked that out for yourself." He leaned in. "In fact I think you already have, Harriet. You've done very well for yourself while I've lived a very basic life. I think my father would have wanted me to have an inheritance."

Harriet lifted her chin. "As it turns out you did. If you lived with Ethel and Ned as you say, you had a roof over your head courtesy of your father's effort."

"And all I did was work while I lived there with never a penny in return. Anyway, that's gone. It never did very well. Ned and Ethel took on a hotel in Port Augusta but I reckon they drank the profits. There's little to show for it now."

"Hardly my fault, Mr Aldridge. My success has been due to my own hard work. Septimus left me very little when he died."

"Whether he did or he didn't I'm not going to argue the point." Jack glanced around the room. He would be taking in her fine china, the silver cutlery and elegant furnishings. Some of her possessions had come from Septimus over the years prior to his death but many she had purchased with money earned through her own efforts as a seamstress. His gaze came back to her. "You are obviously doing well for yourself, Harriet. The question is, what price are you prepared to pay for my silence?"

"You seem to think I am a rich woman, Mr Aldridge. It costs me a lot of money to run this premises, import my stock, pay my staff, it leaves little left for me and I don't keep a lot of cash here."

"I can take what you have for now and come back again for the rest." His hand reached across the table in a sudden move and grabbed her wrist. He looked at the plain gold band on her finger. "Or I can take items in kind. I don't mind. Cash would be better though."

She tugged her arm from his grip and reached for her locket. It was the only thing Septimus had given her that she truly treasured. She would have to withdraw some of her hard-earned cash to pay Septimus's bastard for his silence. There was not only her reputation at stake but Henry's. She had to protect her son. Jack had asked her about children. She hoped that meant he truly didn't know of Henry's existence.

"Very well, Mr Aldridge. I have five pounds in the shop till. You can have that."

"Five pounds." Jack leapt to his feet. "Then I'll be cleaning out your fine silver and whatever else I can carry."

"Calm down," Harriet snapped. "I am sure you don't want the inconvenience of trying to sell my simple goods and chattels. I have a little more money in the bank. How much more do you want for your silence?"

"One hundred pounds."

Harriet gasped. "I don't have that much."

His look faltered and she knew her act had fooled him. "I can take out sixty pounds but that would clean me out except for what I need to pay my bills and wages."

"Do you think I care about that?" Jack came round and pulled her to her feet. "Very well. Get me your five pounds. That will do for now and I will be back this time tomorrow for the rest."

Eleven

"Something's not right, Joseph."

Joseph hovered at the end of their long dining table while Clara paced the floor beside him. Sun streamed through the window but heavy clouds hung in brooding clumps on the horizon. He suspected they would get rain soon.

Clara stopped her pacing and gripped the back of a chair. Her face was pale and lined with worry. She took long slow breaths.

He moved to rub her back but she pushed his hand away and resumed her pacing. She had been upset about this new baby from the start but Joseph had witnessed the labouring process of his other four children and Clara was doing all the same things, if perhaps a little early.

"You're doing a good job, my love." He tried to reassure her but she would have none of it.

"I'm not," she snapped then gasped and gripped her back. "The pain ... is different ... I can't do it."

"Would you like me to get Jundala?"

"No. I want to be left alone."

Joseph stayed where he was. There was no way he'd leave her alone. He watched as another pain gripped her.

Clara let out a guttural cry. Beads of sweat formed on her brow. "It's too soon," she cried.

"Only a couple of weeks." They'd talked about a September baby arriving at the busiest time just before shearing. Now the baby was showing all the signs of being a late August arrival. Clara had paced the floor since the early hours of the morning. Once they had decided the baby was on its way he had asked Mary to take the children on an excursion to their favourite picnic spot.

Once more Clara hunched over the chair and groaned.

Joseph had helped many ewes deliver lambs but when it came to his wife and his child he felt useless. He took a cloth from the bowl of water on the table, squeezed it and went to his wife. He placed the cloth on her brow and she leaned against him.

"I can't do this any more, Joseph," she murmured. "After this one, no more babies."

"I know you're tired, my love, but the baby must be close. Lie down and take some rest while I get Jundala." She let him lead her to the bedroom and help her on to the bed. No sooner had she laid down when another pain gripped her.

He held her hand until she relaxed again. On the box beside the bed Joseph noticed the bottle of tonic. He reached for it.

"Why don't you try some of this, my love."

"I don't have a headache," she snapped.

"I know but it might help."

He held the little bottle to her lips and she sipped, wrinkling her nose. She gripped his hand tightly as another pain swept over her. Joseph saw her through it then went to get Jundala.

He hurried out through the kitchen and out of the back door, almost knocking William over. He gripped his son by the shoulders.

"Why aren't you with Mary and the children?"

"I didn't want to go." William looked down and shuffled his feet.

He was wearing the new boots he'd been bought for his seventh birthday only last month from Mr Garrat's shop. The boy was growing so fast he'd soon grow out of them, no doubt. Still there were three more children to pass them on to, soon to be four.

A cry sounded from the house. William looked up, his blue eyes wide.

"Mother." His voice carried an edge of fear.

"It's all right, son. Your mother is having the baby. I'm glad you're here. I need you to fetch Jundala."

"Yes, Father."

Without another word, William spun and raced away in the direction of Binda's camp. Joseph returned to the bedroom where Clara writhed and moaned. Her hair and face were damp with perspiration. He bathed her forehead and helped her change into a fresh nightgown. She was resting on the bed when Jundala appeared with William and Binda close behind.

Joseph stepped from the bedroom and closed the door on Jundala and his wife, relieved at the presence of another woman to support her. He was beginning to think Clara was right, this birth was different to the others. Binda made cups of tea and the three of them, Joseph, Binda and William, sat at the table in a silence punctuated by Clara's moans and cries from the bedroom. Joseph would have preferred William not be here. He knew Clara wouldn't like it, but he couldn't send the boy away now.

They all looked up as Jundala let herself out of the room and closed the door behind her. She went to Binda and spoke rapidly in her own language. Joseph knew many words of Binda's language but his concern for his wife and the speed of Jundala's speech meant he understood none of what she said. Binda nodded and turned to Joseph.

"Jundala says the baby is wrong way up. It's trying to come out back end first."

"Backwards?" Joseph looked towards the bedroom. Clara had said something wasn't right with this birth.

"She is worried for Clara," Binda said. "She wants me to get the old woman from her tribe who has experience with such babies."

Once more the air was pierced by a deep guttural scream from Clara. Jundala gave Joseph a reassuring smile and went back to her.

"Yes, please go, Binda." Joseph clapped a hand on his friend's bare shoulder. "Go fast."

Thankfully he knew Jundala's tribe were camped not too far away. At this time of the year they were still in the foothills, close to water and an abundance of game.

Binda fixed Joseph with a steadying gaze. "Don't worry my friend."

No sooner had he gone than William spoke. "What about Grandma?"

Joseph looked down at his son.

"She will know what to do." William's look was pleading.

Joseph knew Clara's baby would arrive long before William could make it to Wildu Creek and back but his mother would be a big help with the children. It would give Clara time to rest and get over this difficult delivery. And the trip would give William something to do other than listen to his mother's painful cries.

"I can do it, Father."

"All right. Take the small cart."

"No, I'll take the horse. I'll get there quicker and we can come back in Grandpa's cart."

Joseph patted his son's head. "You're a smart boy. I'll come and help you saddle the horse."

They hurried outside, Joseph to the small stone hut where they kept the horse tack and William to the horse yard. They strapped a swag to the saddle and kit for a fire and a billy.

"If you don't make it before dark find a sheltered place to sleep for the night." Joseph's heart lurched. It wasn't until he thought of his son camped alone at night in the bush that he fully realised the enormity of what he was asking.

"I'll be all right." William's determined look reminded Joseph of the woman he was going to find. Lizzie Baker might be small but she was indomitable and he would be most grateful for her reassuring presence.

In no time at all Joseph was waving goodbye to his son. The ominous clouds had moved closer and William was riding towards them. Joseph felt a lump rise in his throat. He was sending a seven-year-old on a man's mission.

William urged his horse forward. He didn't want to leave his mother but he knew the adults wouldn't let him near her and he wanted to do something useful.

He had seen the look that passed between his father and Uncle Binda. A secret look William didn't fully understand but it had made him fearful for his mother. He didn't know about babies and how they could come out backwards but he had seen enough sheep give birth to understand what was happening to his mother. He didn't want her to have only the help of a couple of native women. He wanted his grandma to take charge. She would know what to do.

By the time he reached the gate in the fence that marked the boundary between Smith's Ridge and Wildu Creek his horse was in a lather. He walked it through the bluebush to the heavier trees that marked the waterhole. To his surprise there were already horses there and then, even more surprising, he saw it was his grandma bending over a billy at a small fire while Eliza, their manager's wife, cleared some foliage from the edge of the waterhole.

"William?" His grandma peered at him. "Is that you?" She looked beyond him. "Are you alone? What's happened?"

William slid from the saddle and into his grandma's outstretched arms. It was such a relief to feel her warm embrace, her hand brushing at the hair on his head. Then he remembered his mission. He pulled away.

"Mother is having the baby. It's early and it's coming out backwards." William saw the flash of concern cross his grandma's face and she glanced at Eliza who'd come to stand next to her. "Jundala asked Uncle Binda to get some old native woman to help her but I thought you could do better."

Once more his grandma glanced at Eliza.

The younger woman smiled at William. "You did well to think of your grandma. My first baby came out backwards and she was a big help to me."

William was relieved to hear that. Eliza's oldest son was a strong young man now who worked with his parents at Wildu Creek. Both he and his mother had survived this coming out backwards business.

The morning light turned grey as big clouds covered the sun. William looked up, glad he'd brought his thick coat. It looked like he might need it to repel rain.

Lizzie sprang into action. "Eliza, you ride home and let the men know what's happening. I'll go on to Smith's Ridge. Tell them not to worry. I'll send word with one of the natives once the baby's arrived."

William felt so much better. In spite of the grey day his grandma's practical presence would make everything right. By the time she was ready he had watered his horse and together they turned for Smith's Ridge. They had only made it as far as the boundary gate when heavy rain began to fall.

The afternoon was so dark William could see the lamps were already lit inside the house. He was relieved they had made it before they lost the light altogether. Thankfully the heavy rain had finally eased when they were halfway home. Now a gusting wind blew. His teeth chattered he was so cold. His grandma slid from the saddle. She gripped the reins to steady herself then thrust them at William.

"Tether the horses. Someone can see to them later. You need to get out of those wet clothes and warm up."

William grinned. His grandma was as wet through as he was. She hurried up the steps to the verandah, dragging off her sodden outer coat as she went.

William was only a few minutes behind her. He'd had trouble getting his frozen fingers to undo the laces on his new boots.

He opened the front door and let himself inside. The big front room was warm but empty. Low voices carried from his parents' bedroom. The door was ajar and he could detect movement but not what the voices were saying. He edged closer. At least his poor mother wasn't crying out. He hoped that meant the baby was out. He listened carefully. There was no sound of a baby's cry either.

Suddenly the door opened wide and an old black woman came out. She was wearing nothing but a possum skin around her shoulders and another around her hips. William gaped at her. Her hands and body were smeared with blood.

She stopped when she saw him, her eyes opened wide and she cried out. Jundala came from the bedroom and Uncle Binda from the direction of the kitchen. Jundala looked at William with big sad eyes. She carried a basin full of pink-coloured water and blood streaked her dress. She murmured something to Binda then put a hand on the older woman's shoulder and guided her through to the back of the house.

Uncle Binda moved towards him but William dodged around him and into his parents' bedroom. One lantern glowed in the corner of the room giving him enough light to see the form of his mother stretched out on the bed, covered by a blanket. Her eyes were closed, her cheeks hollow and her lips dark. Her pretty golden hair was brushed neatly and fanned out on the pillow. His father sat on her other side, his head bowed. William turned at a movement in the corner of the room. His grandma had her back to him bending over the cradle. He tiptoed closer and looked round her. She was wrapping the tiny still form of a baby.

"William," she whispered. "You should wait outside."

"No, Mother." William spun at the sound of his father's stern voice. "He's almost a man. He has to deal with it."

"He's seven, Joseph." Lizzie's voice held a hint of reprimand.

"Come here, William."

He went to his father and stood beside him looking down at his mother. She was so still. William stared at her trying to see a sign from her nose or her mouth to show she breathed.

"Your mother died having your baby brother."

William gasped and pushed himself back against the wall.

"Your brother is dead too."

It was then that William noticed the pile of bloody sheets by the door and another basin of bloody water. He looked back at his lifeless mother. Her pale face was such a contrast to the black women smeared in her blood. Everywhere he looked there was linen red with blood. He didn't understand what had happened here.

"He was round the wrong way," Joseph said. "And he got stuck."

William bit at his lip to stop the cry that wanted to erupt from his throat.

"Your mother wasn't strong enough to push him out because of the bad medicine we got from the vile Mr Wiltshire. The old woman tried to drag the baby out."

William gasped.

"Joseph." Once more there was a warning tone in Lizzie's voice.

"He's old enough to know the truth, Mother." Joseph spoke sharply. "Jundala said Clara had lost control." He picked up a small glass bottle and waved it in the air. "Clara drained it, she was so desperate for relief, but it was the worst thing she could do. The old woman managed to taste a drip. It was some kind of drug that robbed Clara of her strength. Wiltshire is as much to blame for her death as I am."

William stared at his father. Fear and disbelief snaked through him. What did his father mean, he and Mr Wiltshire were responsible for his mother's death? It was the old black woman who'd been covered in his mother's blood.

"Joseph, that's enough." Lizzie came and knelt down beside William and drew him into her arms.

William stiffened. If he let his grandma comfort him he would cry and he sensed that would make his father angry.

Behind him Joseph groaned. William glanced back. Joseph stretched his arms across his wife and laid his head on her chest.

"Oh, Joseph, my dear son." Lizzie let go of William and put a hand on his father's back.

William edged along the wall and crossed the room. At the door he looked back at his grandma comforting his father, who clung to his dead wife. A shuddering sob escaped William's mouth. He ran through the empty house and out the back door. He could see a light shining from the window of the shepherd's hut and smoke wisping from the chimney. No doubt Mary was there with the little ones. It would be warm in there but he didn't want to be with Mary. He didn't need a babysitter.

He stumbled through the late-afternoon gloom, tears flowing down his cheeks. Rain began to fall again and too late he realised he'd run out without his coat and boots. What did it matter? He was wet through already but there was no-one to chastise him. He no longer had a mother to tell him to wipe his feet, take a bath, feed the hens. The memory of the blood and her still body burned in his brain. William made his way to the tack shed. Inside he curled up on the dirt floor with his back against the stone wall and cried for his dead mother.

Twelve

Lizzie stooped over the fire, coaxing it back to life, trying to bring some warmth to the big front room that had been Clara's pride and joy. The flames flickered and Lizzie watched them a moment, resting one hand on the long polished-wood mantel Joseph had set in the wall above the fire. Every muscle in her back ached. The children had needed so much attention. Over the last day and night she'd carried, rocked and soothed. She was out of practice at lifting and holding little bodies for long periods of time.

Out in the kitchen she had two cakes in the oven Joseph had built for Clara and a big pot of broth bubbling on top. Lizzie sucked in her bottom lip to hold back the tears. Everywhere she looked she pictured Clara, so proud of her big new house.

She straightened and put her hands to her hips, then arched backwards. Her throat was also sore. She hoped that didn't mean she was coming down with something like poor William had succumbed to.

The night of Clara's death had been every bit as cold as a winter's eve. By the time she had comforted Joseph and gone looking for her grandson, night had set in and so had more rain. The air was freezing and William hardly any warmer when she'd found him huddled in the tack shed. She'd heated water, bathed him and warmed him up before she'd tucked him into his bed. She'd kept him there most of yesterday. Mary had managed the little girls and Lizzie had looked after Robert and William.

The two younger children didn't understand that their mother wasn't coming back but Violet had been inconsolable and William the same, although reluctant to show it. Now he had a slight fever and a cough to add to his misery. She just hoped all four children would sleep a little longer. The sun wasn't up yet and it was going to be a long day for all of them, one Lizzie wasn't looking forward to. Today they had to bury Clara.

Lizzie had tried her best to shield the children from the sadness but Joseph was insisting they all be part of the funeral. It was the only way they would understand, he'd said when Lizzie had questioned him on it. At least Thomas would be here today, and their dedicated stockman, Timothy and his wife Eliza. Timothy was like one of the family. He had come to live with them as a young man. On one of his visits home to Port Augusta he had met Eliza and she became part of the Wildu Creek family, as did their children who were almost grown now. Lizzie would have plenty of others to help with the food and the children.

Lizzie turned at the sound of the bedroom door opening. Joseph stood in his crumpled clothing, the same clothes he'd been wearing two days ago when she'd arrived. His hair stood out all over his head and his face was haggard. He looked around the room through bleary eyes as if he didn't know where he was.

"Did you get some sleep, son?" Lizzie asked gently.

He turned to her, frowned, then winced as if in sudden pain. His legs wobbled beneath him. Lizzie rushed to his side and helped him to a chair. He raked his fingers through his dishevelled hair and put his head in his hands.

"How am I to survive without her?" he whispered.

Lizzie bent down and wrapped her arms around his wide shoulders. She felt him shudder as deep sobs wracked his body. Bearing witness to his raw grief nearly broke her heart. She was grieving too, for her daughter-in-law but also for her poor son who had lost his wife. Finally his soundless sobbing abated. She let him go and made some tea. They sat at the table together.

"I can't get the sight of her and the sound of her pain out of my head." Joseph stared into his cup of tea. "And the blood."

Lizzie reached across and gripped his arm. "I'm sorry I didn't get here sooner but I don't think there would have been anything different I could have done. Jundala and the other woman had more experience than me."

"It must have been that damn tonic of Wiltshire's." Joseph looked at her with wild eyes. "Clara had no trouble birthing the others."

"Each birth can be different. Sometimes babies get stuck. It can be especially difficult if they're the wrong way round. Clara may have been worse without the tonic."

"No. The old woman said it robbed her of the strength to push." Joseph dug his fingers into his eyes as if he was trying to block the memory. "Clara said it didn't feel right. I should have done something sooner."

"There was nothing you could have done, son."

"Perhaps if I'd taken her to the Port, to a doctor, instead of leaving her with natives."

"Don't go blaming yourself, Joseph. I am sure the old native woman was as capable as any doctor when it comes to birthing. This was nobody's fault."

A cough came from behind them. Lizzie turned to see William hovering in the bedroom doorway. He was already dressed in the set of good clothes Lizzie had laid out the night before.

"How are you feeling, William?" She could see his cheeks were still flushed and his hair damp.

"I'm all right, Grandma," he croaked.

"Come and sit at the table and I will warm some milk for you."

Joseph lifted his head. "The cow."

"Binda was up early too. He said he would see to it."

When Lizzie came back from the kitchen with the milk, Joseph and William sat at opposite ends of the table in silence.

Lizzie put the warm drink in front of William and placed a hand on his shoulder. "You did a very brave thing coming to find me on your own."

Joseph looked up. Lizzie gave him an encouraging smile.

"It was William's idea to get you," he said. "I didn't expect you so quickly."

"Luckily he only had to go as far as the boundary waterhole. Your father and Timothy were moving the lambing ewes to higher ground. He was worried about this weather coming. Eliza and I had offered to check the waterholes and we'd just reached that one and set a fire for the billy when William turned up."

A small cry sounded from the children's bedroom. Joseph turned his head.

"Robert's awake." Lizzie got to her feet and gave Joseph a reassuring smile. "I'll see to him." She crossed the room, trying not to stoop. Every part of her body ached already and the day had hardly begun.

William had never seen so many people in their front room. It was mainly full of ladies. Neighbours had come from all around, including Mr Prosser and his wife who were rare visitors even though their property shared a boundary with Smith's Ridge. The door was open in spite of the cool day and most of the men were on the verandah that wrapped around the front room.

They had buried his mother on a flat patch of dirt under a large gum tree. His father had said she'd always have the morning sun to warm her. There were plenty of flowers to cover the mound of bare dirt. The plains were covered in them and the women had gathered beautiful bunches. His mother would have liked that. She loved flowers.

There had been no priest available so his grandpa had read some verses from the family bible he'd brought with him all the way from England. William knew that Grandpa would record his mother's death in the back of the bible along with all the other births, deaths and marriages he'd documented over the years.

William bit his lip to keep the tears back. He'd been doing that all day but he knew his eyes and nose were red anyway from his cough. Mary wove through the room carrying Robert to his grandma. The women parted to let her through. Close by he heard some muttered whispers. William remained still but strained to listen.

"Walks through here as if she owns the place." It was Mrs Prosser's voice.

"Looks after that baby as if it's her own." The other lady, Mrs Marchant, was from a property further south. Her clothes were the smartest William had ever seen. He didn't recall her ever visiting their home before.

Another set of eyes studied him. Looking around her mother's skirt, her red hair fluffed over her shoulders as she watched him with pale green eyes, was Georgina Prosser. She was a little younger than William and years younger than her brothers.

William felt his cheeks burn under her scrutiny. Then Mrs Marchant's voice drew his attention.

"Poor Clara, such an awful birth," she said, "and they say she was butchered by an old black woman."

A cold shudder swept through William as he recalled the native woman smeared with blood and the bloodied sheets in his mother's room. Suddenly Mary's round face was inches from his.

"William," she hissed. "Your grandma wants you."

He glared back at her then glanced around to see if Georgina was still watching. She must have disappeared behind her mother's skirts and the two older women appeared to be talking about something else now. He stepped around Mary and went to his grandma's side.

"There you are, William," Lizzie said brightly.

He noticed her cheeks were a deeper red than normal. "You remember Mrs Henderson from the property beyond Prosser's Run?"

"Hello, William." A kindly faced woman smiled down at him. "I haven't seen you since you were about Robert's size."

William pulled back his shoulders and thrust out his hand "How do you do, Mrs Henderson?"

A smile twitched on the woman's lips then she shook the hand he offered. "You've certainly grown into a fine young man. Your grandma was telling me you rode all the way to Wildu Creek to get her."

"Only as far as the first waterhole."

"Still very brave of you."

"William, I was hoping you could take Robert outside for me. Find a place out of the wind in the sunshine."

William reached for his brother and his grandma swayed beside him.

Mrs Henderson put out a steadying arm. "Are you all right, Lizzie? Sit down."

Robert squirmed in his arms but William remained rooted to the spot. His grandma's cheeks were flushed but the rest of her looked so pale.

"No doubt you've been working yourself ragged looking after these children." Mrs Henderson tutted.

William frowned. Was Mrs Henderson suggesting he and his siblings were a nuisance for his grandma?

Lizzie gave him a weak smile and patted his cheek. Her hand felt hot against his skin. "I'm all right William. Off you go outside while the day is still warm."

William turned away clutching his squirming brother. His normally strong grandma didn't look well at all and it was probably because of him and the other children. He could look after himself but what was to become of the others? His father would be too busy. He squeezed past Mr Prosser on the verandah and recalled his wife's words about Mary. William gritted his teeth. He knew what his father would do. He would ask Mary to look after them. Anger wormed in his chest. William wasn't going to be cared for by her.

"Lizzie, I'm taking you home."

She opened her eyes and looked up into Thomas's worried face, then at the early glow of first light beyond the window.

"Not now, Thomas." She put a hand to her forehead, her cool palm soothing against her warm skin. Somehow she'd managed to get through the day yesterday but by night time she'd been exhausted. She'd slept fitfully in a makeshift bed in the big main room of Joseph's house. Thomas hadn't wanted her to spend the night in the little hut out the back. From beyond the door Thomas had left open she could hear a child crying. Probably Esther. Lizzie closed her eyes again. Her head ached and her chest was sore from coughing. "I can't face the ride."

"Timothy and Eliza left us the cart. The rain has gone and it promises to be a warm day. I've made you a cosy bed in the back of the cart. If we set off now we will make Wildu Creek before dark."

"The children."

"William is recovered from his fever and the others haven't succumbed."

"But they need care. They've lost their mother."

Thomas took her hand. It felt warm and strong around her own. "Joseph has Jundala and Mary to help with the children for now."

Lizzie coughed and pain wracked through her chest and back.

"You can't do anymore here, my love. You're too sick. I'm taking you home to Wildu Creek."

"Very well." Lizzie was too tired to argue. The last thing she felt like was rattling along in the back of the cart but she knew she was no help to Joseph as she was. Thomas couldn't spare anymore time away from Wildu Creek and she did long for her own bed.

In a very short time Thomas had her rugged up and bundled into the back of the cart, over which he'd rigged a canvas frame to give some protection from the breeze.

Lizzie looked back at Joseph, who held Robert with Violet standing beside him. Mary held Esther. Both little girls were crying, Esther loudly and Violet trying not to, with big tears rolling down her cheeks. William stood a little apart from the others, his face grim.

Wispy clouds passed over the sun giving a momentary grey light. Thomas clasped Joseph's shoulder then climbed up onto the cart, urging the horse forward. Lizzie jerked with the sudden movement. She tried her best to give the sad little family gathered on the verandah a happy smile and a big wave. It broke her heart to see her son leaning against the verandah post for support, his face so sad, his shoulders stooped.

Within minutes they were lost from her sight as the cart followed the track through large trees. Once more she clutched at her chest as a bout of coughing hacked through her. Finally it eased. Lizzie felt so tired and the bed Thomas had made was surprisingly comfortable. She huddled down into the blankets and closed her eyes.

Thirteen

"This is certainly interesting country, Mr Prosser." Henry shifted his gaze from the gently rolling hills scattered with sheep to the backdrop of the rugged mountain range behind. This trip to Prosser's property was his first to the country beyond the plains where Hawker had been built.

"Much better than the plains. They shouldn't be farming there. Some have the strange notion that the rain follows the plough."

"I've heard it mentioned several times. You don't believe it?" Henry shifted his weight in the saddle. His backside was beginning to ache. The horse Prosser had loaned him was steady and reliable but Henry wasn't used to sitting in a saddle. He'd made his way to Prosser's Run in his small delivery cart. With Catherine still in Adelaide and no word of the baby, he had taken the opportunity to leave Mr Hemming in charge at the shop and drive out to Prosser's property, a full day's journey in his cart. Last night he'd enjoyed the Prosser's hospitality and now he was getting a look at their land.

"I think Mr Goyder's information is more accurate. He has drawn a line on the map of the state beyond which he doesn't believe the land and the climate can sustain crops." Prosser reined in his horse and looked back at Henry. "The government won't listen to his advice. They're too eager for the money farmers are willing to pay. I only got this place at a good price because the previous owner was frightened away."

"How so?"

"He believed the government would be pressured by the farmers to carve up some of the flatter country like this for agriculture."

Henry thought about the country he'd ridden through. The thick grass, as high as his knees, had swayed in the breeze in waves like the ocean, broken by the occasional bush or tree. "Is it possible to clear such land and put it under a plough?"

"Possible yes, but I believe foolhardy. Thankfully the dry seasons we've had have saved Prosser's Run from the plough till now." Prosser got down from his horse and held Henry's while he did the same then tethered the animals to a small bush.

The two men walked to a rocky outcrop and looked down the slope of the hill where sheep grazed on the tufts of grass. It was only September but the mid-morning sun was beating down from a cloudless blue sky. Henry sweltered in his jacket. He slipped a finger inside his shirt collar. It was buttoned to the top and finished with his neat narrow neck tie. Prosser was quite a few years older than Henry and had always lived in the bush. He was a tall man with a commanding presence in spite of his more casual attire. Henry envied his open-necked shirt, over which Prosser wore some kind of leather vest.

"Sheep do well in this country?" Henry asked. His thoughts were on the land he'd acquired on the plains. If Prosser was right and it wasn't good for cropping then perhaps he should invest in some sheep and a shepherd or two.

"They do but we've had trouble with wild dogs and natives."

Henry nodded. "I've heard reports the natives take a few sheep."

"More than a few," Prosser snarled.

"Would I have the same trouble on the plains?" Henry was concerned his foray into property ownership was already fraught with difficulties.

"I imagine so."

"I was thinking of quitting the wheat and trying my hand with sheep."

"I certainly think you're wise not to try to grow wheat on those plains. The sheep farmers fare a little better." Prosser turned his shrewd dark eyes on Henry and studied him a moment. "You seem like a man who does well in business and is wise enough to hold his own counsel, Mr Wiltshire."

"That I am." Henry held Prosser's look. The man was obviously deliberating over something.

Finally Prosser spoke. "I have a neighbour who's being careless with his sheep. They stray onto my property and he doesn't miss them."

"You didn't think you should return the sheep to their owner?"

Prosser glared at Henry. "I dislike the man. He's arrogant and not a good neighbour. If there was someone in need of stock who didn't ask too many questions, one of my men could make sure they arrived at their new home." Prosser looked back to the sloping country on his other side. "His management is foolhardy. Treats the natives as if they are part of his family. He lets whole tribes of them camp on his property. Added to that his wife died a month back and he's gone soft with grief."

Henry stiffened. "You mentioned one of your neighbours was Joseph Baker of Smith's Ridge. Would that be him?"

"The very same." Prosser's eyes narrowed. "Do you know him?"

"Yes, and your summary of his character is the same as mine." Henry was quick to take Prosser's side. He sensed there was a deal to be made here. One that would be good for Henry and do a disservice to Baker.

"Well, as we are of the same opinion when it comes to Joseph Baker, we might be able to come to an arrangement."

"Would that arrangement involve stocking my plains properties with sheep?"

"I think so. This is just the beginning for me." Once more Prosser's gaze travelled off to the country to the south. "I intend taking over Smith's Ridge and eventually Wildu Creek."

Henry's eyes widened. "Doesn't Wildu Creek belong to Baker's father?"

"It does. That's some of the best grazing land in the area and has a lot more permanent water than my property or Smith's Ridge. I'm a patient man. One day it will all be mine."

Prosser was also an ambitious man. Henry understood that.

"What would you want in return for this deal?"

"Along with your silence." Prosser pinned him with a sharp look.

"That goes without saying."

"Nothing for the time being but you are a forwarding agent. You must broker a lot of sales for stock, wool, wheat."

Henry pulled back his shoulders. "My clients are growing in number."

"There might be times when it would be helpful for me to know what price others are getting, or how much stock they may be selling, anything that might give me the upper hand in neighbourly dealings." Prosser dragged out the last two words.

"I am most happy to assist, Mr Prosser, but you should know, Joseph Baker is no longer a client of mine and I don't imagine I will get his father's business either."

"That's as may be but we never know what the future holds and I have other neighbours."

"Of course." Henry nodded. He was uncertain where this deal would lead him but he was sure it was in the right direction.

"I imagine we can supply you with stock very soon." Prosser thrust out his large hand and Henry accepted his strong grip with a smile.

"It is a pleasure to do business with you, Mr Prosser."

"If we are to do business I think we should be on first name terms, Henry, don't you?"

"Certainly, Mr … Ellis."

They both turned at the sound of thrumming hoof beats. A horse and rider came into view.

"This is one of my shepherds, Donovan," Prosser said.

Donovan reached them but didn't dismount. Prosser introduced him to Henry.

"Just riding in to tell you the natives have taken at least fifty this time."

Henry tried not to flinch at the uncouth diatribe Prosser let forth. Donovan's horse flicked up its head and pranced in a circle.

"Ride over and get Swan," Prosser said. "I'll get the other men and we'll meet you back here in two hours. They're not going to get away with it this time."

Donovan gave a nod and moved his horse on.

Prosser strode back to where they'd left the horses. "Damned natives."

"Can't they be brought before the law?" Henry followed, horrified to think that Prosser's loss could go unpunished.

"I've tried that. The law is too soft on them. Says they have a right to the land." Prosser pulled his whip from his saddle and slapped it against his boot. "I've developed my own way of dealing with them. It's catching the bastards that's the hard part. But this time it might be easier. Fifty sheep aren't easy to hide."

"It seems a large number."

"It is, but this is a big country." Prosser swung up into the saddle. "Anyway, it won't matter to me much longer. I'm changing to cattle."

"Will that make a difference?" Henry managed to climb up onto his horse with less difficulty than he'd done the first time.

"I won't suffer as many losses from natives and wild dogs at least. Cattle are wary of sounds and smells they don't recognise. They're a lot bigger and in a group they look formidable." Prosser's face twisted into a malicious grin. "They've also got large, sharp horns. More than a match for dingo or black men."

Henry felt a prickle worm down his spine.

"We will go back to the homestead and collect my sons and whoever I can find." Prosser's horse wheeled around. "You'll ride with us, won't you? You might need to experience this if you are to have stock of your own."

Henry nodded and urged his horse on after Prosser's. He had an uneasy feeling. Violence had never been a part of his nature. Not to dish out personally anyway. There had been a couple of times in his earlier years back in Adelaide when he had been bullied. He hadn't mentioned it to his mother but access to her money had meant he could pay someone else to dish out the retribution. He'd earned a reputation for being a man not to be messed with, without needing to dirty his own hands.

When Prosser's house came into view, they reined their horses to a trot. Henry's backside was aching and he had not been able to come up with any excuse not to accompany the men on their mission. He had already accepted Mrs Prosser's invitation to stay one more night. There appeared to be no escape.

"Who's this?"

Henry lifted his head in the direction of Prosser's gaze. A horse and rider were galloping towards the homestead. They all arrived under the big tree at the front of the house at the same time. A young lad Henry recognised from Hawker slid from the saddle and dug a paper from his bag. Mrs Prosser and her daughter, Georgina, came out on the verandah. Everyone was interested in the new arrival.

"What do you have there, boy?" Ellis asked.

"I have a telegraph for Mr Wiltshire."

Henry climbed down from the saddle. The telegraph station had only recently been installed in the room behind his shop.

"Mr Hemming sent me." The lad held out the paper.

Henry took it, and read the few words of black print. A great sense of relief flooded through him. He scrunched the paper in his hand and clapped the other on Prosser's shoulder. "I am a father," he cried. "I have a son!"

"Congratulations." Prosser grasped his hand in a tight grip and gave it a fierce shaking up and down. "Tonight we must celebrate."

Henry extracted his hand. "That's very kind of you Ellis, but I must get back to Hawker."

"What about …?" Prosser glanced at the boy who was standing beside them grinning broadly. "The job we were going to do?"

"I am sure you will manage very well without me. You do understand I must get back and make contact with my wife." Henry looked at Prosser with the brightest of smiles.

"Yes, of course. Disappointing but I understand your desire to return home."

Henry turned to the lad. "You can help me hitch up the cart and ride back with me."

"Yes, Mr Wiltshire."

"He'd better water his horse first and I will get my wife to prepare you something to eat for the journey. My horses can stay here. My daughter will see to them." Prosser waved in the direction of the verandah.

"Thank you, Ellis, you're most generous."

"I won't stay to see you off. I want to get on after those …" Once more Prosser glanced at the lad. "Sheep."

"Of course."

Ellis shook Henry's hand then strode away towards the house. He spoke to Georgina who hurried down the steps and took the reins of the horses.

Henry gave her a nod. She was only young but she led the horses away with the experience of someone much older. No doubt women had to do a lot more outside work on a property. He wouldn't like to think his Catherine would ever have to do anything such as look after the horses. Thinking of her reminded him he had a son.

"Well done, boy." Henry patted the lad's back and led him in the direction of the watering trough. "We'll soon be on our way. Lucky it's a full moon. It will be late by the time we arrive in Hawker."

Henry pointed out his horse to the boy then set off for the house to collect his bag and food. He couldn't wipe the smile from his face. Not only was he a father but in the most timely fashion. The arrival of his son had saved him from the odious task of being a part of Prosser's gang.

Fourteen

Thomas brought his horse and cart to a stop just before he reached Joseph's house. He could see no smoke from the chimney. Chickens roosted on the front verandah rails, a blanket lay crumpled on the ground at the foot of the steps and an upturned bucket lay nearby. From beyond the house he could hear the sound of sporadic chopping.

Thomas tethered the horse. He glanced back at the canvas-covered load in the back of the cart. Lizzie's gifts of food would have to wait. He shifted the bucket and picked up the blanket. It was wet and covered in dirt. He hung the blanket over the rail. Perhaps it had blown from there already. The chickens squawked their protest as he shooed them from the verandah. He stopped at the door. Now he could hear wailing from within. Thomas took a deep breath. He wished Lizzie was with him but she was still recovering from her illness and tired easily. He opened the door.

The sight before him was of utter devastation. Clara's once-tidy house had disappeared. The long table was covered in plates and mugs, the floor littered with items of clothing and no fire burned in the grate Joseph huddled in front of, rocking a sobbing

Robert in his arms. More crying came from the other room and he could hear Mary's soothing tones.

"Joseph."

He didn't react.

"Son?" Thomas called a bit louder.

Joseph lifted his head slowly and turned his sorrow-lined face to his father. Recognition flickered in his eyes. He staggered to his feet. "I didn't hear you."

"I've come to see how you are."

Esther flew from the bedroom. She wore a tatty brown night-dress. "Gam pa," she called and flung her arms around his legs. He patted her hair, which stuck out in an untidy jumble and felt rough. Violet arrived a few steps behind her wearing a clean nightdress. Her hair was neatly brushed and her skin glowed pink. Mary followed, a brush in her hand.

Thomas squatted and enveloped both little girls in his arms, one smelling sweet and the other like she hadn't washed in a while. Mary crossed to Joseph and took Robert with her out to the kitchen.

"Where is William?" Thomas asked.

Joseph looked around the room through bleary eyes as if he was searching for his son.

"He's chopping wood, Grandpa." Violet's sweet little face looked up at him full of concern. "We don't have a fire in the day but Father lets us light it at night."

Thomas gave Joseph a questioning look.

"The days are warm enough." Joseph shrugged his shoulders and Thomas realised how unkempt he looked. He hadn't shaved since the funeral, by the look of the growth on his face. His hair was long and lank, and his clothes stained and filthy.

Thomas prised Esther from his leg. "Would you girls ask Mary to make Grandpa a cup of tea please?"

Violet started for the kitchen immediately and Esther was soon pushing in front wanting to be first.

Thomas turned back to his son. "What of your animals, Joseph?" Thomas was concerned at the sight of his grandchildren. If Joseph couldn't look after them how would the sheep be faring? It wasn't long until shearing.

"Binda and his cousin have been managing. Sometimes Jundala and Joe help, and William. I've ridden out a few times but …" His voice trailed away.

"Is that where they are now? Out with the stock?"

A small frown creased Joseph's brow. "Binda and Jundala took Joe with them to visit Jundala's people but they left Mary here. I don't know how I would manage without her."

"How long have they been gone?" Thomas realised things were much worse at Smith's Ridge than he'd imagined. Binda had always been a reliable help to Joseph, unlike Gulda who came and went, but Thomas had Timothy and his son to help and Gulda's son Tom was proving to be a good worker.

Joseph didn't answer. He leaned forward and put his head in his hands.

"Three days," a younger voice said.

Thomas looked towards the kitchen door. William held an armload of wood, his face still flushed from his exertion.

"Hello, my boy."

"I've been out to check the closest waterholes first thing this morning." William dumped the wood in a box beside the fire and began to set a new one. "There were a couple of sheep stuck after that last rain, but I could only drag one of them out."

Thomas noticed William's clothes were covered in mud. The child was only seven years old, too young to be taking on the chores of a man yet. Still Joseph sat, head in hands, oblivious to the squabbling tones of Esther and the wailing of Robert from the kitchen or William trying stubbornly to coax a fire to life.

Thomas understood grief. He'd buried two babies in their early days at Wildu Creek but he'd still had Lizzie and they'd supported each other. He wasn't sure how to help his son. Lizzie was so much better at knowing what needed to be done. Joseph was in need of her special touch. Once more Thomas wished he'd risked bringing her but she had been so sick after the funeral. He had thought he was going to lose her like Joseph had Clara. It had taken some time but she at last had some colour returning to her cheeks and her cough had gone.

Flames flickered in the grate. Thomas moved closer and placed his hands on William's shoulders. "Sounds like you've been doing a mighty job. I need to talk with your father. Can you ask Mary to boil some water for a bath?"

The boy pulled his shoulders back and turned out of Thomas's grasp. "It's not Saturday."

"I know but I think you could all use a wash."

William glanced in his father's direction. Joseph lifted his head. He looked from his son to his father, sadness etched his face.

"Do as Grandpa asks, William."

The boy's eyes widened and he hesitated a moment then went out to the kitchen, closing the door behind him.

Thomas sat in the chair next to Joseph and met his son's weary gaze. What was he to say? He felt so helpless.

Joseph leaned forward and prodded a stump further into the flames with the poker. "I can't do it." His words were a whisper and Thomas watched as his shoulders began to shake. "I can't do it without her."

Thomas reached forward and clasped his son's shoulder with his hand. His heart ached for the pain he knew Joseph suffered and for his own sorrow at the loss of his daughter-in-law. He'd loved Clara like a daughter. Lizzie had sometimes found her a bit aloof but Thomas knew Clara had been a fiercely independent woman who had been a hard worker and a wonderful wife and mother. Finally Joseph's shaking stopped and he sat back in his chair. Thomas did the same.

"I don't know what to do." Joseph stared at the fire.

After the loss of their daughters Thomas and Lizzie had thrown themselves into their work but that was difficult for Joseph with four young children to look after.

Loud voices sounded from the kitchen and the door burst open.

"Mr Joe." Binda's son, Joe, ran to them and a half-dressed William followed slowly behind. "Father says come quick, Mr Joe."

Joseph looked at the boy but didn't speak.

"What's happened?" Thomas asked.

"Men with guns, came to family camp. Father needs help. Please, Mr Joe." Joe tugged at Joseph's hand. "You come quick."

"What's this about, son?" Thomas's sadness was replaced by concern.

"I don't know." Joseph shook his head vigorously. "Binda said he was going to visit Jundala's family. That shouldn't cause trouble."

"It might be Mr Prosser." William came closer. "They're camped close to his boundary."

"What can I do?" Once more Joseph shook his head. "If they're on my land Prosser should leave them alone."

"Please Mr Joe." Joe tugged at his hand. "Father say you come help, quick."

"Sounds like your friend needs you, Joseph," Thomas said. "I can come with you."

"I'll go."

They all looked at William. Silence followed but for the crackle of the fire and the sounds from the kitchen. Thomas looked around as a low growl rumbled from his son.

"No." Joseph stood up. "I'll go." He strode across the room and lifted his firearm from its rack over the front door.

Thomas frowned. "We'll both go." He turned to William. "You have to be the man of the house and look after your sisters and brother until we get back."

William's eyes blazed but he said nothing.

"Grandma has sent food. It's still in the back of the cart. Can you unload it while we're gone?"

"Mary can help you," Joseph said.

"I can do it." William's hands went to his hips.

Thomas smiled. His grandson had inherited a good dose of his mother's and his grandmother's determination.

"You don't have to do this, Father." Joseph stood in front of him. His appearance might be bedraggled but Thomas was pleased to see some purpose in the set lines of his face.

Thomas gave a swift nod. "I'm coming with you."

Joseph and his father halted the horses in front of the house. Ahead of them Joe's horse wheeled beneath him then settled. Joseph lifted his hand in a wave. His children, with Mary, watched from the verandah as they rode away. He wasn't happy about leaving them alone but he had no choice. He gave his father a sideways look.

"You're sure about this? It's probably nothing."

"I've heard a few stories about Prosser," Thomas said. "I'd like to see for myself what's happening."

Together the three riders urged their horses forward. Joseph let young Joe take the lead. He followed on his large piebald horse and his father followed on a borrowed steady grey. Joseph felt a surge of anticipation. He didn't expect to find anything more than a few agitated natives worrying over nothing much but it felt good to have a purpose. Something had snapped inside Joseph when his father had said Binda needed him. It was as if a door had opened letting a crack of light into his dark world. Just for a short time he could push aside the terrible sadness that had engulfed him since Clara's death.

Joe picked up the pace and they rode as fast as they could across the rolling hills until Joe turned his horse towards the ridges. From here the ground became more uneven and treacherous shale rock skittered beneath swift hooves. They slowed to a trot as they crossed into a dry creek bed where the going was much flatter but scattered with obstacles deposited during times of fierce-flowing water.

They wound their way between huge fallen logs and deep cut-aways littered with rocks until Joe led them up a sloping bank and into a gap cut into the hill by a smaller creek. Joe climbed from his horse; Joseph and Thomas did the same, leading their horses and picking their way forward. Joseph hadn't been this way in a long time. He knew there was permanent water ahead. It's where he'd thought he'd die when he was little more than a boy but Binda had found him and saved his life.

He only let his sheep into this country when there was no water to be found anywhere else. Once they got into these hills they were difficult to find again. He knew that was one of the reasons Jundala's family chose to camp here. They were unlikely to be bothered by the white invaders, as her father and Binda's called Europeans.

A gunshot echoed back along the creek. The young native turned terrified eyes to Joseph.

Joseph gave his reins to Joe and pulled his firearm from the holder on the side of his saddle. Thomas did the same.

"Stay here," Joseph said to the boy.

He and Thomas picked their way forward on foot. Finally the ground evened out again and they passed a waterhole. Three dead sheep lay scattered under a nearby tree and there were hoof prints to indicate many more had been here. Joseph knew they were not his sheep. Further on against the side of a low cliff they came across several of the small dwellings made by Jundala's family. Smoke drifted from a fire that had burned low but there was no other sign of habitation.

They moved on urgently, around tall trees and large boulders through a gap. Voices echoed along the ridge wall, frightened, angry voices, and the dreadful sound of someone wailing.

Joseph hurried on. A group of natives appeared in front of him. He was thankful to see Binda in the lead but his arm was around Jundala who was limping. Behind them Jundala's family followed in a group. Binda stopped, and they all stopped. An angry voice was raised and a man stepped around Binda and waved a spear at Joseph.

"Steady," Thomas said and came to stand beside him.

Binda spoke rapidly to the other native who glared at Joseph but lowered his spear.

"What's happened?" Joseph asked. "Is Jundala hurt?"

"Many are hurt and Jundala's cousin is dead."

"Dead?"

Binda moved closer then to one side, still holding Jundala. The others filed past. The man who had lifted the spear gave Joseph a wild, angry look but continued on.

Next came four men carrying a young man. His head hung backwards, his body showed signs of a battering, and he was accompanied by two women who were both wailing. The younger of the two had long hair that fell in ringlets and finer facial features than Jundala. Several others in the group limped or nursed bloodied arms. At the rear, two young men carried another, the flesh of his right arm a mess of torn skin and blood.

"What happened?" Joseph turned a worried face to Jundala. He was relieved to see she didn't appear to be injured except for one foot which she held off the ground. It was swollen and bleeding and the small toe stuck out at an angle.

"Prosser came with many men," Binda said.

"This isn't his land," Thomas growled.

"What's he doing coming on to Smith's Ridge?" Joseph gripped his firearm tighter.

Jundala shook her head. A huge tear rolled down her cheek. "Cousin take sheep."

"Smith's Ridge sheep?" Joseph had always made it clear to Binda that he didn't mind a sheep or two being used for food if game was scarce as long as the natives asked Binda first.

Once more Jundala shook her head. Her tears flowed freely now.

"Prosser's sheep," Binda said. "Her crazy cousin and some others drove them up into these hills behind Smith's Ridge."

"But it's impossible country." Joseph scratched his forehead. "Why?"

"He's lazy." Binda lifted his chin. "He thought he could keep them here and have a ready food supply."

"So what happened?" Thomas asked.

"Prosser and his men came. They had horses and guns. They rounded up the sheep and Jundala's cousin along with them and fired their guns."

"Damn Prosser." Joseph slapped his hand on his leg.

"He was taking back his sheep." Binda looked from Joseph to Jundala and shook his head. "Crazy cousin."

"There was no need for such violence." Rage surged through Joseph. "A man is dead and Prosser should be made to pay for it."

Binda put a hand on his shoulder. "There is more. Some others went to help but they were trampled and pushed about by the men on horses. Another cousin, Muta, threw his spear. It hit one of the men on the horse. Someone fired at Muta just as the rest of us got there. Muta fell and there was much shouting and confusion. Jundala got pinned between a horse and a tree. The horse trod on her foot. Prosser left with his man pierced by the spear and the rest driving his sheep." Binda shook his head slowly, his deep brown eyes full of sorrow. "It has come to this, a death and injuries. Very bad."

"We should go to the constable." Joseph's father put a restraining hand on his shoulder.

Joseph shook it off. "They will take Prosser's side."

"But a man is dead." Thomas's face was creased in concern.

"A black man." Binda's voice was low.

Joseph turned to his friend. "I will have it out with Prosser."

"No, my friend." Binda shook his head, just once.

"We can't let him get away with this." Joseph felt the rage surge in him again. It was good to feel something other than the wretched sorrow that had enveloped him for months. He felt alive again, with purpose.

"Jundala's family must move away." Binda's voice was deep with sorrow.

"This is my land." Joseph slapped his hand against his leg.

Jundala's crying ceased. In the silence she lifted her head. It was rare for her to make eye contact but her look was defiant and bored right through him.

"You know your family is welcome to stay." Joseph stumbled over his words. Jundala's people had lived here long before any white man had laid claim to the land. "They are not all responsible for one man's foolishness."

"You and I both know Prosser won't see it that way," Binda said.

Joseph glared at his friend. "They can stay. I will protect them."

"No." Once more Binda gave only one shake of his head. "It's nearly time for them to move on to their summer camp. They will set off after the burial ceremony. Jundala will go with them. She will return with the next moon."

"Binda's right, son." This time Thomas's hand on his shoulder was supportive. "You can't be here all the time. Best the natives move away for a while until everything calms down."

The fight went out of Joseph as quickly as it had come. His father's reasoning made sense. He couldn't even look after his own family, how did he think he could safeguard Jundala's?

Binda nodded, took Jundala by the elbow and together they moved on in silence. Joseph and Thomas returned to a terrified Joe who was still minding their horses. They all went back to the native camp where there was plenty to do patching wounds. Joseph walked amongst the injured. Some looked up at him with sadness, others with anger. The sad wailing of the women continued in the background.

Muta had been lucky. The bullet had travelled between his arm and his chest, ripping away flesh but missing anything vital and no broken bones. Jundala would have a sore foot for a while and several other family members nursed injuries.

Binda reassured Joseph there was nothing more he could do now but to leave the family to their sorry business.

It was dark by the time they reached the Smith's Ridge homestead. After all they'd been through Thomas longed for a cup of tea and his bed but all was not quiet. Light poured from the front windows, the curtains still open. Robert's crying was interspersed by squeals from Esther and loud banging.

"What the devil?" Joseph muttered as he strode in the back door and crossed the kitchen to the living-room door.

Thomas followed his son and they both stopped at the sight before them. William was pacing the floor with Robert, Violet was sitting by the fire sobbing and Esther was on the table clutching a pot and a wooden spoon. Mary was desperately trying to get hold of her arm.

"Father." William was the first to notice them.

Distracted, Esther stopped her dance along the tabletop long enough for Mary to catch her. The little girl let out a piercing scream.

"Enough." Joseph's command brought silence. "You should all be in bed. Girls, go with Mary."

Esther made a sound of protest.

"Now!" Joseph's bellow even made Thomas flinch.

Violet's lip wobbled at the tone of her father's voice; the same tone miraculously silenced Esther. Robert began to whimper. Joseph crossed to William and took the little boy from him as Mary ushered the girls out to their bedroom.

"What happened, Father?" William stood his ground.

"I said get to bed."

William held his father's look for a few seconds then turned and left the room. Thomas saw the defiant look on his young face. Joseph paced up and back in front of the fire, jiggling Robert in his arms. Once again Thomas's heart ached for his son and his family.

"You need help with the children, Joseph."

"I have help."

"It's too much to expect of Mary. She's little more than a child herself."

Joseph stopped his pacing. "What else can I do? My wife is dead." His words came out in a bitter rush. Robert started crying again. Joseph spun on his heel and went back to his pacing.

Thomas sighed. He went to the kitchen, added wood to the fire and looked around for something to eat. By the looks of the plates and scattered food, Mary had done her best to feed the children. The girl could be no more than thirteen and now that Jundala would be away it was too much to expect her to manage the house and the children.

By the time the kettle had boiled, Thomas had stacked up the plates and put some cheese between rough slices of bread. He poured two mugs of tea and carried them in to the front room with the food. Joseph sat in front of the fire, a sleeping Robert curled in a blanket at his feet.

Joseph took the offered sustenance with a grateful nod. Thomas sat beside him. They chewed the dry bread in silence and washed it down with the tea.

Finally Thomas spoke. "I've been thinking."

Joseph continued to stare at the fire.

"Why don't I take the girls home with me for a while?"

Joseph turned his weary gaze to Thomas. "You and mother have enough to do."

"I'll admit your mother has been very sick but she's recovered now and Eliza would help. Her children are older and would entertain the girls."

They both looked down at a murmur from Robert. He stretched one small arm into the air then rolled over and snuggled back into the blanket.

"I am sure Mary could manage Robert," Thomas continued. "And William is capable of helping and looking after himself."

Joseph gripped his hands together. "Clara wouldn't want me to give up the children."

"You're not giving them up, son. You could all do with some respite. Once things have settled down and Jundala's back we can decide what to do for the future."

"The children are all I have now."

"You're wrong. You've still got your mother and me. We're your family and we can help. I see out in the kitchen you've had a letter from Ellen. You know your sister loves you. It breaks our hearts to see you all hurting so much."

Joseph leaned forward and put his head in his hands. "I don't know what to do."

Once more Thomas felt so useless in the face of his son's despair. He reached over and placed a gentle hand on Joseph's back. "Let us help you."

Mary came into the room. "Little ones all asleep now, Mr Joe."

Joseph lifted his head to look at her.

"Want me to put little Robbie in his bed now?"

Joseph drew in a deep breath then unfolded himself from his chair and stood to one side. He sighed. "Yes, thank you, Mary. Then you go to bed. I'll watch the children tonight."

Once Mary had left with Robert cuddled in her arms Joseph crossed to the dresser in the corner and opened the door. He lifted out a small silver flask and raised it towards his father. "Fancy a nip?"

Thomas was shocked. He had no idea Joseph drank. He shook his head. "Not for me."

"Don't look so worried." Joseph flipped open the top and took a small sip. "Someone left it here after the funeral. I find it helps." He took one more sip, replaced the lid and wiped the back of his hand across his mouth.

Thomas didn't like drink. He'd never enjoyed the few times he'd tried it and it had been the downfall of Lizzie's brother, Isaac. Smith's Ridge had been the place he'd learned to drink and it had all but consumed him. Thomas felt a prickle creep down his spine. He'd never been fond of the place since his past nemesis, Septimus Wiltshire, had taken it from the Smith family through treachery. Even though the Bakers had it back again Thomas always felt uneasy here.

"It's still half full." Joseph shook the flask then replaced it. "Sometimes I feel so cold inside. A nip of drink warms me." He came back to the fire and sat beside Thomas. He stretched his hands towards the flames then turned to Thomas. "I agree you should take the girls for a while."

"I'm sure it's for the best."

"Just until I can work out what to do."

"Of course."

The sun was still a soft glow on the horizon when they loaded the cart the next morning. Little puffs of steam blew from their mouths in the crisp morning air. There was little talking, Esther the only one whose raised voice interrupted their activity. Thomas wanted to get his granddaughters back to Wildu Creek during daylight. He hoped he was doing the right thing. The girls had been excited at the prospect of a holiday with their grandparents but the forlorn sight of the remaining family was hard to bear.

Thomas shook his son's hand then pulled him into a firm hug. Without a word he climbed onto the seat of the cart. Mary stood on the verandah holding Robert and William stood at the bottom of the steps. Joseph remained by the cart after making sure both girls were firmly tucked in. He gave them a wave. William was stiff, his arms at his sides, his young face serious.

Thomas wished he could stay or come back soon with Lizzie but that wasn't an option. They were both needed at Wildu Creek. They would be shearing soon. He cast another look at Joseph. He still looked weary but his shoulders were back and he'd shaved. Seeing him with the flask of liquor last night still worried Thomas. It didn't bother Thomas that people chose to drink the fiery liquid but he'd seen firsthand the damage too much of it could cause. Somehow one of them had to come back again soon, pay Joseph a visit and reassure him he was not alone.

"Father." Violet let out a desperate call and reached out her arms.

Joseph leaned in and gave her a hug. "You look after Grandma for me." He cupped her chin in his hand and kissed her head. Thomas could see the water in his eyes.

"I will, Father."

Violet's little voice was so earnest it melted Thomas's heart. He told himself once more he was doing the right thing.

"Be good Esther." Joseph ruffled the little one's flyaway hair.

Thomas lifted his hand in a wave then flicked the reins. Behind him, tucked into a blanket, Esther and Violet kept calling out farewells from the cart. The horse picked up speed and they were soon out of sight of the house. The sound of the horse's hooves echoed back to them through the still morning air.

"Will we be there soon?" Esther called.

"It will take us most of the day, my darling girl," Thomas said over his shoulder.

Esther complained.

"Let's sing a song," Violet's sweet voice called. "'Georgie Porgie'"

Thomas joined in and so did Esther. He shook his head. It would take a lot of singing to get them home.

Fifteen

Henry stomped his boots on the wooden verandah at the front of his shop. Dust rose around him. He had just had a most unsatisfactory discussion with his builder, Mr Sanders. The house had not progressed as quickly as Henry had hoped. Catherine and Charles Henry would be coming back to Hawker soon.

Henry said the name out loud. "Charles Henry."

They had agreed on Henry as their son's middle name but Henry would have preferred George as the first name; after George Charles Hawker for whom the town was named. Catherine's grandfather had been Charles and she preferred it. Henry had acquiesced. It was a worthy name for his son.

Now all he wanted was a house that was also worthy. When his wife and child came home Henry wanted them to be able to move straight in to the new house. There was no longer any room at the shop with the telegraph in the room he used as an office and Malachi Hemming now occupying their old bedroom.

Henry took out his watch. He had been away from the shop longer than he'd anticipated. It was nearly closing time. He hoped

Malachi had been busy and yet not so rushed that he couldn't attend diligently to each customer.

Henry pushed open the door. At the sound of the bell Malachi looked up from the box of gloves he was packing. All else was quiet.

"I hope you've managed well without me, Malachi. I've been held up at the house. Mr Sanders is full of excuses at the lack of progress."

"You have a visitor, Mr Wiltshire."

Henry turned from closing the door to see Malachi nod in the direction of the tall seat they kept for customers by the counter. A woman slid from it and stood. Her clothes were plain and patched, her brown hair pulled into an untidy bun but she had an air of determination about her.

"Mrs Nixon, isn't it?" Henry gave a small nod in her direction. She and her husband were another of the pathetic farmers he'd given credit to. No doubt she was here to ask for more.

"It is, Mr Wiltshire." She drew herself up. In spite of her ragged appearance she had a shapely figure from what he could see, and hard work had not robbed her of her beauty yet. Henry judged her to be a few years his senior. "I had hoped to be able to speak with you …" She glanced in Malachi's direction. "In private."

"Of course, Mrs Nixon. Come through to the telegraph office."

Henry stepped across the shop and behind the counter where he held the curtain open to allow Mrs Nixon to pass through. The fresh scent of lavender floated with her. At least she smelled clean, unlike some of the other poor folk who still sought credit from him.

The already crowded room was even more so now that they had a desk for the telegraph. Henry pulled out a chair from the table which took up the middle of his old living area. "Please sit, Mrs Nixon."

He squeezed around to the chair opposite.

"Forgive our cramped conditions. I will soon be moving most of this furniture into my new house." If it is ever finished, he thought to himself. "How can I assist you?"

Mrs Nixon lifted her head and fixed her chocolate-brown eyes on him. "It's your new house I've come to see you about."

"I don't understand."

"My husband has … we've walked off our land."

Henry gripped the lapels of his jacket and prepared for another desperate tale. He wasn't sure he needed any more land at the moment, given the lack of cropping prospects.

"Our neighbour has taken it over. My husband has found work further south trapping rabbits. Our neighbour is allowing me and the children to stay on in our house for a little longer but he wants it for his son who's being married soon."

Henry was tiring of the woman's talk. She was no different to the many others who were leaving their land.

"I can't see what this has to do with me, Mrs Nixon."

"We owe you money, Mr Wiltshire. You've been very kind letting us have credit but we will have difficulty paying it back with the meagre amount my husband is earning now. I will have to move the children to Hawker, camp under canvas if we have to."

Henry moved in his seat. The woman was becoming boring. "Come to the point, Mrs Nixon."

"The point is, Mr Wiltshire, I hear your wife has had a baby and you are building her a fine new house. I am offering my services as a domestic."

Henry felt his jaw go slack. His budget had stretched to hire Mr Hemming and the house was costing more than he had bargained for. "I am not taking on a domestic. My wife manages our home."

"She has a grand new house and a new baby now. And I'm sure a fine lady like Mrs Wiltshire will be wanting to entertain guests in the future. She will no doubt be busy with many things and would appreciate some help." She pulled back her shoulders and jutted out her chin. "I could be that help. Before I married my husband I was a domestic for a lady in Adelaide. In spite of our current circumstances I managed to make our home most comfortable. I can sew and have always had favourable remarks of my cooking."

Henry sat back in his chair. What the woman said was true. Catherine would be much busier. He still expected her to help with the shop on occasion and he had hopes they would entertain once the house was finished. He tapped his fingers together.

"What would you expect from this arrangement?"

"All I would ask in return is a small amount of money to feed my children. The rest of my wage would go to paying off the debt."

Henry tried to think how much the Nixons owed. "That could take some time."

"It could be a trial period. If once I've repaid the debt and you or Mrs Wiltshire decide you no longer require my services, I will leave without a fuss." Once more she lifted her head high. "You have my word on that, Mr Wiltshire."

Henry studied the woman. With her hair washed and brushed and a new dress she would look quite presentable. He stood up. "Let me think on it."

For the first time since she'd begun speaking the confident look on her face faltered. "I have to find work, Mr Wiltshire. I have to feed my children."

"I understand, Mrs Nixon."

"Please call me Flora."

Henry extended his arm towards the door. "Come and see me once you move to Hawker."

"I will, Mr Wiltshire."

Henry followed her beyond the curtain and watched as she left his shop. At the door she turned and gave him one more resolute glance and then she was gone. He crossed to the window and watched as she climbed up onto a small cart pulled by a draught horse.

Malachi moved towards the door. "Shall I lock up now?"

Henry pulled out his watch. "Yes, thank you." He turned as the telegraph chattered to life in the room behind the curtain.

A little while later he sat back in his comfortable armchair in the corner of his old living room with the telegraph scrunched in his hand. Catherine wasn't coming home next week as planned. The baby was still unsettled. Henry drummed his fingers on the armrest. He was disappointed. He missed his wife in many ways. It was a long time since she'd warmed his bed. He was also anxious to meet his son.

Still, their delay could work in his favour. He would be able to push the builder a little harder and perhaps the house would actually be finished before his family came home. Flora Nixon's words replayed in his head. She had been right, Catherine would need help at home. Henry jumped up from the seat, a spring in his step. He could engage the woman as housekeeper and it would cost him very little.

Malachi was tallying the day's takings. He looked up as Henry came to stand beside him.

"A profitable day all up, Mr Wiltshire."

"Very pleasing. I am going home now, Mr Hemming. I will see you in the morning."

"Do you think Mrs Wiltshire will want to come to the shop on her way from the train?"

Henry lifted his shoulders. "Unfortunately Mrs Wiltshire is still too fatigued to make the journey."

Malachi's face fell. "I hope she feels better soon."

Henry knew the young assistant was keen to show Catherine how well he'd been doing in her absence. Clothing in particular was selling well. No doubt in part due to the new display mannequin which Malachi had become a dab hand at dressing.

"I am sure she will. And in the meantime it gives me a chance to have the house finished and ready for her. Much better than the little place I am renting next door."

"Yes. I am sure you're right, Mr Wiltshire." Malachi opened his mouth, closed it again then took a small step forward. "I hope you don't think I'm speaking out of turn but if Mrs Wiltshire is to move straight to the new house she will no doubt want curtains in the windows."

Henry stroked his chin.

"I think you're right, Mr Hemming."

Malachi hurried along behind the counter on the opposite side of the shop. "We have the new swatch of fabrics only arrived last week. If you were to choose some I could order the fabric immediately so they could be made up. Before Mrs Wiltshire's return, with any luck."

"Yes." Henry scratched his chin this time. He was good at many things but he'd never been one to select soft furnishings. That needed a woman's touch. "I agree it would be a grand idea to have everything done before Catherine arrives home but ..." He spun to look at Malachi. "Give me the swatches. I will take them home with me and bring you back my decision tomorrow."

Henry tucked the fabric squares under his arm and made for the back door before Malachi could even say goodnight. A woman's touch was required and he had decided Flora Nixon may just be the one for that. He hurried around to the front of his shop and looked up and down the street. There were several people, horses and carts moving back and forth but he could see no-one that resembled Flora. He wondered where she would go. It was surely too late for her to return to the farm tonight. He didn't think she would have the money for the hotel. She'd said she was prepared to sleep under canvas. Maybe she was already doing that. He spun around and headed towards his temporary accommodation to get his own horse and cart.

Half an hour later Henry approached the first small creek crossing on the southern road out of Hawker. The sun was low in the sky but he could see a wisp of smoke rising from the trees to his left. A little further along he made out the back of a cart. He pulled his own horse and cart and to a stop. He listened. There was no sound, not even from the birds which he knew were customarily in the trees. Henry suddenly felt a little prickle of fear. It could be anyone he'd ridden up on. There were some unsavoury characters about at times.

He climbed carefully from his cart and made his way towards the smoke. Just before he reached the fire he came to a clearing. The draught horse was hobbled there grazing on some grass. It lifted its head to look at him.

"Oh thank goodness it's you, Mr Wiltshire."

Henry spun at the sound of Flora's voice. She dropped the large stick she was holding.

He lifted his eyebrows. "What were you planning to do with that, Mrs Nixon?"

"You never know who might come along out here." She dusted her hands on her skirt and drew herself up. "I can look after myself."

"I'm sure you can but I was concerned for you out here alone. I have a favour to ask of you. I've come to offer you a meal and I thought perhaps you could spend the night in the shelter of my stable rather than in the open. Then you can avoid having to camp out alone and set off first thing in the morning."

Flora studied him closely. "It depends on the favour."

Henry felt heat rise in his cheeks. "Nothing untoward, I can assure you. I want to have curtains made for my new house and my wife is not here to choose them. You said you were good at home-making. I had hoped you might select something."

Flora eyed him strangely. "Mrs Wiltshire might not appreciate my taste."

Henry shrugged. "That's of no consequence. She can always change them later. I have only a desire to make the house liveable for her return."

"When will that be?"

"I am unsure at this stage but we need to act quickly. I hope she won't stay away too much longer. I am no cook myself but the stationmaster's wife has taken pity on me and delivered a meat pie and some baked apples this very afternoon. You could share them with me, take a tour of the house and see what you think."

"Does this mean you are taking up my offer to work for you?"

Henry frowned. She was a very forward woman but if it didn't work out he could soon get rid of Flora Nixon.

"Yes, Mrs Nixon, it does."

"I have two children."

Henry lifted a hand.

"They won't be any trouble," Flora said quickly. "But I will need to have them close by."

"I didn't plan on having three of you."

"They're old enough to chop wood and dig a garden. I can keep them gainfully occupied when they're not at school. You won't even know they're there but you will reap the benefit. Three for the price of one."

"Hmmph!" Henry snorted. "This is very odd, seeing this morning I hadn't planned on even one."

Flora thrust out her hand. "Do we have a deal, Mr Wiltshire? There's no point in me accompanying you back to town if we don't."

Henry's eyes narrowed. She was a shrewd woman but not hard to look at. He could do worse. He accepted her hand and was surprised at its softness.

"Very well, Mrs Nixon. We have an agreement."

By the time they reached his rented accommodation next to the new house it was dark. There was nothing to be gained by looking in the house straightaway since they would need to use the lantern in any case, so Henry suggested they eat first.

Flora asked if she could serve the food. He sat in the small front room reading the newspaper while she was busy in the kitchen. *The Port Augusta Dispatch* often had reports on local happenings. But the only local news in the current issue was a report on the grand rain of more than two inches that had fallen middle of September. While a section of the railway line near Edeowie was rendered impassable the rain did not fall further south where many farmers had already suffered three seasons of little or no rainfall. Henry folded the paper. This was what had driven Flora to his door. Listening to the sounds of her bustling about in his kitchen he decided it was not a bad thing. He missed Catherine and he had been alone a long time.

Sixteen

Joseph bounced Robert on his knee. The little boy chuckled and waved his chubby fists in the air, enjoying the rare midday play with his father. Joseph had hardly seen his youngest son awake for over a week and had determined to spend time with him today. Glad now that the girls were staying with his parents, he was trying to devote some time to the baby of the family. Children needed a mother and Joseph knew his own mother would be doing her best for the girls but what was to become of Robert? They were all trying: Mary had appointed herself his chief carer. Joseph could see the way she doted on the child and if William wasn't busy he would insist on taking Robert.

Joseph kissed his son's soft hair which was the same colour as Clara's, then looked up to the ceiling.

"What do I do, my love? You were such a good mother, Clara."

His murmur drew Robert's attention and a small hand grasped his nose.

Joseph looked up from the child's dimpled cheeks at the sound of horses approaching fast. Mary came in from the kitchen. Fear etched her face as she looked towards the front of the house.

Joseph strode to the front window in time to see Prosser and two other riders come to a halt outside.

"Take Robert to the kitchen, Mary." He handed over his son.

"Baker!" Prosser's bellow carried into the house.

Mary clutched Robert tightly, her eyes wide with fright.

"It's all right. You're safe here. Stay in the kitchen."

Mary fled and closed the door behind her. Joseph swept back his hair and picked up his hat from the hook beside the door. He took a deep breath, swung the door open and stepped out onto his verandah.

"Where are those wretched blackfellows?" Prosser yelled from his horse.

"Hello, Ellis." Joseph pushed his hat onto his head and stepped up to the verandah railing so he was the same height as the men on their horses. He nodded at the other two, Prosser's son, Rufus, and a shepherd, Swan.

"I'm not here for chitchat, damn you Baker. Send out those blacks you're hiding." Prosser's face was the same vivid red as his hair.

Joseph opened his hands and held them wide, secretly cursing himself for not bringing his firearm out with him. "I'm not hiding anyone. What is it that you take issue with?"

"Last week those blacks you allow to camp on your property stole my sheep."

"One of them is dead." Joseph kept his voice steady.

"The thief."

"We won't know for sure now."

Prosser glared at him and puffed out his chest. "I went to claim what was mine and one of them threw a spear at my youngest son."

"Riding in rough, firing weapons: the natives would have been defending themselves."

"Defending themselves! They killed my boy." Ellis's face went a deeper red and spittle formed on his lips. "It took nearly six days but the wound from the spear killed him."

Joseph's heart sank. There had been too much death of late. "I'm sorry for your loss, Ellis."

"Sorry, are you?" Prosser pulled his firearm from his saddle. "You will be."

Joseph pulled himself up straight. His heart thudded in his chest. He didn't believe the man would shoot him but he wasn't sure what Prosser was capable of in his current state.

"Pa?"

Prosser shook off his son's restraining hand and aimed his firearm at Joseph's feet. Joseph stood his ground. There was nothing else he could do. There was no way he could wrench the weapon from Prosser. The angry man could discharge it before Joseph had left the verandah.

"Pa, what are you doing?" Rufus looked worried.

"He's got your brother's murderer hidden here somewhere." Prosser swung the firearm wildly. "Bring him out."

Joseph shook his head slowly, hoping Mary would stay put with Robert. There was no telling what Prosser would do while he was so distraught.

"I am the only one here, Ellis. My friend Binda is out checking sheep but you know he didn't steal your sheep."

"How do I know? They're all the same, these blacks, and they stick together. He's probably been helping the others and you encourage them by letting them camp near my boundary."

"The native family have moved on."

"Where?" Prosser's horse wheeled beneath him and the firearm swayed in his hand. "Come out you black bastards." His bellow echoed around the house.

"They're not here." Joseph spoke quietly and prayed Jundala's family were a long way away by now, out of Prosser's reach. He was also thankful that Binda was not here. He was out checking their southern boundary and waterholes and William had gone with him.

"They can't hide forever. The constable will find them. You can't kill a man and get away with it."

Joseph stared at Prosser over the top of the firearm. Obviously a lot had happened in the last week that he was unaware of and now the law was involved.

"There's a native dead as well. Does the constable know about that?"

Prosser's eyes bulged. "That was an accident and it's not the same as killing my son. He was a man, not some thieving bush animal."

Joseph felt both angry and sick to his stomach. In Prosser's eyes the natives were less to him than his stock. Joseph despised the man's ignorance. He knew there would be nothing good to come out of this. He worried for Jundala and her family.

"We should go." Rufus spoke quietly to his father. "We've searched and we can't find them."

"Smith's Ridge has plenty of hidey-holes." Prosser glared at Joseph. "I know you've got them hidden somewhere."

"I can only assure you I haven't." Joseph moved slowly towards the verandah steps. "I do have work to do."

The end of Prosser's firearm lowered. "I'll find them one day." He was no longer shouting but there was menace in his voice. "You can't protect them forever." He shoved the firearm back in its holder, turned his horse and galloped away. Joseph gave a nod to Swan and Rufus who reciprocated then turned their horses to follow Prosser.

Joseph walked slowly down the steps and around the side of the house in the other direction to that of the retreating riders. Prosser was in such an agitated state, Joseph didn't trust that he wouldn't turn around and come back. The grieving man could be capable of murder and, just as terrifying, Joseph saw his own anger and grief reflected in Prosser's eyes. In his heart he harboured his own ire at Henry Wiltshire and his vile tonic. Joseph blamed it for Clara's death. He had woken from restless sleep on several occasions dreaming he had his hands around Henry's throat.

Joseph walked the length of the outer side of the house and let himself in the gate of the small backyard where they grew their vegetables. He stopped at the back door. Mary must have managed to keep Robert quiet all that time. Who knew what Prosser would have done had he known she was inside with Robert?

He pushed the door open. "Mary?"

There was no reply. He crossed the enclosed verandah and stuck his head in through the kitchen door. "Mary!"

Worried that she might have run off and be caught out in a place Prosser might notice her, Joseph strode into the little bedroom adjoining the kitchen where William and Robert slept. The box bed was empty and William's bedcover was pulled up to the pillow.

"Mary, where are you?"

Fear flowed through him. He was about to look in the other rooms when the quilt that hung to the floor moved. Mary edged out from under it.

"It's all right. They've gone."

She slid all the way out on her back. Robert was fast asleep lying across her chest.

He lifted the sleeping child and laid him in his bed. Mary clambered to her feet, her eyes still wide with fear.

"You did a good job, Mary, thank you."

She came to look at the sleeping child. "He's a good boy, little Robbie." Her voice was a whisper.

"Shall we have our meal now?"

"Yes, Mr Joe." Mary gave Robbie's fair head a gentle pat then shuffled off to the kitchen.

Joseph gave his son one last look. It made his heart ache afresh to think he'd probably not remember his mother's pretty face, her laugh, her hugs and kisses. Joseph sucked in a breath. Once more he reminded himself he had to keep going.

He passed through the kitchen where Mary was preparing food and cleared a place for himself at the messy dining table. He hoped Jundala would come back soon. It was too much to expect Mary to manage Robert, the cooking and keep the house. Jundala would help but she also liked to work outside and was good with sheep. His friend Binda was lucky to have such a capable wife.

Binda had been a good friend, trying to keep Joseph's mind on work. After Thomas had left with the girls they'd made a plan. Joseph and Binda would do a constant rotation around Smith's Ridge paying special attention along the boundary with Prosser's Run. They worked it out so that each night one of them was back at the homestead. So far Mary was managing with Robert and William usually went with one of the men. That was fine for the moment but he couldn't leave his girls with their grandparents forever.

Joseph ran his fingers through his hair and rested his head in his hands. He stared at the mess in front of him. The table was covered with mugs, plates, spoons, a pot with some withered flowers, a book of children's stories Clara had used to teach the children to read. William must have had it out. Lying beside the book was a bottle. Pain gripped Joseph's chest. It was the empty tonic bottle.

Just when he thought his grief was easing it came back, gnawing at his body, wrapping its tendrils around his thoughts, robbing him of strength. He could understand Prosser's rage. He'd been there himself. There was one more thing he and Prosser had in common: another person had had a hand in the death of someone they loved. Joseph knew the anger Prosser felt for the native who had thrown the spear, it was the same anger he felt for Wiltshire who had supplied him with the evil potion that had weakened Clara when she needed her strength; a drug that had rendered her incapable of bringing her own baby into the world. If only Clara hadn't taken that tonic she and the baby might still be alive.

He picked up the bottle in one hand and thumped the table with the other. The anger still simmered close to the surface no matter how hard he worked or how tired he felt.

"Here, Mr Joe." Mary put a plate on the table.

He looked down at the cold mutton and pickles. He was no longer hungry. His eyes strayed to the cupboard where he kept the flask of liquor. Mary stood beside him, watching him.

"Thank you Mary." Joseph glanced up. "Where is yours?"

"I'll eat later, share with Robbie." She stayed where she was.

"Is there something else?"

"We getting low on flour and sugar supplies, even tea. We went through a lot when Missum ..." Mary's voice trailed away and her eyes widened.

Joseph nodded. "It's all right Mary. I will have to make a trip to Hawker soon. Not long now till shearing."

"Okay Mr Joe." She nodded and hurried from the room.

The sound of horses brought Joseph quickly to his feet. Then he relaxed as he recognised William's voice. They were back early. Joseph gripped the bottle tighter. That was a good thing. He would go to Hawker today, alone. Binda could stay at Smith's Ridge with the children. There was plenty to be done in the shearing shed to keep them busy while Joseph was gone. He could pick up supplies and finally have it out with Henry Wiltshire. Tell him what his tonic did and stop him giving his evil potion to anyone else.

Joseph strode through the house, purpose giving him strength. Mary had gone ahead of him. She was already outside greeting her father and William was walking the horses towards their yard but there was someone else with Binda. Joseph came to a stop at the gate. A young native woman wearing a white shirt neatly tucked in to her full skirt took her turn to hug Mary.

Binda turned to meet Joseph, a look of uncertainty on his face. "I hope you don't mind. I've brought my sister Millaki to stay for a while. There's been some … trouble."

Joseph studied the young woman. She gave him a wide smile and looked back at him with sparkling eyes. She wasn't at all shy in his presence like Mary and Jundala.

"You were a toddler the last time I saw you, Millie."

"Yes, I remember you, Joseph." Her grin widened. "You could never say my name properly."

"Mr Joe." Binda gave his sister a gruff look.

"That's all right, Binda. Mr Joe is for children. I am happy for your sister to call me Joseph. I'm glad you're here. Mary says we're low on supplies and with shearing not far away I am going to make a trip to town." Joseph jerked his arm in the general direction of Hawker. The movement dislodged the tonic bottle from his jacket pocket and it fell at their feet. Joseph reached for it and shoved it back into his pocket. Binda watched him, a solemn look on his face.

"Perhaps Millie can help Mary look after the boys while I'm gone," Joseph said.

"I don't need anyone to look after me." William had arrived back and made to push past his father.

"Steady up, young man." Joseph put a restraining arm on his shoulder. "I am sure you're grateful for the food Mary prepares for you after a long day at work."

William scowled at Mary then gave his father a sharp nod.

"Good. I'll be gone a few days so you will continue to do your share."

"I could come with you."

"That could be a good idea." Binda's gaze locked with Joseph's. "You haven't been to town since … for a while. You should have company."

"No." Joseph knew the bottle had made Binda suspicious of his sudden trip to Hawker. "I'll be quicker on my own and William will be better use to you here preparing for shearing. As soon as I get back we will need to start bringing in the outer mobs of sheep to the home paddock. I'll go and get the small cart ready. Mary can tell William what supplies we need and he can write them down."

"I can do it." Millie gave Mary's shoulders a squeeze and made for the gate. "I can read and write white man's words very well."

Joseph stepped aside as they passed.

Binda moved closer, his gaze following his sister and his daughter as they went into the house. "That's part of the problem."

Joseph frowned at his friend.

Binda shook his head. "It can wait until you come home. I will come and help you get ready."

They set off towards the little shed that housed the horse tack.

"There's something else." Joseph kept his voice low. William was not far behind them. "Prosser was here. His son has died from the spear."

Binda paused mid stride. His eyes widened.

"It's all right for now. Although Prosser is irrational with grief."

Binda locked his gaze on Joseph. For a moment it felt as if his friend could see right into his soul. Joseph turned and kept walking. Binda stayed with him.

"Jundala's family are a long way away now."

Joseph nodded. "I'm glad. However I am concerned that in Prosser's current state, any person with dark skin could be in danger. Part of the reason I'm going to Hawker is to speak to the constable. I want him to hear our side of what happened."

"Are you going to tell him it was Muta who threw the spear?"

Joseph paused in front of the shed. "I can only tell him the circumstances and what I saw. Put our side of the story. If it hadn't been for Prosser's rough tactics Muta wouldn't have thrown the spear."

"If Jundala's cousin hadn't stolen the sheep none of it would have happened."

"Maybe not, but I think Prosser is the kind of man who would always be looking to shift your people on." Joseph put a hand on his friend's shoulder. "Stay close to the women while I'm gone."

Binda gripped Joseph's shoulder in return. "I will."

Before long Joseph was on the cart, Mary's list of supplies tucked safely in his pocket as he waved his little family farewell. Millie held a fresh-faced Robert, bouncing him on her hip with Mary beside her. Binda and William stood further away, each watching him closely but not saying a word. He raised his arm in a final farewell, relieved he was on his way to confront Henry Wiltshire at last. The back of his neck prickled. He felt as if the eyes of those he'd left behind followed him even though the track soon wound him out of their sight.

Seventeen

The demanding cries of her baby forced Catherine's eyelids open. She sat up from the chaise longue and looked around her. The book she'd started to read slid from her lap to the patterned fabric of the chair. The late October sun was streaming through the tall windows of the morning room. Her mother would not be pleased to see it had reached the intricate pattern of her Persian rug.

Catherine rose and drew the dark velvet curtain enough to protect the rug from the sun but not enough to block the puffs of sea breeze from the open window. She closed her eyes and inhaled the salty air. How she missed living near the sea.

Her father had purchased this land at Glenelg, separated from the beach by sand hills and bush, little more than ten years ago. Catherine had been just thirteen when the family had moved in to the beautiful two-storey home with its arched windows protected by grand verandahs and lacework balconies. Her mother had decorated it with all manner of fine furniture, rugs and artworks. The thing Catherine loved about it most was the five-minute stroll to Mosely Square with its kiosk and the jetty that stretched out into the ocean.

The distant wails of her baby reached her ears. She opened her eyes and turned to look at the mantel clock just as the door swung open.

"There you are my darling." Her mother, Florence, stepped inside, the fabric of her silk taffeta day dress rustling as she moved. "I thought perhaps you'd be in the garden taking some fresh air. It's such a beautiful day. Have you been reading?"

Florence carried Charles Henry to her. Catherine could see one little fist had escaped his blanket and it waved angrily in the air. She put her hands to her breasts as she felt her milk flow at the sound of his cries.

"Is he hungry again already?"

Her mother jiggled the baby while Catherine untied the ribbons of her soft voile day gown. "He's slept for two hours and then talked to his hands for at least one more." Her mother kissed the baby's forehead then handed him over. "You're so lucky, Catherine. He's a good feeder and a good sleeper and content in between."

Catherine offered Charles her breast. His cries ceased instantly, replaced by the funny little sounds he made as he sucked and swallowed. She gazed at him, taking in the tufts of dark hair peeping out from his bonnet and the soft pink skin of his little cheeks working hard to drain the milk. She bent to kiss the tiny fingers that gripped the flesh at her neck. He was perfect in every way and yet she felt so tired.

"I thought you were going to wash and dress while he slept." Her mother sat beside her gazing adoringly at her grandson.

"All this feeding and changing and waking in the night makes me so tired, Mother."

"You're lucky you have me and Mrs Phillips to help with him. It will be different once you go home."

Catherine looked up at her mother in alarm. "Henry won't expect me until I can manage on my own. The new house will be so much bigger and Charles is so demanding."

"Surely Henry will hire someone to help you with the house?"

"I don't think so." Catherine looked down at her baby again. She had no idea of their financial arrangements. Henry was usually very careful with what they spent. "He's already had to take on Mr Hemming to help with the shop while I've been confined."

"You must ask Henry, my dear. You have your son to think of now." Florence stroked her daughter's hair. "Henry will have to see that you will need help at home."

"There are few people suitable …" Catherine's voice trailed off as she thought of the tiny, dusty collection of rough buildings that made up the town where her husband waited for her return. She closed her eyes. Living in the comfort of her parents' home by the sea at Glenelg it seemed a world away.

There was a tap on the door and Mrs Phillips entered.

"Excuse me, Mrs Hallet. A note has been delivered."

She crossed the room and handed Florence the note. Her sharp gaze swept over Catherine who had the baby over her shoulder patting his back. "Shall I take the dear little mite while you … to give you time to wash and dress for the day."

"Thank you Mrs Phillips." Catherine handed Charles over and tugged her clothes back into place.

"I'll change the dear babe and keep him with me a while."

"You'd best get changed quickly, my dear." Florence put down the note she'd just read. "Your mother-in-law intends to call on you at midday. She apologises for the short notice but she has some business at Glenelg."

"Oh bother." Catherine fanned her face with her hand. "I'm not feeling like a visit from Harriet."

"She wants to fit in one more visit before you leave for Hawker."

Terror coursed through Catherine. "Leave?"

"Tomorrow, my darling. You are supposed to catch the train tomorrow. Had you forgotten the date? You've already delayed your return home by a month."

Catherine's mind was fudge. She had no idea what day it was let alone what date. Her days were filled with feeding Charles, spending time with her mother, enjoying the attention and the visits from her sisters and their children and delightful strolls to take tea at the kiosk. She had little need to know what day it was.

"But I'm not ready, Mother. How will I manage?" Tears brimmed in Catherine's eyes. "I can't go back yet."

"There, there, my darling." Florence pulled her into her arms. "Don't get upset, you'll turn your milk. Perhaps we could send Henry a telegraph. Say you need a little longer to recuperate."

"I can't keep delaying ... can I?"

"You had a long, difficult birth. It takes time to get over that."

Catherine closed her eyes. She didn't want to think about the two days of agony she went through to deliver her precious baby. Charles was the most beautiful gift but she never wanted to endure that agony again. Her cheeks felt warm at the thought of her times in the marital bed with Henry. That would have to cease. There would be no more babies. She would put off her return to Hawker a little longer. Henry would have to understand.

By midday Catherine had bathed and dressed. Her mother had brushed her long dark hair until it shone and then had helped her put it up in an elegant roll, leaving one curl to hang down over her shoulder. She wore her new pale pink linen dress, mercifully cooler than the fabrics of most of her other dresses. It was a princess line, the new fashion Harriet had told her about on her last visit. Catherine had chosen it because it was made without a waist. In spite of that, the skirt was fitted and required her to wear an all-in-one long-lined corset, something she had not missed during her confinement and the two months since. She twisted her head over her shoulder to take in the fabric frills that cascaded down the back of the dress; after so long in loose-fitting clothes she felt more shapely and pretty again. It gave her the confidence to face Harriet who always managed to make her feel anxious.

The mantel clock had only just chimed twelve when Mrs Phillips knocked on the door and showed Harriet into the room.

"My dear." Harriet moved towards her, arms outstretched. "You are positively the picture of health. Motherhood most certainly suits you." Harriet pulled Catherine into a loose hug then let her go and took her by the hand. "And I see you took my advice and had a dress made in the new princess style. It certainly suits you and makes the most of your womanly assets."

Catherine blushed. Henry's mother was talking about her breasts. The new dress certainly showed off her shape although it had been such an imposition to wear a corset again.

"Please have a seat, Mrs Wiltshire." Catherine indicated the high-backed velvet chair but Harriet crossed to the chaise longue.

"Would you care for some tea, Mrs Wiltshire?"

Catherine and Harriet both turned to Mrs Phillips who was still standing just inside the door.

"Not for me, thank you." Harriet sat and patted the seat next to her.

"Nor me, Mrs Phillips, thank you." Catherine sat next to Harriet.

"I can't stay long but as I was in these parts I thought it too good an opportunity to see my grandson. Where is he?"

"Mother will bring him down soon."

"I have left some parcels for you and Charles with Mrs Phillips."

"You spoil us, Mrs Wiltshire."

Harriet patted her hand. "Just some items of clothing I hope you'll find useful in the warmer weather at Hawker."

Catherine didn't want to think about the heat. It had been enough to endure the end of the summer when she'd first moved with Henry to Hawker. A full summer season was ahead of her, and how would she keep Charles cool? It was so much nicer in her parents' home at Glenelg with its thick stone walls and high ceilings and windows that allowed the sea breeze to flow through. If the house was too hot some evenings they packed a blanket and a picnic and sat on the beach to eat.

"Thank you." Catherine resisted the urge to fan her face. Suddenly she felt very hot. There were no cooling breezes at Hawker.

"I have one more thing for you." Harriet reached into her purse and withdrew a small red velvet drawstring bag. "I think it's time you wore this."

Catherine accepted the bag and opened it. She tipped it and a gold chain with a locket slipped into her hand. She recognised it as the one Harriet usually wore.

"But this is yours, Mrs Wiltshire."

"It belonged to my husband's mother. Now that you are Henry's wife and have borne him a son I would like you to have it."

Catherine had always admired the delicate gold locket with its fine filigree and an intricate 'H' etched in its centre. "That's so kind." She lifted it to her neck.

"Here, let me."

Catherine turned her back and lifted the long lock of hair from her neck so that Harriet could do up the clasp.

"There." Harriet reached forward and gently tapped the heart with her finger. "I never met my mother-in-law. Her name was Hester. I always felt happy to share her initial. Your maiden name was Hallet and of course you are married to Henry so the letter 'H' is still relevant." Harriet's finger lingered on the locket. "Keep it safe."

Catherine wondered at Harriet's strange, almost fearful, look. "But of course I will." She looked down. The heart sat just above the rise of her breasts. "It's beautiful. Thank you." Tears brimmed in her eyes. She'd always found Harriet rather prickly but it was a very kind thing to give something that was obviously so special to her.

The door opened and Florence came in carrying Charles.

"And here is my grandson." Harriet stood up. "Hello, Florence."

"Good afternoon, Harriet. Would you like to hold him?"

"Of course."

Harriet accepted the bundle of soft white fabric that enveloped the baby.

"He's grown so much since the christening."

"They do change so quickly." Both grandmothers smiled down at Charles.

Catherine felt the milk surge in her breasts. Oh Lord, she thought, she would have to undress to feed him. Why hadn't she thought of that before she'd chosen to wear her new dress?

Harriet crossed to the window where the partly drawn curtains allowed more light.

"He is looking more and more like Henry. He has the same pointy nose." She looked up and beamed at Catherine. "I'm so glad I got another opportunity to see you both before you go back to Hawker."

Catherine sent a worried look to her mother.

"Their return may be delayed," Florence said.

"Really?" Harriet's smile became a frown. "But Charles is over two months old. Henry will be desperate to meet his son."

"Of course, Harriet, but you are a woman and a mother, you understand how difficult bearing a child can be and how tiring. Catherine needs our care right now. She needs to be strong to return to her duties at Hawker."

"Her duty is to be with her husband."

Catherine felt sick. Her clothes were too tight and the room felt stuffy. "I'm only delaying a little longer. Charles is very demanding."

Harriet looked from the sleeping baby to Florence and then to Catherine. Her eyes glittered. "I can see that." She crossed the room to Catherine. "You are a capable young woman. That's one of the reasons Henry married you." Harriet fixed her with a steely look. "I am sure you know where your duty lies." Harriet bent down and kissed her grandson's forehead then handed him to Catherine. "I must go to my appointment. I can see myself out." At the door Harriet stopped. "I look forward to visiting you next time in Hawker. I am most interested to see the grand house Henry has built for you." Then she was gone.

Catherine felt a rush of guilt. Charles began to squirm in her arms and then let out a sharp cry. Catherine looked at her mother and tears rolled down her cheeks.

Florence was quickly at her side, holding her close. "There, there, my darling, don't upset yourself. All will be well. We've already sent the telegraph to Henry. He will understand you need a little more time."

Catherine's lip wobbled. She wasn't so sure that her mother was right.

The stonework of the house reflected the late-afternoon sun, giving it a golden glow. Henry swept his gaze along the newly painted verandah rails gleaming with deep green paint, to the shining glass of the large front windows with their brass latches and then to the grand front door. Solid wood, polished to the same tone as the golden stone, and with a large wrought-iron knocker above a central door handle. It had stretched his purse and he'd had to bully and cajole the builders to finish but it was done at last. All ready for his wife to return home with their son, Charles Henry.

Henry spun on his heel and walked back down the new stone path. The trouble was, it appeared his wife was not returning home any time soon. This morning he had received a telegraph saying Catherine was delaying her return once more and in the afternoon he had received a telegraph from his mother saying he should come and visit his wife and son. Whatever was going on, it was time Catherine came home.

He blamed her mother Florence for encouraging her to stay away. Florence had never wanted her daughter to live in the wild bush country, as she'd called Hawker. Henry had worked hard to prove to Catherine's family that he could provide for her very well in Hawker.

He stepped through the new gate and latched it then stopped to look up at his new house. A surge of pride puffed out his chest. All was in readiness. Flora had done a fine job of selecting the fabric for the curtains and had even been the one to sew them. There were rugs on the floor in the two main rooms. He had moved in what furniture they had and their personal effects. He was sure Catherine would want to add her own touches but at least the house was ready to live in. She could change things later if she wished.

Henry turned away and made the short journey next door to what had been his rental accommodation. Flora Nixon and her two children were now installed there and he was going to enjoy one of her home-cooked meals before retiring to his new house for the night. Tomorrow, instead of meeting the train, he would be travelling on it. Catherine could delay no longer. Her place was at his side and he wanted to get to know his son. If she wouldn't come home Henry would go and fetch her home.

Eighteen

Joseph strode along Hawker's main street. The mid-morning sun beat down from a blue sky dotted with puffy white clouds. He had made good time getting to town, only stopping when he'd lost the light totally last night and was on his way again as the sun was only a faint glow in the morning sky. He had purchased all that was on Mary's list and more from Mr Garrat's shop where he'd heard all about the recent cricket match and the many farmers on the plains whose crops looked set to fail yet again. He made a visit to the saddler, and now he was headed towards the rough one-room dwelling that served as the police station. Behind him the whistle of the departing train pierced the air. His next stop was to see the constable.

A cart passed close beside him and two dogs ran behind it. Joseph looked down just in time to avoid a pile of horse dung, only one of many scattering the area. There were other such traps for those on foot to be wary of. Sanitation in the town was poor and the smell was particularly bad today. Joseph tucked his head down and tried not to take too deep a breath.

Outside the police station he paused at the sight of a partially clothed native chained to a post. The chap leaned against the post with his head down, the sun beating down on him from above.

At Joseph's approach his head moved slightly. Large brown eyes peered out from under a mop of dark curls then the head dropped down again.

Joseph felt a chill run through him in spite of the warm day. The native's glance had been empty, as if neither the man at the post nor Joseph existed.

The door to the hut was open. Joseph glanced once more at the poor native before he removed his hat and stooped through the low doorframe. There was a man in uniform seated at a crude desk.

"Constable Cooper?" Joseph asked.

"I am he." The constable stood. He was a head shorter than Joseph, thin of frame with clear blue eyes and a bushy moustache. "And you are?"

"Joseph Baker from Smith's Ridge."

The constable's sharp gaze swept over Joseph as he accepted his hand and gave it a firm shake.

"I was soon to be on my way to visit you, Mr Baker. Perhaps you've saved me the journey." Cooper held his hand a little longer and looked steadily into his eyes. "The death of young Prosser needs to be investigated."

"Along with the death of a native in the same incident."

The constable let go of his hand but held his gaze. "I had been informed of native involvement but not of another death. Please have a seat."

Joseph glanced around. The only chair was the one the constable resumed his place on. In the corner of the hut was a wooden bed neatly made up and covered with a grey blanket. Joseph sat on the end.

Cooper settled himself back in his chair. "Since I arrived there have been several occurrences that have needed my attention. Business people tell me there has been ongoing petty theft and in the last week we've had several incidents. It has delayed me leaving Hawker."

"The man chained to the post?"

"Standard procedure. He will not sit quietly. It is the only way I can keep him safe and secure until the magistrate arrives tomorrow."

"Innocent until proven guilty?" Joseph was already concerned it may be a mistake to talk to the constable about the incident between Prosser and the natives on his land.

"Of course." Cooper picked up a ledger and opened the pages. "Now what can you tell me about the murder of Ellis Prosser's son?"

"I wasn't there. The man who works for me, Binda—"

"A native?" Cooper raised his head, his look one of interest.

"I've known him a long time." Joseph pulled himself up a little taller on the bed. "Binda saved my life twice. I still trust him with it."

"Go on."

"Binda's wife's family camp near a waterhole on Smith's Ridge from time to time. Binda was with them when Prosser and his men came on to my land looking for a supposed thief."

"Mr Prosser had approximately fifty sheep stolen and found them in country at the back of his property."

"I know it. It's inhospitable country. Prosser has no fences. It is possible that sheep could find their way there. They would be difficult to find again."

"Or they could have been moved there by someone who wanted to conceal their whereabouts?"

Once more Joseph met the constable's sharp look.

"Yes."

"What happened when Ellis Prosser came to the native camp?"

"I wasn't there. Binda sent his son, Joe, to get me. My father was staying with me at the time. He accompanied me to the camp but there was no-one there. We went looking and came across the native group returning to their camp. Several of them were badly injured and they carried one man who was dead. He was battered and appeared to have been crushed. Binda told me Prosser and his men had rounded up the natives, fired their guns in the air. Everyone was frightened and the dead man was squashed between a horse and a rock wall."

Cooper leaned back in his chair and studied Joseph. "But you were not there when this happened?"

"No. I only saw the results of the altercation."

"And where is the dead native now?"

"I don't know. The family have their burial rituals. It's their own business."

"And you didn't see which native threw the spear that killed Mr Prosser's son?"

Joseph continued to hold the constable's steady gaze. "No."

Cooper sat up suddenly and looked at the open book in front of him. "Your story is different to Prosser's. He paints the natives as the aggressors."

"He would." Joseph glanced at the pages but he couldn't read anything from where he sat. "Ellis Prosser is not inclined to like natives."

"But you are?"

"I am inclined to treat all men fairly unless they give me reason to do otherwise." Joseph stood up. "A man's word is worth more than how he looks."

Constable Cooper rose to his feet. Even though Joseph was taller the constable's presence was commanding. He held Joseph's look as though thinking things over.

"Thank you for your information, Mr Baker. I will continue to investigate but I have the feeling it will be difficult for me to get to the true bottom of this incident. Two men are already dead, it seems. Perhaps in a crude way justice has been served."

Joseph pushed his hat back onto his head. He wasn't sure whether to be relieved or enraged at the constable's response. He nodded. "Perhaps."

"I also understand you are now a widower, Mr Baker."

A knife of pain stabbed through Joseph. Every now and then he forgot about Clara's death and when he remembered it was fresh again, as if it had just happened.

"My wife died giving birth several weeks ago."

Cooper offered his hand. "I'm very sorry for your loss."

"Thank you." Joseph accepted the shake and turned away to duck out through the door.

"Mr Baker?"

Joseph looked back. The constable was standing stiffly, framed in the doorway that wasn't too low for him.

"I hope that I can come and visit Smith's Ridge one day. I am interested to know the country further out than that around Hawker."

Joseph nodded. "You would be welcome, constable." He turned to give one last look at the chained native and opened his mouth in surprise. The post was empty, the chains that had bound the native's wrists dangled free and a pair of trousers lay crumpled on the ground.

Cooper let out a growl as he noticed his prisoner was gone. He strode to the post and picked up the chain.

Joseph walked away a smile playing on his lips. The cuffs were designed for thicker-wristed Europeans. No doubt the fellow had wriggled free. He hoped the native had the good sense to clear well away from Hawker and Constable Cooper's reach.

Joseph's humour was short lived. His next job was to confront Henry Wiltshire over the bottle of tonic he had supplied for Clara. Perhaps that was something he should have mentioned to the constable but what could he do? Best Joseph faced Henry personally and had it out with him.

Joseph sucked in a long breath. The stench of something rotten made him wish he hadn't. He picked his way along the street until he made Wiltshire's verandah where he stopped to straighten his shirt collar and brush off his jacket.

He pushed the door open firmly, setting off the bell above his head in a shrill jangle.

A pale-faced young man with dark hair brushed back from his forehead and a reedy moustache looked up from the counter. His lips turned up in a thin smile.

"How may I help you, sir?"

"I'm here to see Mr Wiltshire."

"I'm sorry but you've just missed him. Perhaps I can help you?"

Joseph studied the scrawny-looking chap a moment. "No. My business is with Mr Wiltshire. How long until he returns?"

"I am not sure, sir. Possibly a week. He has just taken the train to Adelaide to collect Mrs Wiltshire and their new son."

Joseph felt as if he'd been punched. The room closed in around him. He'd come here to accuse Wiltshire of poisoning his wife only to find the man had a baby and his wife had clearly survived the birth. Wiltshire obviously hadn't drugged her with his vile potion. Not that Joseph wished her any harm. She was far too nice a person to be married to Henry Wiltshire.

"Are you all right, sir?" The assistant came around the counter. "Are you sure there's not something I can help with? My name is Malachi Hemming. I am Mr Wiltshire's assistant and he has placed full trust in me."

Hemming's voice sliced through Joseph's pain. The man peered from beady little eyes. His look reminded Joseph of Wiltshire.

Joseph drew in a breath then let it hiss out over his teeth. "Henry Wiltshire may very well put his trust in you, Mr Hemming, but I would not reciprocate the gesture if I was you."

Hemming blinked then opened out his hand towards Joseph. "Whatever the problem is, sir, I would like to try to help."

The door opened behind Joseph. A stout woman bearing a basket entered the shop. Joseph glanced in her direction then back at Malachi Hemming. He leaned closer and spoke in a low voice. "The only thing I suggest you do in his absence is rid your shop of his vile tonics."

Malachi glanced past him, no doubt concerned at the presence of another customer. "I'm not sure what's happened, sir, but Mr Wiltshire only sells the very best remedies."

"They are poisonous." Joseph felt the fury building inside him. He poked a finger at Hemming's chest. He wanted justice for Clara and their baby.

"I'm sure there's some mistake." Hemming's eyes swivelled back and forth between Joseph and the new customer.

"Are you Mr Baker from Smith's Ridge?" The woman with the basket had come to stand beside him, her face full of concern.

"Yes."

"Oh, Mr Baker. I am Mrs Taylor, the stationmaster's wife. I was so sorry to hear about your wife's passing. And did I hear you right in suggesting that the tonic you have bought from Mr Wiltshire was the cause? I thought she died after a difficult birth."

Joseph looked from Mr Hemming's agitated face to Mrs Taylor. "She did, but she was not helped by the tonic that Mr Wiltshire gave her."

"Oh, my poor man." Mrs Taylor patted Joseph's arm. "Childbirth can be a difficult thing. I myself had a terrible time delivering my last baby. The babe didn't survive and I nearly died myself. It was several years ago now but grief is a terrible thing. We look for someone to blame but we can't change God's will."

Joseph felt as if he would burst with outrage. What did this woman know about what happened to Clara? And how dare she lecture him on God's will.

"My husband is a firm believer in the Hathaway Oil that Mr Wiltshire sells." Mrs Taylor prattled on, oblivious to the rage that churned inside Joseph. "It has brought great relief to his aching legs. Once again I am so very sorry for your loss Mr Baker, but I am sure you can't blame Mr Wiltshire's medicinal tonics for it."

Joseph opened his mouth to speak but nothing came out. The woman looked at him benevolently as if he was a child in need of gentle correction. Mr Hemming remained silent but Joseph noted his face had changed from concern to an almost smug look.

With a wrench of his arm Joseph pulled from Mrs Taylor's grasp, gave a final glare at Malachi Hemming and turned on his heel. Behind him he heard the woman gasp.

"Well I never," she said.

Joseph didn't look back. He strode out the door and onto the wooden verandah then along the road, not looking left or right until he reached the place he'd left his horse and cart. His chest was heaving and his hands shook as he took the lead that tethered his horse. For a moment Joseph rested his head against the warm neck of the animal and it stayed put as if sensing his need.

Slowly his breathing calmed and he relaxed. Joseph had prepared himself to have it out with Wiltshire and now, robbed of the opportunity, the fight had gone out of him leaving him with only the aching sorrow. He climbed up onto the seat of his loaded cart. At least he had his supplies. He wasn't sure much good would come from his visit to the constable, and his trip to Henry Wiltshire's shop had been a total waste of time. With a click of his tongue and a flick of the reins he headed cart and horse for home.

Nineteen

Henry left the grand arches of the Adelaide railway station and made his way along to King William Street. Walking the path beside the wide road, all manner of carts passed him in both directions, drawn by every kind of horse, from a single trap with a fine bay to a carriage pulled by two sleek black thoroughbreds and many large wagons drawn by huge draught horses. Henry had become accustomed to the quieter life of Hawker. Adelaide bustled with life.

He made his way to the new bridge over the Torrens, which had only opened a few years before, and paused to look down at the succession of pools of brackish water that were grandly called a river. Even from the height of the bridge he got a waft of the malodorous ponds below. Water only flowed during winter and here it was the first days of summer. It would be a long time before water trickled below the bridge again. He gazed along the muddy banks in the direction of the sea, six miles away. It wasn't only the country in the north that suffered from deficiency of water. South Australia lacked abundant water wherever people had settled.

By the time he made it to his mother's new location in North Adelaide he was weary and his throat parched. It was almost closing time as he entered her shop on O'Connell Street. Several women looked up as he entered, but only one of them approached him as the rest returned to their end-of-day tidying.

The woman advancing on him was tall, with her brown hair in a neat bun. She wore a soft cotton shirt, buttoned to her neck, and a black skirt. She moved with careful elegance. "Good afternoon, sir. How may I help you?"

Henry removed his hat and gave a slight nod. "I am here to see my mother, Miss Wicksteed."

"Oh my, Mr Henry, I didn't recognise you." Colour flooded the woman's pale cheeks. "I beg your pardon."

"No need." Henry grinned at the woman who had been the first staff member to be employed by his mother once her business picked up. After his father had died and they'd moved from Port Augusta to Adelaide it had taken some time to become established. Since then her business had grown to the point where she had shifted to these fine new premises. "I haven't been away that long."

"My but you've changed." She looked him up and down. "Grown taller, filled out … I'm not sure what it is but married life must certainly suit you."

"I'll take that as a compliment."

"Please do, and I must congratulate you on becoming a father." Miss Wicksteed clasped her hands together. "What joy to have a new son. Your mother has been busy sewing for him."

"Thank you, Mrs Wicksteed." Henry looked over her shoulder. The women behind the counter were eying him curiously but turned back to their work under his gaze. They were all new since his mother had opened her North Adelaide shop. "Is my mother in?"

"Yes, Mr Henry. She's in the house. She didn't say she was expecting you. Is it a surprise?"

"A quick visit. I am here to collect my wife and son and accompany them on the journey back to Hawker."

"Mrs Wiltshire says your shop there is doing very well."

"It is." Henry took a step forward. He had more to do than make idle conversation with his mother's employee. "If you'll excuse me, Miss Wicksteed. I am only here for a short time."

Once more the woman blushed. "Oh, forgive me, Mr Henry. It's been so delightful to see you again but you will be wanting to see your mother of course." Miss Wicksteed extended an elegant arm in the direction of the polished-wood door behind the counter. "Please do go through."

Henry nodded at Miss Wicksteed and the other women behind the counter as he passed and let himself through the door. The next room was long and narrow with several windows that let in ample light during the day. Stretching down the centre was a long wooden table. Several bolts of fabric were piled at one end. Under the windows three sewing machines were set up. Through the open door on the opposite side he could make out a tall cheval mirror and a chaise longue covered in deep maroon fabric. He assumed it would be the room where his mother's clients took tea, looked at designs and fabrics, and had their fittings.

He kept walking and quietly opened the door to the next room. It was beautifully furnished with comfortable chairs, an intricately patterned rug and rose pink curtains and was obviously his mother's private sitting room. She was sitting close to the window, her head bent over the garment she was plying with a needle,

"That can't be good for your eyes, Mother."

The fabric fell from her hands and her head shot up. Her expression was almost fearful. She blinked.

"Oh, it's you Henry." She used the high armrest of the chair to help her to her feet.

"Were you expecting a different gentleman caller?"

"I am far too old to entertain gentlemen." She smiled and limped towards him.

"Is your leg worse, Mother?"

Harriet blew out a sharp breath. "No. It's often stiff when I've been sitting a while. How wonderful to see you."

Henry accepted the hug from her open arms.

"You didn't expect I would come after receiving your telegraph?'

"I hoped you would but I hadn't reckoned on how quickly." Harriet lifted her chin and studied him. "Have you been to see your son?"

"I have only just arrived. I thought I would spend the night with you and go to visit my wife and child tomorrow."

"That's very wise. Would you like a cup of tea? I made a pie today. We will have that for our meal later."

"I would very much enjoy a cup of tea. The last one I had at the railway station was all but cold."

Harriet crossed to a door at the back of the room. "How long do you plan to stay?"

"Only tonight. I've booked passage on a steamer that leaves for Port Augusta tomorrow afternoon. We shall take in some sea air and then continue on the train to Hawker."

Harriet took a step back towards him, her gaze holding his. "So Catherine doesn't know about this yet?"

"No. I plan to surprise her."

Harriet's eyebrows raised. "It may be a bigger surprise than you'd planned."

"In what way? Your telegraph was brief."

"They are expensive."

"Is there something going on that I don't know about? Catherine's letters are full of news about Charles Henry and nothing else."

"Sit down, Henry. I will make some tea and we can talk."

Henry opened his mouth but his mother left quickly in spite of her limp. He didn't know whether to be worried about her comments or not. Surely there was nothing wrong with either Catherine or the baby. Henry would have been told by now. Instead of sitting he inspected his mother's sitting room. It was furnished sparsely yet tastefully. A large mirror hung over the mantel on which sat some small oval-framed portraits. One was of his mother. He remembered it from their days in Port Augusta. Another had been taken at the same time, a picture of Henry as a young man, and the third was a photograph of Henry and Catherine on their wedding day. He picked it up and studied it. It was a full-length portrait rather than the head and shoulders picture that now adorned the new sitting-room wall in Hawker. Henry placed it back carefully on the mantel and looked around.

Harriet came in carrying a tray. He reached out to take it from her but she ignored his offer of help.

"What are you looking for?" She placed the tray on a low table between two comfortable-looking chairs.

"There is no portrait of Father."

"I've told you before, Henry. Your father wasn't ever interested in having a portrait taken. I only have those of you and me because I had a client who was a photographer and he took the photographs in exchange for some sewing I did for him." Harriet poured the tea.

"I don't really remember him."

"Your father?"

Henry nodded.

"That's not surprising. He was away for much of your life and he died sixteen years ago."

"Now that I am a father it makes me think of him."

"Perhaps that is a natural thing." Harriet smiled. "I do remember missing my mother so much when I had you."

"But at least you remember your mother. I feel as if the little I recall is slipping away."

The cup wobbled on the saucer as Harriet passed it to him. "Now is not the time to be digging up the past, Henry. You have the future to plan for and I think you may have your hands full with that for a while."

"What is all this delaying about, Mother?" Henry placed the cup and saucer back on the table. He no longer felt like sipping tea. "Is there something wrong with Catherine or Charles Henry?"

"Not that I can tell. They both appear fit as fiddles." Harriet's sour look changed to a smile. "I have given Catherine the locket that your father gave me. It was his mother's."

Henry knew the locket well. His mother rarely took it off. "That was very generous of you. I know how much the locket meant to you."

"Now that Catherine is your wife and has given you a son I think it's time it passed on to the next generation. It's safer there."

Henry studied his mother. 'Safer' was a strange thing to say.

"Charles Henry is so like you were as a baby." Harriet's mouth softened and her eyes twinkled. "He's long with a slender little face and a shock of dark hair."

A pang of envy swept over Henry. His child was past two months and he still had not held him in his arms. "What is going on, Mother?"

Harriet sat stiffly back in her chair. His question had come out sharper than he intended.

"What is it that is delaying Catherine's return to Hawker, to her home?"

He studied Harriet as she took a sip of her tea then maddeningly she replaced the cup and saucer on the table before she spoke.

"A new mother's devotion to her child is overwhelming. It can sometimes … well, change the way a woman regards her husband."

Henry leapt to his feet. Fear pounded in his chest.

"Are you saying Catherine no longer loves me?"

Harriet waved a hand at him. "No, no, that's not what I mean. Sit down."

Henry frowned at his mother and lowered himself to the chair again. "What do you mean then?"

"I think she has become accustomed to being taken care of."

Henry puffed out his chest. "Do you think I don't take care of my wife?"

"Of course not, Henry. I know you have provided for Catherine very well although her mother may not fully agree."

So it was Catherine's mother who was meddling. Once more Henry leapt to his feet.

"For goodness sake stop jumping up and down like a jack-in-the-box." Once more Harriet waved a hand at him.

Henry ignored her flapping and remained on his feet. "Speak plainly, Mother."

"What I mean is that Catherine has not taken responsibility for anything but her child since the birth and even then she has her mother and the woman they employ to help her. It must seem daunting to Catherine to return to Hawker and the duties she knows will await her there."

"Is that all?"

"It may seem of little importance to you but Catherine is not such a strong young woman."

Henry placed a hand on the mantel and studied the portrait of his wife. Desire coursed through him at the thought of her returning to his bed. He kept his body turned away from his mother while he tried to gain control of his wayward emotions. His mother didn't know the real Catherine, especially not the one he knew in the privacy of their bedroom. "Catherine is made of tougher stuff than you know, Mother. I am sure her rest with her family has done her the world of good but it's time for her to bring our son home. Tomorrow morning I will go and collect her—"

"She will need time to pack."

"I will go early. The steamer doesn't leave until the afternoon tide."

"Very good, Henry. You are the master of the house and you need to take charge. And I'm sure you're right. Catherine will settle in again once she's back home."

And warm within my arms, Henry thought smugly to himself. He went back to his chair and picked up his cup of tea. "I am most interested to hear about your business, Mother. Perhaps there are some ideas I can adapt for my shop in Hawker?"

"Perhaps." Harriet raised her cup in the air, smiled and took another sip of tea.

Catherine put aside the book she was reading and pushed it under the cushion. There were heavy footsteps on the stairs. She could hear her mother's voice and that of a man. Not her father, he had left for work some time ago.

She got up from the chair under the window of her bedroom where she'd been enjoying some quiet after a fretful night with Charles. He'd woken several times and Mrs Phillips had offered to take him out for a walk this morning while Catherine took breakfast in her room and dressed. She'd had the breakfast but was still in her bed clothes.

"You can't go in. You have no right to burst in on her unannounced."

Catherine's eyes widened at her mother's voice. Who was this man who had come upstairs and was apparently now outside her door? She clutched her shawl tightly.

"I have every right."

The voice was—. The door flew open and Catherine's hand went to her cheek. "Henry," she gasped.

He hesitated a moment, taking in her no doubt dishevelled hair, the shawl she had draped over her nightgown, her bare feet.

"My dearest." He took the space between them in three strides and his strong arms gathered her in. His lips were warm on her cheek.

"Really!"

Florence's indignant tone made Catherine pull away from Henry. She peered around him to take in her mother's stunned face. Henry twisted his head to look too.

"I am sorry I had to force my way in, Mrs Hallet, but I haven't seen my wife for nearly three months. I am sure you understand how much I've missed her. We have much to say to each other. Please allow us some privacy."

Catherine almost giggled at the look on her mother's face; her mouth opened wider and her eyes were round. Catherine felt a surge of excitement at Henry's forthrightness. She had forgotten the strength of his arms, the softness of his lips.

"It's all right, Mother," Catherine said. "I am quite safe with my husband."

"Well." Florence wrung her hands. "Well, of course you are. I will make some tea. Perhaps you can come down and join me in a moment, Henry, allow Catherine time to dress."

"I am quite capable of assisting my wife while she dresses."

Catherine pursed her lips together. By the colour of her face, she thought her mother would explode.

"Well," Florence said again. "I will make the tea and wait for you both downstairs." She backed out of the door and pulled it firmly shut behind her.

Catherine giggled. Henry stifled the sound with his kiss. Before she knew it he was backing her towards the bed. Catherine stiffened.

"Henry, what are you doing?"

"Surely we can spend a little time together. I haven't seen my pretty wife for so long." His hands slipped inside her nightdress and his lips nibbled at her neck. "You smell so sweet, Catherine." A small groan gurgled from his throat.

"No, Henry." Catherine pushed him away. "We can't. Not now. Don't you want to see your son? Mrs Phillips will be back any moment. She's taken him out for some air. He had such a restless night."

The hunger she saw in Henry's eyes made her panic. She wasn't ready for this. She bent to retrieve the shawl that had slipped from her shoulders and pulled it tight around her.

"How long are you staying, Henry?"

"We must leave by midday."

"We?"

"Yes, I've booked us passage on the coastal steamer. It departs the port on the late-afternoon tide." Henry clasped both of her hands in his. "I thought it would be a more comfortable journey for you, my dear, and for our son of course."

"But I'm not ready." Catherine's heart raced.

"We have time." Henry smiled benevolently. "I can help you, my dearest, and you don't need to pack everything. I am sure your mother would be happy to send on anything you leave behind."

"Our little house will be so crowded."

"That is something I was going to surprise you with but allay your fears, my dearest." He lifted one of her hands to his lips and kissed it. "Our new home is finished. I have been living there this last week. All is ready for your return."

Catherine glanced wildly around the room. She couldn't go, not yet. Her gaze came to rest on the baby's cradle. "Henry, I'm not sure you understand how much it takes to prepare and look after a baby." She went to pull her hands from his but he gripped them tightly.

"And I'm not sure you understand, Catherine." His eyes darkened and the smile left his lips. "I want my wife and son by my side at home in Hawker where they belong. I am leaving here at midday and you will be at my side."

The command in his final words sent another shiver down her spine. Her heart continued to beat against her chest like a trapped bird. The sound of a baby's cries broke the silence between them. They both turned at a tap on the door.

"Come in." Henry's voice carried the tone of the owner of the house rather than a guest.

Mrs Phillips came in carrying a wailing Charles in her arms. Henry was at her side in an instant. He reached out his hands for the baby.

"My son," he said.

Mrs Phillips looked past him to Catherine. Catherine gave a small nod. Henry would soon see there was little to be done when Charles was screaming for the breast like he was now.

Henry carried the baby to the bed where he laid him on the cover and unwrapped the blankets. Catherine could see Charles's little hands waving angrily in the air. Once more she felt the milk gush in her breasts. Nothing would calm him now until he was fed.

Henry slid his hands beneath his son. "Well, what a fine set of lungs you have young man." He raised the baby up, studied his scrunched red face then gently put him to his shoulder, supporting the tiny head with one fine-fingered hand and patting the baby's back firmly with the other.

"Hello, Charles Henry," he murmured into the baby's tiny ear. "I am your father."

The wailing ceased almost instantly. Catherine's eyes widened. Mrs Phillips gave a small cough.

Henry turned his head slightly in her direction. "Thank you, Mrs Phillips. Can you tell Florence I will be down soon to take some tea with her? Then I'd be most grateful if you could return to begin packing while Catherine is taking care of our son's needs."

Mrs Phillip's eyes flashed but she simply gave a small nod and left the room, the only sound the crisp rustle of her skirt.

Henry looked at Catherine, the benevolent smile firmly back on his face. "Make yourself comfortable, my dear. I am assuming the reason for all that bellowing and the snuffling now at my neck is because our son is hungry."

Catherine sat. "He is often so of late."

Henry watched while she undid the ribbons of her nightgown then he handed Charles to her as if the baby was made of delicate eggshells. Immediately Charles began to wail again. Catherine placed him on her breast. Henry put a gentle hand on the baby's head then on hers. "He's a feisty little fellow, isn't he?"

"He keeps me very busy," Catherine said as forcefully as she could muster.

"I will leave you in peace." Henry kissed the top of her head then strolled to the door. He paused and turned back. "I will ask your mother to pack some food for the journey. I've ordered a carriage." He pulled out his watch, looked at it then slipped it back in his pocket. "We will leave here, the three of us, at midday precisely." He stepped out the door and closed it softly behind him.

Catherine looked down at the baby tugging on her breast and two big tears rolled down her cheeks. The time she'd spent in her family's care was over.

Henry accepted the teacup perched on the delicate saucer from his mother-in-law. "Thank you, Florence."

She gave him a small nod, her own cup remaining on the intricate table that held the tea tray. They were seated in the front room that faced the sea and Henry could hear the distant sound of the waves through the partly open arched windows.

"I hope you don't mind me speaking out, Henry, but I must on my daughter's behalf."

He looked over the rim of his cup at her powdered face and waited.

"This is a delicate matter." Florence perched awkwardly on the edge of her seat. "Bringing a child into the world is not always easy for a woman. Catherine was in pain for several days."

Henry returned the cup to the saucer. "She had the baby here so she could be attended by a physician."

"And she was. Catherine had the best of care but some women experience more complications. First babies can be especially difficult."

"What are you saying, Florence?" The woman was most perplexing. Perhaps the birthing of his son had caused some internal problem for his wife. "Is Catherine … unwell … or hurt in some way?"

"No, no." Florence's cheeks turned pink and her chin lifted a little higher. "It is taking her some time to recover, that is all. And to adjust to the challenges of being a mother."

"I will be able to assist her with that."

"But surely you are at work all day providing for your family."

"I have employed a housekeeper." Henry gave a smug smile as Florence sat back. "Our new home is not as grand as yours of course but I think you will find it most suitable for people of our standing in the community." He puffed out his chest. "My shop is patronised by those people who are held in high regard in Hawker."

"There don't seem to be many women in Hawker who are … appropriate companions. Women need other women to talk to so that they don't burden their husbands with day-to-day trivialities."

Henry put a finger inside his collar and adjusted it more comfortably on his neck. "On the contrary, we have several acquaintances who are looking forward to Catherine's return." He agreed with Florence to some degree but wouldn't admit it. Mrs Taylor had asked after his wife just prior to his departure and Johanna Prosser had sent a gift of a small wooden rattle. They might be older than Catherine but were fitting friends given Henry's position and future standing in the community.

"Hawker is so far away."

"You must come and visit us. There is a regular train service now." Henry put his cup and saucer back on the table and stood. He would have no more delaying tactics. The sooner he got his wife and son home the better. "Thank you for the tea, Florence. Would you have your cook prepare some food for us to take on our journey? I am going down to inspect the new lighthouse at the end of the jetty. I expect my wife and son to be ready to depart as soon as I return."

Florence's cheeks turned a deeper shade of pink. She glared at him a moment then gave a slight inclination of her head. "As you wish."

"I'll see myself out."

Henry's footsteps rang on the tiled floor of the entrance hall. He retrieved his hat and scarf from the intricately carved hall-stand and eyed himself in its mirror. He was pleased with what he saw. There was still a long way to go to match his father-in-law's wealth but he would do it. One day perhaps they would take regular summer holidays in a house like this of their own near the beach but for now Catherine's place was at his side. There would be no more meddling from Florence. Henry spun on his heel, swept his hair back from his forehead and pushed his new hat onto his crown, then he stepped out into the spring day.

Twenty

Joseph swung his legs over the side of his bed and groaned. Light poured in around the edges of Clara's heavy blue curtains. He put his head in his hands and pressed his fingers to his throbbing temples, glaring through one eye at the empty flask lying on the floor at his feet. He should have camped one more night to break his journey but last night the moon was bright and he was close enough to know each rut in the track and let them guide his horse and cart home.

Binda had heard him return and had come to help with the horse and cart but they'd said little to each other. It was late, Joseph was tired and had no news worthy of sharing. He crept into his bed but sleep had eluded him. That's when he'd thought of the flask. A nip would help him, but one mouthful wasn't enough and he must have eventually drained the rest of the contents judging by the way his head felt.

There was noise beyond his door, chatting and laughter. He strained to listen. It was William who was laughing, a sound Joseph hadn't heard since ... well, it seemed a long time since there'd been any laughter in this house. Without the little girls here it was only Robert who had quickly adapted to the loss of his mother and chortled often at whatever took his fancy.

Joseph had had no word from his parents since Esther and Violet had gone to stay with them over six weeks ago. He had a sudden desire to see his little girls but quickly pushed it away. The shearers would be here in a week and there was much to do. In the past his father's overseer, Timothy, had come to help at Smith's Ridge for shearing and then Joseph had always headed to Wildu Creek to help there. No doubt that would still be the plan but without Clara to cook and look after the children he wasn't sure how it would all work.

Once more William's laughter reached him. Joseph stood, dragged his fingers through his hair and pulled on his clothes. He opened the door and paused at the sight before him. Their big living room was empty of people but now he took in what his eyes hadn't seen in the semi-dark last night.

Sunshine streamed in the dust-free windows showing the floor swept neat as a pin and bare of clothing, shoes and food scraps. The big long table was clear of everything except a jar of the wildflowers that sprouted from the plains and the hill country at this time of year. The fireplace was clean and set ready to be lit. Once more the sound of laughter drew Joseph's attention. He followed it to the kitchen. William stood at the table. Opposite him was Mary, beside her Robert perched on a chair and at the head of the table was the other native woman, Millie. Joseph had forgotten she'd arrived as he'd left for Hawker. All of them were focused on the table as puffs of white hovered in the air between them.

"What's this?"

"Father!" William spun, his eyes bright and his hands covered in flour.

Robert gurgled something that sounded a lot like 'papa'.

"We're making pies, Father." William beckoned him over. "Come and see."

Joseph moved closer and put an arm around Robert who was wavering precariously on the chair. He looked from Mary, whose lips were turned up in a shy smile, to Millie, whose white teeth shone from her laughing mouth.

"Welcome home, Joseph," she said.

"See, Father." William tugged on his arm. "Millie had dough left over so we are each making our own little pie."

Joseph looked down at the table where several oddly shaped creations sat on a baking tray.

"Mine is an elephant shape." William pointed proudly to a round blob with several pieces sticking out of it. "Mary's helping Robert make a kangaroo. It's very good isn't it?"

Joseph looked at the shape in front of Mary which did indeed closely resemble a kangaroo.

"My brother said to tell you he's gone to check the fence at the top of Prosser's Run." Millie glanced at him. "I hope it was all right to make use of the supplies you brought back?"

Joseph took in the happy group. Clara was always so careful with every last jot of provisions but if this small wastage was what it took to bring some light into his children's lives then he was not going to complain.

"Of course." Joseph stuck a finger in a small pool of flour. "As long as we have enough to feed shearers in a week's time." He put a dab of flour on William's nose and then Robert's.

William rubbed at his nose and Robert sneezed.

"Time to put these pies in the oven and clean up now." Millie turned away to test the oven. A delicious smell wafted from whatever was inside before she closed the door again and reached for another piece of wood.

"Are you responsible for the cleanliness of my house?" Joseph put a hand to his stomach as it rumbled. He'd hardly eaten since he left Hawker two days ago.

"Mary helped me." Millie grinned. "I have some egg-and-bacon pie ready to eat. Would you like some?"

Joseph looked in astonishment at the pie she indicated on the bench. He could see the chunks of bacon and whole eggs inside the already-cut pastry.

"We had some," William said. "Millie cooks like Mother ... it was very nice." William shuffled his feet.

Joseph's heart ached for his son. "Sounds like I had better try some then."

"You go and sit at the table." Millie flapped her hands at him. "I will bring it to you."

Mary took Robert off to clean him up and William followed Joseph to the front room.

Joseph sat in his usual seat, grateful that the pounding in his head had eased. William took a seat on the long stool beside him.

"Has everything been all right while I have been away?"

"Yes," William said. "Uncle Binda stayed in the hut with Millie the first night. I went with him to check the close water-holes the next day. We've only made short trips so we are not far from home, in case ..."

He stopped talking as soon as Millie appeared with the food. She placed a generous serving of pie in front of Joseph.

"Thank you, Millie," he said and was rewarded by her brilliant smile.

William waited until she was gone before he continued speaking

"We've cleaned out the shearing shed and checked the yards. Today Uncle Binda left early. He wanted to inspect the fences between us and Prosser's Run ready to move sheep closer to the home paddock."

"We'll have to start that tomorrow." Joseph took a mouthful of pie. William was right, it was every bit as delicious as Clara's. Jundala always had trouble with the pastry and the consistency of the pie but Millie had it just right. "Very good pie," he murmured once he'd swallowed two mouthfuls.

"Jundala and Joe haven't come back yet. Uncle Binda thinks they might stay away for a while." William rested his hands together on the table. "Millie has been very busy in the house. I don't think Uncle Binda is very pleased with her. I've heard them arguing a few times."

"What about?"

William shrugged his shoulders. "They spoke in their language. It was too fast for me to understand."

Joseph paused before pushing the next forkful into his mouth and pondered on that while he ate. Binda had intimated there was something he wanted to tell Joseph before he'd left for Hawker. No doubt his friend would share with him what was going on in good time.

William leaned closer. "Millie is different."

Joseph eyed his son. He wanted to smile at the boy's earnest expression but he sensed that would be the wrong thing to do.

"In what way?"

"She's native but she wears dresses."

"Jundala and Mary wear dresses."

"Jundala only does when she's working in the house and Mary's are always ..." William paused. "She never looks right in them."

Joseph thought about that. Millie was of medium height, almost as tall as her brother. The dress she wore fitted her perfectly and she moved around the house with ease in it. "I think that's because Mary's don't fit her properly." Joseph also thought that both Jundala and Mary were more comfortable in their traditional clothing which didn't entail very much at all, especially in the warmer months.

"She speaks good English and she can read and write. She's been reading to Robert and me each night you've been gone. Just like Mother used ..."

Joseph reached out a hand and was shamed when he saw William flinch. What had he become that his son was frightened of him? "It's all right son." He placed a hand on William's shoulder and gave it a gentle squeeze. "You don't have to avoid mentioning your mother."

William stared down at the floor.

Joseph felt as if the food he'd swallowed had turned to rock in his throat. "She will always be in your heart. In all of our hearts."

"Robert doesn't miss her." William looked up, his eyes darkened. "He thinks Mary is his mother."

A stab of pain knifed through Joseph. "I'm sorry, William. There is nothing I can do about that."

"He should have gone to Grandma's with the girls."

"Robert is a baby. It would be too much for Grandma to have him as well."

"Mary's not his mother." William banged his hands on the table. "She's ... she's ... black and Robert is white." He turned worried eyes to his father. "Do you think he will end up brindle like Mr Prosser said?"

Joseph might have laughed had he not felt anger surge through him once more. He removed his hand from William's shoulder, closed his eyes and gripped his head with one hand. Damn Ellis Prosser and his evil tongue. Why couldn't people see beyond the colour of another's skin before they judged?

"I'm sorry, Father."

Joseph's eyes flew open. Once more William had fear on his face.

"It's not your fault, William, and you have nothing to be sorry for. Men like Ellis Prosser don't deserve our attention."

"He's our neighbour."

"He might be but he's not a good one. Your Uncle Binda is a much better man than Mr Prosser will ever be. He doesn't judge a person by the way they look and neither should we."

William studied his hands for a moment. "It's not so much what she looks like I suppose," he said. "She bosses me and I'm old enough to make my own decisions."

Joseph raised his eyebrows.

"And." William leaned closer and lowered his voice. "She often smells. We have to have a bath every week and change our clothes but Mary wears the same dress without washing it for a long time."

Joseph felt the rage ebb away. His son was growing up early. Circumstances had made him part man already and Joseph could understand not wanting to be told what to do by Mary who was little more than a child herself. As to the clothes, the same happened with Binda and Jundala. Clara had always made sure they had clothes to wear but they often wore the same apparel without washing it for long periods of time. Joseph had a fair idea it was the clothes that smelled rather than his friends.

"You've been raised differently, William. Mary's not like you nor you like her yet we try to get along. Her father is my closest friend."

"I thought Uncle Timothy was your friend."

"Yes, he is also a good friend but he works for Grandpa and I don't see him as often."

"His skin is the same as ours."

Joseph sighed and shook his head. "William, you are too much bothered by the colour of a person's skin rather than what's inside."

They both turned at the sound of raised voices from the kitchen then Binda came into the room.

"I am glad you are back, my friend." He crossed the room and stood beside Joseph. "Prosser has been at it again. Some fence is knocked down."

Joseph thumped the table making the fork clatter on the plate. "Damn the man, why can't he leave us in peace?"

"It's in a difficult place to see. A lot of thick bush around. There are tufts of wool on the wire and the hoof prints have been disturbed. Maybe the sheep knocked the fence down, maybe kangaroo, maybe a man." Binda shrugged his shoulders. "It is difficult to tell."

"But what do you feel in here?" Joseph stood and put a hand to his own chest.

"It looks deliberate to me. I found horse prints further down the fence line. They were on our side of the fence and not our horses."

"We must bring in our stock. We've already delayed shearing by a month."

"There are only the two of us."

"And me."

Joseph felt a swell of pride as his son leapt to his feet. He gave a nod. "Timothy will be here any day. That will make four of us."

Binda, who was usually the one full of confidence, shook his head. "Still not enough."

"Mary and I can help."

They turned as Millie came into the room, her hands on Mary's shoulders.

Binda's eyes bulged so much Joseph was fearful they would pop out.

"I can ride."

Binda made a strange strangled sound.

"Thank you for the offer, Millie." Joseph smiled at the young woman whose eyes were alight. "If it's all right with you, I will put you in charge of food. It's a big job but it appears you are most capable."

"Thank you, Joseph. I would like to help in whatever way I can."

She smiled sweetly at him then at Binda. Joseph had never seen his friend so agitated.

"Binda and I should ride out. Check the lay of the land and plan our next moves." He guided his friend through the kitchen, past the outside verandahs and along the path out of the yard. They came to a stop under a straggly group of eucalypt trees near the horse yard.

"Now, Binda." Joseph turned to face his friend. "Perhaps you'd better tell me the story of your sister."

Binda glared back at him. It was rare to see his body stiff with anger.

"I only brought her here because my father was ready to kill her."

Joseph frowned. "Literally?"

Binda continued to glare. "Millaki is attracted to the ways of white men."

"You say that as if it's a bad thing."

"You know my father."

Joseph nodded. He remembered Yardu as a terrifying man, ready to kill the white invaders who threatened his country.

"The more he tried to keep his people away from your people the more interested Millaki became. Eight years ago she was supposed to marry the man she had been promised to. A hawker came close to where my family were camped. Millaki hid in his wagon. It was a long time before my people discovered she was gone. By then Millaki was a long way off. She got herself a place working at one of the big properties in the south. She learned to speak your language, wear your clothes, clean your house, cook your food. When my father finally found out where she was he sent me to find her." Binda's hand, which had been raising higher in the air with each sentence, suddenly dropped. He frowned. "Something had happened. She won't say what. She moved to another place but she wasn't happy there. I think they treated her badly. She came home but our father didn't want to see her and she was very unsettled. She no longer fitted into her old life. I suggested she come here for a while."

Joseph thought about his tidy house and his full stomach. "That's acceptable to me."

"She caused problems with my family. I don't want her bringing trouble here."

"I don't see how Millie managing my household will cause me trouble."

Binda looked back in the direction of the house, his usually straight stance slightly bowed. "I don't know what will become of her. She can't go home. Doesn't want to. She's stuck between your people and mine."

Joseph's heart ached for his friend. It suddenly hit him that in reality Binda's fate was the same as Millie's. Unwilling or unable to return fully to their traditional lives and yet rejected by European society.

"Millie will be welcome here for as long as she wants to stay. I need someone to keep house and help Mary with the children. Jundala prefers the outdoor work so when she returns she will be free to do more of that if she wishes. I will pay Millie for her services, of course."

"White man's money." Binda gave him a sceptical look.

"We will come to an arrangement like I have with you. Money as well as food and clothing." Joseph offered his hand. "My friend."

Binda held his gaze a moment then accepted his hand. They shook and Joseph pulled his friend close in a hug.

"Now that we've settled that I think there are other urgent matters to deal with." Joseph pushed his hat firmly on his head.

"Sheep."

"Yes, sheep. It's time to bring them in for shearing." In spite of the work he knew lay ahead and the dull ache in his head Joseph felt a lightness of heart. Physical labour was a good way to forget about everything else.

Twenty-one

Joseph put his hands to his hips and stretched backwards. Every muscle ached. The smell of wool and the astringent odour of sheep urine saturated the shed. All around him the bleating of sheep filled the air but the blades that had clipped and snipped for nearly two weeks were silent. Shearing was finished. He looked about him. The ringer gave him a nod then scrutinised the six shearers, some cleaning their blades and the rest stretched out on the floor. They'd worked hard.

The men were quiet now, reflective even; quite different to the jovial conversation they'd kept up during their weeks of work. The two shed hands plus William and Joe were still busy sweeping the boards and collecting the dirty wool that had been tossed to the floor. It had been a gruelling few weeks but everyone from the tar boy to the boss had kept their good humour and that had been the prevailing feeling in the shed. Joseph was pleased. Some teams they'd had in the past had been rough and ready but these men had taken pride in their work.

Thomas was checking the fleece spread on the table before him. He looked up, caught Joseph's look and smiled. "This wool is better than last year's. You should do well from your wool cheque this season."

Joseph felt a sense of pride swell. He had been experimenting with different breeding practices and perhaps they were showing some promise. Then just as quickly as it rose the happiness fell, dampened by the thought that there was no Clara to share the success of all their hard work, and also that his sheep numbers were significantly lower than he had expected. Even so, his attempt at breeding sheep better suited to the conditions looked like it had paid off.

"You're finished in good time too." Thomas moved around the table plucking at the fleece.

Joseph narrowed his eyes. "Our count is down a few hundred more than it should be."

"You don't think the natives …"

"Not at all." Joseph cut his father off. "I think Prosser has helped himself to some of my sheep but I've no way to prove it. He's too shrewd."

"But the fence …"

"You know how easy it is to destroy a fence, Father. And Prosser does it where we're least likely to find it for a while."

"Well you've certainly still got enough sheep to make a grand amount from. I thought I'd be able to give you a couple of days work but I've barely arrived in time to help at all."

"You sent Timothy. With Millie and Mary in the kitchen, Jundala has been free to help Binda in the yards. Besides someone had to look after Wildu Creek."

"Father!"

Joseph spun at the squeals of delight coming from his two daughters as they flew across the wooden boards together, their arms outstretched, skirts and ribbons flying. He bent down and wrapped them in his arms, kissing first Violet and then Esther, holding them tight as he swept them to his chest. Their hair shone and they both smelled so sweet he suddenly remembered his own filthy clothes and set them both back on their feet.

"Where did you two come from?"

He looked across at his father's grinning face then back to the door. He felt a ripple of shock at the woman who entered. It was his mother but she looked painfully thin and her hair was streaked with grey. Immediately he felt remorse at leaving his daughters in her care. It had only been two months but she had aged several years since he'd last seen her.

"Mother." He put one hand carefully to her elbow and bent to kiss her cheek.

She accepted his kiss but pulled her arm from his grip. "Don't put those filthy hands on my sleeve, Joseph. Lucky I put pinafores on the girls."

"What are you doing here?" He looked from his excited daughters who were giving William hugs, to his father and then back to his mother. Eliza, Timothy's wife, watched from the doorway.

"I guessed it would be nearly time for the cut out party." In spite of her pale fragility her eyes shone. "I can see I've arrived just in time."

"Who is looking after Wildu Creek?"

"Young Tom is a keen worker and Gulda and Daisy are there. I thought we should be together for this occasion. Something happy to pin our hopes on."

"I hope you haven't gone to too much trouble." Joseph was still shocked by her pale face and the extra wrinkles he noticed under her eyes.

"It's never any trouble to cook for cut out."

"Millie and Mary have been doing the same. I think we'll have plenty."

"Millie?" His mother's eyebrows arched.

"Binda's sister is staying with us for a while. She's an excellent cook."

"And housekeeper? I noticed a row of shirts strung on the line and a rug hanging over the back fence. I thought it was odd. You'd all be too busy for that."

"Millie has been a big help."

More than Joseph had expected. She had lifted the spirits of the whole household, except perhaps Binda who was prone to watching his sister when she was near like an eagle seeking prey. Robert was happier, William lost his sullen look when she was about and Joseph had been delighted to hear her laughing with Mary and Jundala last night as they cleaned up in the kitchen. Even though he'd been achingly tired he'd lain in bed listening as they chatted and giggled. He had no idea what they were talking about but the happy sound lulled him into a deep sleep.

"I will go and see where she would like the food then. Are we to eat in the house?"

"Too many of us now I think."

"It will be a mild evening. What about under the gum tree near your back garden fence?"

"It sounds fine to me." Joseph reached out and took her small hand in his. Hers looked so delicate in his huge, dirty hand. "Let the young ones do the heavy work."

She lifted her free hand to his face and gently brushed his cheek. "Don't worry about me, Joseph. I'm not in my dotage yet."

"Hello, Grandma." William had come to stand beside them, one little sister dangling from each arm.

Lizzie patted his shoulder. "How much taller you are, William, and you've grown stronger. I expect you've been working as hard as the men."

Joseph looked down proudly at his son, who had definitely done his share of hard work, then at his two daughters. He bent and kissed both their cheeks. "You've grown taller, Violet."

"And me, Father?" Esther pulled her shoulders up as high as she could next to Violet.

"Yes you too, Esther."

"Time to talk later." Lizzie spun on her heel and called to the girls. "Violet, Esther, come along. We've lots to do to prepare supper for these hungry workers. With everyone helping we'll have a splendid feast ready in two shakes of a lamb's tail."

Both girls immediately followed their grandma. It didn't surprise him to see Violet do as she was bid but seeing Esther go so willingly was another matter. Perhaps she also had matured like the rest of them.

By the time the food was ready there was a big group gathered under the gum tree. The shearing team were eight in number, plus Binda's family of five including Millie. Joseph and his children were another five, and the Wildu Creek visitors were six, as Eliza and Timothy's son and daughter had also come.

The women had found some railing planks and put them between barrels to make a large table which was loaded with all kinds of vegetables, pies and terrines. The chairs and benches had been brought out from inside and there were cut logs turned up for those who didn't have a seat. A fire was lit a small distance away, no doubt with kangaroo and mutton cooking slowly in its coals. And they'd hung lanterns from the tree and the nearby fence posts. Lizzie had decorated the table with gum leaves and some of the pretty purple branches from the shrubs that were flowering now.

Joseph watched his mother as she carried a large plate, offering the contents to each person gathered. She chatted happily, making sure people were welcome and fed, playing the hostess for him. A lump caught in his throat. Time moved on and his parents weren't as agile as they once were. He'd noticed his father retired early after a day's work now, and was slower to get going in the mornings. His mother's aging had been much more sudden. She'd appeared so frail when she first arrived but now, in the half-light between day and night, she looked more like the woman he remembered.

Joseph spoke to the shearers and thanked them for their work. Their boss was a tough man but fair. He'd kept a steady eye on them and nearly two weeks of shearing had passed with only a few minor injuries to sheep. One man had cut his hand but it had only slowed him up for a while. All in all it had been a successful shearing.

He looked down as a small pair of arms wrapped around his legs. Esther had attached herself to him and by her mournful look he could tell she was tired. He hoisted her to his shoulder and immediately she snuggled close. He relished the sweet smell of her and the softness of her hair against his neck. He took a deep breath to hold back the melancholy that threatened him once more. Tonight was meant to be a celebration. His mother had been right. It felt good to have something happy to think about.

Violet came from the house carrying a board with a loaf of freshly baked bread; behind her followed Mary also carrying a large plate of food. Joseph noticed her hair shone and she wore a clean dress. And then came Millie. His eyes widened at the sight of her. Her hair which usually flowed past her shoulders had been swept up into a bun and was studded with a small sprig of white flowers. Her deep brown eyes sparkled and her mouth was wide in a happy smile. She looked positively radiant as she handed around a plate with cheese and assorted condiments.

He could tell by the looks on the men's faces he wasn't the only one to notice how pretty she looked in her dress with deep maroon stripes and a bodice that hugged her small breasts and nipped in at her narrow waist where it joined the wide skirt that swished as she walked.

"She wears white women's clothes well, my sister."

Joseph twisted his head at the murmur of Binda's voice. He nudged his friend with his spare elbow. "She's better looking than her brother."

"We've both got fine-looking sisters."

Joseph's thoughts went to his little sister, Ellen. A woman now with a child of her own he'd yet to meet. She had certainly got the good looks in his family.

"Millie seems happy here." Joseph adjusted the heavy weight of the now sleeping Esther in his arms. "I am most grateful for all she's done for my family, especially managing the house like she does."

Binda turned his big round eyes to Joseph. "I suppose you will want her to stay."

Joseph frowned. "I thought that was the idea."

"I had hoped she would find a position with another family."

"Why?" Joseph glanced at Millie then back at his friend. "Has she told you she's not happy here?"

Binda shook his head. "I'm not happy."

"Why not?"

Once more he turned his gaze to Joseph. There was a deep sadness in his eyes. "She's my sister but she is ..." He sighed and looked back in Millie's direction. One of the men said something that made her laugh. It was a bright happy sound. "Trouble seems to follow her wherever she goes."

Joseph was going to ask what Binda meant but Millie had arrived in front of him with her plate of food.

"Mary," she called over her shoulder. "Come and take little Miss Esther to bed so her father can eat in peace."

Joseph tipped Esther carefully into the crook of his arm. She was indeed asleep. Mary held out her arms and he slid the child to her.

"Thank you, Mary," he said and lifted a plate from the table so that he could take some of the food Millie offered.

"You should try some of that quandong paste with your cheese." Millie nodded her head at the deep red mixture in a small pot. "Your mother made it and it's delicious."

Joseph put a scoop of the paste on his lump of cheese. "Thank you."

"Why don't you sit down, rest for a bit? Walter over there has a harmonica. He's going to play later." She flashed a smile at him. "We could dance."

"Don't be cheeky," Binda growled. "Joseph is not one of the working men, he's the master of this place."

"Is he?" Millie turned a mischievous look at her brother. "I thought you were the boss."

"Millaki!" Binda snapped at her but she'd already spun on her heel and moved on, her skirt billowing behind her.

Joseph couldn't help but chuckle at the fury on his friend's face. "Little sisters," he said. "They are a trial."

"Some more than others." Binda glowered at Millie's back a moment then turned to Joseph. "Where are the shearers going next?"

"Prosser's Run but they won't be there long. Evidently Prosser has sold off a lot of his sheep and only has a small mob left."

"Why would he do that?"

"He's changing to cattle. I even heard he's going to start building fences."

Binda scowled. "I'd like to get a close look at the sheep he has left."

"So would I, my friend, but we'd be wasting our time. Anything that was ours would be long gone. He'd make sure any sheep he had were his own brand."

They were interrupted by murmurs of delight as Jundala and Mary uncovered the fire pit and removed the meat that had been baking there for several hours. The smell of it set Joseph's mouth watering. He hadn't eaten since the midday break and he suddenly felt very hungry.

He shovelled the last of the cheese into his mouth and clapped Binda on the back. "Let's eat."

Thomas got slowly off the bed and stretched. His back always ached these days even after rest. He winced as he twisted to pluck his trousers from the hook behind the door.

"Is your back giving you trouble?"

He glanced at Lizzie who was watching him from the bed they had shared in the hut Joseph had built for Binda. "Nothing a night in my own bed won't fix. Besides I never sleep well here."

"How can a god-fearing man like you believe in curses, Thomas?"

"I don't. Smith's Ridge doesn't have very good memories for me, that's all." He ignored her sceptical look. "What about you, Lizzie my sweet? I think you tossed and turned a lot last night."

Lizzie sat up, swung her legs to the floor and put her hands to her back. "As you say, the bed is not as comfortable as our own at Wildu Creek."

Thomas laughed. "Perhaps we are getting old. Once upon a time we would have slept anywhere and woken refreshed."

"Well, at least the noise didn't keep us awake. It all went quiet not long after we left the fire."

Thomas pulled on his trousers. "Timothy and Eliza would have started for home by now and the shearers were planning to move on to Prosser's Run early. No-one wanted a late night."

"It will be quiet at Wildu Creek." Lizzie hooked back the hessian sack that served as a curtain. The early morning light shone through her nightgown revealing her thin silhouette. Thomas frowned at the sight. She had never regained the weight she'd lost when she'd been so sick. It bothered him that she was still so thin.

"Life will be easier for you if the girls are staying here."

Lizzie turned to him. "It was no bother, Thomas. I loved looking after the dear little lambs."

"I know." He crossed the room and wrapped her in his arms. He was gentle, afraid she would break. "But we've just admitted we're not as young as we used to be, and it's better they're with their father."

"I hope so." Lizzie pulled back a little and looked up at him. "Did you know Joseph drank?"

Thomas had wondered when she would mention their son's drinking around the fire last night. "A couple of mouthfuls doesn't hurt a man after all the hard work he's put in."

"It was more than a mouthful. He was unsteady on his feet when we went to bed."

Thomas shrugged his shoulders. "I am sure it was just the chance to relax for a while." He pulled Lizzie in again and kissed the top of her head. He had been shocked himself to see Joseph pull out a flask when the shearers did.

"I often think Joseph reminds me of Isaac." Lizzie's voice was muffled against his bare chest.

"He is like him in some ways." Thomas knew Lizzie was thinking about her younger brother's battle with liquor. "But they are very different in others. Circumstances and a terrible experience drove Zac to drink. He overcame it."

"Not forever. If he hadn't been drinking—"

"He may not have drowned, I know, but then perhaps he would have anyway. Plenty of sober men have lost their lives crossing swollen creeks."

"I worry about Joseph."

"I think you'll find he's made of stronger stuff. Already he appears much happier. He has something to live for. It was a tragedy to lose Clara but he knows he must go on for the children if not for himself."

Lizzie moved away and began her own dressing. "He has plenty of home help now at least."

"Mary and Millie?"

"Millie seems to have everything under control. I wonder where she slept last night. She has been sleeping in here with Mary."

"At Binda's hut, I suppose."

"I hope so." Lizzie's voice was firm, her back stiff as she fiddled with the buttons of her bodice.

"Where else would she be?"

Lizzie turned. "I hope Joseph didn't let her sleep in the house."

"Well, there's plenty of room …"

Thomas's voice faltered as he took in Lizzie's stern look, her lips pursed in the way she did if she was extremely put out by something. Not a common occurrence. "You don't think he would …"

"Take her to his bed?" Lizzie put a hand to her chest. "He wouldn't be the first white man to take a native woman as his …" She flapped her hand in the air. "Mistress."

Thomas felt his mouth drop open. Surely that wouldn't happen here. Black or white, it was not appropriate. He took a step forward then back. He gripped his hands together then dropped them to his sides.

"Look at you, Thomas Baker. You look like a man with ants in his pants." Lizzie giggled. "Or perhaps a boil on his bottom."

He looked across the room into the twinkling blue eyes of his wife, remembering the time they'd first met when he had indeed had a boil on his rear end that she had lanced. "You're teasing me." He took two strides to reach her and encircle her in his arms again. He bent and kissed her, softly at first then more insistently. Finally they took a breath.

"Well." Lizzie smiled up at him. "Perhaps we shouldn't have been so quick to get out of bed after all."

There was the sound of scuffling and a rattle of the outer door. "Grandma, Grandpa?"

"Our dear little Esther still demands attention." Lizzie tugged at her hair and twisted it up into a bun which she deftly clipped in place. "Coming, my sweet lamb." She swept past Thomas but he grabbed her hand. They hadn't been intimate since Lizzie had been sick. In spite of her frail appearance she was obviously much better.

"When we get home there will be no children to occupy your time." He kissed her hand. "We shall have an early night."

Lizzie gave him a slight bob. "Yes, my lord." She grinned and was gone before he could reply.

Twenty-two

Catherine struggled up from the comfortable chair she'd settled in. She'd only meant to close her eyes for a few minutes. She looked around the tidy sitting room. Their furniture was sparse in this bigger room but met their needs for now. Henry had said they would add to it eventually. Henry! Her glance flew to the clock on the mantel. It was nearly supper time, then with a rush of relief she remembered he'd gone south to visit one of his properties. He wouldn't be home at all tonight.

She sucked in a deep breath. The smell of something delicious wafted around her. She straightened her skirt and patted her hair then listened. No crying but she could hear Flora singing softly in the distance.

Catherine closed her eyes and sent a silent prayer of thanks for Flora Nixon. She had no idea how she would have survived these last two weeks without her housekeeper. Henry had built her this house. It was certainly grand by Hawker standards but it entailed so much more work than their little house behind the shop.

And then there was the shop. Henry had wanted her help there almost as soon as they'd arrived home. Business had grown in her absence. Henry's work took him away from the shop more and more and Mr Hemming had deliveries and the telegraph to manage as well as their customers. Catherine had put in the odd hour here and there but today was the first day she'd spent any length of time in the shop. It had been so hot. The first month of summer had produced some very high temperatures already. She had forgotten how hot Hawker could be. That was another reason for her tiredness.

Tears welled in her eyes and rolled down her cheeks. How she wished she was back in Adelaide with her dear mother and Mrs Phillips. She was startled by a knock at the door and turned away quickly, scrabbling for her handkerchief, as Flora came into the room.

"Oh you are awake, Mrs Wiltshire. I hope you are rested. This young man is ready for his supper."

Catherine pulled a smile on to her face and turned to her housekeeper. "Thank you, Flora." She settled herself in the comfortable chair she'd just vacated, undid her buttons and held out her arms. It seemed all she was good at was feeding her baby.

Flora crossed the room and poured a glass of water from the jug on the dresser. She placed it on the small table beside Catherine's chair.

"Thank you, Flora."

"I've made you a meat pie for your supper."

"Is that what I can smell?" Catherine gave Flora a wobbly smile. "It will be delicious I'm sure."

"It will keep warm on top of the oven so you can have it later whenever you feel like it." Flora crossed the room and peered through the front window. "It's a lovely evening." She drew the deep green brocade curtains.

"My husband tells me you helped select the fabric for the curtains."

Flora ran her hand down the edge of one curtain and straightened it. "I hope my choice meets your approval."

Catherine swept a glance at the curtains. Before Charles came along she would have delighted in selecting the furnishing for her new home but now she wasn't the least bit interested. "You've chosen very well."

Flora crossed the room. "I'd best be getting home soon or my two will be squabbling. They get very cranky after a day at school."

Catherine felt a pang of guilt that Flora was here with her and her own children where left alone. "Thank you for all you've done but there's no need to stay any longer. Charles and I will be perfectly all right." Brave words when at the thought of managing the demanding baby alone all night tears brimmed in her eyes again. Henry often walked the baby in the night if he didn't settle. How would she manage alone?

Flora stayed where she was, close to Catherine's chair.

"Forgive me for saying this, Mrs Wiltshire, but you look so tired." She smiled kindly. "Why don't you let me take Charles home with me tonight?"

Catherine gaped at the woman.

"I can make a little bed up for him in my room," Flora said quickly. "I managed to have my children sleeping all night by three months. If he gets upset I can always bring him to you."

Charles let go of Catherine's breast, snuffling and grunting. She quickly swapped him to the other side.

"I am sure you would benefit from a full night's rest."

Catherine looked from Flora to Charles and back again. Once more she felt tears brim in her eyes.

"Oh, Mrs Wiltshire." Flora knelt down beside her. "I didn't mean to upset you, only I know how tiring it can be getting up to babes in the night. Once he's sleeping through you'll feel so much better, you'll see." Her look was full of kindness.

Catherine sucked in her bottom lip and patted at her tears with her fingers. "You really are so kind, Flora. You don't know how much I long for a good night's sleep."

Flora patted Catherine's shoulder. "Yes," she said softly. "I do. In your own turn you and Mr Wiltshire have been so good to my own children, without this job ..." Her voice trailed off and she stood abruptly. "I'll go home now and prepare a bed for Charles, then I'll come back later and collect him. He'll be perfectly safe with me."

Catherine watched her go and then listened to the sounds of her leaving the house. Flora was a truly kind woman. Charles squirmed and fell away from the breast, his little belly full. Catherine put him to her shoulder, got up and paced the room as she patted his back. She felt as if a weight had been lifted from her shoulders. What bliss to have a whole night alone in her bed to sleep. Now she was glad Henry was staying away overnight.

After the rough boat trip from Adelaide to Port Augusta where she'd felt so sick, and then the train journey in the heat that sucked the moisture from her body as quickly as Charles did her milk, all Catherine had wanted was to fall into bed once they arrived at Hawker but Henry had other ideas. He'd taken her on a tour of the shop and then the house. Charles had been asleep by then and when they reached their bedroom Henry had thought he would take her to bed. Catherine had been shocked and pleaded exhaustion.

Since then two weeks had passed and she had managed to keep a distance between them. Even in bed she had made an excuse or feigned sleep but she knew she could not keep him away for much longer. She could see the need in his eyes, feel the pressure of his tongue when he kissed her and the lingering touch of his hands.

Catherine shuddered. Charles's birth had been long and difficult. She had been sore for so long she couldn't bear the thought of the pain Henry would cause her, but she knew the time of delaying was running out along with his patience. At least for tonight she was safe and she could sleep, perhaps all night if Flora could manage Charles.

★

Henry slid down from his horse and rubbed his hands up and down his backside. He wasn't a good rider, much preferring to use the horse-drawn cart but in this instance riding had shortened his time away from home. He dealt with the horse with only the light of a partial moon to guide him and made his way to the house. It was a large dark monolith against the night sky. Even in darkness it looked impressive. He passed by the lean-to walls of the bathroom and laundry. Later when he had more money he would have them made of stone like the rest of the house. There was also provision for a cellar to be dug with access from the laundry.

He slipped off his jacket and made his way to the kitchen where he lit a candle. He was hungry but for more than food. He wanted to bed his wife. Since she'd been home she had been elusive. The sight of her pink lips and deep brown eyes, her pale shoulders and her full breasts, tantalised him daily. He had missed her so much he thought he would explode at the very sight of her but she kept him at arm's length. During the night it was either Charles at her breast or she was asleep.

He pulled off his boots then took the candle and made his way along the wide hall to their bedroom at the front of the house. He was very tired but the thought of Catherine's ripe body gave him energy. The bare floorboards beneath him gave little protest but they would need a runner to soften the echo of the long hall.

In the bedroom he could make out Catherine in the bed. She was covered in a light blanket, her arms resting on top. He held the candle closer and watched the rise and fall of her chest. She was sound asleep. He removed the remains of his clothing and blew out the candle, the mundane tasks helping him to resist the urge to rip back the covers and climb on top of her as he badly wanted to do. Instead he slid carefully between the linen sheets, greeted by the vague scent of lavender and carefully wrapped himself around his wife.

Catherine was instantly awake, stiff in his arms.

"It's all right, my love," he whispered. "It's only I, your devoted husband returned home early."

"Henry." She pushed him away. "You gave me such a fright."

He reached for her again. The room was dark but he could make out the shape of her eyes wide open watching him. He slid his hand between the ribbons of her nightgown and fondled her full plump breasts.

She gripped his hands. "What are you doing?"

"It's time we were husband and wife again, my love." He leaned in and kissed her. "In the full sense."

"I'm so tired."

"I know, my love, but this will relax you." He caressed her breasts then slid his hands down her stomach, pulling up her gown to reach the softness below. Desire coursed through him and all he could think of was entering her. He threw back the covers and wrenched her nightgown from her fingers.

"No, Henry. I'm not ready." Her plea was barely more than a whisper as he pushed into her.

"You soon will be, my love."

He held himself up on his outstretched arms, lifted himself up and down carefully at first until he could hold himself back no longer. In his frenzy he heard her moans. She enjoyed his attentions. He'd known she would come round. He plunged again and again, oblivious to anything but the pleasure her body gave him. Very quickly he exploded within her and collapsed, spent beside her.

He lay panting, satisfied at last and happy to think they would do this again soon. As his heart slowed its thumping he was aware of Catherine, straightening her nightdress and easing the covers back over her. He reached out a hand and patted her.

"That was wonderful, my love."

He heard no reply but the fatigue that he'd felt earlier swept over him again and with a smile on his face, he drifted off to sleep.

Henry's eyes flew open. The first pink glow of morning light ebbed from the edge of the curtains. He glanced over at Catherine. Last night had been wonderful and the way he felt right now he was ready to do it all over again. She was curled away from him, obviously still asleep. He took pity on her. She had probably been up to Charles in the night. He would let her sleep in.

He took his shirt and trousers and made his way to the kitchen. There were enough coals to get the fire started and before long he had the kettle boiling.

He was just about to put his cup of tea to his lips when the sound of the baby stopped him. He stood up, prepared to pick up his son and take him to Catherine but the crying seemed to be coming from the back of the house instead of the front.

His mouth dropped open at the sight of Flora Nixon hurrying through from outside with the baby clutched to her. It wasn't so much that she was carrying his child from wherever she'd been but what she was wearing that surprised Henry. She had a loose gown over the top of what must be her nightdress.

"Oh, I'm sorry, Mr Wiltshire." Flora paused in the doorway cuddling the crying baby to her. It was the first time Henry had seen Flora flustered. "I didn't know you were home."

At the sight of her Henry felt desire rise in him again. Dear God, this woman wasn't even his wife but she looked so delightful.

"I arrived late in the night." He turned his back to her, aware of the bulge in his trousers, pulled on his shirt and went back to his tea to give himself time to regain his composure. He stood in front of the fire with his cup and turned back to Flora. She still hovered in the doorway, clasping her gown together with one hand and holding his son with the other. She was a fetching sight. "Where have you been with my son?"

"Mrs Wiltshire was so tired from the night feeds. I suggested Charles was old enough to sleep through. I took him with me to give your wife some rest."

Flora was babbling. He liked seeing her flustered. He hadn't seen this side of her.

"And did he?"

Flora looked at Henry, her mouth half open, a questioning expression on her face.

"Did the baby sleep through the night?"

"Oh, no, but he didn't fuss too much. I got him back to sleep."

With that Charles gave an extra loud wail as if to dispute what she said.

Henry put down his cup and held out his arms. "Let me take him."

Flora hesitated then hurried across the room and handed Charles into his arms. She stepped back and her gown fell open to reveal a white cotton nightdress that was so threadbare he could almost see through it. She clutched at her outer gown, quickly wrapping it around her, and backed away.

"I will return soon to prepare breakfast."

"Thank you, Flora."

She turned and fled. Henry found the whole incident rather amusing. He lifted his son into the air level with his face. The baby stopped crying.

"Well, well, young man." Henry bounced him gently up and down. "Aren't you the lucky one? Sleeping with Mrs Nixon." Henry kissed the top of his son's head as the child began to cry again. "Time to wake your mother I think."

Henry carried the baby up the hall, unable to remove from his mind the glimpse of Flora Nixon's breast, and the shapely figure silhouetted in the gown.

Twenty-three

Joseph leaned against a tree watching his children play in the shade by the creek. Parrots chattered in the branches over their heads and behind them the hill sloped away to the plain dotted with sheep. Lizzie sat in a chair keeping a close eye on Robert who toddled on stocky legs trying to keep up with his siblings. Ellen had gone up to the house to put her sleeping baby to bed and her husband, Frederick, and Thomas were deep in conversation about ships.

They had all enjoyed a late breakfast together and the giving and receiving of Christmas gifts on this flat area above the creek where so many Baker family events had taken place. His mother liked to call it her outdoor room. Over the years various shades had been erected to add to that presented by the large gums and his father had created all kinds of outdoor chairs, varying in design and the degree of comfort they offered.

Joseph cast his gaze over the almost-dry creek below and across the valley to the plains. The meandering creek was studded with the tall gums. Barely a trickle now, it could also be a raging torrent carrying all kinds of debris in its brown wake. Wildu Creek was the place of his childhood. There were so many happy memories here. Lately he'd been silently conceding that his father may be right about Smith's Ridge. Not that it was necessarily cursed but over the years it had accrued so many unhappy family memories. He and Clara had been happy there but now Clara was gone.

"Penny for them."

Ellen had returned and stood beside him.

"Nothing worth reporting." Joseph gave a brief shake of his head. "Thinking about our happy childhood."

Ellen tucked her arm through his and leaned her head against his shoulder, a lock of her dark hair falling across his white shirt. They were like cheese and chalk with their colouring. He was fair like their mother and Ellen dark like their father.

Ellen drew in a deep breath. "Wildu Creek was a special place to grow up in."

"Now you're a town girl." Joseph gave her a nudge. "Bet you don't run up and down the place barefoot like you did here."

She nudged him back. "I'm not a little girl anymore. I'm a woman now."

Joseph gave a snort.

"It's certainly different living in town but I'm happy to live anywhere Frederick is."

Joseph looked over to where her husband was deep in conversation with Thomas. Frederick was a shipping clerk and Thomas had developed an interest in the ships that docked at Port Augusta since his more regular visits to stay with Ellen. "He's a good bloke."

"Oh, Joseph." Ellen flung her other arm around him and hugged him close. "I'm so sorry. You must miss Clara even more on days like this."

"It's all right. I'm glad you are happy." Joseph closed his eyes. Esther's giggle made him open them again. William had built a little group of buildings from sticks and they were playing some kind of pretend game with stones for horses, and bits of bush for trees. In spite of their mother's loss his children were healthy and mostly happy. It still amazed him to see the transformation in his youngest daughter. Since her stay with his parents, Esther had been a much happier child. She still asked for Clara sometimes of course and cried for her mother but in general she was so much easier to live with. "I don't know what Mother did to Esther when she stayed here but she's come back a different child."

Ellen let him go and studied the group before them. "Mother never stands any nonsense."

"I didn't think Clara and I did either but somehow Esther was always in a mood."

"Father's the soft touch." Ellen shook her head. "My little Isabelle is not out of the cradle and she has him hanging on her every sound. When she smiles at him I think he's going to burst with happiness."

"He has always loved babies."

"Oh dear." Ellen grabbed his arm. "I keep putting my foot in it don't I? You lost your own baby when you lost Clara."

"Don't fuss, Ellen. Life goes on. You can't stop talking in case you hurt my feelings." Once more he nudged her. "Although life would be much quieter."

She chuckled. "And boring."

They both watched the children again. Lizzie plucked Robert to her lap to prevent him from knocking over the game that had the other three children enthralled.

"How are you managing Robert?" Ellen slipped her arm through his again. "The day-to-day practical things must so hard without Clara. Mother said Binda and Jundala are still with you?"

"Yes. They have been a big help with the animals and the outside work. Their son Joe helps and their daughter Mary is good with the children. She's thirteen now."

"That's still young."

"I have a housekeeper as well."

"Really?" She peered up at him. "Mother didn't mention it."

"It's a new arrangement. Mother and Father both met her when she first arrived at shearing time. She's Binda's sister, Millie."

"An Aboriginal woman?"

"What does that matter?"

Ellen shook her head. "It doesn't. It's just that I've never found them much good at keeping house."

"Daisy and Jundala perhaps, but they've always stuck close to their traditions. Keeping house holds little interest for them. Millie is different. She has worked for a family on a property in the south and is well skilled at cooking, managing the house and looking after the children. She enjoys it and she's a much better cook than Jundala or Mary or me." Joseph patted his stomach. "She looks after us well and the children are happy."

"Well, that's all that matters then."

Once more their gaze went to the children and their game.

"Yes it is." Joseph nodded his head. He wasn't sure how they would have survived if it wasn't for Millie. And it wasn't just her ability with cooking and cleaning that he appreciated. It was her constant happy presence around the children. The younger ones loved Millie and even William enjoyed her company. She couldn't replace their mother but she filled a gap in their lives and for that he was most grateful. Even Binda appeared to have left behind his earlier misgivings about his sister's staying and life had settled in to some kind of comfortable routine since shearing.

"What are you two nattering about over there?" Lizzie struggled up from her chair holding Robert in one arm and nearly fell back again.

Joseph rushed to her side. "Careful, Mother."

"I wouldn't drop him."

"I'm not worried about Robert. I'm sure he'd bounce. It's you I'm concerned for. Can't have you hurting yourself before we've eaten your wonderful Christmas dinner."

Lizzie's eyebrows shot up. "Your son needs some distracting. A walk perhaps?"

"I'll take him." Ellen reached for the toddler. "Come to Aunty Ellen. I think there's a puddle further down the creek you can splash in."

"Can we come?" Esther and Violet called together.

"Now look what you've done," Joseph said to his sister.

"The more the merrier." Ellen laughed and blew a raspberry kiss on Robert's plump cheek. "What about you William?"

"No thank you, Aunt Ellen."

"Very well." She took Esther's hand. "Come on girls. Don't tell your father but when we get to the creek we're going to take off our shoes."

Both girls squealed in delight, their excitement as much for being part of the teasing of their father as for the thought of playing in the water.

Joseph shook his head at their departing backs.

"Perhaps you could come inside and help me with a few things I need to do for this Christmas food you're looking forward to."

"Of course, Mother."

"Do you need me, Lizzie?" Thomas looked up from his conversation with Frederick.

"No, you stay here. I only need one set of male muscles for the moment."

Joseph offered her his arm and they walked across the patch of bare ground to the front of the house.

William watched his father and his grandmother walk away arm in arm. Snatches of his grandmother's happy chatter drifted back to him as they went. Now that they'd left there was little point in staying. His grandfather and uncle were only talking about the differences in the ships that came to the port. That didn't interest William.

He should have gone to the creek with his Aunt Ellen. She was always good fun to be with but part of him had wanted to stay with the men. If he sat quietly it was his observation that the adults in his life usually forgot he was there and adult conversation was often full of interesting fragments. He discovered all manner of things that he digested and put back together later.

"I hear there are many farmers struggling in these parts."

William paused his building. His Uncle Frederick was changing the subject from boats. William was out of the two men's line of sight so he didn't even have to pretend he was playing.

"Those on the plains are having a tough time of it but most of us in sheep country are doing well although Joseph suffered some significant sheep losses this last year."

"Through lack of feed and water?"

"No. We've not had the best year but we've maintained feed and our water supplies are strong. The losses are too high to be put down to wild dogs and natives."

"What else is there? Disease?"

"One that goes by the name Ellis Prosser. Joseph's neighbour."

"He's stealing Joseph's sheep? Can't the police do something?"

"If we had proof I am sure the constable would follow it up but Ellis and those who work for him are too clever. We haven't caught them in the act and we can't prove it."

William was a little disappointed. He'd heard this discussion several times already between his father and Binda. The conversation was nothing new.

"It is very beautiful here." William could tell his uncle was looking beyond the creek to the mountains in the distance. "But it is so remote. I don't know how you live here all the time."

Thomas chuckled. "It was the last place I expected to end up when I came from England nearly forty years ago. Back then I thought Adelaide the most remote place on earth but this country claimed me for its own."

"You don't ever want to go back to England?"

"Why would I? There is nothing for me there. Everything I love is here. My family, the land; although we have been sorely tested at times."

"No doubt Ellen has been a handful."

Thomas chuckled. "I meant by the land. Back in the sixties we suffered through a terrible drought. We could have lost everything, nearly did but for the help of good friends. What stock we had left we sent south. It was a grave time."

"But you hadn't been here long then. You're more established now."

"Perhaps, but we also had some dry seasons only a few years later. That was when Joseph took it into his head to go off in search of permanent water on Smith's Ridge. Luckily he found it and he survived but it's not enough. Nothing can save us unless it rains and we haven't had a lot of that in the last couple of years. It reminds me of the sixties."

William pondered his grandfather's words. He knew his own father had nearly died when he was only a few years older than William. The land had been so dry he'd set off to look for the springs of water he was sure existed in the rugged country at the back of Smith's Ridge. He'd found a permanent waterhole but would have died had Uncle Binda not found him. William had heard that story many times but it was always in a lighthearted, joking way between Uncle Binda and his father.

"Joseph seems to be coping." Uncle Frederick changed the subject again.

There was a pause before Thomas spoke. "I think so."

"Are you worried about him?"

William sat perfectly still.

"No. Perhaps a little concerned. It's a big task raising four children alone and managing Smith's Ridge. Lizzie and I do what we can but it's a day's ride between us. And we have our hands full with Wildu Creek."

"But Mother Baker said he had some help."

"Yes. He has a good friend, a native called Binda and his family."

"Ellen has spoken of them."

"Binda also has a sister who I think is proving very helpful with the house."

"Do you think it would be wiser for him to employ a … someone of his own kind?"

There was a pause before Thomas spoke. "I think it's working out all right."

"The children seem happy and cared for."

"They are but children find it easier to move on, become absorbed in the day to day."

"You still worry for Joseph?"

"Lizzie is concerned … we both are. He never was a drinker but since Clara died we've notice he imbibes more regularly."

"Oh, I hope you didn't mind me bringing the mead?"

"Not at all."

"Last night was just meant to be for some Christmas cheer."

"It was and even Lizzie and I enjoyed a few sips but Joseph doesn't stop at that."

William frowned. Worry wormed in his stomach. His grandfather hadn't seen the small flask his father kept in the dresser at home. Joseph filled it from a bigger container he kept hidden in the shearing shed. William had followed him one day and seen him. Some nights after he thought they were all in bed his father sat alone drinking until the flask was empty.

"No doubt last night he felt able to relax. Here with his family."

"Yes. I told Lizzie there's no harm in the occasional tipple."

Squeals of laughter echoed along the creek.

Frederick stood up and walked to the bank. "That sounds like my mischievous wife."

Thomas went to stand beside him. "The children adore her, as do I."

"You are not alone there."

William edged backwards until he was beside one of the large trees then he turned and hurried back to the house. His father was drinking liquor regularly, a lot more than his grandparents realised. What did that mean? Did it put his father in danger? Could it kill him like it had Great-uncle Isaac? William didn't know what he could do about it but he had already lost one parent, and he wasn't prepared to lose another.

And niggling away at the back of his mind was his grandfather's warning about drought. William hoped his words were the concerns of an old man but his grandpa was very sensible and not one for idle speculation. He didn't usually say something unless he felt there was truth in his words.

"There you are, William."

William stopped at the steps leading up to the verandah and looked up at his father who was carrying a tray loaded with mugs and a large jug.

"Your grandmother needs help carrying food. We're going to eat again. She wants us to be outdoors while the weather is pleasant."

"Yes, Father." William bounded up the steps. He hoped his face looked happy. His grandmother had a funny way of extracting things out of him and he wasn't prepared to share his concerns with her, especially those about his father's drinking.

Twenty-four

The dining room of Henry and Catherine's home was tastefully decorated with red velvet bows at each window. A swathe of pine which had been studded with smaller bows and little gold balls decorated the mantel. Merry voices filled the air and drew Henry's gaze back to his guests.

Seated around his table were Ellis Prosser and his wife, Johanna; Sydney Taylor the stationmaster and his wife, Agnes; and Reverend Mason, the visiting Church of England priest; a small but worthy gathering for their first official dining event in their new home.

Henry looked down the length of his new dining table. Covered in one of his mother's beautiful white damask tablecloths, set with their fine dinner plates and groaning with Christmas fare, one would never know it was made of pine instead of the cedar or mahogany he couldn't afford.

From the other end of the table Catherine caught his eye and gave him a sweet smile. She looked delightfully pretty in a pink dress she had brought back with her from Adelaide. The heat had left the day, something they were both grateful for. Even though the thick walls and wide verandahs helped keep the house cool there had been a week of excessively hot weather leading up to Christmas. Yesterday the wind had come from the south, allowing them some respite and a chance for the house to cool.

Catherine and Flora had been cleaning and cooking for days in preparation. There had been a big discussion about whether to serve hot or cold food. In the end they had decided on cold. Catherine and Henry had greeted their guests with a refreshing punch and Henry had welcomed Ellis Prosser's gift of a bottle of red wine which they would drink with their meal.

Once they were all seated Flora had passed around ham-and-tongue mould, Aberdeen rabbit sausage and beetroot-and-mint terrine, all of which looked bright and festive and tasted delicious. That had been followed up with platters of turkey and ham and cold potatoes. Rather than pudding Catherine had decided they should have mince pies, dainty cakes and fruit to follow.

Now they were all replete, relaxed and sipping an after-dinner madeira, sherry or in the Reverend's case, a lemonade, made fresh this morning by Flora. Agnes Taylor was admiring the Christmas tree in the corner of the room.

"Wherever did you find such a fine specimen on this treeless plain?" she asked.

"I have Ellis to thank for that." Catherine inclined her head to him.

Prosser, who was seated on her right, placed his hand over hers. "We have an abundance of pines on our property. It was no trouble to get you one."

Henry noticed the way the man leaned in a little closer to Catherine and how she slid her hand away from his.

Flora appeared in the doorway with Charles which set Agnes and Johanna into raptures of delight. Catherine rose and the men stood.

"I think we ladies will retire to the sitting room."

"Splendid." Ellis Prosser tapped his pocket. "I have some fine cigars, gentlemen, if you'd care to imbibe. We'll need an ashtray and perhaps another glass of sherry, Henry?"

Henry went to give his son a kiss before the ladies departed and then he made his way to the sherry decanter. He was prepared to be amenable to Prosser's officious manner but he made sure he didn't snap to it like a servant. He had benefited several times already from his business dealings with Prosser and he hoped to do so again. Prosser needed to remember they were more in the way of partners than master and servant.

"How are your cattle settling in?" Henry poured sherry into three glasses. The Reverend continued to sip his lemonade and declined a cigar.

"More about how my men are settling to them. Not the same to move about as sheep. They have horns." Prosser gave a derisive chuckle. "Something a few of my men have found out the hard way."

Sydney Taylor took a puff of the cigar Prosser had lit for him and spoke to Henry. "And you've turned some of your cropping properties over to sheep, I've heard."

"Just the one south of Cradock. It worked in both our favours. Ellis was looking to destock and I was looking for sheep." What no-one knew was that Prosser had sent most of his stock to markets in the south and made good money on them. Many of the stock on Henry's southern property were from Smith's Ridge and he had bought them from Prosser for half the money they were worth to Joseph Baker, a deal that had given satisfaction to both Henry and Prosser. "Finding feed for them has proved difficult of course. The land is quite bare but we are managing with a relatively small number of stock for now."

"Are you sure it was wise to convert cropping country to grazing?" Sydney blew a puff of smoke into the air. "The farmers I've spoken to have had a fairly good harvest."

"They're close to Hawker perhaps." Henry stroked his chin. "Even Wilson had some average results but around Cradock the crops were very poor."

"There are most certainly some very desperate families there in need of our prayers," the Reverend said.

"Fools, all of them," Prosser barked.

"That is surely harsh, Mr Prosser. These families have taken up their land and put everything they have into it in good faith."

Prosser blew a cloud of smoke towards the Reverend. "Encouraged by a misguided government who has no understanding of the conditions."

"Your property borders that Baker fellows who lost his wife recently, doesn't it?" Sydney changed the subject. "How is he getting on?"

"Grief affects us all differently." Prosser's face darkened.

"I'm sorry, Ellis." Sydney put a hand on the other man's arm. "I didn't mean to stir up sad memories."

"I don't believe Johanna and I will ever get over the loss of our son."

"The police have not been able to bring his killer to justice?" Henry asked.

"Constable Cooper has done little to track down the culprit." Prosser puffed himself up, his face nearly as red as his hair. "We grieve for our son every day but Baker appears to be managing fine without his wife."

Sydney shook his head. "My wife spoke to him in your shop a while back, Henry. She said he was quite delusional with grief."

Henry held his breath. Malachi had informed him of Baker's claims that the tonic had killed Baker's wife. Nothing more had come of it and sales were as brisk as usual for the variety of lotions and tonics he stocked.

"He may well be delusional but I am confident he has made up for the loss of his wife." Prosser's lips turned up in a lurid sneer.

"How so?" Sydney asked.

Prosser looked from Henry to the Reverend then back to Sydney. "He's got a woman living there."

"Be damned." Sydney slapped his leg.

"He has young children." The Reverend looked sternly at each of them. "No doubt he would need a housekeeper."

Prosser stabbed a finger in the air. "She's more than a house-keeper. And not only that but she's black." Prosser spat the last word as if it was poison.

Henry wasn't surprised. He had always thought Joseph Baker was mixing his favours and he'd been right.

"One should be sure of one's facts before speaking ill of others, Mr Prosser." The Reverend had gone quite pale.

"Oh I'm sure," Prosser growled. "I had reason to call in at his house only last week. Baker wasn't there but his black woman was. Full of airs and graces and acting like the lady of the house with the youngest Baker child on her hip."

Henry shook his head. "Shameful."

Catherine appeared in the doorway, Charles in her arms. She hesitated, looking from one man to the other.

"Hello, my dear." Henry hoped she hadn't heard their discussion.

Catherine smiled sweetly. "I am putting the baby to bed, gen-tleman. Then we ladies hoped you might join us in the sitting room to sing some carols. Our shop assistant, Mr Hemming, has been dining in the kitchen with Mrs Nixon and her children. I've asked him and Flora to join us."

Henry opened his mouth to speak but Catherine caught his eye.

"I think that's very humble of you, to invite your workers to join us, Mrs Wiltshire." The Reverend's pale face was stretched in a wide smile.

Henry didn't think so but he could hardly contradict the priest.

"You'll lead us in the singing won't you, Reverend?" Catherine asked.

"I'd be delighted." The Reverend shot across the room as if eager to escape.

"Please don't hurry. It will take me a few minutes to put Charles down but in the meantime Flora is about to bring out some of her delicious mead."

Prosser clapped his hands. "Well that should lubricate our throats. What do you say, Sydney? Are you up to some singing?"

"I think so. It is Christmas after all."

Catherine disappeared from the door and Prosser and Sydney made their way out towards the sitting room. Henry paused a moment, thinking of Baker. The man may have been feeling desperate enough to take a black woman to his bed or maybe they'd been cohabiting for some time. He remembered the first time he'd met Joseph. He had been brazen about his connection with the natives then.

If the truth be told Henry was almost envious of Baker. Since Catherine had returned from Adelaide he could count on one hand the number of times they'd coupled. He was a married man for goodness sake but he felt constantly frustrated by Catherine's lack of interest in that part of their marital life.

"Oh, I'm sorry Mr Wiltshire, I didn't realise you were still in here."

Henry looked around at the comely Mrs Nixon hovering in the doorway.

"Is it all right if I start clearing the table?"

"Of course."

Henry watched her cross the room and begin stacking the plates. She kept her back to him but he could tell by her movements she was aware he was watching her.

"Catherine says you have some mead for us."

Flora stopped her work and turned. He stared at her. She met his gaze with a look that suggested she could see right into him. He enjoyed her boldness. In fact, to his surprise, it aroused him.

"I have served it in the sitting room. I would like to clear up in here before the singing starts." She turned back to her work.

Henry watched her a moment longer then left her to join his guests. He hoped some boisterous carol singing would burn up some of his restless energy.

It was nearly midnight by the time he stood beside Catherine on their front verandah farewelling their guests. Feeling jubilant at the success of their first official dinner and mellow from several glasses of mead he slid his arm around Catherine's waist and nuzzled her neck as they stepped back inside. He felt his wife stiffen.

"Henry, please," she whispered and slipped from beneath his arm.

He followed her into the sitting room where she put out the candles, keeping one to guide her. Henry turned off the lamp in the window and followed her to the bedroom. Once more he encircled her with his arms.

"Henry." She pushed him away. "It has been such a busy week and now today with all our guests I am simply exhausted. I must get some sleep."

"Charles sleeps all night now."

"I know but it's after midnight and he will still be awake at dawn. I am so desperately tired, my love, and my head aches. You understand, don't you?"

Her big round eyes shimmered in the candlelight. It only served to inflame his desire for her. He took her in his arms and pressed his lips to hers, trying to arouse that same desire in her but she struggled against him.

"Henry, stop." She stepped back. "I am your wife, not a common strumpet to be taken at your pleasure."

Henry was so shocked at her words he was speechless.

She turned away. "I am going to bed to sleep," she snapped. "I think perhaps you should take the spare bed tonight."

He watched her in disbelief as she removed the pins from her hair. What had happened to his sweet malleable wife? And where had such language come from? Damn, he felt not the least bit tired. Part of him wanted to slap her, show her she was his woman to be taken to his bed whenever he chose but he thought better of it. She was tired, overwrought from all the preparations. He would leave her be for the moment. He turned and left the bedroom. Down the hall there was light shining from the kitchen. Behind him the bedroom door closed. Henry walked towards the light.

It was extremely warm in the kitchen. Flora Nixon was standing at the scullery washing the last of the dishes. The jug of mead sat on the table. He loosened his necktie and poured himself a glass. Flora spun at the sound. Her sleeves were rolled up and the top buttons of her shirt were undone revealing the pink skin of her neck. One wet hand reached for the gap in her open shirt.

"Mr Wiltshire, you startled me."

"I'm sorry." He raised the glass of mead. "Care to join me?"

"No, thank you. I have a few more jobs to do before I retire."

"I give you permission to have the rest of the evening off. It's Christmas." He poured another glass. "Come, join me."

Flora hesitated then she wiped her hands on her apron and accepted the glass.

He raised his higher. "Merry Christmas."

"Merry Christmas."

She took a sip from her glass. Henry half-emptied his.

"This is very good mead, Flora."

"Thank you, Mr Wiltshire."

She took another sip and Henry drained his glass and refilled it.

"You must miss your husband."

Flora met his glance as she put her glass to her lips. She took another mouthful of mead.

"My husband is a hard worker but circumstances ... well let us say they haven't made him an easy man to live with."

Henry thought about that. His only memories of his own father conjured up thoughts of a man, gruff and remote. Was that why his mother never spoke of him? Perhaps her life had been similar to Flora's. Often alone, raising a child; and yet his mother had done well and provided for all his needs.

"Did you say he was trapping rabbits?"

"Yes. He has to go a long way south. He says the farmers there are having terrible trouble with them." Flora smiled. "But he called on us a few days ago. Brought the children some sweets. The Aberdeen rabbit sausages I served tonight were courtesy of my husband."

"That was very generous."

"Mrs Wiltshire paid for them."

"Indeed."

"He could only stay the day and then he set off again." Flora drained her glass and set it on the table. "I was going to talk to you about that. He's not bringing in very much money. It is a struggle."

"You have free accommodation in exchange for the debt your family owes."

"For which I'm very grateful but the children are growing so fast and young Hugh especially is always hungry. Mrs Wiltshire is so kind about letting me take leftovers home ..." Her voice trailed away. It was one of her rare vulnerable moments.

"But still it's not enough." Henry's eyes roamed from Flora's pink cheeks, down her neck and took in the curve of her breasts. Not full like Catherine's but shapely all the same. "Perhaps your husband should take the children with him."

"Oh no. That would be no life for them. He does the best for us he can …"

Once again the unspoken 'but' hung in the air.

An idea began to take shape in Henry's brain. Perhaps it was the mead; it was so brazen he shocked himself and yet like Flora he had his own desperate needs. "It must get very lonely for you without your husband."

"We manage."

"The nights must be …" He waved a hand in the air. "Empty."

Flora lifted her chin. "My children are the most important thing, Mr Wiltshire."

"Of course, and you would do anything for them." Henry moved into the space occupied by Flora between the table and the scullery.

"Yes, but …"

Henry took another step towards her. Only a few inches separated them. Flora Nixon stared back at him, not backing away further. Excitement coursed through him at the boldness of his idea.

"Perhaps there is a way that would benefit us both."

Flora's eyes widened. He slipped a hand around her waist. She met his gaze but she didn't move.

"In what way?"

Henry barely registered her question. He could tell from her look she understood him and she wasn't pulling away. He lifted one hand to her breast. She gripped it with her own hand and stared into his eyes. "What would be the benefit for my children, Mr Wiltshire?"

"We can work it out." He leaned in closer. There was a faint smell of perspiration mingled with lavender.

She pressed herself against him. "We work out the arrangement first." She murmured in his ear.

Henry growled. "Very well." He lifted his head from the kiss he'd been about to plant on her neck. "What is it you require?"

Flora drew herself up. "My debt paid in full."

"What!" Henry almost choked.

"And a full wage."

"You ask too much."

Flora placed a hand on his chest and then moved it slowly down to his waist. Her look was shameless. "Not for what I am offering in return." Her hand slid lower.

Henry groaned. Right now he would give the damned woman anything she wanted as long as she came willingly to bed. "This will need to be a very regular occurrence."

Flora lifted her hand. "As long as my children and your wife are unaware of our ... arrangement."

"Of course." Stupid woman. As if he'd tell his wife he was bedding another woman. He grabbed her hand and pushed it back to where she had removed it from his rigid cock.

Once more she lifted her hand. She stepped away and turned off the lamp. He hurried to blow out the candles. He was fed up with delay. He caught her arm and pressed her to the wall, one hand on her breast and the other pulling her head to meet his lips. He would have some relief for his manly needs at last.

"The spare bedroom would be best I think," she spoke softly in his ear.

He lifted her skirts, grabbed her buttocks and hoisted her up. She wrapped her legs around him. The sensation drove him wilder with desire. He carried her across the hall into the small bedroom and closed the door behind them.

Twenty-five

1883

Dust hung in the air, stirred up by several horses and carts ahead of them on the track to Bennie's paddock. There had been some rain a week back but the pleasant autumn sunshine had soon dried the ground. Catherine flicked her fan despondently in front of her face. Her silence conveyed her displeasure. Henry had insisted she accompany him to the races. It was the opening meeting of the Hawker Jockey Club and most important that they be seen there.

He found a place to tether their horse and cart and offered Catherine his arm to get down. She was slow in doing so and almost collapsed against him as her feet reached the ground.

"My dear." He put two steadying hands on her shoulders.

"I'm all right." She adjusted her hat and looked around. "I didn't think there would be many here."

Like Catherine he swept his gaze over the scene before them. There were already groups of people gathered under the tall trees at the edge of the paddock and many more lined up at the refreshment booths that had been erected. Horses were being led around a yard to one end of the paddock with several others tethered nearby. Flags fluttered from fence posts and temporary poles. The whole affair was quite festive.

"The who's who of our district." Henry puffed out his chest. "Today is a very important occasion. Holding our own race meeting marks what a progressive community Hawker is."

"I do hope there will be a place for me in the shade." Once more Catherine fanned her face, which looked pale and puffy under the delightful tall hat with a narrow brim his mother had sent from Adelaide. It was black with red plumes on the side which matched the red trim of her grey jacket. His wife was bound to be one of the best-dressed women here.

Henry had thought she had feigned illness to get out of accompanying him but now that he studied her more closely she didn't look her usual self. He offered his arm. "I will make sure of it, my dear."

They passed through the gate. Henry was a little taken aback that they should have to pay six pence each to enter; he was after all a sponsor of one of the races. They strolled past the refreshment booths and a tent that had been erected over a wooden floor for dancing for those who wished to stay on once the races were over, until they reached the stand of large gums. There Henry spied Ellis Prosser's red hair near one of the larger trees. He steered Catherine in that direction.

"Here you are at last, Wiltshire." Prosser thrust out a hand.

"My fault we're late, Ellis." Catherine smiled and her face lost its vexed look. "I was a little slow in my preparations."

Prosser took her arm and looked her up and down brazenly. If they weren't such good friends Henry would take offence.

"Well it was worth the wait." Prosser said. "You look resplendent as always, Mrs Wiltshire. We have saved you a seat. Come and meet everyone."

Johanna Prosser greeted them. She was very smartly dressed in a black-and-white jacket and skirt with a matching hat. No expense had been spared on her outfit Henry wagered.

"Have you met our new medical resident?" Prosser indicated a thin young man talking to the Taylors.

"Not yet."

"Dr Bruehl, allow me to introduce the best merchant in our area, Mr Henry Wiltshire and his wife, Catherine."

"Doctor." Henry offered his hand to the doctor, admiring his two-piece tweed suit. The doctor had no doubt brought it with him. Harriet had only recently sent Henry sketches of similar jackets and suits that were becoming common in Europe.

"Please, you must call me Siegwart," the doctor replied, his English heavy with a German accent.

"Lovely to meet you, Siegwart." Catherine turned her charming smile on the serious-faced doctor who gave a quick upturn of his lips in response.

"You know the Taylors of course, and our head teacher Mr Harry. Have you met the Marchants?"

"Of course." Henry nodded to the others and shook the pastoralist's hand. He had a property south of Prosser's and was a good customer.

"Well what a fine day." Prosser tucked his thumbs into his waistcoat and strutted forward rather like a peacock. "Now that you're here Henry I think it's time we gentlemen inspected the horses. There are to be three races and we have a total of eighteen entries. Not a bad effort for our first meeting."

Henry showed Catherine to a chair with the ladies. He watched as she settled herself carefully. Catherine wasn't usually one to pout but she was certainly acting in a fragile manner.

"Off you go, Henry." Agnes Taylor waved at him. "We will look after your lovely wife."

Henry turned away to follow the men.

"Your husband is one of the most devoted I've come across." Agnes's voice prattled behind him.

"They are still only a few years married, Agnes. You remember those days." Johanna Prosser chuckled.

Henry strode after the men, wondering at the boldness of her conversation with her young daughter sitting nearby. He smirked. If Johanna Prosser only knew the truth she'd have something to natter about. He troubled his wife less these days when it came to fulfilling his needs. The accommodating Flora Nixon knew all the right ways to please him in bed and that their coupling was clandestine made it all the more desirable.

"My horse is in the first race." Prosser indicated a bright bay horse of fine proportions being led around by a lad. "I purchased Duke from a breeder in New South Wales."

"A fine animal indeed." Sydney Taylor turned a triumphant smile on the group. "I can see there would be no need to place a wager anywhere else, gentlemen."

In spite of that assurance, Prosser insisted on inspecting the other runners, after which they retired to the refreshment booth. One of the enterprising local publicans had set up a tent and brought some barrels of ale. They all partook except for the doctor and Mr Harry who both chose lemonade.

"Quite a turn out," Mr Harry declared once they had found a place away from the crush at the bar. "I recognise some from quite a distance away."

"Everyone from farmers, to blacksmiths and saddlers, to the likes of us fine fellows." Sydney raised his glass to the others. "To the Hawker Jockey Club."

They all echoed his sentiment and took a drink.

Henry gave Prosser a wary look as he nearly choked on his ale.

"The audacity of the man." Prosser's already florid hue darkened to crimson. "Bringing his black woman here amongst decent folk."

Henry followed Prosser's gaze to the area in front of the finish line. People milled about and on the edge of them stood Joseph Baker, with his son and— Ellis was right. A young native woman dressed in a blue-and-brown patterned skirt and jacket, with a deeper blue hat set at a jaunty angle on her head, stood beside him. They were talking to some farmers Henry recognised from Wilson.

"But there are other native people here." The doctor nodded to where a group had set up camp with a small fire.

"They keep to their kind and all is well," Prosser said.

"I hear she's his housekeeper," Sydney said.

"That's the story he puts about," Prosser growled.

Henry felt the colour rise in his own face. "It's scandalous behaviour."

"It certainly is." Prosser stomped his foot on the ground causing a puff of dust to rise around them.

"Perhaps they are married?"

They all looked at the doctor with varying degrees of shock.

"Taking a black woman discreetly has been known to happen," Prosser huffed. "But any white man with a sense of decency wouldn't marry one of them."

"The horses are being led to the start," Marchant said.

Immediately the focus was on the horses and Prosser led the way to the edge of the track. Henry followed the others. The gall of Joseph Baker, bringing his woman to this auspicious event. Henry's indignation simmered just below the surface.

William pushed his way to the front of the crowd. This horserac-ing business had caused the biggest commotion he'd known in

Hawker. It had been a big surprise to him that his father had decided to make the journey to attend and that he'd also agreed William should go too. The only problem had been Millie. Joseph had asked her to come with them and it had caused a heated discussion between him and Uncle Binda who had thought she should stay home. William had not been able to hear why.

The shouting of the crowd pressed around him and William strained to look along the track as the horses thundered towards him. It was a warm day and the smell of leather and horse sweat enveloped him as the horses swept past, cloaking the cheering spectators in a cloud of dust.

There were cheers and groans, shouts of joy and mutters. A jubilant farmer next to William picked up his wife and kissed her. "You clever woman," he exclaimed. "My Lady won by a good head."

Around him others muttered and dropped their tickets in the dust. People drifted away, back to the booths and the shade of the trees. William decided not to find his father. He'd noticed some of the stares and whispers Joseph had attracted with Millie at his side. William quite liked Millie. She was good fun and didn't treat him like a baby and boss him about like Mary tried to, but he was very aware that here amongst the people of the district the colour of her skin made her a cause for gossip. Perhaps that was why Uncle Binda hadn't wanted her to come although William had noticed several groups of native people here.

He picked up a stick and drew a trail in the dirt then found a small patch of grass and sat in the shade of a wagon. He gathered other bits of stick and before long he had a small construction growing on the ground in front of him.

Another race was about to run, this time with hurdles. William stayed where he was. The view would probably be better from this distance and he was on higher ground than those that ranged the edge of the track. There were only three horses in the race. Once it was all over he went back to his building.

A frilly pink skirt appeared next to him. "What's that?"

William looked up at the girl who belonged to the dress. The pale green eyes in her pert little face were studying his work. Georgina Prosser had grown taller since he saw her last.

"A stable for horses."

"They'd have to be very small horses." She was matter of fact. "Luckily I have some."

William gaped at her as she opened a little drawstring purse and took out two tiny horse figurines. "I wanted to bring them to the races." She smiled and her face shone. "They were supposed to bring good luck but I'm afraid Father's horse didn't win. He's not happy. He paid a lot of money for it. He's gone back to the refreshment booth so now Mother's not happy because he's drinking liquor. I have escaped for a while."

William continued to stare up at her. He wasn't sure if he was expected to respond.

"Can I stable my horses in your building?"

Georgina crouched down as if she was going to sit. William leapt up.

"Here." He slipped his vest from his shoulders and spread it on the ground. The grass was only patchy around them. "You'll get your dress dirty."

"Thank you." She settled on the vest next to him. "Pale pink is a silly colour to wear to a day at the races. I told my mother I wanted to wear my dark green dress or the ruby-red one but she wouldn't listen."

William concentrated on his construction. His sisters had three dresses. Two that they alternated at home and one for best. If they had come to the races they wouldn't have had a choice about what they wore.

"You don't talk much do you?"

William's cheeks felt warm. Georgina was studying him closely, her hair fluffed out around her face under her straw hat with a ribbon that matched her dress exactly. "I don't have anything to say."

"We are neighbours but we haven't been properly introduced. My name is Georgina Prosser." She held out one hand.

"I know." William looked down at his own hands. They were dirty from his building work. He brushed one on his trousers and gave her hand a quick shake. "I'm William Baker."

"Yes, I remember you." She looked at the small stable and yards and slid her horses into the bays he had built. They fitted perfectly. "Do you like horses?"

"They're just horses. I've never thought about it."

"Then why are you building a stable for them?"

"I like making things, buildings and yards, working out how they fit together and what kind of roof works best." William was usually busy with work and if he wasn't working Millie had him practising his letters and reading. The rare times he had idle hands he loved to imagine constructions and then try to recreate them with whatever he had at hand, usually sticks and bush and rocks that he bound together with mud if he had water. Today he'd stuck to sticks.

"I like to sketch horses," Georgina said. "When I'm older father is going to buy me a fine Arab."

William didn't know what to say to that so he remained silent.

"Do you ride?" she asked.

"Of course." William pulled his shoulders back. "I'm eight years old."

"So am I."

"I am nearly nine." His birthday was less than two months away.

"I just had my birthday. That's when I got this dress. Mother thought I needed it." Georgina tugged at the sleeves disdainfully. "I wish father had bought me the Arab instead."

William peeked at the girl from under his hat. She was far too small to manage such a strong horse. "Do you ride often?"

"Every day, and Father lets me take care of several of our horses even though my mother says I should stay in the house. I much prefer to be out with the horses."

"Georgina!"

"Oh crumbs." Georgina jumped up and brushed at her skirts. "That's my mother. I'd better go before she gets herself in a stew. "

"Don't forget your horses." William picked the two figures from the stick construction and handed them to her.

"Thank you." She slid them into her purse. "And thank you for letting me join in your game."

William watched as she hurried away. She didn't speak like a child and she seemed much nicer than her father. He smirked. For all her bravado she certainly jumped when her mother called.

He cast his gaze to the track. Another race was about to run. This one was called the Farmer's Purse and he knew his father had wagered some money on one of the runners. He stood and watched the race unfold before him. There were six horses this time, and once more he watched the milling crowd cheer and then disperse, some jubilant and some with long faces.

Movement a little further away caught his eye. Standing apart from the people and horses were two men. William recognised his father and the other was hard to distinguish from the distance but perhaps he was the man from the shop they no longer visited. The two men were standing opposite each other and William's normally level-headed father was moving from foot to foot.

He looked around for Millie but he couldn't see her. Then the other man pushed Joseph hard in the chest making him stumble. William ran in their direction.

"I've had enough of your accusations." Henry watched as Baker steadied himself from the push. Henry hadn't shoved him that hard but the man had been off balance already. He'd imbibed some liquor by the look of him but then so had Henry. He knew his own movements were slightly impaired. "My tonics are the finest that can be bought."

"They might be the finest but they were poison for my wife."

"You don't seem too worried about her now. I see you have a black woman to keep you warm in her place."

Henry took a small step back as anger clouded Baker's face and he raised his fist.

"How dare you discredit both my wife and my housekeeper in that way!"

"I am only repeating what other well-bred folk have said and I dare in the same way that you dare to spread untruths about my tonics."

"You are a wretched, vile man." Joseph spat the words at him.

"And you are not fit to be with decent people, you and your whore."

Henry got ready to fend off the blow he knew was coming when suddenly Baker was attacked from behind.

"No, Father."

The boy latched on to his father's arm.

Henry took the opportunity to swing a punch that connected with Baker's jaw and sent the man reeling. Henry felt instant pain across his knuckles. He'd never hit a man before and it hurt.

"What's going on here?" Sydney Taylor looked from Henry to Joseph, who was being helped up by his son.

"This fool attacked me." Henry clenched and unclenched his hands at his sides, trying not to show the pain he was in.

Sydney shook his head at Joseph who was trying to push his son away. "You'd better come quickly, Henry, your wife is unwell."

Henry turned to Sydney immediately. "What is the matter?"

"I don't know." Sydney lowered his voice. "Ladies' business. They've taken her to your cart. The doctor is with her."

Henry clapped a hand on Sydney's shoulder. "Thank you."

He left Baker to his son and hurried along the track which was scattered with people leaving now that the last race had run. When he reached the cart, Catherine was propped up in the back, her face pale and her eyes closed. The doctor and Johanna sat with her. He felt a sudden pang of guilt that he hadn't listened to her protests that she hadn't felt well.

"What is it, doctor? What's the matter with her?"

The doctor stepped down from the cart. He moved away a few steps and Henry followed.

"I believe your wife may be with child, Mr Wiltshire."

Henry glanced towards the cart. A wave of relief swept over him. Another baby, of course. Catherine had been unwell in the early stages of her confinement with Charles.

"I think she has overtaxed herself," Dr Bruehl said. "I want her to rest and I will come and see her tomorrow."

"Of course, doctor." Henry shook his hand. "Thank you. I will make sure she is well taken care of." Henry strode back to the cart. He thanked Johanna and helped her down before adjusting the blanket around Catherine and setting the cart for home.

There was not a breath of wind. All the movement on the track leading back to town was stirring up the dust which hung in the air. Behind him Catherine moaned and clutched at her stomach. He looked back at her propped in the small tray and slowed the horse.

"My poor dear," he murmured. It would be a long and uncomfortable ride home but he couldn't help the stab of excitement he felt at the prospect of a brother or sister for Charles. He grinned. And he had backed two winners today. Quite a good day all round it seemed.

Twenty-six

"Now let me look at your jaw."

Joseph lifted his chin towards the lantern Millie held aloft.

"Not much of a bruise there," she said.

"I told you it was nothing. Wiltshire landed a lucky punch. If William hadn't grabbed my arm—"

"William was very worried about you. Brawling in public like a ..." Her eyes flashed in the lamplight. Her knowledge of English was good but there were some gaps.

"Ruffian?" he offered.

"Like a man who has lost his good sense." She put the lantern down and sat on the log they'd pulled close to the fire.

Joseph watched her poke at the fire with a stick then pour herself another mug of tea. His eyes were drawn to the flames. The drink he'd consumed had worn off during the cart ride to their first creek camp site. He'd been left with a dry mouth, a headache and, even though he wouldn't admit it, a throbbing jaw courtesy of Wiltshire's knuckles. In spite of all that, he felt extraordinarily cheerful. It was rare for him to enjoy Millie's company alone. Well, almost alone. William had often been so quiet on their ride to and from the races one could forget he was there sometimes.

No doubt, like Wiltshire, the gossips didn't think an eight-year-old boy a suitable chaperone but when they were at Smith's Ridge there were so many of them he rarely got the chance to talk with Millie for any length of time without interruptions. At least on this journey they'd done plenty of talking and that's when he'd understood.

He had felt different towards her for some time now and as they'd journeyed to the races he'd recognised what that difference was. He'd grown to love Millie and all her ways. The realisation had come as a shock to him. It was quite different to the way he'd loved Clara. With her there had been a strong physical attraction right from the start. William had been conceived on their wedding night or soon after. Joseph had loved Clara for the strong wonderful woman she was, not just for her body but their physical desire had been an important part of their marriage.

That was not what had attracted him to Millie. And yet, God help him, he would happily take her to his bed but he didn't want her to be any more the source of gossip than she apparently already was. Joseph's hands curled into tight fists as he recalled Wiltshire's words. He cared nothing of what other people thought about him but he would not have them think badly of his family or Millie.

He glanced at her huddled over the fire and delight replaced his dark thoughts. His love for Millie had grown from the way she cared for his children, took an interest in what happened on the property, made sure he was well fed and his clothes were washed. She had adopted the ways of Europeans and yet there was no mistaking her native roots, not just because her skin was black but because of her natural connection with the land. She may live like a European yet she existed easily in the landscape that was Smith's Ridge. Clara had often struggled with the heat, the dust, the flies. Not Millie, she mixed the two cultures, taking her knowledge of both to create someone new that was uniquely Millie.

She turned to look at him, a shawl draped around her shoulders, her face glowing from the warmth of the fire. "What are you doing standing back there in the cold?" she asked. "The days might be warm but the clear night sky sucks away the heat. I've poured you a mug of tea."

He went and sat beside her and took the tin mug she offered. It had sat a while so it was cool enough to wrap his fingers around. He took a sip and wrinkled his nose.

"What's this?"

"Tea." Her smile split her face. "With a little something extra for aches and pains.

"I told you I feel quite well."

She raised an eyebrow and looked back at the fire. He took another sip, the taste was a little bitter but bearable. He extended one hand closer to the flames feeling at a loss for words. Now that he'd admitted his true feelings to himself he was unsure how to speak to her lest he say something wrong. Binda had said something had happened to her at the property down south where she'd worked. Joseph had suspected it was something to do with a man. He didn't want to do or say anything that would upset the balance of their lives.

"You do a lot of thinking, don't you?"

He looked up from the flames. Once more Millie's big dark eyes were studying him.

He shrugged. "With four children the time to ponder is short."

"What things do you ponder?"

He kept his gaze on hers. "You, my dear Millie."

She looked away and instantly he regretted his words. Perhaps it was too soon to tell her how he felt but they had so little opportunity to be alone. Frantically he thought of something else to say.

Millie stood. "We should talk."

He looked up at her, hope surging in his heart.

"Not here." She nodded in the direction of the cart where William was sleeping. "He's a little sleeper that one."

Joseph liked the way her English was sometimes not quite right. Her native dialect still influenced her speech, but he wasn't about to correct her.

"There is a moon." Millie lifted her face to the sky. "How about we go for a walk?"

She pulled her shawl tighter and moved around the fire. Joseph picked up his jacket and followed, unsure if he was about to be told off or encouraged. His heartbeat quickened.

They walked for a while along the dry creek bed in silence. Once away from the fire, their eyes adjusted and the moonlight was enough for them to see their way clearly. Millie led them to the pale grey trunk of a huge gum that had fallen and now stretched part way into the creek. She leaned her back against it and waited for him to come to a stop beside her.

She looked beyond him up at the sky. The moonlight made her skin shine but for the first time since he'd met her he saw a deep sadness in her eyes. He sensed her inner turmoil. He was desperate to know what troubled her but he wouldn't rush her.

Finally she lowered her gaze to him and spoke. "There is a lot you don't know about me."

"I could say the same."

She grinned, the sadness swept away in an instant. "Perhaps."

"I know that you are a wonderful housekeeper and you take good care of my children."

She shook her head slightly and stared into his eyes with a look that suggested she was far older than her years. "When my brother found you and brought you to our camp I thought you were a magical being."

She reached out and traced one finger slowly down the side of his face, along his jaw to his chin. Her touch was so gentle and yet his skin tingled where her finger had been. Her hand dropped away.

"I wanted to find out everything about this boy with strange skin and words I didn't understand."

"I remember you were often hanging around."

His attempt at humour was ignored.

"When you left, a great sadness came over me. I think now that perhaps I loved you even then."

Joseph gaped at her. "How old were you? Three or four? It's bad enough your father says I'm the reason his son lives in two worlds. I don't want him to think I was the cause of your choice as well."

"Don't worry." She flashed him a smile. "He already blames you."

Joseph shook his head. No wonder Yardu's hostility towards him was so strong. Not only was Joseph the reason Binda had moved away from his people but it appeared he was also the reason Millie had too.

"When Binda left I wanted to go also. I was too young but when Binda came to the camp for visits I would get him to teach me your words. When I was older the chance to get away came. I hid in a hawker's wagon and got a job in the house of a family closer to Adelaide. I didn't think my father would find me there. By the time he did I was my woman. He sent Binda to bring me home but Binda understood why I wouldn't go. It was a big property, lots of sheep, lots of people working there, Aborigine, English, Chinese, even a German. The family who owned it treated us all well. I was happy there." Once more Millie glanced at the night sky and fell silent.

Joseph watched the changing expressions cross her face, as if she were grappling with an inner demon. "Did something bad happen to you there?" He felt compelled to ask even though he wasn't sure he wanted to hear the answer.

Millie dragged her gaze back to his. Tears brimmed in her eyes but they didn't fall. "I fell in love. Not a little girl fondness ... truly in love."

All kinds of wild thoughts whirled through Joseph's head. If she was no longer with this man did that mean he'd hurt her?

"What happened?" he asked in a whisper.

Millie let out a deep sigh. "I had been there four years when James arrived. He was the owner's nephew. He was my age, not long from England, keen for adventure and ..." She smiled. "He laughed a lot. How he would laugh, and soon everyone would be laughing. He much preferred the conversation of the workers quarters, he said the big house was too quiet. It was him who helped me improve my English even more. We'd spend any time we could together and we fell in love."

Once more Millie fell silent; looking up at the sky, remembering something Joseph was not a part of. He waited.

"James's uncle found out. He was very sad for us. Said we could not be together. James was only in Australia for two years then he was to return home to help with his father's business. The family sent me to another property. To protect me, they said. James would have to go back to his life in England and I couldn't go with him. James managed to visit me a couple of times but when his uncle found out he was sent home to England immediately." Tears filled Millie's eyes again. "My heart was broken."

Joseph desperately wanted to wrap his arms around her but he'd never done anything more than bump her accidently in passing. Her heartache was intense. Unsure what to do, his arms remained limply at his sides.

"Anyway the new property wasn't the same. Not just because James had gone from my life but the owners weren't nice people. Treated their workers badly, especially my people. I decided to go home. My father wasn't happy. He made it difficult for me and

I had made it difficult for myself. I was used to your ways and couldn't settle for the life my family lived." Millie pushed away from the trunk and stood just in front of him, looking deep into his eyes. "When I came to Smith's Ridge I recognised the sadness in your eyes, Joseph. I remembered the boy I thought I loved and I wanted to make you smile again." She reached out a hand for his, gently clasping his fingers in hers. "I see you, Joseph Baker. Your heart sings again and it makes mine sing."

"Does that mean—"

"That I like you very much."

Joseph felt a mixture of relief and delight. They'd both had sorrow in their lives, other loves lost to them. He reached for her other hand. Her grip was strong but when he tried to pull her closer, she resisted. Her eyes darkened.

"I am still sad sometimes for James. He is gone from me and I don't want that pain again."

"I understand that pain, Millie, but I am also my own man. I love you. I won't let anyone or anything hurt you."

"I am sure you mean what you say, Joseph, but we are not alone."

He felt a prickling at the back of his neck but resisted the urge to look around.

"You have family," she said. "Friends, neighbours. They will not feel happy for us."

He laughed inwardly. His mind had gone straight to spiritual beings rather than the people they lived with. "It may be a surprise at first—"

"Think about it, Joseph." She squeezed his hands. "Look at what happened today. The fight you had was about me, wasn't it?"

"I had another issue with Wiltshire."

Her eyes stared deeply into his.

"Well, partly, but he is a pompous ass of a man who believes he's a cut above everyone else. I don't intend to cross his path again and I don't care a jot about what he thinks." Joseph leaned a little closer, willing her to see what was in his heart. "It's how we feel that matters, Millie. If we love each other my family will accept that and anyone else who doesn't will be of no importance to me."

"Don't be so quick with your words, Joseph. We need time to explore our feelings. You are a deep thinker. I like that. Think on this, on us and what our being together would mean, for longer."

Joseph inhaled deeply. He was happy at least to know she had not been physically harmed in the past and that she didn't reject his love outright. If she wanted to move forward slowly he would accept that for now but there was something he was desperate to do.

"Millie?" He pulled her gently towards him and this time she didn't resist.

"Yes."

He leaned his head towards her. "May I kiss you?"

Her lips parted in a smile. "Yes."

They drew together and Joseph savoured the taste of her, the feel of her slim body in his arms. Just for a while there was nothing else to think about but holding Millie close.

Twenty-seven

1885

Joseph looked down from his horse at the bloodied carcass of a sheep. Blood stained the ground around it. It was a fresh kill but already the flies crawled all over it. He slid from the saddle and moved closer. No smell yet but the heat of early January would bring on the decay quickly.

He looked up as Binda came through the bush from the other direction.

"Dingo." He looked from Joseph to the pitiful remains between them. "Big male. I lost his tracks on the ridge."

Joseph pursed his lips. The wild dogs had been all but eradicated with baits and traps in the early days. There had been good summer rain in the ranges and grass was plentiful. Rabbits had increased in numbers and they in turn had become easy food for the dingo along with his sheep. This was the third carcass they'd found since the new year had begun only a few weeks back.

"Such a waste." He turned back to take his shovel from the pack on his horse. "We'd better bury it. Don't want it ending up in that waterhole down the hill if we get more rain."

Binda found a place where the soil was clear of rock and while Joseph dug the hole Binda cut what wool he could from the dead animal and stuffed it in a small hessian bag. Finally the job was done. Joseph took a long draught from the water bottle and offered it to Binda. They both stood in the shade of a tree and stared at the mound. The dingo had eaten little of the sheep.

"Such a waste." Joseph shook his head.

"Dingo only eats to fill his stomach. He knows he can easily get more food."

"This was the offspring of one of my experiments." Joseph bent and tugged a tuft of wool from the bag. He slid it through his fingers feeling the oily lanolin on his skin. "Sturdy for these conditions and yet the wool is so strong and fine."

"Maybe I should camp up here for a while," Binda offered.

"It's the middle of summer."

Binda grinned. "Best time here. Plenty of food, plenty water."

Joseph nodded. "I would appreciate you keeping a watch for a while. I'll get some traps next time I'm in Hawker."

He spun at a footfall. Two sheep came through the bush. They stopped at the sight of the two men and the horse then settled to munch on the sweet grass.

"You're a bit jumpy." Once more Binda grinned at him. "Expecting someone?"

"I was …" Joseph's voice trailed off. He was hot but even so heat spread to his cheeks. He had continued to court Millie very discreetly but he knew there was little her brother Binda missed. Nothing had been said about it though. If Binda thought Millie was being too familiar with Joseph he continued to reprimand her. Joseph took care to be nothing but respectful but after the Christmas just passed – the third since Millie had come to live with them – he'd asked Millie to marry him and she'd accepted. Their love didn't have to be a secret any more. "Millie's been gone a while."

Binda waved his arm. "This is her country. She can look after herself."

"But she was only going to visit your family for a few days."

"Maybe she's decided to stay, not come back."

Joseph's heart gave a thud. Millie had told him she was going to tell her father she planned to marry Joseph. Yardu wouldn't be happy and he was sure Millie wouldn't want to stay any longer than she needed. He'd wanted to go with her but she'd laughed at him, said her father would have steam coming from his ears and nose at the sight of Joseph.

Binda's sharp gaze locked with Joseph. "My Mary can keep house for you."

"Mary has been wonderful but—"

"You don't need Millie." Binda stamped his foot and stood tall.

Joseph rarely saw him angry. He opened out his palms to his friend. "I love her, Binda."

"You think you do." Binda shook his head vigorously from side to side. "Millie is smart and pretty. I knew as soon as she set her eyes on you she would try to charm you. I've seen her play her games, giggling and touching your arm when she thinks I'm not looking."

"We have kept our feelings to ourselves as much as we could."

Binda snorted. "She's my sister but she will be no good for you and you no good for her."

"Why?"

Binda stretched his arm out beside Joseph's. Even though Joseph's skin was dark from the sun he was still fair in comparison to the black of Binda's skin. "This is why."

Joseph stared at his friend. Anger surged within him. He flipped over his wrist and waved the scar at Binda. "Does this mean nothing to you?"

"You are my blood brother but nothing can change the colour of our skin. We chose this friendship."

"Yes, and Millie and I chose ours. No-one forced us. She charmed me yes, but in a good way. We love each other. I thought you would understand."

"Millie will not bring you happiness."

Joseph's anger ebbed as quickly as it had peaked. "She already has. Millie has brought happiness back to my life and to my children."

"Others will not understand."

"If you don't I'm certainly up against it."

"Your people only tolerate us if we can work for them."

"My people?"

"Those who have stolen our land."

Joseph's hands fell to his sides. "Stolen? Jundala's people are always welcome here. Your people too. Yardu is the one who chooses to keep away."

"It is not a choice." Binda's dark eyes glittered. He remained perfectly still. "The land is fenced, the waterholes are used by many sheep, rabbits and sheep eat the food of the animals he hunts."

Joseph was speechless. He had no idea his friend felt this way. "I'm sorry, Binda. I was born here. I don't know any other life."

"I do." Binda's lips turned up in a small grin. "I am my father's disappointment, living in two worlds." He lifted his hand and gripped Joseph's shoulder. "You are a good man but you are only one person. Many others do not treat our people well. It is these people who will make life bad for you and Millie if you marry. You will not belong to them or to her family. No-one will want you."

"I can't turn off my love for Millie and I won't let what others think dictate my life."

Binda gripped his shoulder tighter. "I am proud to call you my brother."

"So we will continue to be friends?" Joseph was still shocked by Binda's outburst.

"We will. I want you to be sure you understand." Once more Binda squeezed his shoulder. His dark eyes, barely a foot away from Joseph, stared steadily. "You will be treated like a black man if you marry my sister. You might not like it."

Joseph and Millie had already had this conversation on several occasions. "We are not children, Binda."

Binda's hand fell away. "Your mind is made up and so is Millie's."

"You've spoken to her about our marriage?"

"Before she left."

Joseph felt panic constrict his chest. Perhaps Binda had said something to make Millie stay with her family. "What did you say?"

"That I would talk to you. Try to make you see sense."

"And what did she say?"

"She laughed. Said she would see me when she came back."

Immediately Joseph's gaze went to the top of the ridge. It was the direction Millie would return from.

"Why don't you go home that way? She should be coming any time now. You might meet up with her. Unless our father has tied her to a tree and beaten her with a stick."

Joseph looked back at his friend. There was a sparkle in Binda's eyes.

"I am hoping that's unlikely."

"He is a determined man. I think that's where Millie gets her strength from. For all his anger he would not hurt her but I think he will no longer want to see her again."

Joseph felt bad about that.

Binda gave him a little push. "Go on. Millie was destined for a different life. It might as well be with a good man like you."

Joseph gripped his friend's hand. "Thank you. I will come back tomorrow with some supplies."

"Tell Jundala where I am. She will want to come up here too."

Joseph gave a nod and mounted his horse. He gave Binda a wave and moved down the gully away from the sheep that had been joined by two more. He circled through the bush and then followed the slate-covered ground that led to the top of the ridge. He took a deep breath. The heat of the day released the scents of the leaves and flowers. Above him the azure-blue sky was studded with small strips of wispy cloud and an eagle drifted on the currents.

He loved this country, and couldn't imagine living anywhere else which made him think again of Binda's words. Was Smith's Ridge really stolen land? If that was the case every pastoral lease and farm was stolen. Even Hawker itself was standing on land that did not belong to those who built there. He shook his head. Not every inch could belong to the natives.

Joseph turned his horse's nose east and followed the ridge top pondering the dilemma of it all. He stopped to wipe the sweat that trickled down his face and took another drink. Down in the small curve of the rocks below him a shadow moved. He blinked and rubbed his eyes, focusing on the spot, wondering if he might come across the wild dog.

The shape moved out from behind an arm of rock and strode to a large gum beside the creek. Joseph gaped. The shape was female and looked a lot like Millie but the thing that surprised him most was that even from his distance he could see she was naked. Her back was to him. He watched her pause on the edge of the creek and slip into the water.

Once more heat from within swept up Joseph's chest and to his cheeks as he forced himself to look away. When he had kissed her goodbye a week ago she had been wearing her favourite green patterned skirt and light brown blouse. He slipped from his horse and led it quietly back along the ridge until he could find a place where he could get down to the flatter country. What was he to do? He had never seen Millie naked. Jundala and Gulda's wife Daisy often wore little clothing when they worked outside but they were at least partially covered. From what he could see Millie was wearing not a stitch. Thank goodness her back had been to him.

Millie climbed out of the creek into a patch of sunshine and squeezed the water from her hair. It had only been a quick dip to wash away the smell of campfire and the layers of dust that coated her skin. She had enjoyed the temporary freedom of camp life with her family but it came with other restrictions. Her journey to see her family had not been an entirely happy one. When she'd first arrived she'd seen the hope in her father's eyes that she had returned for good, hope that had turned to anger and then to sadness when she'd explained she was going to marry Joseph Baker. Yardu had ignored her from that moment.

Thankfully the rest of her family had not been so intolerant, especially the women. Her mother had been sad at first but when Millie had joined her aunties and cousins to gather berries and yams, they became immersed in the pleasure of their task and each other's company. That was the only thing Millie missed, she thought, as she dragged her fingers through her wet hair then twisted it up onto her head; the company of the women. She had spent most of her time with them, listening to their stories, laughing at their jokes and sharing the burden of any sadness. At Smith's Ridge, Jundala mostly worked outside. Mary was good company but so much younger. Millie missed the camaraderie of women.

She took her neatly folded clothes from the hole in a large gum tree where she'd left them, shook them out carefully and laid them out on a fallen trunk. Slowly she slipped each item on and turned her thoughts to Joseph Baker, the man she loved and would marry. She didn't need other company. Joseph and his children were her family now and maybe there would be another baby one day. Millie did up the last of the buttons on her blouse, tucked the ends into her skirt and set off for the house that would soon be hers. Happiness made the journey short.

Joseph stopped his horse. It snorted and tossed its head. He decided to follow the track through the trees to the lower hill country and walk the horse in the hope Millie would catch him up. He couldn't stop his mind from replaying the vision of her dark skin shining as the sun caught it before she slipped into the water. He enjoyed the memory of her long hair, loosely flowing in glossy waves over her shoulders, the nip of her waist, her slight hips.

He rubbed at his eyes trying to erase the image but he couldn't and his body responded, out of his control, making it difficult to sit in the saddle.

"Hello."

The sound of her voice so close startled him. He turned his head slowly, terrified she would still be naked and yet part of him hoping she was.

There stepping out of the bush was Millie, dressed again with her hair coiled up on her head, even darker now that it was wet. He got down carefully from the saddle.

"Hello to you."

She flung herself into his arms. Joseph gave her a quick squeeze and let her go. His wayward body was already far too responsive to the sight of her.

"How are your family?" He chose his words carefully not wanting her to know he had spied on her.

"Well, except for father who must have an upset stomach. He rumbled and glared and groaned the whole time I was there."

"Because of us?" Joseph smiled and took her hand as they fell into step together.

"Yes. I am a bad daughter." Her dark brown eyes were liquid like a deep pool.

"I am sorry, Millie."

She grimaced. "I wish he could be happy."

"You didn't expect him to be?"

"No but a small part of me hoped." She put her other hand to her breast.

Joseph's heart ached for her. He had to trust he would be enough to keep her happy. After seeing the ease with which she shed her clothes and blended with the bush he wondered how comfortable it was for her to live with him.

"Are you sure you want to marry me, Millie?"

She stopped walking, making him stop behind her. The horse he was leading dutifully did the same.

"Yes."

Once more Joseph felt as if he could fall into the depth of her dark brown eyes. Binda's words came back to him. Millie was destined for a different life. "But you are giving up so much."

"The land will always be in my heart but I like these clothes, a high roof over my head, cooking and sewing. They make me happy. I love my family but I also love yours. Robert's hugs are so special, and Esther's determination and Violet's eagerness to please. William is so like you." She reached a hand up and gently traced the curve of his cheek, over the rough stubble of his unshaven face to the tip of his chin. "And I love you."

Joseph couldn't help himself. He took her in his arms and kissed her, savouring the softness of her lips, the slightly salty taste of her mouth. He groaned and with two hands on her shoulders gently moved her away from him. He would not take advantage now.

"We should marry soon." Millie's eyes were wide, her breathing quick.

"Yes." He nodded. Once more he took her hand, snatched up the reins of the ever-patient horse, and they set off again following the rough track through the low bush. "Binda is in agreement."

"How did you make that happen?"

"We talked."

"I am glad. He is my brother but also your friend. I don't want to spoil that."

"There is only my family to tell now," Joseph said. "The children will be happy."

"Except perhaps William?"

"William likes you very much."

"I know but as a friend, not as your wife."

"William will have to accept our marriage the same as everyone else." Joseph looked at the bush ahead but he could feel Millie's gaze upon him.

"I hope your parents understand better than mine."

"They will be happy for us." Joseph spoke with a conviction he wasn't certain of. His parents got on well with the local natives and called them friends. He hoped they would be accepting of his planned marriage. He squeezed Millie's hand and brought it to his lips.

"The children have missed you."

She smiled back at him. "It will be good to get home."

Twenty-eight

Harriet had asked Mrs Simpson to pack the seamstresses up thirty minutes early and usher them home. The first week of March had been excessively hot. It was stifling in their workroom and the lingering smell of their sweat had pervaded her house. They were on time with current orders and she thought the bonus of an early finish would be most welcome.

She closed the door on dusty O'Connell Street and made her way to the haberdashery counter where Miss Wicksteed was overseeing a junior who was serving a lady's maid in need of items for her mistress. Thankfully the shop smelled sweet as ever. Harriet always kept it stocked with perfumed soaps and the scent lingered and disguised other less pleasant odours.

"All well here, Miss Wicksteed?" she asked.

"Yes, Mrs Baker. Annie is doing a fine job."

The maid nodded her agreement and Annie's face broke into a proud smile. Harriet waited a moment, listening to their discussion over the merits of one cotton over another. The maid had black hair and her skin was dark but her features were not native, perhaps oriental. Harriet had made it very clear to her staff they were not to allow coloured people of any description in her shop but this woman appeared exotic and had been newly appointed to her position as lady's maid to the mayor's wife.

Harriet still felt prickles on the back of her neck when she thought of the evening nearly four years ago when a dark hand had slipped around her door and Jack Aldridge had paid her a visit. For a long time after she'd hardly ventured outside her premises alone. Then whole days and in more recent times whole weeks would go by and she wouldn't think of him and yet the sight of the dark-haired woman had sent her recollecting again.

At the next counter another of her senior assistants was helping a well-dressed lady to adjust a new lace collar she was trying and along from them another assistant was showing a customer a range of hosiery.

Harriet's silk day dress rustled softly as she walked. She glimpsed an image of the pale green fabric as she passed one of the small mirrors installed on the side wall. She was more than happy with the colour and the design was perfect for her petite figure. It had been quite some time since she'd allowed herself a new dress after being fleeced of so much of her hard-earned money by the vile Jack Aldridge.

She had lived life watching over her shoulder ever since but he'd never returned. It had taken a lot of hard work and careful money management to keep her business on track but she'd succeeded. She had a nice amount of money in the bank again and her nest egg which she wouldn't touch unless there was absolutely no other way.

Harriet moved to the side counter and straightened some bolts of fabric. When she had first begun her dressmaking business in Port Augusta she had got into the habit of putting a small amount away as a safeguard. By then Septimus was a rare visitor to their home and while he usually made sure they were taken care of she couldn't trust that he would always provide for her and Henry.

The money had been useful setting them up in Adelaide after Septimus had died. Since then Harriet had stashed little bits away again as she could spare it. Slipped into a silk purse and tucked up in the springs of the sitting-room chair, it was her assurance of a comfortable future should something happen to her business.

She thought of Henry and the letter he had sent which awaited her in the kitchen. He didn't write often but when he did he regaled her with stories of Hawker life, his business and the latest achievements of Charles Henry.

"Time to close up, Mrs Wiltshire?"

Harriet turned at Miss Wicksteed's question. The customers had gone and the girls were gathering their bags and hats.

"Yes, Miss Wicksteed, thank you. I will lock the door behind you."

She stood beside the door saying goodnight to each one. Annie was the last before Miss Wicksteed who brought up the rear.

"Well done today, Annie." Harriet smiled and nodded. "You have the makings of a fine sales assistant."

"Thank you, Mrs Wiltshire. I do enjoy working in your beautiful shop. Good night."

Miss Wicksteed said her goodnights and Harriet was quick to shut the door behind her and push the bolts across. She felt uneasy tonight. She didn't know why but it made her hurry through her tasks, tallying the day's takings against the dockets and making sure all was ready for business the next day. Finally she went through the door into the workroom. Her leg was giving her pain today which didn't help her mood. She shut the door behind her and cast a quick glance over the silent machines and cutting table. All was tidy but still odorous and warm. She hoped for a breeze overnight and she would rise early and open the windows to air the room before the girls arrived to start work. She stepped into her sitting room and shut the door on the stuffy workroom.

Her house was warm and airless. She decided to open her sitting-room window. It faced a narrow path at the side of the building and although there was no cool air yet it might be fresher at least. The kitchen was even warmer with the fire and she resented having to add a little more wood to boil her kettle. She picked up Henry's letter and crossed to the back door. It was early evening and her kitchen only had a small window. It was hard to read in the gloom and she was not prepared to light a lantern yet. Keeping a fire going was bad enough.

She slid the letter from the envelope and opened the door. She stood just inside the frame where there was more light for reading while she waited for the kettle to boil. She fanned herself with the envelope and glanced over his opening words and his detailed description of Charles's new teeth. She stopped at the next paragraph. Catherine had miscarried again. She re-read his words. It was obvious he was sorely disappointed Charles was still to be an only child. Catherine was slow to recover this time and because the heat was still excessive she was going to take Charles and stay with her parents at Glenelg for a short holiday. She hoped to call on Harriet when she was feeling better.

Harriet looked at the date at the top of the letter then put it aside while she made a pot of tea. Poor Catherine, this was her second miscarriage. As a mother Harriet felt for her but she had warned Henry she didn't think Catherine was a strong person. Harriet didn't particularly want to see Catherine, they had so little in common, but she would be pleased to see her grandson again.

She set everything out on a small tray, added the letter and carried it out to the back of her house, into the tiny walled yard with a plum tree and a locked gate that led to the lane behind. There was some small movement of air at least. With the window and door open Harriet hoped some fresh air might be drawn through the house.

She set her tea tray down on the small table beside the chair she kept outside and settled herself. Her leg felt instantly better once she sat. Harriet poured a cup of tea and took up the letter again.

Henry wrote of the booming trade he was doing and urged her to send more of her fine linens as soon as she was able and any shawls and hats she could source. Harriet flicked her eyes over his details about the town. He was very effusive in his description of the opening of one of the two new flour mills in Hawker and also of the new stone railway station to replace the wooden building that had burned down. He attended every official function in Hawker and was full of praise for the town. Harriet held little hope that he might sell his business any time soon and return to Adelaide.

The last page was in the way of a request. The light was fading fast now and Harriet had to peer closely to make out his words. He needed capital to be able to take up a lease in the hill country near Hawker. All of the pastoral leases ran out this year and he was keen to take one up. Harriet shook her head. He was yet to repay her for her previous loans. He had built Catherine a fine house and was furnishing it lavishly by all accounts. He already had a smattering of smaller properties. Harriet worried he was overstretching himself but he seemed to think diversification was the way. His letter was most insistent. He wanted her help with money again.

Harriet put the letter in her lap and sighed. She had only recently built up some savings again since Jack had cleaned her out.

A movement at the door startled her.

"What are you doing sitting out here in the dark?"

Her heart filled with dread at the voice. She peered through the gloom at the smiling face of Jack Aldridge. It was if her earlier thoughts of him had conjured him up. His tall body was framed inside her open back door.

"How did you get in?"

"A very convenient open window."

Harriet's hand went to her throat. She had forgotten to put the chock in the window to stop it opening further.

Jack dug his hand in his pocket. Harriet was startled by the sudden flare of a match. He held it towards her.

"I think it's time to light the candle."

He reached down and lit the candle she kept on the table, flicked the match away and leaned back against the kitchen wall. Harriet watched his every move as if he were a snake about to strike.

"That's better. You have very clear eyes, Harriet. I like to be able to see them. I've become very good at telling when people are lying to me by studying their eyes."

Harriet's gaze narrowed. She could hardly see his eyes. His face was in shadow while she knew hers would be illuminated by the candlelight.

"What do you want, Mr Aldridge? I hope it's not money because I've had little chance to build up any savings since you were here last."

He remained silent, watching her from the shadows. Suddenly he moved and she jumped.

"Oh dear, you are excitable tonight." He smirked. The shadows gave his face a gruesome twist. "I hope you haven't had bad news."

Harriet looked down at the letter in her lap. Her heart beat faster. He had simply shifted from one foot to the other but she was so wound up it had alarmed her. She took a slow deep breath. She couldn't let Jack find out about Henry. Now there was young Charles to think about as well. She slid the letter under her teacup.

"A friend sending news. Nothing alarming. However your presence here is. I gave you a great deal of money for your silence. What have you done with it?"

"All gone." He laughed. It was a mirthless sound.

"Have you tried finding work?"

"Many times, Mrs Wiltshire, but it never lasts. My employers always seem to find issue with me. Something to do with the colour of my skin I think."

Harriet felt a pang of guilt. She would most certainly not employ or entertain as a customer anyone of native skin. Still there were plenty of people who did. It was not her problem if Jack Aldridge couldn't get work.

"You don't look like a man without employment." She had noted the fine cut of his jacket, the quality of his pants and boots, and the grooming of his beard.

"With thanks to my benefactress." He bowed slightly and she could see his face more clearly. He was mocking her. In spite of his dark skin there was no doubting he was Septimus's son. He had the same strong lines of the narrow nose and the piercing eyes.

She sat back in her chair and stared at his shadowy face. "We had a deal, Mr Aldridge. I paid you well. You were never to come back."

"Perhaps you can't trust me. But then again maybe I can't trust you."

Harriet's brain scrambled. He'd come from the house. Had he found her money stash in the chair?

"You have a very nice sitting room."

In spite of the warm night Harriet's blood ran cold. Not her nest egg. He can't have her nest egg.

"Nice portraits on your mantel."

"Portraits?" Harriet could only think of her money.

"A younger you. You're still a very striking woman, Harriet. Then there's a boy and another of the boy, now a man, on his wedding day perhaps?"

Oh no, Henry. Harriet reached for the locket that was no longer around her neck, she glanced at the letter under the teacup. "I told you my husband died a long time ago."

"Yes you did but you neglected to mention you have a son who it appears is very much alive."

"The portraits are a friend's son."

Jack was very still then he crossed the small space between them in an instant and leaned in. He smelled of cigars and liquor.

"I'm not much of a reader, Harriet. The Aldridges didn't think it important for me to learn but I can manage the basics."

He tugged the letter from under the cup and opened it out. Harriet knew it was the last page she had read that he would be seeing.

Holding the letter close to the candle Jack peered at the paper. He began to read, his voice slow as he stumbled over the words. "I do hope this finds you in good health Mother, your loving son, Henry." Jack turned cold eyes on her. "Shame on you, Harriet. I have a brother and you tried to keep him from me."

Dread spread through Harriet and a terrible realisation. She was never going to be rid of Jack Aldridge. No matter how much she paid him he would always come back for more and now he had extra bargaining power.

Jack tossed the letter back on the table but it slid and the pages fell to the ground at her feet.

"I will give you more money." Harriet lifted her chin and focused her gaze on his. "But you are to leave my son alone."

Jack stroked his neatly clipped beard as if he were contemplating her words. He turned and paced the small backyard. The next time his back was to her, she pushed the pages under her chair, hidden by her skirt. It appeared he wasn't a proficient reader but if he did peruse the letter further he would discover where Henry was.

Jack came to a stop in front of her again. "Money alone is not enough. It is gone so easily."

He smirked and Harriet knew his pacing had all been an act.

"What do you want, Mr Aldridge?" Her bravado had deserted her.

"I think I am entitled to at least half of whatever my brother has. I am sure you have set him up well. My father would want the same for me."

"You've cleaned me out once already. How am I to set you up in a business?"

"Oh no, Harriet. I don't want my own business." He stood tall and once more his face was in shadow. "I want half of yours."

Harriet felt the blood drain from her face. "How can … how will …" Words failed her. Once more she grasped for the necklace that was no longer there.

"It's simple: you will give me half your daily takings."

"Half. You don't know about business, Mr Aldridge. I told you I have to pay staff, pay for goods. Some days there is very little left over for me."

"You will pay me a wage."

"A wage? What for?"

"I will be your new employee. It will make a change from shearing sheep, lugging wheat bags and chasing stock. I am sure there must be the odd job you can find me. I am not averse to heavy lifting. I will be an official employee who receives a wage and half of whatever your daily take is."

"I have no need to employ you. My other staff will be suspicious."

Jack shrugged his shoulders. "You'll work it out. You have a way of twisting the truth for your benefit." He leaned in closer again. His brooding eyes focused on hers. "The problem is, Harriet, I don't trust you. So I will need to be nearby, keep an eye on things so that I get my correct share."

Dread settled over Harriet like a cloak. She struggled to keep her brain focused.

"You must give me time to think of a suitable job, a reason for your presence. I will need to prepare my staff."

"I am guessing it will be quite a shock for them when you employ a black man." Once more his laugh was mirthless, his breath sour in her face. He stood back. "Very well. I have some unfinished business myself. I will need five pounds and I will be gone for two weeks. When I return you will welcome me as your new employee."

"I have money inside." Harriet picked up the candle, eager to be rid of him. As she stood her leg wobbled beneath her and Jack took her arm.

"Steady. I don't want any harm to come to my new partner."

He guided her inside. She lit the lamp and took down a tin from the kitchen mantel. She kept a small amount of money there for housekeeping. Aware that he watched her every move she tipped the contents onto the table. Coins rolled in several directions at once. He slapped them to the table. She counted out nearly three pounds. He looked at her with raised eyebrows.

"I have a little more in the till." She took up the candle again.

He followed her through the workroom and into the shop. She slid her hand behind the curtain at the back of the counter and felt for the tray. He took the candle from her and yanked back the curtain. There were two one-pound notes and an assortment of coins in the tray. It all added up to four pounds, eight shillings and three pence. She knew because she had counted it herself. Jack took the notes and then began to scoop out the coins.

"Please leave me something. I will need some money for the start of business tomorrow."

He hesitated then let the curtain fall back into place. "I will be on my way now, Harriet." He moved across to her shop door, drew the bolts then turned and gave her the candle. "I will be back in exactly two weeks to start our new partnership."

He slipped out of the door into the darkness. Harriet pushed it closed firmly behind him and slid the bolts back in to place. She blew out the candle and peered through the glass panes but could see nothing in the darkness. Letting out a breath, Harriet leaned her shoulder against the door, weak with relief that he was gone. Then she remembered the window. She hurried back to her sitting room, slammed the glass shut and turned the lock.

What was she to do? Her eyes watered but she took out her handkerchief and dabbed them dry. Harriet had discovered at a young age she had little use for tears and had only succumbed to them a few times in her life. She was in a bind but there had to be a way out. Whatever it was she just hadn't thought of it yet.

How would she explain Jack's presence to her staff, to Henry should he visit? She had always avoided native people, now she had to take one into her shop. Damn Septimus and his bastard son.

She glanced across at Henry's portrait. There was nothing for it. She would have to ask for his help. She would have to tell him about Jack but she didn't want to commit her embarrassing tale to paper. No, she would have to travel to Hawker and tell Henry in person. If Catherine was in Adelaide they would have a better chance of speaking freely. Harriet didn't want her daughter-in-law burdened any more than she already was. She was also quite sure Henry wouldn't want his wife to know about her dead father-in-law's indiscretions.

Tired as she was Harriet began to make preparations. She would need to leave quite a list for Miss Wicksteed if she were to catch the following day's train to Hawker. It was two days travel there and two days back. She could only afford to spend a day with Henry. She would send him a telegraph to expect her on an errand of great urgency.

Twenty-nine

His mother had said March was a terrible time of year for a wedding but when Joseph took Millie's hand in the shearing shed at Wildu Creek, he didn't care that the morning was already hot and that sweat trickled down his back inside his new shirt. Millie was smiling her beautiful smile and her eyes were wide with delight and love for him. He felt the same way about her and that was all that mattered.

Reverend Masters had kindly detoured to Wildu Creek on his monthly visit to conduct Church of England services in the district and now read a bible passage on the virtue of marriage. The Reverend had been a little taken aback when he'd first met Millie but she'd quickly charmed him and assured him she, like Joseph, was devoted to their future together.

Joseph's family, under his mother's directions, had cleaned the shearing shed and decorated it with the few bits of greenery they could find. His mother had created an arch using the branches of trees for them to stand in front of. Somewhere she'd found some switches of tiny white flowers to weave around the branches and Millie wore a sprig of them in her glossy dark hair.

Behind them stood their family and a handful of close friends. Joseph knew they all harboured varying degrees of reservation about his marriage to Millie but he felt sure of their support none the less.

The Reverend lifted his hand in the air and said a prayer over them. "Almighty God, who at the beginning did create our first parents, Adam and Eve, and did sanctify and join them together in marriage; Pour upon you the riches of his grace, sanctify and bless you, that ye may please him both in body and soul, and live together in holy love unto your lives' end. Amen."

Behind them came a chorus of amens. Millie smiled up at him and Joseph pulled her gently into his arms and kissed her. They had only ever kissed during their rare moments alone. Joseph had been very careful that their developing relationship was virtuous – he knew they faced enough hurdles without adding to the gossip – but since Millie's return from her visit to her family it had been harder and harder to stop at a simple kiss. Now his kiss was passionate, as he felt his new wife respond. There were claps and cheers, and reluctantly Joseph released her except for the grip he had on one hand. They turned to face those gathered as the Reverend declared them the new Mr and Mrs Joseph Baker.

Esther and Violet rushed forward and flung their arms around them. Robert came too, pushing between them. Thomas and Lizzie hugged them both and then others lined up to congratulate them.

Between hugs Joseph noticed William still sitting on the chairs that had been placed in the shed for the service. Even though he was only ten he appeared to carry the weight of the world on his shoulders. Joseph caught his eye and winked. William gave a small smile in response and then he was lost from Joseph's sight as Binda and Jundala came forward, offering their congratulations.

Thomas clapped his hands and they all turned to look. "Please move down to the other end of the shed for some refreshments. The ladies have been cooking for days and Lizzie tells me there is some cool lemonade ready for you."

Joseph took Millie's hand and leaned closer. "Happy?" he asked.

"Yes." Once more her brilliant smile lit up her face. "Very."

They moved to the other end of the shed where the big door was open and a slight breeze cooled their skin. Ellen came and hugged them both, her two little girls clinging to her skirts.

"I am so happy to welcome a new sister-in-law." Ellen kissed Millie on the cheek. "The lace collar on your shirt is so pretty. It goes well with the flowers in your hair and I love the diamond pattern in your skirt. You make the prettiest bride."

Millie glanced at Joseph. She was very confident when it was just them at Smith's Ridge but she was never one to be the centre of attention like she was today.

"I trust the groom meets with your approval, dear sister." He deflected Ellen's attention.

"By far the handsomest man here."

"You can only say that because you husband isn't present."

Ellen's face turned serious. "I'm sorry Frederick couldn't be here but his work has taken him to Adelaide for a week. He sends you his very best wishes."

"Thank you, Ellen," Millie said.

Joseph wondered at his brother-in-law's absence. While Ellen had grown up with natives, Frederick had not been long from England and then had enjoyed Adelaide life before he married Ellen and they took up residence in Port Augusta. He was always very stilted with their native friends on his rare visits to Wildu Creek. Joseph suspected his brother-in-law wouldn't approve of his marriage to Millie. Frederick's trip to Adelaide may have been carefully timed.

"Do come and eat." Lizzie came to drag them away to the big table that had been set up and was positively groaning with food. Violet took Millie's hand to show her the special floral arrangements she'd helped prepare to decorate the table.

"Thank you, Mother." Joseph bent to kiss Lizzie's forehead.

"What for?"

"This." He cast a hand towards the table then looked back at her. "And for everything."

"You're welcome."

"What are you two talking about?" Thomas slipped an arm around Lizzie's waist.

She reached up and gave Joseph's cheek a gentle pat. "Just wishing our son every happiness."

Thomas thrust out his hand and shook Joseph's. "Yes, that's true, Joseph. I know I was … well a—"

"Doubting Thomas?" Lizzie looked up at her husband and chuckled.

"Well, you know we had misgivings, Joseph." Thomas nudged his wife. "We both did."

"Nothing against Millie, you know we love her already." Lizzie's face shone with happiness.

"I understand." Joseph nodded. Like Binda they had expressed their concern at a mixed marriage and the difficulties it might bring for Joseph and his family.

"Once we understood the depth of your love and commitment to each other your father and I would put no further obstacles in your way. Would we Thomas?"

Joseph gave his father a wry smile. He had been able to convince his mother quite quickly that he loved Millie but his father had taken a little longer. He suspected it had been Lizzie who had brought Thomas around. Joseph would have married Millie anyway but it was better that his parents had given them their blessing.

Lizzie linked her arms through those of the men. "Come on. Let's enjoy some of this marvellous food."

It was a splendid spread, their wedding brunch timed to avoid the heat of midday and to allow Joseph and Millie time to ride home. After consuming more than his fair share Joseph found himself seated on a bench along the shed wall between his father and Timothy. William sat on Thomas's other side.

"We need to talk about the leases before you go, Joseph." Thomas's brow was creased in a frown. "It's not that long until we have to put in our bid."

"It is hard to imagine after all your hard work over thirty-five years that you could lose it all to someone else." Timothy shook his head.

"We won't lose Wildu Creek." Thomas sat back. "We have enough saved to ward off any other prospective lessee."

"I'll be honest, Father," Joseph said. "I don't know how I'm going to keep making the lease payments."

"It's a struggle everywhere in the current climate. Our stock are being eaten out by rabbits and I shot a wild dog in the hills behind the house just two days ago. We rid ourselves of them in the past but the rabbits are attracting them and sheep are easy picking. Even the eagles are doing some damage."

"It's the same at Smith's Ridge, only worse," Joseph said. "And I've very little put aside."

"Everyone's struggling from what I hear," Timothy said. "Ellis Prosser's overseer was telling me just last week they were selling off cattle and the farmers on the plains are really doing it tough."

"If there's no-one to bid against you, we could hold on to Smith's Ridge," Thomas said. "I've a small amount I can put towards it."

"I don't want you to throw good money after bad, Father. I would like to hang on to the place but not to the detriment of Wildu Creek."

"But where would we live?" William's question reminded them all that the boy was listening to their conversation.

"It might not happen," his grandfather reassured him. "But if it did you will always have a home here at Wildu Creek. It's big enough for all of us."

"It is, Father, but not enough work for all of us. I've thought about this and I might have to take a team and cart wool and grain to keep food on the table."

"I won't hear of it, Joseph. I'm not getting any younger and there's plenty to do. If you lose Smith's Ridge you will come to work on Wildu Creek."

Joseph was aware of Timothy shifting restlessly beside him. Thomas was being kind but Joseph wouldn't be the one to displace Timothy who had worked for them for a long time. The way things were, Wildu Creek couldn't support another extra family for long. He didn't like the thought of it but if he couldn't keep his lease, he would have to find work elsewhere. How he would manage the children he didn't know. He looked over at his new wife who appeared to be in earnest conversation with Eliza. It might be that Millie would have to stay with the children to look after them. He couldn't ask his parents to take on any more.

"Damn those meddling fools in Adelaide." Thomas slapped his knee. "The government and even the general public regard us as easy targets for increased taxes and extra charges just so they can balance their budget."

"Goodness, what are all these serious faces about?" Lizzie appeared in front of them, smiling from one to the other. "It's time to cut the cake so we can all have a piece with our cup of tea."

Joseph groaned and clutched his stomach. "Mother, we've eaten so much already."

"Come along." Lizzie took his arm and helped him to his feet. "Millie." She waved to her new daughter-in-law. "Come and cut the cake."

Thomas put a hand on his shoulder. "We will talk again when we bring the children home in a few days."

Joseph nodded and let his mother guide him to where she'd set up a large fruit cake with a sprig of the tiny white flowers on top, the same as Millie's hairpiece. Millie picked up the knife. Joseph placed his large sun-browned hand over her slender black one and together they cut the cake. There were more cheers and clapping and congratulations. Once the cake had been shared around, Joseph thought it time to leave. He and Millie were to have a few precious days alone at Smith's Ridge and he wanted to make the most of them. There was still work to be done and Binda would be there of course but he would be out checking their dwindling stock. Thomas and Lizzie would wait for cooler weather and come with the children in a few days.

They kissed the children goodbye. William stood ramrod straight as Joseph shook his hand but allowed his new mother to place a kiss on his cheek. It was a happy crowd that waved them off, except for Esther who was wailing because she wanted to go with them.

Millie had changed into trousers and mounted her horse with ease even though she had only learned to ride since moving to Smith's Ridge. She'd never taken to side-saddle. Joseph thought how good she looked on the small chestnut horse, still wearing her white shirt with the lace collar and now tan trousers and the broad-brimmed leather hat she favoured. More like an explorer than a new bride. They grinned at each other, eager to be on their way. With final waves they headed off, keeping to the large gums beside Wildu Creek for a while until they turned inland towards home.

Joseph had a mixture of feelings. On the one hand he felt so happy he could burst and on the other there was the worry about the looming end of the twenty-one year lease they had on Smith's

Ridge. It was the only way he had to feed his family but he could lose the lot to another bidder.

"What is it, Joseph?" Millie had ridden closer to him and gave him a searching look from under her hat.

"Nothing." He leaned across and kissed her.

"Hmmm." She licked her lips. "You taste like dust."

"Good clean dust I hope."

They rode on a little further in companionable silence.

"You're frowning again." She gave him a small poke.

"I am worried about Smith's Ridge. How I will provide for you all."

"You think too much. Let's enjoy today." Millie urged her horse off to the right around some trees calling over her shoulder. "Tomorrow can take care of itself."

"Where are you going?"

"It's shorter this way."

Joseph shook his head and turned his horse to follow.

It was dark by the time they reached the house at Smith's Ridge. The last part of their journey had been slow once the sun went down with only a sliver of moon to guide them.

Once inside, Joseph pulled Millie into his arms but she wriggled away. She lit the lamp in the living room.

"Please wait." She kissed his cheek and went to the bedroom. "I want to wash the dust from me."

He watched as she closed the door. Suddenly he felt unsure. In that room he'd spent so many hours with Clara and their children and Clara had died there. He'd lived in it like a hermit ever since. Millie had tidied and dusted what she could from time to time and changed the bedsheets. Damn. He scratched the back of his neck. Why hadn't he thought to tidy up and change the linen at least?

He went to the cupboard and took out his liquor flask. He hadn't had a drink for a few days and he sure needed one now.

The door opened behind him. He looked up to see Millie framed in the doorway wearing one of his shirts that covered her top half but not her long slender legs.

"Come, husband." Millie's look was decidedly cheeky. "You don't need liquor to give you the courage to come to bed do you?"

He put down the flask, replaced the lid and followed her into the bedroom. He halted just inside the door. The bed had been moved to the other end of the room under the front window. A candle flickered on the small cupboard beside it. There was a new quilt neatly folded at the end and fresh sheets. Where the bed used to be was the hanging rail with their clothes. A water jug and washbasin sat on top of the small chest of drawers that now stood neatly closed under the side window. The curtains were the same but had obviously been washed. The whole room was changed and tidy and, he suspected if he looked closer, much cleaner than when he'd left it two days ago.

"How?" He turned a full circle. By the time his gaze came back to the bed, Millie had removed the shirt and slipped under the sheet. Her dark hair, loose from its clips, fell over her bare shoulders and sprawled across the white pillow. God, how beautiful she looked.

"Jundala helped me once you were out of the house. I hope you don't mind. We thought a change was good."

He could only shake his head. He was speechless.

She sat up holding the sheet to her and patted the quilt at the end of the bed. "I've been sewing this since you asked me to marry you. It has our names on it and the children's."

He only gave the brightly coloured quilt a brief glance. It was hard to keep his gaze from her. She turned and blew out the candle. He shed his clothes as quickly as he could and slid under the sheets. She met him halfway, her lips seeking his, her hands pulling him close, as they explored each other's bodies. He knew he had to take his time, go gently, for Millie had never been with a man before and the last thing he wanted to do was hurt her but he didn't know how much longer he could hold back. To his surprise Millie rolled him to his back and straddled him. She looked down at him with such love in her eyes Joseph knew everything that had led them to this moment had been right. He reached up and drew her to him, covering her lips with his own.

"Dear sweet Millie," he murmured in her ear. He would love her forever.

Thirty

"I can't believe it, Mother." Henry pounded his fist on his dining table. It was new and strong, made of mahogany. His hand smarted. "You said you had important news to discuss. I thought you were coming to Hawker to work out the arrangements for our joint venture into leasing a property. Not to tell me that I had a half-brother and a black one at that."

"Lower your voice, Henry." Harriet glowered at him. "Your front windows are open and your housekeeper only a few rooms away. Do you want all of Hawker to know our shame?"

Henry pushed back his chair and paced up and down then stopped beside his mother's chair. "Are you sure it's true? I know you've always had an aversion to coloured people. Are you sure this Aldridge fellow hasn't made this up to frighten you into doing what he wants?"

"He knows everything."

"Everything?" Henry collapsed back into the chair beside Harriet. "Please God, don't tell me there's more."

"Pull yourself together, Henry. I am quite convinced Jack Aldridge is who he says he is. There is also a likeness."

Henry turned to face her.

"He has your father's nose, his eyes." Harriet fell silent.

"I thought things were bad enough. Mr Hemming tells me that Mrs Taylor had been into the shop with news that the Church of England priest has arrived in town after coming from Wildu Creek. While he was there he married Joseph Baker to his black mistress and now here you tell me my father did the same."

"He didn't marry her," Harriet spat. "I was his lawful wife."

"How could you let him do this to us, Mother?"

"I don't know how Jack Aldridge found me."

"Not him. My father. Why did he go off looking for a black piece on the side?"

Harriet's hand flew up and she slapped Henry's face. "You will not speak like that."

Henry put a hand to his cheek. He couldn't ever recall a time when his mother had hit him.

Harriet's eyes narrowed. "Your father left us, not the other way round. He was away for long periods of time. I always believed it was on business. It's as much a shock to me as it is to you that he had another family."

"Family? There's more?"

"No. Jack said his mother and brother are dead."

"Thank God." Then another thought popped into his head. "Does he know about me?"

"He's only just discovered you exist."

"Catherine." Henry thought of his wife in Adelaide within easy reach of this man. "Does he know about Catherine and Charles?"

"He saw your wedding portrait."

Henry put his head in his hands. His two most precious possessions were in harm's way.

"He doesn't know Catherine's name nor that you have a child and he doesn't know where you live." Harriet took a deep breath. "I am sure you are safe for now."

Henry looked across at her. "So what's to be done? Presumably you have a plan to rid us of this man."

Harriet lifted her chin. "Not yet. That's why I've come to you."

Henry leapt up from his chair. "He could have followed you here."

"Of course he didn't. He's gone away somewhere. I have at least another week before he returns to my door. If we think it through together—"

They both spun at a knock on the door.

Flora stepped inside. "Would you like me to prepare some lunch, Mr Wiltshire?"

Henry strode to the window. The sight of Flora unnerved him. With Catherine away he had enjoyed his housekeeper's body in his own bed but now that he'd heard about his half-brother it suddenly occurred to Henry that he could father a child with Flora. Damn, he didn't want that to happen. He would have to stop his liaisons with her, gratifying as they were.

"Thank you, Flora." His mother took the lead. "We will eat here in the dining room."

From the corner of his eye Henry saw Flora glance in his direction then she left, closing the door behind her. He turned to face his mother.

"My father isn't the first man to father a bastard, nor will he be the last. I say we call Aldridge's bluff. He might cause some curiosity for a while but with no money coming his way, he will surely lose interest and crawl back into whatever cave he came out of."

"You haven't met him. We won't be easily rid of him." Harriet fiddled with the gloves she'd removed earlier and had set on the table in front of her. Henry studied her dithering movements. It was not like her to fidget. Then he remembered her earlier comment. There must be something she wasn't telling him about Jack.

"You said Jack knew everything, Mother." He crossed back and looked down at her. The grey in her hair was much more visible from above. "As if there was more."

She looked up and he saw real fear in her eyes.

He slipped back into the chair beside her, worry worming its way inside him. His mother was rarely afraid. He reached for her hand.

"Tell me."

"I was completely unaware of your father's other family. Just before he ... he died I went looking for him at the inn in the hills. He wasn't there but we had once lived in a hut tucked in rugged country behind the inn. It's where you were born. I thought perhaps he might be there so I continued on."

Henry's concern grew as he felt his mother's hand tremble in his. "You found him there with his mistress? That must have been a terrible shock."

Harriet nodded. She stared towards the window. Henry squeezed her hand. How dreadful for her to be reliving the horror of what she'd discovered. "Go on," he said softly.

"There was no-one inside when I got there but I heard shouting from behind the hut. Your father cried out, I could see he was being dragged away by two native men, I took his gun but when I got outside I saw Dulcie ..."

"Dulcie?"

Harriet turned her pale face to his. "She helped me ... when you were born and assisted in the house."

"A black woman?"

Harriet nodded.

Henry was appalled. His mother had always kept well clear of natives and taught him to do the same.

"Dulcie was holding a toddler and beside her was a bigger boy. He called out to your father ... he called him Papa. It was then I realised the children's skin was much lighter and I thought about the long periods of time Septimus stayed away ..." Harriet pulled her hand from Henry's, her fingers curled into her palms. She pressed them to her lap. "Dulcie had worked for me. We were not friends but ..." Harriet took a deep breath and looked Henry firmly in the eye. "I walked back through the house to my cart and I ... I rode away."

Henry met her look, his blood felt like ice in his veins. "You let them kill your husband?"

"I didn't know they would kill him. I was shocked, angry, I—"

"As you had every right to be." Henry uncurled her fingers and held both her hands in his.

"I had to think of you," Harriet said quickly. "I didn't want you tarnished by your father's deeds."

"I am grateful for that, Mother." Henry couldn't believe his ears and yet he could. He no longer cared he only had vague memories of a brooding father who was rarely home. Harriet had turned towards the window again. He squeezed her hands gently. "So this Jack Aldridge ..."

She looked back at Henry. "Is your father's son, I'm quite sure of it. And he ... he ..."

"He saw you walk away."

Harriet nodded. Dread coursed through Henry. He suspected it wasn't going to be as easy to rid them of Jack Aldridge as it had been the bullies of his younger years. There was a sound at the door. It swung open and Flora came in carrying a tray.

"Thank you, Flora." He met her enquiring look with a stern response. He had also been in the habit of sharing his concerns and thoughts with her after they had been together in bed. In light of his mother's revelations he would have to learn to be more guarded.

Flora began to lift the plates of cold mutton, potato and pickles from the tray.

"Leave it." Henry flicked his hand at her. "We can manage."

Perhaps because of his abruptness, Harriet pulled herself up and gave Flora a charming smile. "Thank you, Mrs Nixon, this looks most appetising."

Henry followed Flora to the door and shut it firmly once she was through. He shook his head. His plans to take up a lease were fading fast. If his mother kept having to pay off this Aldridge fellow there would never be an end to the money he would take.

Harriet had arranged the plates and cutlery on the table. He sat at the place she'd set for him at the head.

"I'm sorry, Henry. I had hoped to keep all this from you."

"What a burden it must have been, Mother. And you've worked so hard all your life. Jack Aldridge is not our family and yet he will drain us of money."

"Not only that, he insists I find work for him."

"What? Where?"

"In my shop."

Henry's fork clattered to the plate. "What kind of work?"

"He wants to keep an eye on things. He doesn't trust me. The only work I can think of is some kind of doorman and parcel carrier. He's strong. He could be of use when we take delivery of fabric and other heavier items."

"No, that cannot happen." Henry couldn't believe she was considering such an option. "What will your clients think?"

Harriet clasped her hands, her food untouched. "I have no other option. Better I have a half-caste doorman than he tell everyone he's your half-brother and that he witnessed my … my involvement in your father's disappearance."

"This is so unfair. You didn't murder my father."

"But Jack Aldridge was right. I've thought of it many times myself. If I had fired a warning shot, the natives probably would have let Septimus go."

"Or come at you while you reloaded."

Harriet shook her head. "There's no point in going over the past. Jack Aldridge is part of our present and there doesn't appear to be any way to be rid of him."

Henry picked up his cutlery and began to eat. Harriet stared at her food.

"I really had big hopes of picking up one of the pastoral leases." Henry was speaking to himself as much as his mother. "There are a few which Ellis Prosser and I believe will become available. The current lessees won't be able to afford to continue."

"You already have several investments in the district." Harriet reached across and put a hand on his arm. "I had hoped you would move back to Adelaide."

He smiled at her. "One day, Mother."

Harriet sighed and took up her fork. "Why would you want one of these leases? If their current occupants aren't managing them what makes you think you can?"

"I've had a lot of help from Ellis Prosser. His advice has always been wise. I have land on the plains but if I had some in the hills I could move stock around, perhaps cattle like Ellis instead of sheep. Often the hill country gets rain when those on the plains don't. Ellis would find me a good overseer. One of the properties we've had our eye on is right next door to his. Smith's Ridge is—"

Henry stopped at Harriet's gasp.

"Smith's Ridge?" She frowned. "That was the name of your father's property. I knew it was somewhere out in this northern country but I had no idea where."

"It's a day's ride by horse. Longer in a cart." Henry tried to get his head around what she was saying. "How did father end up with it?"

"I knew little of your father's dealings but after his death I did discover he had wronged the family who originally invested in the lease. I returned the lease papers to the family. I've no idea if they took up the option."

"There are no Smiths there now."

"That wasn't the name." Harriet put a finger to her lips. "It was Baker."

"Joseph Baker." Henry nearly choked on his mouthful of food. What a terrible day this was. Now he discovered a property that could have been his had been given to the odious Baker.

Harriet reached across to pat his back. "Not Joseph, his name was Thomas."

"The father? He has the lease next door to Smith's Ridge."

"Yes that's right."

Henry flopped back in his chair and put his hands to his head. Prosser had only said recently that he was confident Baker didn't have the resources to renew his lease. They'd discussed it at length. Prosser had his eye on a property in the ranges north of Hawker. He had gone off the idea of taking on Smith's Ridge himself since his son had been speared but he was happy to support Henry's bid to gain the lease.

Harriet placed her cutlery neatly on her plate. "Perhaps that's our answer."

Henry sat up. "What?"

"My idea is a long stretch but it could work. It would keep him out of sight but still where you could keep an eye on him." Harriet's hand lifted to her bare neck then dropped. "It would mean pooling our resources and presenting it to him in such a way that he would be tempted."

"What are you talking about, Mother?"

"Jack's inheritance."

Henry shook his head. "I don't understand you."

"Let him work Smith's Ridge."

Henry pushed back his chair and started pacing again. Smith's Ridge was part of his plan but not one he had intended sharing with a bastard half-brother. He came to a stop in front of Harriet who was watching him closely. "Jack has no money except what he's extorting from you. He can't take up a lease."

Harriet leaned forward. "But we could and he could manage it."

"Are you saying we give him the property?"

"Not give but we will work it out so it looks that way to him." She smiled. "There will be provisions of course, clauses that he won't understand. He doesn't read well. There is much to be sorted out but it could just work."

Henry scowled at his mother. "I don't want him anywhere near my family."

"I am also your family." Harriet's eyes flashed with anger. "I have put a lot of money into your ventures. If Jack works for me and continues to blackmail me, not only will my business suffer but you will get not another penny." She tapped the table with the palm of her hand as she said the last three words.

"Damn Jack Aldridge." Henry struggled to keep his simmering anger in check. He slid back into his chair, rested his elbows on the table and pressed his fingertips together as if in prayer. Perhaps Harriet's idea would make the best of a bad lot. Somehow they could insist Jack stayed out of sight at Smith's Ridge. Much better than allowing him to work in Harriet's shop and siphon off her money. Money that was Henry's inheritance, not Jack's.

He stroked his chin. "There's no guarantee we would win the lease."

Harriet's gaze changed. She looked at him with eyes full of hope. "There must be other properties? I can put up the money."

"We would have to sort out a lot of things."

"I know a lawyer who is a good customer." Harriet was smiling now. "He buys for his mistress as well as his wife. I am sure he would help and be discreet."

Henry studied his mother. Her quick gaze was locked on his, her cheeks pink with anticipation. "Are you sure you want to do it this way?"

"I have no other option." Harriet drew herself up in her chair. "And I'm prepared to pay whatever it takes."

Henry covered his surprise. She made it sound as if she had access to a lot more money than she'd ever let on before. He nodded his head slowly up and down. "Very well, Mother. We will send Jack Aldridge to Smith's Ridge. And then we will work out how to be rid of him … permanently."

Thirty-one

It was an odd group that arrived at Wildu Creek on a cold winter's morning: Joseph, Binda and William herding the last of the good Smith's Ridge breeding stock, and Millie, Jundala and all the children with the cart and wagon loaded with their possessions. The cow and extra horses trailed behind.

They'd left Smith's Ridge three days ago and Joseph had given no backwards glance. The journey was slow with the stock and he and Millie had made it a kind of holiday for the children. They ate what Binda caught for them and sat around the campfire each night singing until the littlest ones fell asleep. It had been a happy time considering, but with their arrival at Wildu Creek came the start of new responsibilities.

Joseph looked towards the creek and what his mother called their outdoor room, the scene of many happy family events. The canvas that was usually strung over his father's more recent permanent structure had been put away for winter but the outdoor furniture he'd crafted was still scattered under the tall gums. A little way from there was the wooden hut that had been the first house Thomas had built and where Timothy and his family now lived. The newer stone house was on slightly higher ground giving the verandah a good view of the creek and the lower land stretched out before it. Joseph's mother and Eliza stood on the verandah waving a welcome.

His spirits lifted a little. In some ways it was a relief to be back here at Wildu Creek. He hoped it would mean they could leave the sadness of Clara's death, the failure of keeping Smith's Ridge, behind them and make a fresh start. Of all of them Millie deserved that. Clara's memory was strong at Smith's Ridge.

"We didn't expect you would make it this soon." Lizzie had crossed the yard towards him. "Your father is checking sheep up on the back ridges."

"We left a day early." Joseph had to shout to be heard over the animals and excited children.

"We've been camping, Grandma." Esther's voice was the loudest although Robert was fast matching her with his funny warbling tone.

"We will yard these animals." Joseph turned his horse to follow Binda and William who were herding the sheep towards the holding yards of the Wildu Creek shearing shed. Jundala was already leading the cow towards the small paddock that had been fenced for Lizzie's cow and, with Lizzie and Eliza taking the children from the cart, Millie was seeing to the horses. He kept his gaze on his wife until the buildings blocked his view. Yes, he had so much to be thankful for.

A short distance from the shearing shed Joseph reined in his horse and dismounted. Where once there'd been a patch of bare ground there now stood a long low hut.

Gulda came to meet him. His hair was greying but he still had the same cheeky smile Joseph had known all his life.

"Welcome home, Joseph." Gulda drew him close in a warm hug. "It's good you've come."

No sooner were they apart than Gulda was pulling his pipe from his pocket and filling it with tobacco. Joseph inhaled the smell as the older man lit up. Gulda had only taken up smoking after a shearer had given him a pipe a few years ago. Now he rarely went anywhere without it although Daisy had banned him from lighting it in their hut after he burned the last one down with his discarded match.

"I hope so." Joseph lifted his hat and swept his hair back from his face. "What's this?" He waved a hand towards the hut.

"Mr Tom been wanting to make a hut for shearers. With you coming he decided to get a move on." Gulda's grin widened. "Timothy, me and Mr Tom made it. Very good, hey?"

"It certainly is." Joseph walked towards the hut.

His father had been talking about building something for the shearers to camp in but as it would be used only once or twice a year it had never been a priority. The hut was long and had a verandah stretching right across the front with all doors opening on to it. Joseph looked inside the first room. It was the biggest with windows and a fireplace and a door in the back wall.

"Plenty of room in there." Gulda blew another puff of smoke into the air. "These other rooms are for beds."

He opened a door and Joseph stuck his head inside. The room was big enough for a double bed or two singles and not much more. There was one small window in the opposite wall.

"There's plenty of rooms." Gulda waved his hand towards the last three doors then clapped a hand on Joseph's shoulder. "It's good and strong. Good house for your family."

"It certainly is." Joseph felt a small sense of relief. He had wondered how they would all fit into his parents' house. At least his family had somewhere of their own to live.

Gulda leaned against a verandah post and puffed on his pipe. "Mr Tom glad you're coming. Daisy and me, we're going away for a while. See her family in north country. We'll be gone many months."

Joseph wondered at that. Gulda and Daisy often went away but they didn't stay away for such long periods.

"Both our Tommie and our Rosie have new babies." Gulda pulled his pipe from his mouth, a distant look in his eye. "We're going to spend time with family."

"I'm glad for you." Joseph shook Gulda's hand again. "I'd better help get these sheep penned. Thank you for all you've done."

He went back to his horse, gave Gulda a wave and set off for the yards.

That night Joseph sat by the fire with his parents in his old home. Millie had retired early with the children and he had promised he wouldn't be long. He was weary himself but he wanted to spend a few quiet moments with his parents.

The day had been exceptionally busy. By the time Thomas had returned home the animals were yarded and the furniture unloaded. Everyone had helped Joseph and Millie make the shearer's hut into their home. Their bed had been set up in the first of the bedrooms. The boys were in the room next door then the girls and Mary had the last of the bedrooms. Gulda had helped Binda make a bush hut close to his own. They had all shared a stew for dinner from Lizzie's huge pot that had been simmering over the fire all day. For the time being everyone was settled but Joseph knew it wouldn't stay that way.

"Thank you for building the accommodation." He looked up from the flames. "Although I don't know where the shearers will fit when they come."

Thomas chuckled. "They're not expecting it so it won't make any difference. The place is yours until we work out what's best."

"We're both so happy to have you all here." Lizzie looked fondly at her son. "I don't believe that rubbish of your father's that Smith's Ridge is cursed but things have a way of working out."

"It's good that Millie and the children will have their own space while I'm away."

Thomas and Lizzie looked at each other then back at Joseph. "We've been thinking about that. We—"

Before his father could continue, Joseph cut him off. "The way things are Wildu Creek can't support another two families. Binda can help out with hunting food and he will look after stock, especially if Gulda's going away, but I will have to find some work off the property to bring in some money. I have a wife and four children to feed."

"No." Lizzie's response was sharp.

Thomas reached for her hand. "What your mother means is we have a way for you to stay."

Joseph raised his eyebrows. His parents had made many sacrifices all their lives. He wasn't allowing them to make more to save him some labour.

Thomas leaned in. "Wildu Creek is as much yours as it is mine. The money we had saved to help you keep Smith's Ridge is still there. It's enough to keep us for quite some time providing the season improves. Instead of leaving your family behind to find work, stay here and work. Whatever you do benefits us all."

"No, Father. It's a kind offer but you've said yourself you don't like the look of the seasons we've had lately. If we get another drought you will need everything you've saved to survive."

Once more his parents looked at each other. This time his mother leaned closer.

"We need you, Joseph."

"I'm not a young man anymore." Thomas squeezed Lizzie's hand. "We both feel the work more. Gulda is a kind friend but he's never been as reliable as Binda and the older he gets the more he wants to spend time with his family. I know how he feels."

Thomas locked his gaze on Joseph. "Timothy and Eliza and their children work hard but it's not enough."

Joseph sighed. "You really mean you want me to stay?"

"We can work closely together again, just like we used to." Thomas's face shone in the firelight. "And you can continue your breeding program here. You're already seeing improved results. I'd like to be part of that. Together we can breed a better sheep with fine wool. An animal more suited to the conditions here."

Joseph stood turned his back to the fire and studied his parents who were watching him eagerly. "You're sure?"

Lizzie gripped the arm of her chair and rose to her feet. "Of course we're sure, son."

Relief flooded though Joseph and he beamed from one to the other. "Then, yes, I'll stay."

Thomas got to his feet and Lizzie clapped her hands in excitement.

"But!" Joseph held up his hand and they both paused to look at him. "Should things take a turn for the worst I will definitely leave to find work elsewhere."

"Yes, yes, of course." Lizzie flapped her hands. "Oh do let's have another cup of tea. What a pity Millie was too tired to stay. Still, it's best the children have her close the first night in a new place. Tomorrow night we'll have a celebration dinner." She reached up and kissed Joseph's cheek then hurried out to make the tea.

Thomas sat again. "No-one had arrived at Smith's Ridge before you left?"

Joseph shook his head. "No and I didn't want to be there to meet the Aldridge fellow I'm told has taken the lease. We will have to meet our new neighbour eventually but I'd like time to adjust to this new arrangement first."

"Of course. Have you heard anything about Aldridge?"

"Only that he's from Adelaide and no-one appears to have met him yet."

"No doubt we will soon enough." Thomas tapped his fingers together and stared at the fire. "I hope he's someone we can be on friendly terms with."

Joseph nodded. He sat back, enjoying the warmth of the fire and the thought of another cup of tea before he ventured out into the cold night.

Later he slipped quietly into his new bedroom. Millie had left the lamp burning low. All he could see was her dark hair above the brightly coloured quilt that covered their bed. He stripped to his undergarments, turned out the lamp and slid quickly beneath the sheets, seeking her warmth.

Millie nestled back against him, her body perfectly curved against his.

"I'm staying at Wildu Creek," he whispered in her ear.

She reached back and pulled his arm around her. "I knew you wouldn't go away," she murmured.

He kissed her neck and his hands drifted to cup her soft round breasts. She responded to his touch. Very quickly their bodies came together in perfect unison with each other, then nestled together they both slept their first night at Wildu Creek in peace.

Thirty-two

Jack signed his name on the document and watched as Henry signed his.

"So that's it." Henry offered his hand.

Jack gave it a firm shake staring into his half-brother's eyes. Henry was a hard man to read but he appeared genuinely pleased at this arrangement and Jack was more than happy to go along with something that would see him on his own piece of land.

His legs straddled one of the benches that stretched either side of the huge table taking up most of the space in the big Smith's Ridge living room. It was the only furniture that had been left in the house, probably too big to remove. He stood up, stretched and walked around the large room. The sound of his boots echoed on the wooden floor. It was cold away from the sunshine which poured through the windows. He'd need to get some wood and light a fire or he'd freeze tonight.

"You'll have to find yourself a wife." Henry stood up also. "They tell me it can get lonely out here, and cold at night."

"Well I don't imagine I'll find a woman easily in these parts." Jack gave a sardonic smile. "Unless the neighbours are friendly?"

It had been on the tip of Henry's tongue to suggest there were plenty of natives in the area but he thought better of it.

"I've told you it's important you keep to yourself. Make sure you prove your worth before you make any overtures to the neighbours. People in these parts have had trouble with natives. It's best they don't know your heritage until you've shown you're trustworthy."

"Settle down." Jack spun to look at Henry. "I know what we arranged. I will see how it suits me."

Henry met his gaze with a steady look of his own. "We have a signed agreement, brother."

"Not worth the paper it's written on."

Surprise registered on Henry's face.

At last Jack had managed to dislodge the mask. He grinned. "That would only be if we didn't agree, of course."

Henry turned away to pick up the papers. When he turned back his face was composed. "As long as we work together we will both benefit."

"I am happy to accept your plan, for the moment."

Jack watched as Henry folded the papers and slid them into the pocket of his jacket. When Henry had welcomed him as a long-lost brother, Jack had been suspicious, especially as Harriet had originally been so quick to try to be rid of him. But Henry had proved to be different. He had explained that while Jack was no relation to his mother, Henry and Jack were half-brothers, and he had been most welcoming. He'd said it had been his idea they take on Smith's Ridge as partners. He'd also told Jack that he didn't get on with the previous lessee, Joseph Baker, and Henry was concerned that if Joseph knew he and Jack were related he would make things tough for Jack.

Jack had laughed at that. He took no nonsense from anyone but he was prepared to go along with Henry for now.

"So my overseer and a shepherd will be here tomorrow?"

"Or the next day. There's little feed on my Cradock property and the sheep are in poor condition. It could take Donovan and Brand a bit of time to move them."

Jack watched Henry walk to the window and peer out.

"Well, let's unload my cart." Henry said. "I must return to Hawker. It will be dark before I get there."

"Missing that pretty wife of yours?"

Henry turned to look at him, his expression unreadable. "Catherine does not like to be alone at night."

"Well, she'll have to be tonight." Jack crossed the room to pick up his hat from the table. "I need help to unload the wagon. It will take us a while."

Henry frowned. "Donovan and Brand can do that when they get here."

"You've just said that could be days. I'm not sleeping on the floor. Besides your wife has your child and the delightful Mrs Nixon for company and we've got a nice pie of hers to share for our supper."

"You know a lot about my family for a man who hasn't met them."

Jack tapped the side of his nose. "Blackfellas, we have a sixth sense."

Henry glowered at him then gave a snort. "More like you slipped in to town from your camp last night and peered in through my windows."

"Can't blame a man for wanting to see how the other brother lives." Jack pushed the hat firmly onto his head.

"I told you we cannot be seen to know each other and you must never come to my house again."

"Worried people will find out about your bastard brother?"

"Not so much people as my wife or Mrs Nixon. They are close. What one sees the other soon knows and then my mother would find out."

"I'm not scared of Harriet."

"Neither am I but my business is tied to hers. If she finds out about our arrangement she could cut off the money."

Jack's eyes narrowed and he scratched at his chin. Harriet would surely wonder about the ease with which he had taken her money and left. Still, he'd go along with Henry. If it all fell apart he could go back to fleecing Harriet.

He smirked at Henry. "Blackmail works wonders with your mother."

Henry looked him up and down. "But what would be the point of that when we can achieve our goals without her knowledge but with her money. My mother has always kept the purse strings tight. It took me some time to convince her this deal was a good one. If she thinks you're involved that will be that."

"Where does she think I've gone?"

"Gone?" Henry tugged at his collar, something Jack noticed he did from time to time to delay answering a question.

"She's obviously convinced that whatever you've supposedly offered me has guaranteed my silence and my absence from her life."

"I told her we spoke man to man—"

Jack laughed out loud and drew himself up. "I didn't think Harriet was so gullible."

"She's not but I convinced her that you didn't really want to be tied to Adelaide and that the payment she gave you would allow you to travel to America." Henry glared at him. "Her utmost wish is that you won't return from there."

"So we are partners in deceiving your mother?"

"We are."

Jack put his hands to his hips and tipped his head back a little. "Remind me once more what you will gain from this."

"A property in this good country."

"My property."

"Eventually but for now we need each other. I've got stock that need feed and you have no stock nor the funds to buy any. Once you've got your own, mine should be fattened up enough for market. Then I will be looking for my own lease somewhere else in good grazing country."

"You could have leased Smith's Ridge yourself. Left me out of it."

"Yes but that was before I discovered I had a brother who's entitled to some kind of inheritance. Our father used to have this property. It's only right that we get it back. I'm not a pastoralist. You've had experience on the land. Donovan is a good overseer and Brand has come with excellent references but I need someone here who can be my ears and eyes." He paused and lifted his chin, his dark eyes locked on Jack's. "My brother."

"Well, brother, I need your help to move in. Think of it as some time for us to get to know each other before you leave me out here in the wilderness."

"I'll admit it's isolated but hardly the wilderness." Henry held his gaze a moment longer, indecision on his face then he grimaced. "Very well, I will stay but I must be gone early tomorrow morning."

Henry lay in the bed that was to be Brand's when he arrived. He curled himself under the layer of blankets trying to keep some warmth in his body and wished he was home tucked up next to Catherine. In spite of the chilly wind that blew up the valley he'd worked up a sweat unloading the wagon. Now he felt clammy. He couldn't wait to get home to Hawker tomorrow and soak in the new bath they'd had installed.

It had taken the best part of the afternoon to unload the food, crockery and tools Henry had provided from the wagon and cart.

Then there'd been the rough assortment of furniture to place. Unbeknown to Jack, Harriet had supplied it. Some of the furniture Henry remembered from his childhood. Harriet must have been hoarding it somewhere. An old cupboard that held the dishes had been put in the kitchen with a small table and a couple of chairs. There were some old stuffed armchairs and even a chest that he recalled being in their house at Port Augusta. The beds and other pieces weren't new but she had sourced them from somewhere. Harriet had been only too happy to ensure her plan to install Jack at Smith's Ridge worked. It had amazed Henry how much money she had put forward. She must have had a nest egg stashed away. It rankled to think he didn't know about it.

Henry rolled onto his back and thought about the man lying in the next room. Now that he was alone he could let down his guard. It had taken a lot of restraint to maintain a semblance of camaraderie with the man he resented calling brother. If the truth be known Henry resented Jack Aldridge for breathing the same air.

Their first meeting in Harriet's backyard in Adelaide had been difficult. Henry had imagined some ignorant native he could easily bluff but Jack had been smarter than he'd imagined, a quick thinker, always on the alert. Henry had thought his plan may have been foiled before it had a chance to begin but he hadn't reckoned with Jack's obvious desire for family. Jack kept it hidden under his tough exterior but once Henry had found his weakness the fellow was putty in his hands.

After that it had been easy to convince Jack of his own excitement at the discovery of a brother and explain away Harriet's abhorrence as natural for a woman who'd been hurt and wronged by her husband. She wasn't prepared to accept Jack for now but Henry had told Jack he was hopeful she'd come around.

In the meantime he had this proposition: instead of working as a doorman for Harriet, Jack could be his own boss on a property. Henry could see straight away the idea appealed to the man who had been treated as second class most of his life. With some more money from Harriet, Jack had been happy to keep out of the way. Once Henry had secured the lease of Smith's Ridge it had been easy then to get Jack to Hawker and then on to Smith's Ridge.

Ellis Prosser was the only major sticking point. Henry had needed his help. Knowing Prosser's extreme hatred of natives it had taken some thinking to come up with an idea to explain Jack's presence and then even more work to sell it to Prosser. Henry had finally come up with the story that Jack's mother had been Indian and Jack the result of a liaison with Catherine's uncle who lived in India. Jack had an almost oriental look, after all.

Henry had explained the family felt they owed him something but didn't want him close so they'd sent him to Australia. Jack was the pretend manager of Smith's Ridge until such time as the family felt their debt was repaid and then he would be given a good reference and encouraged to move on. While Prosser was a bull-headed man he could also be charitable when the mood took him and since it was Henry who was asking, he was prepared to accept a coloured neighbour as long as it was only temporary. Henry had assured Prosser it was and that Henry would eventually take over Smith's Ridge once Jack left.

Taking on the lease, paying Jack a handsome wage and employing a shepherd had cleaned out Henry and Harriet's current resources so Prosser had loaned him his overseer, Donovan. It had been Prosser's suggestion so that there would be someone at Smith's Ridge to report back to him and thus to Henry.

Fatigue swept over him and he felt sleep closing in. All Henry had to do was hold together this web of deceit until such time as he could be free of Jack. He didn't know how yet but it would happen. It had to.

★

Henry was up early the next morning, still tired after a restless night but eager to be on his way. He shared a mug of tea with Jack but declined the rabbit his half-brother had sizzling in the pan over the fire.

"I hope Brand and Donovan can cook." Jack wasn't in such fine humour this morning.

"Didn't I tell you? Donovan has a wife." Henry dragged on his thick outer coat. "She's with them while they drove the sheep. She will see to the cooking once she arrives."

"So that's why Donovan wanted the hut up the back." Jack's face lit up with a lecherous look.

"You'll do well to keep your thoughts to yourself. Donovan and his wife must be close to fifty."

Jack wasn't deterred. "Maybe they'll have a daughter."

Henry made for the door. He hoped Jack wouldn't go causing trouble out here but there was no going back now. The plan was well and truly in motion.

The air was bitter outside the hut. Henry worked as quickly as his stiff fingers would allow to hook up his horse and cart. He drove the cart down to the front of the house. Jack came out to the verandah and leaned on the rail, two hands clasped casually in front of him, jacketless, oblivious to the cold.

Henry gave him a wave. "I'll be back in a month with provisions and to see how things are going."

"Stay the night again." Jack called after him. "I enjoyed it."

Henry gave the reins a flick and his cart lurched forward as the horse set off at a trot, with Jack's laugh echoing behind him. He huddled in and gripped the reins tightly. Until he came up with a way to be rid of Aldridge, the foul man was close but out of sight.

Thirty-three

1886

Catherine closed the shop door and drew the bolt. She leaned against it a moment and gained her breath. The close heat of the interior made her feel light-headed.

When she turned, Malachi Hemming was coming from the room behind the curtain.

"I see no point in staying open a moment longer, Mr Hemming. It's such a terrible day out there. There's not a soul about and it's nearly four o'clock." She looked down at the dirt that had blown in as their last customer had departed a good hour before. Dirt was everywhere in Hawker. There had been no rain to speak of since the previous September and it was already May. Only yesterday two of her older customers had been talking of the Great Drought of the 1860s and saying the conditions were the same. Every time the wind blew, which was quite a regular occurrence over the last few months, it brought billowing clouds of dust with it, fine particles that seeped in everywhere. Rain was needed badly.

"If you're sure, Mrs Wiltshire. I am happy to keep the shop open if you wish to go home early."

"No." Catherine crossed the floor to pick up the broom they kept permanently propped behind the counter. "You can have an early finish too."

Malachi moved from one foot to the other.

Catherine knew he was worried about what Henry would think of closing over an hour early. Henry never closed early no matter what. "Mr Wiltshire won't be home until tomorrow night at the earliest. In fact he could be away a few days. He's gone to inspect Smith's Ridge and take them some supplies." She smiled at the young assistant. "I won't tell him if you don't."

"But he will be back for the race meeting?"

"Oh yes. That's still several days away." Catherine began to push the broom across the floor. "Henry wouldn't miss the annual Hawker races for anything."

"I should very much like to see it one day."

"Perhaps I will stay at the shop and you can go in my place, Mr Hemming. I find the whole affair noisy, dusty and very tedious."

"Oh ... well ..." Once more Malachi shifted from foot to foot.

Catherine felt badly. She hadn't meant to raise his hopes. "Perhaps not this year, Mr Hemming," she said quickly, "but we must think on it for next." Henry had already insisted on her having a new dress made at his mother's shop in Adelaide. It should arrive any day on the train. "Now come, let's finish up."

"Very well, Mrs Wiltshire." Malachi reached for the broom. "But please let me do the tidying up. You go home to Master Charles."

"Thank you, Mr Hemming. I'm most grateful." She handed over the broom. "I will see you in the morning."

"I can open up in the morning." He gave her a tiny smile. "No rush for you to be here."

Catherine let out a sigh. Her back ached from being on her feet all day. "Thank you again, Mr Hemming." She went through to the back of the shop, tied on her bonnet and let herself out the kitchen door.

Immediately the heat and the dust enveloped her and then the flies found her. It really was a wretched day, she thought as she made her way along the path. She clasped her hand to her mouth as the stench from the privies that lined the back lane combined to overwhelm her. She hurried away towards the road that led to her house, careful where she put her feet. Several pigs roamed nearby and had left a foul trail of dung behind them.

At least the new stone wall Henry had had built around their yard kept unwanted animals from her garden, what there was left of it. The wrought-iron gate that had been inserted between two stone pillars was hot to her touch as she pushed it open. When Catherine finally reached the sanctuary of her home she was relieved that the temperature was quite a bit cooler inside and the air much cleaner. She removed her bonnet, undid the top buttons of her shirt and leaned against the wall, absorbing its coolness. The house was silent. No doubt Flora had taken Charles to her house once her children came home from school.

Catherine went to the kitchen, poured herself a mug of water and sat at the kitchen table. Even with the fire flickering in the grate it was still cooler in the kitchen than outside.

There was a thud at the door, laughter and footsteps. Flora's children, Hugh and Martha, came into the room swinging Charles by the hand between them. They stopped abruptly at the sight of her.

Flora appeared behind them. "Oh, we weren't expecting you home for another hour, Mrs Wiltshire."

"Mama." Charles squirmed from between the children and rushed to her open arms.

"Hello, my darling boy." She planted a kiss on his chubby cheek. "I hope you've been good for Flora."

"He's an angel." Flora put a hand each on her children and patted their shoulders. "You go home again now."

"Oh, no." Catherine knew Flora thought her children shouldn't be in the house if the Wiltshires were at home. "Charles was having such fun with the children and I'm sure this house is cooler than yours, Flora. Let them stay." She smiled at Flora's son and daughter who were only a year apart in age and nearly the same height. Then she set Charles back on his sturdy legs. "Take Martha and Hugh to your bedroom, Charles. I am sure they could help you build a fine tower with the new building blocks Papa bought you."

"Come on." Charles skipped back to the children, squeezed between them again and led them away.

"Thank you, Catherine." Flora smiled. She only used her mistress's first name at Catherine's insistence when it was just the two of them. "It has warmed up a lot in our little house. The children are usually so good but they get irritable in the heat."

Catherine was pleased to repay some of the kindness that Flora extended to her. "You're lucky your two have each other. I dislike being pregnant but I am sorry I haven't been able to give Charles a brother or sister. He will be four in September. And Henry badly wants another child."

Since the failure of yet another pregnancy last year Henry had been much more demanding in bed. He no longer trailed kisses down her neck, nibbled at her breasts or caressed her body, all things she'd enjoyed before Charles. These days he used her simply for his own gratification and so she often lay still beneath him, willing him to finish quickly. In spite of her discomfort and disinterest she knew she would fall pregnant again eventually. In fact, the way this heat made her feel it wouldn't surprise her if she was with child again already.

"I would have liked more children but now I'm glad I've just got the two. They're enough to feed and clothe." Flora put the kettle on the fire and went to the pantry where she took out food for Charles's supper.

"Why didn't you have more?" The question was out before Catherine had time to think. "I mean your husband is away a lot now but before … when you were in the same house all the time …" Catherine put a hand to her cheek. "Oh dear, I'm being very rude asking you such personal questions but I seem to be with child quite regularly even though they don't last and yet I see people with only one or two children and wonder if they have the same trouble."

Flora made a pot of tea and put a cup in front of Catherine. "I don't mind telling you," she said.

"Please, sit down for a while and have a cup with me. Henry is away. We are not in a rush."

Flora got herself a cup and sat next to Catherine. "I had my first two babies in less than two years and was soon pregnant with a third. My husband …" She poured herself some tea. "He was more attentive then. Later, with the poor seasons, the way it was on the farm, he lost hope, it changed him." She stared into her cup a moment. "Anyway, something went wrong with the third baby. I carried the poor sweet thing nearly to my confinement but it died inside me."

"Oh, Flora." Catherine reached out her hand and put it over Flora's. "A fully grown baby, how terrible." Catherine hardly mourned the babies she'd lost. In her mind they were not yet real. She simply wished one of them would grow into a proper baby. Perhaps another child would be enough and Henry would no longer desire her body.

"Made a terrible mess of my insides. I was in a bad way. I nearly died. Think I would have if it hadn't been for the potions of an old native woman."

"A native?"

"There was no-one else to help me. A family of natives used to pass through our place once or twice a year. Lucky for me they were nearby when I needed help. The old woman looked after me. If not for her, my children would be motherless."

Catherine's eyes widened at the thought of being taken care of by a native. Henry wouldn't have allowed it.

"Anyway, there were no more children for me. Whatever happened I never fell again no matter how much we ... well it just wasn't meant to be, and I've got my two, I'm thankful." Flora took a sip of her tea.

"Yes, that's right. We must be grateful for what we have and I am so glad my husband found you, Flora. I don't know how I'd manage without you."

Flora gripped her teacup tightly with two hands and placed it back on the saucer. "You're too kind, Catherine. I'm not ... well I'm sure you'd manage or find someone else."

"Perhaps but they wouldn't be as nice as you. You are happy here, aren't you?"

"Yes, very happy."

"You are so much more a friend to me than a housekeeper. I don't know what I'd do if you left."

Flora went to speak but Charles's excited cry cut her off.

"Mama, mama, come and see." He ran to Catherine and began tugging on her hand.

"Just a moment, Charles." Catherine looked back at Flora. "Were you going to say something?"

"Only that I like you very much too and—" Catherine let out a scream as a sharp set of teeth bit into her hand.

"Charles! That's very naughty." Catherine lifted her hand to see a perfect set of teeth marks indented in her skin.

"Come and see now!" Charles stamped his foot.

"Oh dear, what's the matter?"

"Come and see the castle Hughie built."

Catherine sighed and took his hand. "Very well." She stood and turned to give Flora a smile but her housekeeper was already busy scrubbing the carrots.

Charles yanked on her arm. "Come on."

Catherine let him pull her along. He really did need a brother or sister. He was becoming very demanding. Henry could always manage him. With the terrible weather and Charles being so difficult she could feel one of her nasty headaches coming on. She could take a dose of the tonic Henry gave her but it always made her so sleepy and it would be some time before Charles went to bed. She could only hope Henry would not be away too long.

Henry pulled off his boots, brushed off his clothes and walked through the back entrance to the Smith's Ridge house. He pushed the door shut behind him to stop even more dust entering with him. On a small table just inside the door was a basin with a small amount of dust-covered water. He rinsed his hands and face and dried himself on the cloth hanging on the back of the door. In the kitchen Mrs Donovan stirred a large pot on the stove.

She glanced up as he came in. "Good gracious, it's you, Mr Wiltshire. You've chosen terrible weather to travel in."

Perspiration dripped from her face and she batted at it with her apron.

"It doesn't appear quite as bad here as in Hawker." Henry stopped to pour himself a mug of water from the jug on the table. "When I left there yesterday morning I could barely see my hand in front of my face."

"Hmm." Mrs Donovan nodded and kept stirring whatever the delicious-smelling brew was in her pot.

Henry's stomach rumbled. He'd broken camp at first light without bothering to have so much as a cup of tea let alone eat anything. Now he was parched and hungry.

He eyed the pot. "None of the men are here?"

"No. They've been going out in this dust every day trying to make sure the animals have water but it's becoming harder and harder."

"I've brought you fresh supplies although some of it won't be faring so well in this heat."

Henry looked at her expectantly. The woman ignored him and looked back to her pot.

Henry pursed his lips and sniffed. "Can you spare me something to eat before I begin to unload?"

"Of course. This wombat's still a bit tough." She put the huge stirring spoon on the bench. "But I've got a pie in some luscious brown gravy ready. Sit yourself down in the front room. It's a bit cooler in there without the fire."

Henry made his way to the big living area. It was still sparsely furnished but neat and tidy. Mrs Donovan no doubt kept house as well as prepared the food.

She brought him in a plate with meat and dark brown gravy oozing out from below a golden-brown piecrust. He eyed it a moment then took a small spoonful. It slipped down his gullet leaving a delicious flavour on his tongue. The woman was right. It was good. She came back with a pot of tea and a mug which she set on the table in front of him along with some bread and dripping.

"What do you think of my parrot pie?"

Henry nearly choked.

"It's Mr Donovan's favourite. Will that do you?"

"Yes, thank you."

She went back to the kitchen. Henry peered at the pie a moment. He took another cautious mouthful then ate the rest hungrily. He mopped up the remains of the gravy with the bread before finally sitting back feeling contentedly full.

There was a thud at the front door. He rose to his feet as the door was flung open, letting in a wild-looking man and another cloud of dust before it was closed again.

"Henry!"

"Jack?" Henry studied his half-brother. Jack's hair hung in long waves under his once-black hat and his dark eyes glittered above the handkerchief covering his mouth. He tugged it down so it hung like a scarf around his neck.

"About time you paid me a visit. Did you bring the whiskey?"

"Yes."

"And the tobacco?"

"It's all there."

"Good, because there's not much else to do in this godfor-saken place." Jack strode across the room, his boots echoing on the wooden floor. "Mrs Donovan!" he bellowed. "Bring me some of whatever you've cooked and two mugs."

Henry studied Jack's lean frame. He looked fit in spite of the dirt and the terrible weather. "Six months ago Smith's Ridge was your piece of paradise."

Jack spun back to look at him. "That was before the heavens decided we should have no more rain. Where's the whiskey?"

"Still in the wagon."

"Be damned." Jack thumped the table with his fist making everything clatter.

"Steady up."

"We may as well unload now. I have no idea where Donovan and Brand are or when they'll return." Jack strode towards the kitchen nearly colliding with Mrs Donovan carrying a tray.

"Leave it on the table." Jack looked back at Henry. "Well come on. I'm not doing it by myself and Mrs Donovan only cooks and cleans. No heavy lifting for her. Isn't that right, Mrs Donovan?"

The woman didn't answer but continued to the table where she set out the food and mugs and collected up those Henry had finished with.

Reluctantly Henry rose to his feet and went to pull on his boots.

By the time they were done, the wind had eased. A thick bank of clouds covered the sun and the day had cooled considerably. Henry looked to the west, in the direction of Hawker. The clouds didn't look as thick out that way. Rain was badly needed but not before the races. He didn't know how his new horse would fare if the track was wet.

Back inside Henry watched while Jack began to eat the now-cold pie.

Jack paused with his spoon halfway to his mouth. "Pour some of that whiskey."

Henry didn't usually drink in the afternoons. He was always far too busy working but he decided to join Jack. He poured some whiskey into the two mugs Mrs Donovan had left for them. He took a sip, Jack a mouthful.

Henry placed his mug back on the table. "So, how are my sheep?"

Jack snorted. "You may as well have left them wherever you had them. There's little feed here."

"None on the plains either. Grasshoppers have decimated what little crops that grew and the rabbits have taken the rest."

"Rabbits are eating the feed here faster than the sheep and water is getting harder to find. We've lost several sheep to wild dogs."

"No trouble with natives?"

Jack pushed away his empty plate and sat back. His dark, brooding gaze locked on Henry. "No."

"Good. Then all you have to do is wait it out. The rain will have to come eventually."

Jack continued to study him. "How long are you staying? If this change holds we can ride out and look at some of the fences we've built. Makes it much easier to keep watch on the stock."

Henry was interested to see what his money was being spent on. "I can only stay two nights. I want to be back for the Hawker races. I have a horse running this year."

"Races?" Jack sat up with a lurch. "Hawker has races?"

"Of course. We might be a long way from civilisation but we are a progressive community."

"I enjoy the races."

Henry felt a chill run through him. Why had he mentioned it? "You can't come."

Jack's eyebrows arched. "Can't I?"

"Remember our agreement." Henry took another sip of whiskey.

"I've been here for nearly nine months." Jack tossed back the whiskey and slapped the mug down on the table. "I think it's time the new owner of Smith's Ridge had an outing."

Henry opened his mouth to complain but Jack slapped a hand over his, gripping it tightly.

"The more I remain closeted up here, the more curious people will get. The races are a perfect chance for me to show my face." He gave Henry's hand one last squeeze then let it go. "Don't worry, Henry." Jack let out a deep laugh. "I'll keep out of your way."

Henry kept his lips turned up in a smile but underneath he bristled. He wasn't at all happy for Jack to attend the races but there was little he could do about it.

Thirty-four

The sun was shining through gaps in the plump white clouds and the strong winds and accompanying dust that had plagued them for weeks had abated. Jack felt a sense of anticipation as he approached the paddock where the Hawker races were to be held.

He'd ridden all day yesterday and camped the night at the last creek before Hawker. This morning he'd done his best to freshen up before dressing in his good trousers and jacket. He smiled as he looked down at his clothes. Harriet had been a gift that kept on giving. Sometimes over the last few months he'd wondered if he'd done the right thing letting Henry persuade him to live at Smith's Ridge. It was a lonely existence. He missed the company of a good woman in his bed, something he hoped he would find today. Hawker must surely have a supply of young women, one of whom would succumb to the charms of Jack Aldridge.

He tethered his horse away from the gate with the others and made his way through the crowds to the refreshment booth. He was aware of a few glances in his direction, some curious, some disdainful. As a half-caste man who'd always lived in a white man's world he was used to it, and barely took any notice. He always dressed well and usually had enough charm to win over the staunchest of enemies if needed. He of all people knew appearances could be deceptive.

He bought himself an ale and stood just outside the booth surveying the colourful scene before him. The movement of people and horses stirred up the loose dust so there was a slight haze in the air but it didn't appear to dampen the enthusiasm of the crowd.

All around him voices rose in happy greetings, laughter and general merrymaking. Only over at the ring where horses were being led around did the scene appear more serious. Jack headed in that direction.

To one side he picked Henry's head, leaned forward in deep discussion with a tall redheaded man. Jack hadn't met him yet but from Donovan's description he was guessing the man was his neighbour, Ellis Prosser. Jack pulled the brim of his hat down and kept to the back of the crowd watching the horses. He had bet on a few races in Adelaide but he'd come along today more for something to do than to squander his money on a horse race. He much preferred cards.

The laughter of children and chatter of female voices drew his attention to a wagon set up under some trees a little way from the horses. He made his way over to where a group, mainly women and children, were gathered around a man who was doing magic tricks. Jack watched for a moment then directed his gaze to the crowd.

Standing opposite him in the semi-circle around the magician was a native woman. He'd seen several others here at the races, but they had looked out of place amongst the European crowd. This woman fitted right in, except for the colour of her skin. She wore a pretty patterned dress that followed her curves and nipped in neatly at the waist. Her black curls were tucked up under a bonnet and she chatted easily to the woman next to her, an older white woman.

Well, well, Jack thought to himself. At last a woman worthy of his interest. He slowly made his way around the crowd, stopping to applaud the magician with the group, then moving on until he was standing just behind her. She stood straight, her dark skin in sharp contrast to the pale blue of the dress and the cream lace collar. When the next bout of clapping began, Jack lifted his elbow and bumped against her back.

She turned to look at him and he was instantly mesmerised by her large brown eyes.

"I beg your pardon." He lifted his hat and held out his hand. "How clumsy of me."

"Please don't worry. I'm not harmed." She gave him a quick smile, ignoring his hand and turned back to the magician. Her speech was clear, with little trace of her Aboriginal heritage. Perhaps she had been raised by white people like he had. This was getting more and more interesting.

"I was carried away with watching this fellow. He's very talented isn't he?"

She looked back again. This time her gaze held his a little longer. "Yes."

"I'm Jack Aldridge." Once more he offered his hand. He was surprised when she suddenly grasped it firmly in hers.

"Mr Aldridge?"

"Yes."

"From Smith's Ridge?"

"Yes."

Finally she let his hand go. "I'm Millie Baker from Wildu Creek." Her face opened up in a wide smile. "Your neighbour."

Jack was stunned. It was absolutely the last thing he'd expected her to say. Henry had suggested he keep away from the Bakers. Maybe Millie was part of the reason. "Forgive me, Miss Baker. I have kept away as I thought you may not be too happy to meet the person who had taken over your lease."

"It's Mrs Baker, and please don't worry, Mr Aldridge." She leaned in a little closer. "In some ways it was a relief for us to leave. Smith's Ridge had some sad memories for my husband."

Jack opened his mouth but before he could speak she had turned away and was tapping the arm of the woman next to her and speaking in her ear. They both looked back at him.

"This is my mother-in-law, Lizzie Baker."

Once more Jack extended his hand, growing more intrigued by the minute. Mrs Baker's white skin was a vivid contrast to her daughter-in-law's. She shook his hand firmly.

"Mr Aldridge. How lovely to meet you at last. I am sorry we've been remiss in not inviting you to visit us but times have been … well, very trying in the last few months. How have you settled in at Smith's Ridge? Is there a Mrs Aldridge? We—"

Millie put a hand on her arm. "Mother Baker, please let him have time to reply," she said gently.

"Oh, yes of course."

Both women smiled at him.

"I am one to talk on a bit, Mr Aldridge. Do forgive me."

"Nothing to forgive, dear lady." Jack turned on his best smile. "In answer to your questions, yes, I am very settled at Smith's Ridge although I agree the times have been challenging and no, sadly, there is no Mrs Aldridge."

Loud oohs and aahs resounded around them from the crowd. "Millie, did you see that?" A young fair-haired boy jumped up from where he'd been sitting in front of the women. "Oh, I'm sorry."

"William." Millie put a hand on his shoulder. "This is our neighbour, Mr Aldridge."

The boy stared at Jack a moment, his look almost disdainful, then suddenly he shoved out his hand as if remembering his manners. "Hello."

"William is the eldest of my husband's children." Millie beamed down at the boy.

More and more intriguing, thought Jack. He wondered if she had children of her own and where William's mother was but it would not be polite to ask.

There were loud calls from the horse ring.

"The hurdles are starting." William half-turned his back to Jack. "Shall we go and watch?"

"Of course." The two women spoke at once and laughed.

"Nice to meet you, Mr Aldridge." Millie gave him a smile before she moved off.

"Do call in and see us soon." Mrs Baker senior put her arms around William's shoulders and turned him in the direction of the track.

Jack had noticed the steely look the boy gave him. What was that about?

The three Bakers moved away together and the rest of the crowd around the magician dispersed, his show over for now. Jack followed along behind. So the rather attractive Millie was his neighbour. He wondered what kind of white man she'd married. He couldn't wait to take up their invitation and find out more about the Bakers. Who knew? Millie might not have a happy marriage and a visit from Jack Aldridge might be just what she needed.

"Hello, Mr Baker."

Thomas looked up from the ticket he was studying. Johanna Prosser had stopped in front of him accompanied by a younger woman. They were both dressed in frills and bows, far too much frippery for his liking.

"Mrs Prosser."

"Have you met, Mrs Wiltshire. Her husband Henry owns the best shop in Hawker."

Thomas paid more attention to the younger woman. Of course, that's why she'd looked vaguely familiar. He'd only seen her once before when he'd gone with Joseph and Lizzie to Wiltshire's shop.

He inclined his head. "I don't believe we've been formally introduced. Good afternoon, Mrs Wiltshire."

Catherine Wiltshire gave him a shy smile. She had kind eyes and a delicate mouth. It was hard to imagine her as the pompous Henry's wife. He glanced lower as the sun glinted off the chain around her neck. It was gold and from it dangled a beautiful filigree locket in the shape of a heart. His eyes widened and he leaned closer.

"Mr Baker!" He was startled to attention by Johanna Prosser's indignant voice.

"I beg your pardon, Mrs Wiltshire." He straightened feeling heat in his cheeks both from anger and embarrassment. "My own mother once had a locket just like the one you are wearing."

Mrs Wiltshire's gloved fingers clasped the locket. "Oh, I see. Well this one has also been in my husband's family a long time. It was his grandmother's. Her name was Hester I believe."

Thomas glared at the young woman. Her look was guileless. No doubt she was completely unaware of the lies she'd been told.

"Well, we should be off." Johanna Prosser gave him a wary look and took her friend's arm. "The next race is about to begin."

"Ladies." Thomas lifted his hat and watched them walk away. No matter how many times Lizzie told him he must forget how Henry's father Septimus had duped him out of some of his family's precious possessions it was most difficult. Especially when his own mother's precious necklace was around another woman's neck instead of that of his dear Lizzie.

William watched as the last of the horses thundered past the finish line. There were the usual shouts of joy and a murmur of moans as some delighted in the outcome of the race and others rued their losses. His father and grandfather would be happy. Both of them had decided to put a wager on a small horse called Thunder. They had laughed at their choice, hoping it was a good omen and it would win and bring down much-needed rain. Thunder had won, much to the delight of three farmers from Cradock who owned him.

"Well I never," a haughty voice hissed nearby. "That's the black woman Joseph Baker married. Fancy him bringing her here to mix with decent folk."

William spun to search out the voice but he came face-to-face with Millie. The crowd surged and she got bumped. William put out his hand to stop her from falling. Anger coursed through him but when he looked beyond Millie no-one was paying them any attention.

"Are you all right, Millie?" William felt a mix of concern and resentment. He liked Millie but other people couldn't see her goodness. His father should never have brought her here and let her be the target of gossips. Now he had to be the one looking out for her.

"I am quite all right, William. Thank you for your arm." In spite of her smile he thought she looked shaken.

"Disgusting!"

Once more William searched the faces but none were looking their way. Was someone talking about Millie or the race?"

"Please, William." Millie put a hand on his arm. "Don't worry on my behalf."

"People are so rude. Father shouldn't have brought you."

Millie's large brown eyes studied him closely. "I am enjoying the race day, William. Would you prefer I'd have stayed home?"

"No." William looked down at his boots. His head said yes. He felt bad for Millie but also for himself. He knew people stared and talked about his father marrying a native. He liked Millie but it was hard to be with her on days like this.

"It's all right, William."

She tapped him under the chin and he looked up. She gave him the kindest of looks.

"We seem to have lost your grandma in the crowd. I think I'll go back to our picnic spot." She leaned a little closer. "Please don't mention this to your father. We've all been having such a lovely day, he'll only get upset."

Millie turned and the few people left around her gave her a wide space. William saw a man shake his head. He watched Millie as she walked purposefully across the bare ground towards their picnic spot, a lone figure with her head held high. William's insides were in turmoil. He looked around but no-one paid him any notice. His cheeks burned with shame but he couldn't help feeling relief that she was gone.

Millie reached the rug they had spread in the shade of some trees and let out the breath she'd been holding. No-one else had returned to their picnics yet. She was grateful to be away from prying eyes for a while. She lowered herself to the rug and arranged her blue-and-maroon patterned skirt around her. There were several other picnic rugs and baskets set out around theirs, vacant now and so making the distance between them and the Baker's position more obvious.

Millie wriggled back to lean against the trunk of a tree, watching the crowd mingling along the edge of the track. The sound of voices and laughter wafted up to her. Three young women walked past arm in arm. They chatted happily. One cast a sideways glance at her then turned back and murmured something to the other two and they picked up their pace. Millie sighed. She knew the colour of her skin would always be an obstacle for these fair-skinned people who looked down their noses at her. That didn't bother her as much as her lack of female company, especially at events like this.

She was also concerned for William. She liked Joseph's older son very much. He was developing into a fine young man, strong and hardworking. He had a good heart like his father but she could see how much he struggled with what other people thought about his father's marriage to her.

"Millie!"

She looked up at the sound of Joseph's voice and her heart skipped a beat. He strode towards her, his pale moleskin trousers hugging his long legs and his brown jacket over an open-necked white shirt flapping as he walked. He was waving something at her and his grin was as wide as his face. She dismissed her troubled thoughts and waved back.

He tossed his hat aside, flopped down on the blanket beside her and laid some notes in her lap. "Thunder won." He took her hand and kissed it. "You are my lucky charm."

Millie chuckled, noting the dark pouch in his shirt pocket. "I thought it was your special rock that brought you luck."

He shuffled around and lay his head in her lap, looking up at her with a wicked glint in his eyes. "You're much cuddlier than a rock."

She bent forward and he lifted his head till their lips met. A tantalisingly brief touch yet it was as if a spark had leapt between them and ignited desire in her body. Millie leaned back against the tree, one hand resting on his head, and closed her eyes. She cared little for what the rest of the company thought of her, she was Joseph's wife and that made her the luckiest woman around.

William wandered amongst the people still mingling at the edge of the track. Through a gap he saw a smart green bonnet with tresses of red hair flowing out beneath it. It had to be Georgina Prosser. He edged in her direction. He hadn't seen her since his last trip to the races three years ago. She was standing beside her father. This time she was wearing a deep green dress and matching bonnet which heightened the colour of her hair

"Be damned if I'll let them get away with it." Ellis Prosser's voice was loud. People turned to look in his direction and William moved a little closer. "I can't see how that hack could beat my fine Lightning or even your Charlie Boy, Wiltshire. It's rigged."

The man beside Mr Prosser turned slightly and William recognised the shopkeeper who had called them vagabonds. Thank goodness Millie had left.

"I don't see what we can do." Wiltshire scratched at his chin. "It all appeared above board."

"Humph!" Ellis Prosser snorted. "I need a drink." He looked down at his daughter. "Georgina, go and find your mother."

Georgina stayed exactly where she was as her father strode away. Once he was out of sight she turned and hurried in the direction of the horse yards. William followed her, laughing to himself over the way she hitched up her skirts so she could move faster. By the time he caught up with her she had her hand over the rails of the yard, stroking the nose of her father's horse.

"What went wrong?" she asked the jockey who was seeing to the horse.

"I don't know, Miss Georgina. I gave him his head like your father said but once he got caught in the dust … well no matter what I did he wouldn't go forward."

"Poor Lightning." Georgina kissed the animal's nose. "The dust has certainly been stirred up again today by all this movement." She looked at the jockey. "Perhaps he's become frightened of it. We've had some terrible dust storms lately."

"Perhaps." The jockey went on about his business.

Georgina spun and leaned back against the rail. It was too late for William to conceal himself.

"Hello." She looked him up and down. "Are you spying on me?"

"No." William pushed his hands into his pockets and poked at the ground with the toe of his boot. He glanced up. She was watching him closely. "I've come to see the horses."

"William Baker." She smiled. "I thought you looked familiar. You've grown much taller."

"So have you."

"Have you built anything lately?"

William frowned.

"I recall you were good at building."

"Oh yes." William smiled at the recollection of them sitting in the dirt at the first Hawker race meet. "I don't have much time to play any more."

She gave him a look, the kind of look Millie gave him when she thought he was being too bossy with his siblings.

"We've moved to Wildu Creek now," he said. "I have to help with the work that needs to be done."

"I envy you."

He stared at Georgina in complete surprise.

"I would love to do more outside but apart from help with the horses, Mother won't let me." She put her hands to her hips and just as he had, she poked at the dirt with the toe of her boot. "Next year they are sending me to school in Adelaide." She said the name as if it was poison. "I don't want to go. I won't know what to do there. I love Prosser's Run."

William felt sorry for her. He'd had to leave Smith's Ridge but at least they still lived on the family property at Wildu Creek. He couldn't imagine living in Hawker let alone Adelaide.

"It won't be for long. You can come back once school is finished."

"Mother has her heart set on me marrying someone in Adelaide."

"Marrying?" William was horrified. "You're far too young to be married."

She lifted her chin. "In five years I'll be sixteen."

He smirked. "Still too young to be marrying someone."

She glared at him a moment then grinned. "I'm never getting married. All my mother does is what my father says. She never thinks about anything for herself. I'm not going to be like that."

"Good for you."

"Georgina!"

She looked past William. "It's my brother. I'd better go. Mother has probably sent him." She moved forward, level with William. "Good luck, William. I hope we meet again."

"Goodbye," he said. She was gone before he could say anymore. He knew his father didn't like Mr Prosser but William found he liked Georgina Prosser, even if they rarely met.

On the other side of the horse yards, William saw a familiar head. Jack Aldridge their new neighbour was making towards the nearby bush, his arm around a young woman who'd been selling food in one of the booths. William started to follow then thought better of it. They would be quite away from everyone else over there and the space was open between him and the bush. Much harder for him to conceal himself and pretend he was just checking out the sights if he was discovered.

He turned away and made his way back to the place under some trees where his family had set out their picnic. Jack Aldridge was an unusual man, not just because he was not a full-blood native like Millie and Uncle Binda. There had been something about his manner that William didn't like. In fact the look on the man's face when he'd held out his hand had made William's skin prickle. He didn't know why but there was something about Mr Aldridge that he just didn't like and it had nothing to do with the colour of his skin.

Thirty-five

1887

Joseph stood in the shade of a gum looking across at the low walls that were the beginnings of the house he had started building for his family. He had set it against the side of a hill, parallel to the back of his parents' house and a fair distance away. The main rooms would be at the front and a passage would lead to a kitchen and a cellar dug directly into the hill. There was also to be a room alongside the laundry with a bathtub where they would be able to transfer hot water from the laundry copper. He was so proud of his plans but frustrated it was taking so long. His father had suggested it might be quicker if it was a little smaller but Joseph wanted something special for Millie; a house that would be the envy of those who had turned their noses up at his wife.

They rarely went to social functions beyond their own family events, but when they did he always bristled at the people who couldn't see past the colour of her skin to the kind, funny, gentle, loving woman he knew.

"What are you doing out here in the heat?"

He looked around at Millie crossing the yard towards him from the direction of the hen house. Her apron was pulled up like a bowl, no doubt containing the few eggs their hens were still laying.

He wrapped an arm around her shoulders as she came to a stop beside him. "It's cooler out here than in our quarters."

"Come down to your mother's house. There's plenty to do to be ready for tonight's dinner."

"What's this Aldridge fellow like?"

Millie had already told him as much as she remembered but Joseph was curious. He hoped having a neighbour who was part native would be a good thing for her.

"I've already told you all I remember. He's about your height, long dark hair with skin the colour of toffee. Oh and he was well-mannered and … friendly."

"And there's no Mrs Aldridge?"

"Well there wasn't last May at the Hawker races but anything could have happened since then."

"His note didn't mention a wife."

"Then I expect he's coming alone." She looked up at him. "We're going to a lot of fuss over one extra person for dinner."

"Christmas was quiet with Mother and Father down in Port Augusta at Ellen's, and Eliza and the children away with her family. Mother wants to make this a special get-together."

"Christmas was two weeks ago."

"Mr Aldridge's impending visit has got her moving. Not that any of us want to do much in this heat. Even Father says he can't recall it ever being so hot as it has been this last month."

"It's certainly boiling weather. If I don't collect the eggs as soon as they're laid they're hard-boiled just lying in the nest."

Joseph chuckled and kissed the top of Millie's head. No matter how bad things looked she could always make him laugh.

"When this house is finished we will have some grand parties, Millie."

"We don't need a fancy house."

His gaze went back to the partly built stone walls. "We won't be getting one any time soon."

They began walking down the slope towards his parents' house. Little puffs of dust rose with every step. "I might still have to go and find work elsewhere."

"Your father doesn't want you to."

"I know but we've little income. This heat has shrivelled up any chance of feed. Even the rabbit numbers are dwindling. We've sent some breeding stock down to my uncles at Penakie but even there the land can't sustain too much stock and what we've got left here won't survive much longer unless it rains. We need money coming in."

"But what would you do? Many people are the same as us, they will be looking for extra work."

"Word is that gold is being found at Teetulpa."

Millie stopped suddenly and turned to face him. One hand clutched the apron that held the precious eggs and the other went to her furrowed brow, shading her eyes from the late-afternoon sun. "You wouldn't go there? It's so far away."

"Not that far. There could be all kinds of opportunities. It's close to the stock route to New South Wales and on the route they're building the railway from Peterborough to Cockburn. Yunta will service the railway. There're plenty of work opportunities. But I'd rather try for gold." He put two hands on her shoulders. "If I could find some gold we wouldn't have to worry about supplies so much and there is so much more we could do here."

"People have died there."

"Where did you hear that?"

"I read it in the paper your father brought home from Port Augusta."

Joseph had also read the report keenly. On his last trip to Hawker before Christmas, the town had been buzzing with talk and several parties had already gone to the new field. "Well then, you'll know it wasn't the mining that killed them."

"No, typhus from the lack of clean water."

"I can look after myself, Millie. And I have you and the children to think of."

"We don't need more, Joseph." She slipped away from him and kept walking, her back ramrod straight. "And so far we haven't gone without food or clothing. The children are happy—"

"It's all right." He caught up to her at the back door. The verandah roof gave instant relief from the heat of the sun. "I'm just thinking about it."

"Don't wish for things that aren't important, Joseph." She lifted her head and brushed a kiss across his lips. "All we need is to be all together, as a family."

Jack noticed the difference almost immediately he passed through the gate in the fence between Smith's Ridge and Wildu Creek. Unlike his, this country was dotted with bluebush and saltbush and a variety of other hardy plants. They were sparse and small and stripped at ground level at first, no doubt from rabbits, and their tops and sides well chewed by sheep and kangaroos, but the further he rode the more there were. By comparison, Smith's Ridge had little vegetation in the low country. Brand was camped up in the hills with the remains of Henry's stock, where there were still small pockets of permanent water and some vegetation. This kind of flora, sparse as it was, would enable sheep to be kept in small numbers.

Jack was making this journey in the middle of summer because he was bored with his own company. Donovan and his wife had gone off somewhere to see family for a few weeks which left Jack alone at the house. He'd kept himself busy fixing yards, patching a broken window and doing any odd jobs he could find out of the heat but he was fed up with being on his own.

He'd been planning a trip to Hawker when a traveller had come through trying to sell a rough collection of pots and pans. The man had said he was going on to Wildu Creek. Jack hadn't bought anything but had given the pathetic fellow some flour, tea and sugar in return for delivering his message to Wildu Creek. At last he was taking up Mrs Baker's kind offer of hospitality. He had little to offer as a thank you but he had managed to shoot two rabbits last evening. He'd cleaned them and wrapped them in damp linen cloths inside a hessian bag. He hoped they, along with a packet of the special tea Henry imported, would be some kind of acceptable thank-you gift.

Jack had started out from Smith's Ridge at first light, resting for a short time in the middle of the day before continuing his journey. By mid-afternoon he noticed a smoke smudge in the distance, slightly darker than the dust, and assumed it signalled he was close to the homestead. He left the slopes and pointed his horse towards the large trees that followed the creek.

His first glimpse of Wildu Creek homestead made him bring his horse to a halt. It was a little settlement all of its own. There were considerable buildings: a wooden hut and a stone house close to the creek with yards and tanks and some small stone buildings nearby. Through the trees further up the hill, behind the stone house, a much bigger building had been commenced and then, more distant, was a long wooden hut and a shearing shed with sturdy yards surrounding it. The whole place was tidy and well-cared for.

He rode up a well-worn track that took him behind the wooden hut, and along the side of the stone house to the back, where he took in an enclosed yard with fruit trees and the remains of a vegetable garden. Beyond that were another yard and stables made of stone and wood. Further on, he could see a yard with two cows and chickens scratching in the dirt beside a low wooden structure. Wildu Creek was certainly far more substantial than Smith's Ridge although the dust hung in the air just the same.

Jack dismounted and was surprised at a voice from behind him.

"Hello, Mr Aldridge."

He looked around and was delighted to see Millie Baker coming towards him from the direction of the partly built house. She looked charming in a low-cut dress which hinted at her well-shaped breasts and hugged her narrow waist. A young boy walked beside her, tugging at the collar of his crisp white shirt.

"Mrs Baker." Jack removed his hat and gave a short bow. He appraised her closely from beneath his lowered lashes. He hadn't been with a woman since the races and that had been a long time ago. Mrs Donovan was good at keeping house and playing cards but old and not much to look at. His charm didn't work on her. Jack's preference was for white flesh but Millie Baker was still a welcome sight. "How lovely to see you again. You are positively the picture of beauty."

"No doubt you spend a lot of time with little company, Mr Aldridge." Millie grinned and turned to the boy. "Robert, go in and ask William to come out and see to Mr Aldridge's horse."

The boy gave Jack a shy smile and did as she bid.

Millie nodded towards a post near the back fence. "You can tether your horse there. William will take good care of him."

Jack did as she suggested.

"Please come straight inside, you must be quite exhausted from your ride. January is always hot but this year even more so. There's some water in the washhouse and a fresh cloth if you'd like to rinse off the dust."

"Thank you." He took the bags from his horse and held them out. "Some rabbits and some tea. I hope both will be useful."

"That's very kind of you." Millie took both bags and led him to the back of the house where she showed him where to wash. "Please come inside as soon as you are ready. Everyone is anxious to meet you."

Jack washed quickly and peered at himself in the small mirror hanging over the basin. He had shaved yesterday and only had a dark shadow around his jaw. Mrs Donovan wasn't too bad at cutting hair, although his was wet with perspiration. He dragged his fingers through the thick black locks, sweeping them back from his face, then grinned at his reflection.

"You'll do, Jack."

The washhouse was part of the long room, made from wooden planks built across the back of the house. He took off his boots and left them beside the line-up at the back door and entered the kitchen. Both Mrs Bakers looked up from their preparations.

"Welcome, Mr Aldridge." Mrs Baker senior's smile was animated. "We're so pleased you could come." She undid her apron and slid it over her head. "Please come up to our dining room. Everyone else is there."

Jack cast another long look at Millie before he turned to follow her mother-in-law through the house. He wondered how many she meant by everyone.

Joseph studied the man at the end of his parents' table. Jack, as he'd stated everyone should call him, even the children, was certainly good at entertaining the ladies. He had Millie, Eliza and even Lizzie hanging on his every word. Timothy and Thomas were also listening to his latest story with amused looks on their faces but Joseph noticed William, who at twelve had been allowed to eat at the table with the adults, was not paying much attention.

Laughter erupted as Jack finished his story about riding a donkey and falling off. He was obviously happy to make fun of himself but he didn't strike Joseph as the type of man who liked to be laughed at.

The sun was low in the sky outside and the inside light was suddenly dull.

"Time to light the lamps."

Millie stood. "Help me clear the plates please, William."

Joseph watched to make sure his son did as she bid. Sometimes of late William thought himself too big to help with household jobs but the boy rose immediately and did as Millie asked. He appeared to have grown taller yet again. The new trousers they had given him for Christmas just over two weeks ago would soon need to be let down if he kept that up.

"I see there's a substantial new house being built."

Joseph turned his attention back to Jack.

"Yes, for Millie and me and the children."

"We've tried to talk him out of it." Lizzie gave her son a benevolent smile. "There's only Thomas and I in this house now and it would be easier to build an addition."

"We're a big family, Mother." Joseph didn't want to have this conversation in front of their neighbour. "How do you find the house at Smith's Ridge, Mr ... Jack?"

"More than comfortable. I believe you built that one too?"

"I had the help of some builders but yes, a lot of the work was mine. Clara, my first wife, designed the layout." Joseph was aware of Millie hesitating beside him before she took the plate he held up. He tried never to mention his dead wife by name in her presence.

"I only have my shepherd, Brand, to share it with." Jack's voice filled the break in conversation. "And he's not there often. The Donovans live in the wooden hut at the back. It's a big house for only one." He looked up at Millie who at that moment was clearing his plate and gave her what Joseph could only describe as a meaningful look.

Joseph got to his feet. Jack might be a visitor but he was precariously testing his welcome.

"Perhaps we can go out on the verandah. It might be cooler out there by now."

"What's that noise?" William's face was scrunched up in puzzlement.

Before anyone could answer the floor began to vibrate beneath them. Joseph grabbed at the table. The walls of the house rocked. Millie cried out and there was a deafening crash as the plates she'd collected hit the floor along with the cover of the lamp his mother had been holding. The wick Lizzie had just lit went out and the light from outside dimmed. Screams could be heard from the verandah where the younger children had been playing.

Joseph was torn between trying to reach his wife who was clinging to Jack Aldridge and saving his children. Before any of them could move further the vibrations stopped. The last rays of the setting sun suddenly reappeared and filled the dining room with an orange light highlighting the motes of dust floating in the air.

For a heartbeat there was silence and then the front door banged open and footsteps could be heard in the passage. Mary ushered the frightened children into the dining room. She ran straight to Millie, hysteria in her voice as she spoke in her native language. Millie let go of Jack and opened her arms to Mary who flung herself against Millie's neck.

"It was an earth tremor." Thomas's calming voice spoke over the clamour. "It's all right children." He moved to where his wife was trying to re-light the lamp. "Careful of the glass, Lizzie."

Joseph saw his mother's confused look before he bent down and wrapped Robert, Violet and Esther in his arms. "You're safe," he soothed.

"We've had tremors before," Thomas said. "Nothing to be frightened of."

"Not as strong as that, Grandpa." William stood in the middle of the room, his eyes wide. "The house has never shaken like that before."

Mary babbled something more. Millie wrapped both her arms around her niece. Her gaze met Joseph's over the children's heads and his heart gave an extra thud. In all the time he'd known Millie he'd never seen such a look of fear in her eyes.

Thirty-six

Henry held Catherine close. "It's all right, my dear. It's passed." Over her head he looked at the picture hanging at a precarious angle on their sitting-room wall. Above it two dark lines ran jaggedly towards the ceiling, hopefully only minor cracks. Apart from that there appeared to be no damage in this room, at least.

Catherine clung to him, her body trembling.

"Catherine." He gave her a gentle shake and dragged her arms from his. "It's over I tell you. We are not harmed. Go and check on Charles. I must go to the shop and make sure everything is all right there."

"Don't leave us, Henry."

He forced her hands to her sides and held them there. "Take hold of yourself, Catherine. It was an earth tremor, nothing more. Look in on Charles. He has no doubt slept through the excitement."

"Excitement!" Tears shimmered in her eyes. "We have endured this terrible heat and now this most terrifying earthquake. I've had enough, Henry. It's time we sold up and moved back to Adelaide like you told my mother and yours that we would do."

Henry clenched his teeth and pulled his hands from Catherine's. She rarely raised her voice but her fear had displaced her manners.

"That is enough! Stop this hysteria at once and look in on Charles. Then you should take a draught of tonic and go to bed. I might be late if there are things to be tidied at the shop."

He strode to the front door, moved the empty vase that had obviously slid in the quake back to its place on the hall table and let himself out into the hot, still night. Immediately he could hear voices, some raised in panic, others more excited. It appeared many of the residents of Hawker were outside.

He looked towards the cottage where Flora and her children lived. No sign of anyone there but a light shone in the front window. Flora was a sensible woman, but he would look in on her on the way home.

Henry moved as fast as he could in the fading light. On the corner of the main street he passed a group huddled around a woman who was crying hysterically. A man stood to one side, his hands clutched to his chest, declaring the end was nigh over and over again. On closer inspection Henry recognised him as the clerk from the bank, not a previously pious man he'd thought.

Henry gave the group a wide berth and made for his own shop. He went through the back door and called out.

"Mr Hemming, is everything all right here?"

"I'm in the shop, Mr Wiltshire," came the reply.

Henry walked through the tiny kitchen and into the small room behind the shop that was once again restored to an office for Henry and a living room for Mr Hemming. Now that Hawker had a purpose-built post-and-telegraph office the telegraph had been moved there. It had been a pity to lose the extra business it had brought, especially with the difficult seasons the whole area had been experiencing.

A lamp shone from the shop at the front of the building. Henry had assumed the curtain between the two rooms had been pulled back but as he reached the doorway he realised the whole thing had fallen down. He looked up in surprise at the two holes in the plaster above the door where hooks had once been in place. They had supported the wooden rod that suspended the velvet curtain which now lay at his feet.

"Not much damage, Mr Wiltshire." Hemming was wielding a broom, collecting a small pile of glass. "Two of the sweets jars must have wobbled off the counter, a few things have fallen over, but the only real damage appears to be the crack above the door."

"Crack?"

Henry lifted the lamp Hemming had set on the counter. What he hadn't noticed when he'd looked up at the holes was a large crack running down from the ceiling and spreading out over the doorframe.

"That will need to be fixed."

Henry gritted his teeth. Lately it seemed as if money slipped through his fingers and none of his businesses were making much of a return.

The land he owned at Cradock and Wilson barely brought in enough to cover what he paid the men he employed to manage it. He was plagued at every turn by lack of rain, which meant his crops were poor and his stock had to compete with grasshoppers and rabbits for whatever feed remained. His problems were the same as most of the plains country and people weren't spending money in his shop like they had.

He looked over Hemming's head as he bent over the broom. They were carrying less stock and some of the shelves looked bare. Hemming and Catherine did their best to keep the place clean but the infernal dust was everywhere. In the dim light of the lamp the place looked shabby. What had happened to his fine establishment?

There was a sharp knock on the door.

"Wiltshire? Are you in there?"

Henry was surprised to hear Ellis Prosser outside his door. He moved around Hemming and drew back the bolt.

"Ellis. What are you doing here?"

"I came to see how you have fared." He peered round Henry at the interior of the shop.

Henry stepped quickly outside. "Not too badly, Ellis. Nothing that is not fixable. What brings you to town?"

"I put my wife and daughter on the train today. Georgina will start school in Adelaide when the new school year begins. I am staying the night at the hotel. This quake has caused a ruckus. I was planning to call on you in the morning. Come and have a drink with me now."

"At this hour?"

"I'm sure our custom will be welcome. The hotel at Edeowie has closed and I've heard more closures are likely. The publicans here won't want to follow their fate."

Henry turned back to his shop assistant. "Leave the rest, Mr Hemming. You can retire. I will come early in the morning and we will assess the damage in the daylight."

"Very good, Mr Wiltshire." Hemming came to bolt the door as Henry pulled it shut.

There was quite a crowd at the hotel, including the pious clerk who, by the look of him, must have decided to drink himself to inebriation while he awaited the end.

Prosser bought them a draught of whiskey and they found themselves a space in a corner away from the bar. He got straight to the point.

"Donovan's been to see me about your man at Smith's Ridge."

Henry looked around but there was so much noise in the bar there was little chance of them being overheard. "What did he have to say?"

"Very little." Prosser took a swig from his mug. "Apart from him being arrogant which rankles with Donovan, he says Aldridge mostly works hard, listens to Donovan's opinion and doesn't cause much trouble."

Henry found it hard to believe that a man like Jack Aldridge would settle so easily to life at Smith's Ridge but part of him was relieved. Jack continued to be out of sight while Henry worked on a way to be rid of the man for good.

"What does he do out there?"

"Works like I said. You implied he might be a bit shy of hard work but Donovan says he does his share. Drinks a bit, beats them at cards regularly and treats Donovan's wife as if she's his servant but in all he had nothing to report on Aldridge. You know I can't usually abide coloured fellows but Aldridge has obviously had a suitable upbringing. If it wasn't for the colour of his skin you could pass him off in normal society as a solid member of the family."

Henry took a sip of the whiskey. The strong liquid burned its way down his throat but did little to aid his unease. He'd thought by now Donovan would have been able to supply him with some insight into his half-brother that might help him to be rid of him. So far Jack had given little away and not put a foot wrong, except to come to the Hawker races last May. Henry had seen him in the distance that day but Jack had kept out of his way and there'd been no sign of him in Hawker since.

"Your stock are not faring so well."

Henry looked up from his mug to meet Prosser's sharp gaze.

"Donovan tells me you suffered heavy losses just before Christmas."

"They will only get worse." Henry took a slug of whiskey this time, willing the liquor to ease his concerns. "There's no sign of rain and none likely any time soon. We've had four days in a row here in Hawker with the thermometer over one hundred in the shade."

"It's been the same at Prosser's Run."

"How are you faring?"

"No better than anyone else in the district. My son has packed up and gone after this gold they say is easy picking at Teetulpa. I told him he was a fool but he wouldn't listen. We just have to wait it out. Rain will come again. I sold a lot of cattle over a year ago. We are managing to keep the breeding herd alive." Prosser leaned in. "You should think about changing to cattle. They'd be better on Smith's Ridge than sheep."

"At the moment there's no feed for any kind of stock. Brand has taken the last of my sheep into those rugged hills behind. There's still water there and some feed."

"Cattle are easier to find in country like that."

Henry pursed his lips. It had been Prosser's idea he buy the horse he'd named Charlie Boy to race, and all that had come of that were more costs. He'd had to find a property down south to agist the blasted animal.

Prosser downed the rest of his drink and looked at Henry expectantly. Henry took the last few gulps from his mug, picked up Prosser's and made his way through the crowd to the bar.

They bought another drink each so by the time Henry made his way home he was feeling pleasantly warm inside if a little unsteady on his feet.

As he approached his front gate he looked past it towards Flora Nixon's cottage. He was in the mood for a woman's body and Flora knew just how he liked to be treated. They had more regular visits again now that he'd gathered from Catherine that their housekeeper was unable to bear children. But there was no longer a light in the window and without prior arrangement he couldn't just turn up there. Her children were older and quite knowing and her husband did return on the odd occasion.

Reluctantly he turned his gaze homeward. Catherine would be sleepy by now from her tonic, he could surely coerce her into fulfilling his needs. He'd made some enquiries the last time he'd been in Adelaide buying supplies for his shop. The man he purchased his tonics and oils from told him the tonic contained laudanum and assured him it was simply a relaxant. It explained why sometimes Catherine was more amenable after taking the draught and showed more interest in coupling, like she had in the days before Charles.

Just as he reached the gate he stubbed his boot against something solid and went sprawling to the path. His hand landed in something soft and squishy and a malodorous smell wafted with it as he brought his hand up closer to his face. No doubt some dog muck. The streets were scattered with it. He got to his feet, holding the offending hand away from his clothes, and looked back to see what had tripped him.

The three-quarter moon had drifted free of the clouds and showed him what he had not noticed before. One of the urn-shaped structures which had sat atop each of the gate pillars had broken off and lay at his feet.

"How?" His question remained unanswered as he bent to pick up the lump of superbly fashioned plaster. Too late he remembered the muck on his hand. He lifted the ornament and carried it inside the gate where he propped it against its pillar. It must have been dislodged by the quake.

With the awful smell reminding him of his need to clean up before he climbed into bed with his wife, Henry stumbled his way around the side of the house in search of something he could use to wipe his hand. Then he would go inside, wash and seek out his wife to do her duty.

Thirty-seven

It was only Millie who joined Joseph at the cart in the crisp pre-dawn gloom of late March. He'd said goodbye to everyone else last night and he didn't want the children here making a fuss and getting upset to see him go. If the truth be known it only made it much harder for him to see them so distressed but the hardest part was yet to come, saying goodbye to his wife.

Joseph faced a long, lonely journey to the goldfields but he had no choice. No rain had fallen. Wildu Creek was the same as most of the other properties in the area, struggling to support the families who relied on it. Better he go now and have some chance at finding gold before half the state ended up there.

He checked once again that his load was secure. He was taking one of their carts and two horses: one of the old draught horses to pull the load and his own horse tethered behind. The cart was loaded with everything he thought he would need for six months. Some of it had come from Wildu Creek, including the picks and shovels, food supplies and firewood. He'd been advised the latter was in short supply at Teetulpa. The rest he had bought at Mr Garrat's shop in Hawker. Garrat was doing a good trade in tents and panning dishes and the like. Joseph hadn't darkened Wiltshire's door but word had it his business was struggling. Farmers had no money and no use for his fine goods in the current climate.

Joseph came round the cart and face-to-face with Millie. She had a shawl around her shoulders and her long hair was still tousled from a restless night. They'd woken very early, neither of them able to sleep well, and said their goodbyes with their tender lovemaking. Now he reached for her hand and she wrapped herself around him, holding him tight one last time. He did the same and felt the lump of his lucky rock in his shirt pocket. She slipped her hand over it.

"You have your rock?"

"Safe in the new pouch you made for it."

"And the water?"

"Yes." He eased her from his arms and looked into her deep brown eyes. Ever since they'd heard the news that Rufus Prosser had died of typhus at the goldfields, his family had each in their own way asked him not to go, except for Millie. "I will keep well."

"I know your mind is made up, Joseph, so I won't say anything more than I love you and safe travels."

He bent down and kissed her. He didn't want to leave without once more having the taste of her on his lips.

"Goodbye, my love." He drew away and climbed up onto the cart where he gave the horse soft encouragement to move. The old boy ambled forward immediately as if sensing there was no need for long goodbyes. Joseph didn't look back. No matter how hard it was to leave he knew Millie and the children would be safe with his parents and her brother. Joseph's job was to find gold.

He hadn't gone far when a familiar figure emerged from the bush. Joseph halted his horse.

"Binda. What are you doing out here?"

"I'm going to keep you company."

"You're needed here, my friend."

"I'm not going with you." Binda led his horse behind the cart, tethered it beside Joseph's then climbed up on the bench beside him. "I'm coming as far as tonight takes us, then I will return to Wildu Creek."

Joseph nodded at his friend and set the horse off in its steady forward motion again. He looked at Binda who was grinning back at him and a sense of relief flooded though Joseph. It certainly would be good to have company, even if only for one day.

William lay in bed listening to the soft sounds of Millie's tears. He had heard his father pull on his boots and try to leave quietly but the door squeaked and his boots creaked on the wooden verandah. William had wanted to go out and plead once more to be taken with him but he knew he wouldn't wear his father down on this. The goldfields were no place for children. William had baulked at that. He was twelve and in his mind a man but his father had insisted William's job was to stay behind with Millie and the children and help his grandfather as much as he could.

Robert snuffled and groaned in his sleep. William rolled over and stared at the wall. He felt it a terrible injustice that he should stay at home. Uncle Timothy and Uncle Binda were both here, they could help Grandpa and look after the family. Joseph had said he would be home again before Christmas. That was so far away, nearly nine months; it seemed a lifetime to William. He tossed and turned some more before finally getting up. All was quiet from Millie's room. Like him she would no doubt be thinking of the long time ahead of them without Joseph. William hoped perhaps she had gone back to sleep.

He pulled on his clothes and picked up his boots, letting himself out into the golden light of dawn. The air smelled fresh and was cool against his skin but he knew it wouldn't be long before the sun would be beating down on them again as it had relentlessly for months.

William moved away from the hut and then stopped. He put his hands to his hips and looked around. The shearers' quarters where they lived was a distance from the main house down by the creek. Except for the chatter of birds and the crow of Grandma's rooster there was little sound. He wondered how far away his father was already. He moved a few steps across the open ground to a group of gums and stopped again. He should go and see to the cows but his gaze drifted to the partly constructed building. His father had hardly done anything more to it since the earth tremor had weakened one of the shorter internal walls.

William crossed the space between the trees and the construction. He knew his father's vision for the house wasn't shared by everyone else in the family but William liked the idea. He stood in what would be the front door space and turned. From here you had a grand view down the gentle slope of the hill to the meandering creek and the plains. In the distance were the mountains, a pink haze in the morning light. This was only the first floor. Joseph had planned it so that one day there would be a second floor. Imagine the view from there, he'd said. William remembered the excitement in his father's voice.

He perched on the low front wall and poked at the dirt with his boot. Now his father wasn't here to build the walls higher and, even if he was, there was no money to pay for the doors and windows and someone to help them put them in. He ran his fingers along the rough stone. He had helped find the stones, mix the mortar and build the walls. Perhaps he could keep doing that. He stood up and turned around. The back walls against the hill needed building higher to hold back the dirt. The planks supporting the reinforced wall his father had fixed after the quake were still in place. He could use them to shore up the dirt.

He made up his mind then and there that this would be his job. When his father came home with enough gold to finish the house William would have kept it going up in the meantime. Warmth spread through him, not from the sun that was still low in the sky but from the thought of doing something useful and something that would make his father proud.

William's attention was drawn to the chicken yard beyond the new house. The rooster was carrying on as if something was amiss. William picked up a stick and hurried in that the direction.

He stopped in surprise when he saw Mary locking the gate on the chickens. She held a wire basket full of eggs. The rooster was on the other side of the gate, still making an awful racket.

Mary kicked the wooden gate. "Damn rooster. Millie says you might lose your head one day soon."

William smiled. The rooster was particularly feisty and gave the women a hard time when they collected the eggs.

Mary turned. Her eyes widened as she noticed William watching her.

He cleared his throat. "You're up early." Suddenly he felt as if he was spying.

"Need plenty of butter and eggs today." She bent to pick up the metal milk bucket at her feet.

"Here, let me carry that for you." He closed the distance between them in quick strides.

Mary's eyes widened a moment. She nodded, handed over the bucket and looked away.

"What are you going to make?"

"Millie's going to teach me how to make soft pastry like she does." Mary glanced at him. "I want to be a good cook like her. One day I want to get a job, maybe a housekeeper."

William saw the gleam in her eyes before she looked away again. He couldn't imagine Mary not being there to boss him around, although when he thought about it there'd been little of that for some time.

"Are you planning to leave?"

"Maybe … one day."

They reached the little stone hut where she would separate the cream and make her butter. He put the bucket down.

"Thank you, William." Mary gave him a quick smile.

"You're welcome, Mary."

William turned to walk away then stopped and looked back. Mary had already disappeared inside the little shed. He realised she no longer annoyed him and he no longer resented her. Mary had been with them for as long as he could remember. It would be strange if she left and was no longer a part of their lives. Still, things were changing a lot.

The soft sound of singing came from the shed. William grinned and made his way back in the direction of the cow yard. There was a paling there that needed fixing. Like Mary he had plenty of work to do.

It had been a week since Joseph left home and his sixth day of travel alone. Binda had been a welcome companion at the start of his journey. When Joseph had declared he wanted to marry Millie the bond between the two men had been tested but Binda's reservations had long since disappeared and travelling together they had talked and joked like old times which had raised Joseph's spirits. He'd told Binda once more about the gold he hoped he'd find and what he'd do with it. Binda had put a hand to his forehead and declared he had a bad case of gold fever. Teasing aside, when they had parted company the next morning Joseph had been more in control of his feelings and full of anticipation for the job ahead.

Now, several days later, he'd reached the small settlement of Yunta, which was a hive of activity. Not only was it on the stock route but it was also a stop-off point for the gold fields as well as becoming a service town for the new railway. There were camel trains, wagons, horses and people moving along the rough road between the scattered buildings that made up the flat, dusty settlement.

Joseph found a place to leave his horses and cart not too far from the hotel. He decided he would buy himself a good feed. After today any meals would entail whatever he prepared from his supplies.

Inside, the small establishment was busy in spite of the early hour. Joseph ordered a big plate of bacon, eggs and potatoes and a pot of tea. He found a spot on the end of a bench at a long table. He nodded to the man opposite who returned the acknowledgment but didn't stop eating. The fellow's hair was long and lank, his clothes thin and tatty, and by the smell of him he hadn't bathed in a long while. He was mopping up his plate with such exuberance Joseph suspected it might also have been the first meal he'd had in a while.

Finally the man finished, his plate so clean it would hardly need a wash. He sat back, belched and smiled.

"That was the best tucker I've had in a long time."

"Have you been on the road?"

"No mate. I'm just back from the mine."

"Teetulpa?"

The fellow's eyes narrowed and he gave a sharp nod. "Where are you headed?"

"Teetulpa."

The man eyed him closely again then got to his feet. "Good luck, mate." He nodded, plucked a ragged hat from the seat beside him and hurried out the door.

"Miners, they don't like to talk much and Mad Mick even less than most."

Joseph glanced at the man who was seated next to the place Mad Mick had vacated. He was of much tidier appearance, with a neatly clipped beard and dressed in working clothes but clean ones. Joseph offered his hand. "Joseph Baker."

"Sam Rossiter."

"You're not a miner then, Mr Rossiter?"

"No." He gave a self-satisfied smile. "Railway is much more reliable. Wouldn't want to end up half-crazy like Mad Mick."

"That would require hard work."

Rossiter glared at the man opposite him who sat along further on the same bench as Joseph. "I work as hard as any man, Hegarty."

Joseph's attention was drawn away by the arrival of his food. His stomach rumbled at the loaded plate.

"Enjoy it mate." Rossiter hooked his thumb over his shoulder. "If you're headed out to Teetulpa you might not get a decent feed for a while. I hear the pubs out there are set up for liquid refreshments only." He gave another of his smug smiles. "Which is for the best. Typhus seems to afflict those who drink the water. Three more men died of it just last month."

Joseph paused, a forkful of bacon halfway to his mouth. Rufus Prosser had been one of those men.

"Don't take any notice of Sam." Hegarty shook his head. He was broad across the shoulders with forearms like tree trunks. "I've worked for the government at Teetulpa. They employed fifty of us to dig a dam." He puffed out his chest. "Finished it in ten days we did."

"Pppph!" Sam showed his disgust. "Still not clean water, Hegarty."

Hegarty thumped his hand on the table. "It is as of yesterday. The Water Conservation Department has just finished two condensers. They've started supplying fresh water to the fields."

"That's good to know." Joseph continued eating. There were many things packed in his cart but a big supply of water wasn't one of them. He had a barrel full and that was all. At least he could tell Millie. She was particularly worried about the water. He would write to her as soon as he was settled.

Sam climbed up from the bench. "Good luck, Baker." He shook his head. "You'll need it."

Hegarty looked around. There was only the two of them at this end of the table. He slid along the bench a little closer to Joseph.

"Sam Rossiter's not man enough to leave his job and go and search for gold for himself. He's envious of those that do and quick enough to fleece it from them in a card game when he can." He held his hand out to Joseph, who stopped eating long enough to shake it. Hegarty's grip was firm. "Where are you from, Baker?"

"A property north-west of here near Hawker."

"You know anything about prospecting?"

Joseph pondered the question while he chewed another mouthful. He knew how to breed sheep that produced fine wool but he knew little about finding gold other than what he'd gleaned from others. "I'm a quick learner."

He sensed Hegarty slide a little closer. The man appeared friendly enough.

"You'll do well to mind your own business and keep your mouth shut about anything you find. There are plenty out there who would murder their own mother for a handful of gold."

From the corner of his eye Joseph saw the man pull a small glass bottle from his pocket. He kept it shielded in his large hand. "This is what you're looking for."

Hegarty had Joseph's full attention now. The jar was half full of tiny rock chips, some black but most gold. Before Joseph could get a better look Hegarty had slipped it back in his pocket.

"I've sold my lease and I'm on my way to Adelaide. I don't trust that bank manager on the field to give me a fair price."

Joseph hadn't thought as far ahead as actually selling his gold.

"I wish you luck." Hegarty lumbered to his feet. "And if I come back to Teetulpa I'll look you up."

Joseph watched Hegarty wend his way through the crowd. The bar was full of a mixture of all kinds of men, from some not dissimilar in appearance to Mad Mick to a well-dressed chap propped at the bar, with an ale in his hand no less. Joseph took a long draught from the mug of tea that had come with his food. He had rarely drunk a drop of liquor since he'd married Millie. He no longer looked for it but after meeting the three men here, he got the feeling that might change on the goldfields.

It was late the following morning when Joseph came over the final rise and got his first view of the goldfields. He'd known he was getting closer by the increase in volume of horses, carts and men, either going in the same direction as him or heading away along the well-beaten track. The journey between Yunta and Teetulpa had been through rugged and barren country. Now the eager anticipation he'd been feeling deserted him. Spread out before him was a flat, treeless plain dotted with small hills of dirt and tents as far as he could see. Moving amongst them were small, dark shapes, men in their hundreds if not thousands. His heart sank. How was he going to be lucky enough to be the one of those who found gold amongst so many others?

Thirty-eight

Catherine paused inside the open door. Her heart gave an extra thud at the sight of a man in her front yard talking to Charles. She had only left her son for a few minutes to fetch some cool lemonade.

"My father owns the best shop in Hawker."

Charles's proud little voice reached her as she stepped out onto the verandah. The scuff of her shoe drew Charles's attention along with that of the tall stranger. Once more Catherine's heart beat stronger as the man turned the full force of his gaze on her. His lips turned up in a smile and his eyes sparkled as he looked her up and down. It was a warm morning but Catherine felt extra heat in her cheeks. No-one had looked at her with such candid appraisal in a long time, not even Henry.

She moved across the verandah and it was then she realised his dark skin was not from exposure to the sun but from mixed blood, she was sure. From her vantage point she looked up and down the street. It was Saturday morning and very quiet. Not another soul in sight, thank goodness. If Henry got word of a coloured man at their house he would have a fit. Any little thing seemed to upset him of late and this would be no little thing to

Henry. He had no tolerance for native people and had even grown worse in his disdain for them.

"Mama, Jack is lost and he's been playing ball with me." Charles raced across the dusty yard where once there had been grass and came to a stop at the edge of the verandah.

Catherine put the tray she had been carrying on the small table and looked from her son's excited face to the man who was still studying her brazenly.

"That was very kind of you, Mr …"

"Aldridge, Jack Aldridge." He removed his hat to reveal thick black hair and dipped his head. "Forgive the intrusion, madam. The young lad's ball rolled out just as I was passing and before I knew it I was involved in his game."

Catherine glanced towards the gate which was open. She had thought it closed but since the earthquake back in January it had been difficult to keep shut and sometimes swung open of its own accord.

"Well, thank you Mr Aldridge. Can I help you with directions? Hawker is not a big place, who were you looking for?"

"I fear I have been made a fool of." The man's mouth twitched and he lowered his gaze as if he was embarrassed. "And it is my own fault."

"In what way?"

He took a few steps towards her and replaced his hat firmly on his head so his face was in shadow. "I am passing through Hawker on my way north and I …" He glanced down at Charles who was listening eagerly.

"You may have a mug of lemonade, Charles." Catherine put a guiding hand on her son's shoulder and watched as he moved to the table where she'd left the tray. "And a piece of cake." Charles had already picked up a slice and was shovelling one end in his mouth. She looked back at Mr Aldridge.

He leaned a little closer and lowered his voice. "I overindulged at the hotel and got drawn into a card game. I am not much of a player but I did win. One of the men who owes me said he lived in this street." Jack scratched at his clean-shaven chin. "Said his name was John Smith."

Once more Catherine glanced towards the street. "There are not many houses in our street. I don't recall the name."

"No." Jack put his hands behind his back and looked at the ground. "I suspect there is no John Smith."

"Oh."

"I fear I've been made of a fool of, Mrs …?"

"Oh forgive me." Once more Catherine felt the full force of his gaze. "Wiltshire."

The man looked so disconcerted her heart went out to him. "Would you like some lemonade and a seat in the shade before you set off on your way again?"

"That's very kind of you, Mrs Wiltshire." He was quick to step under the verandah roof.

Catherine indicated a chair and once he was settled passed him the other mug of cool lemonade. "There's cake too if you would like." She couldn't believe she had invited a complete stranger to refreshments on her verandah.

Charles put his empty mug on the tray. Crumbs clung to his lips. Catherine reached out with a napkin to brush them off but he pushed her hand away. "I want to go back to my ball, Mama."

"Of course, but take your hat." Catherine lifted it from the back of the chair and watched her son bound back to kick his ball. He was so like his father; dark hair, a sharp look and a mouth that pursed just like Henry's if something displeased him. Charles's manner mimicked Henry's and he could even be short with her from time to time. The boy was a smaller version of his father.

Catherine sometimes wondered if she had been anything more than a vessel to carry him in.

"Is it always this hot in September?"

"The days can be very warm." She looked back at the man stretched out on her small chair looking so comfortable as if he belonged there. For a moment she glimpsed Henry's face in his and then it was gone; probably her guilt that she was entertaining a stranger without her husband at home.

"Charles said you have a shop."

"Yes, in the main street not far from the railway station."

"And a large home." Mr Aldridge swept his gaze along the verandah. "Not many here built of this stone."

"It's a relief in this climate."

"I have only passed through Hawker on two other occasions. Your business must do well here."

"My husband tries to stock quality goods. We are a long way from Adelaide but people still enjoy variety and distinction." Catherine found herself sounding like her husband and if the truth be known she was actually stretching the facts. Henry had cut back a lot on the variety of items they stocked. Few people could afford his more expensive goods over the last year or so and she hadn't been needed to help as much in the shop unless Henry was away. It suited her fine. After losing her last baby it had taken her months to recover her strength and then had come the extremely hot summer. She couldn't abide the heat and spent most of her days inside, reading or sewing or playing with Charles, longing for the cool evening breezes of Glenelg.

Jack's gaze locked with hers. For a moment Catherine felt as if he could see inside her head. She put a hand to the locket that hung around her neck then dropped it to her side.

He took another mouthful from the mug. "You don't have a drink, Mrs Wiltshire?"

"Oh, no. I will have mine inside. It's getting too hot out here. Just five minutes more," she called to Charles.

"I don't want to go in." He stopped not far from the verandah and looked at Jack. "Would you like to play again, Jack?"

"It's Mr Aldridge, Charles, and no, he cannot play." Catherine cut in before Jack had the chance. Something about his manner made her think he would have indulged the boy. "Mr Aldridge has things to do and so do we." She made it quite clear she was drawing this little party to a close in spite of Charles's pouting face.

Jack got to his feet with the ease of an athletic man. "Perhaps I could have a quick kick before I set off."

Catherine looked up and down the street again. She didn't expect Henry home until midday but he could turn up at any time or someone could walk past. How would she explain letting this man play with their son?

"We do have to go in, Charles."

Jack stopped the ball with the side of his boot and kicked it back to the boy then he lifted his hat in a farewell gesture.

"Thank you for your kindness, Mrs Wiltshire, and for the game, Master Charles." He swept his appraising look over Catherine again then walked out the gate and down the road with long strides.

She watched until he was out of sight.

"Do we have to go inside?" Charles's whining voice drew her attention.

"Yes, we do. You father will be home soon."

"Perhaps he will play ball with me." Charles glared at her and kicked at the verandah post with the toe of his new boots. They were already scuffed and dusty.

Once more panic rose inside her. Henry mustn't find out about their visitor. "I don't think you should ask your father today. He didn't sleep well last night and he will be tired when he gets home.

We won't mention Mr Aldridge's visit. Now let's go inside. It's time to prepare our meal."

Catherine picked up her tray and ushered Charles inside. She looked back at the empty street. She felt as if someone was watching her. Jack Aldridge's visit had been unsettling. She closed the solid wooden door firmly and turned the lock.

Jack stepped out of the shadows. Like he'd observed Catherine do from his vantage point beside a cottage, he glanced up and down the street. Two squealing pigs ran across the road further along closely followed by a yapping dog then quiet settled again. The wind had picked up a little, raising puffs of dust, but not a soul stirred.

He had become fed up with the lonely existence at Smith's Ridge and had treated himself with a trip to town. Brand was permanently camped in the hills and Donovan was out working on fences with the odd visit to Brand. Donovan's tough biddy of a wife was away visiting her daughter. Jack had come to Hawker for company and to find a woman to bed but he'd decided to spend the day checking on Henry's assets before he visited the hotel tonight.

Jack had arrived outside Henry's house at first light from his camping spot out of town. He'd watched as his half-brother had left, dressed for work, then a little later the woman who was his housekeeper and two children set off together from the cottage beside Henry's house. A couple of horses and carts had passed by but he'd kept out of sight. Finally Catherine and Charles had come outside. He watched Henry's pretty wife seat herself in the shade and the boy crying out for her to look at nearly every kick he made. Finally Jack heard her say she was going in to get refreshments. He'd taken the opportunity to wait for the boy's back to be turned then he'd pushed open the gate and the next kick of the ball had sent it his way.

It was easy enough to befriend Henry's son. Jack had always been able to beguile children and charm women. Catherine had been a little shocked to see him in her front yard but she'd been easily reassured. Jack had enjoyed his little play at getting close to Henry's family. Of course it was a risk that Catherine might mention his visit to her husband but Jack didn't care either way. There was little Henry could do about it. It would be a reminder to Henry that Jack wasn't totally out of reach. Jack would keep his silence about their connection for as long as Henry's money flowed or until Jack took over the lease of Smith's Ridge. Apart from the isolation he was enjoying the life. He didn't mind getting his hands dirty, especially knowing the place would one day be his. It was an opportunity he'd never thought possible until Henry had suggested it.

The last time Henry had come to Smith's Ridge with supplies he had hinted that he might not be able to keep paying Jack and the lease. Jack had soon reminded him of their deal. He grinned at the thought of Henry's screwed-up face when Jack had grabbed him by his fancy collar and pinned him to the wall. Jack had seen a glimpse of fear in his half-brother's eyes before he had shoved Jack away and regained his composure.

He glanced across at Henry's house behind its grand fence. There was an urn broken off one of the gate pillars and the gate didn't appear to shut properly. The garden was almost dead but that wasn't a surprise with the lack of rain. Henry's wife and child were dressed well enough and both looked well fed. Catherine was a little plumper than the last glimpse he'd had of her at the Hawker races the year before. He'd also noticed she was wearing the locket that had disappeared from around Harriet's neck. The older woman hadn't hid it as he'd thought but had obviously given it to her daughter-in-law.

It looked to Jack as if Henry was doing well. Well enough to come up with the money needed to pay Jack and keep Smith's

Ridge. Jack made his way back towards the main street. Where Henry's street was quiet, the main road through Hawker was the opposite. A camel train passed by on the other side loaded with wool and further towards the railway station were two wagons, also piled high with wool, while the bullock teams that pulled them stood patiently. Jack waited for a horse and cart to pass before he crossed the street and found a verandah roof to stand under. People and horses moved up and down the street. The odd dog roamed by, sniffing at the variety of animal dung that littered the road. He leaned back against the wall and pulled down his hat to obscure his face. From here he had an excellent view of Henry's shop.

At nearly midday Henry and the man who worked with him began loading up a small cart. Jack was pleased when the assistant was the one to climb up on the cart and call to the horse to set off. Henry stayed in the shade of his verandah roof a moment. He appeared to be looking in the direction of another general store where several people were coming and going. No-one came to his shop. He turned and Jack moved quickly across the road and was at the door before Henry had quite closed it. Jack pushed his way inside and was rewarded with a look of shock on his half-brother's face.

Henry's alarm quickly turned to anger. "What are you doing here?" He looked over Jack's shoulder and quickly pushed the door shut and drew the bolt. "I could have had customers."

"It appears you haven't had any for at least a half an hour."

Henry's eyes narrowed. "You've been watching me?"

"Would you prefer I'd just walked in regardless of who was in your shop?"

"You shouldn't be here at all. What do you want, Jack?"

"I fancied a trip to town."

"We agreed you'd stay at Smith's Ridge, keep out of sight until it can become yours."

Anger flared in Jack at Henry's pompous manner. He jutted his jaw at Henry. "I'm not staying there indefinitely. I could take over the lease now."

"With what?"

"The money I've been saving."

"But we agreed once you took over the lease you would be on your own." Henry's voice was placating and his expression smug. "That means I stop paying you and you have to pay all other costs yourself. Your employees, supplies, stock."

Jack clenched his jaw. For a moment he had forgotten all the other extras Henry paid for. Then he thought of his previous benefactress. "I can always go back and visit your mother. I am sure she'd gladly pay to help keep me at Smith's Ridge."

Henry turned away and busied himself at his counter. "There would be no point. Business in Adelaide has fared no better than here." He looked back at Jack, his dark eyes brooding. "I have tried myself to get money from my mother in recent times. She has given me what she can. That supply has dried up for now."

Jack watched as Henry straightened a shelf of neatly folded shirts. He felt sure his half-brother was lying but he didn't push it. Harriet's reputation was widespread and Jack felt sure she would have done well with the mid-year Jubilee celebrations for both Queen Victoria and South Australia; all those Adelaide ladies would have been purchasing new dresses for the various balls and dinners that had been reported in the papers.

"Since you're here you can take some supplies back with you." Henry was behind his counter now, once more studying Jack with his dark eyes.

"I only have my horse."

Henry pursed his lips. "Then I will make the trip out in a few weeks."

"We can manage till your visit."

"You will have two less mouths to feed soon. Donovan and his wife are leaving."

"When did they tell you that?"

"They didn't. Ellis Prosser did. His son died at the goldfields and he needs a good overseer. Donovan used to work for him." Henry straightened some half-empty jars of sweets on his counter. "He wants him back."

"How am I supposed to manage without a housekeeper and one man down?"

"Times are tough, Jack. We are all making allowances. Once the rain comes again things will improve."

Jack held Henry's gaze a moment then moved around the shop. Everything was tidy but most of the shelves were half-empty and some bare. Perhaps Henry was telling the truth and he really was struggling. Jack would leave him be for now but decided he would make the trip to town more often. He had the feeling Henry Wiltshire needed closer watching.

Henry closed the new wooden door that separated his shop from the house as soon as Jack had slipped out the back way. Damn Jack Aldridge. Henry hoped no-one had seen a coloured man enter his shop. What few good customers he had were discerning. He couldn't afford to lose them. Not that they had a lot of choice in Hawker and Garrat didn't care who he let into his shop.

Henry had to maintain a civil appearance. He had an inclination to become a councillor when Hawker finally got the governor's approval for the home rule they'd been seeking for some time. Names would be put forward to the governor later in the year for his consideration of fit and proper candidates to be considered for such important positions. Henry wanted to be one of them.

As soon as Hemming returned from making his deliveries, Henry left his assistant to do the final tidying up and made his way home. Jack was foremost in his mind.

Henry hadn't been lying to Jack when he'd said money was short. He was overstretched in every direction and would sell off his Wilson and Cradock properties if he could get any money for them. He had spent a lot of money on his house and extras to keep up appearances such as the racehorse Prosser had talked him into. His store was run-down and Garrat was getting a lot of his custom. Smith's Ridge was a drain on his already overstretched finances. Donovan leaving had made no difference. He'd been there courtesy of Prosser. It was only ever meant to be a short term arrangement. Prosser liked to have eyes on his neighbour's doings but he had lost interest with the death of his son. He'd been training Rufus up to take over Prosser's Run. With the loss of a second son Prosser had gone quite mad with grief. Henry thought it best to keep his distance for a while.

He stepped into the coolness of his house and took a deep breath. Things had to get better. They just had to. He couldn't keep asking his mother for money. Unlike his, her business was booming. He'd lied to Jack about that but she was already helping to keep Jack at Smith's Ridge by assisting Henry with the lease payments. She worried about the drain on her finances. Henry had to keep reassuring her that they would be rid of Jack Aldridge eventually and Smith's Ridge would be theirs alone.

"Henry, is that you?" Catherine called from the kitchen. "I am about to serve our meal."

"Yes." He took off his hat, hung it on the hook and made his way to the kitchen.

Charles came running down the hall towards him, a ball tucked under his arm. "Father, Father!" His voice was high-pitched with excitement.

"Steady up young man." In spite of his son's overexuberance in the house, Henry gazed at him proudly. Charles had been made in his image. He was already strong, good-looking and quick-witted to boot.

The boy came to a stop in front of Henry, his face lit up. "I had a game with a man in our front yard—"

"Put your ball away, Charles, and wash your hands." Catherine's voice was also high-pitched.

Henry took in her pink cheeks. She turned away from his gaze.

"A man?" Henry looked back at his son who hadn't moved.

"Jack ... or Mr Aldridge, Mother said I must call him." Charles flicked a glare in her direction. "He kicked the ball with me. Can you do that Father?"

"Perhaps later when it's cooler. Go and wash your hands as your mother asked."

Charles hurried off to do his bidding.

Henry tried to keep his voice calm. "What was this ... Aldridge fellow doing here?"

"He was lost, that was all. He was looking for a man who had deceived him in a card game by the sound of it."

"And you allowed a stranger to play with our son."

Catherine picked up a plate and put it down again. He could see she was getting distressed.

"It ... he came into the yard when I was inside getting a drink for Charles. He didn't stay long. Charles is excited because an adult showed him some attention. With Flora out for the day he missed having the children to play with."

"So the man didn't bother you? He didn't say anything untoward?"

"Not at all. He was most polite." Catherine picked up the tray she had filled with dishes for their meal. "He wasn't here for long." She stepped past Henry and set off towards the dining room.

Henry let out the breath he'd been holding. So Jack had actually been brazen enough to come into his yard, speak with his wife and play with his child, and yet not let on his connection to Henry. Was he sending Henry a warning or just playing a game? Whatever the reason Henry had become complacent thinking Jack was out of the way at Smith's Ridge. He would have to be much more vigilant and look harder for a way to be rid of his half-brother.

Thirty-nine

Joseph huddled in the shade thrown by his tent and folded Millie's letter. His seat was a rock covered with a folded blanket. Behind him, stretched out for miles across the barren landscape, were the tents and flimsy structures of the diggings where thousands of men laboured, desperate to make their fortunes. The sounds of their endeavours filled the air. The post office where Joseph posted his letters home was said to process thousands of letters a month and was connected to the telegraph. There was also a bank, a crude hospital, a hotel and regular church services for various denominations. The field had attracted all manner of men from honest god-fearing fellows to thieves and even those who would jump a claim as quick as look at you.

Joseph hadn't intended to stop work yet but the arrival of the mail had encouraged him to take a break from the constant digging and scraping. He munched a piece of damper that he hadn't stopped to eat at midday and pondered all that Millie had written.

They were well at Wildu Creek although Robert had come down with a terrible cough which had also afflicted Lizzie. They were both recovered except that Lizzie still succumbed to fits of coughing from time to time. The land was dry. They were maintaining their remaining stock in the hills and gullies at the back of Wildu Creek where there were small amounts of permanent water. Binda spent a lot of time there. Thomas and Timothy spent their days building fences to divide Wildu Creek into paddocks. Everyone was tired of the heat but their spirits remained high. The children missed him and the younger ones especially asked after him every day. The girls worked hard with their writing and spelling but Robert would rather climb trees than work in his copybook. William worked diligently with his grandfather and was spending his spare time on a special project. Joseph had pondered briefly what that might be but Millie had ended with her words of love and his thoughts went to her instead.

Now weary but restless he closed his eyes, conjuring up her smiling face, her warm lips. He missed his family but it was Millie's happy voice and soft body that he thought of the most on the lonely nights. He stretched, opened his eyes to the brightness of a cloudless sky and tucked the letter back in his pocket alongside his leather pouch with his lucky rock. It had not brought him much luck at Teetulpa, unless he counted his continuing good health lucky.

After several months, the small glass bottle in his trouser pocket contained only a pitiful amount of gold grains and a few tiny chips. Each time he felt he should give up and return home he found just enough more to raise his hopes again.

During his first month here he had quickly discovered sifting through the dirt with a knife was the best way to uncover gold in the dry conditions at Teetulpa. He'd constructed a simple four-legged structure that loosely resembled a table. Like those around him he dug bucketloads of soil and piled it in heaps close to his tent, then shovelful by shovelful he scraped through the soil with his blade. He went over the sand and gravel on his table several times before he scraped it to the ground.

Joseph had become used to the crude life of the settlement. He kept to himself during the day but at night he sought the company of a few men with claims nearby who had come from the land like he had. There was little to do but drink and share stories about their various homes and families. He was usually so tired he was ready to fall into his swag after a few rounds of the local publican's home-brew but some nights, when he was feeling particularly lonely, he would stay longer until the drink numbed all feeling and he had to stagger his way home.

He'd learned to keep his mouth shut about his work. Hegarty had been right when he'd said there were men here who'd murder their own mother to get their hands on gold or, even if not that desperate, there were others prepared to steal from those who'd been lucky enough to find gold.

Joseph glanced back at the piles of dirt between his tent and his table. He itched to get back to it now. It was like that. You found nothing so you became despondent then a glimmer of gold sent you into more painstaking searching. He was well and truly hooked. Just one more shovel full, just one more sift through. He did it all day, every day, until he lost the light. He pushed the last of the damper into his mouth, washed it down with some cold tea and went back to his table. He still had an hour or more before the sun went down.

He had been there a while, bent over the dirt pile as he scraped his knife through it, his hat the only shade, when muttering started up to his right. The back of Joseph's neck prickled but he didn't look up from his table. He only had one close neighbour since the departure of the young bank clerk on the other side. The poor young man had drunk himself silly and been carted off by two constables.

Joseph's remaining close neighbour was Bart Jones. They'd introduced themselves when Joseph had first set up next to Jones's even cruder camp. The man had very little; a few hessian bags strung up with sticks were his only shelter. Jones was a thin, wiry man with a patchy beard and eyes that darted back and forth, rarely focusing on Joseph when they spoke. Joseph soon discovered he was quite mad. He knew Jones would be watching him now but would look away as soon as Joseph turned.

Their claims were on the edge of the field on a washaway coming off a small gully. The washaway was little deeper than three feet and Joseph had staked his claim right on top of it. The bank clerk's tent had fallen down now. It had been left behind when he'd been carted off. It was unlikely they'd see him again which was just as well. All his other possessions had been stolen but the tent remained. Joseph had half a mind to offer it to Jones but the man was paranoid and just as likely to lie down in the trench again and hide. That's what he'd done the last time Joseph had tried to offer him a share of his food.

Jones often ranted at this time of the day. The poor man was probably hungry but Joseph had given up trying to share his food. The only time he saw Jones eat was first thing in the morning and then nothing more than the damper he burned black in the coals of his fire and black tea. Joseph had tried to share some of his salted meat and dried fruit but Jones had acted as if Joseph was trying to poison him. He was probably harmless enough but Joseph didn't trust him. Finally the muttering abated and the sound of a shovel was all that could be heard.

As soon as the sun was low in the sky Joseph packed up and went in search of the man whose tent they would drink outside tonight. Millie's letter had deepened his sense of loneliness and the futility of his search. Her words played over in his head as he made his way around other men's claims, skirting holes and piles of dirt. Perhaps he should throw it in. Take the little gold he'd found and return home before he went crazy like Jones.

"Baker, come and join us." One of his drinking partners was already at the fire with some crude chairs drawn up. Several other men arrived as Joseph did. Most he knew but there were often a couple of newcomers. Tonight a new fellow accompanied one of the regulars.

Once they'd all exchanged their usual guarded stories of what they'd found that day they settled down to share tales of the homes they all missed.

Joseph stared into the fire waiting for the drink to have some effect. "I'm thinking of returning to Wildu Creek."

Only the new man on his right heard him. "Have you made enough to go home?"

Joseph turned his weary gaze to the fellow. He was broad across the shoulders with a full beard and eyes that glinted in the firelight. It was the kind of direct question you didn't ask on the goldfields unless you were new.

"No." Joseph looked back at the flames and took another swig of the liquor the local publican brewed behind his bar; a large tent, open on one side with a rough bar from where he served by the mug or by the gallon jug. That was what the men were passing around and filling their mugs from tonight.

"I didn't mean to offend you," the man said. "I've only arrived this morning and I'm still trying to work out what goes on. They told me in Adelaide there was lots of gold being found here."

Joseph instinctively patted his pocket. "If there is mate it's not by me."

The man's gaze went to Joseph's pocket but Joseph was distracted by a nudge from his other side.

"Your turn to buy the jug, Baker." It was one of the long-standing regulars Joseph drank with. Joseph knew he should go home but he couldn't renege on his turn. He struggled to his feet, took the jug and made his way along the rough path that led past the crude wooden hut that housed the bank, the couple of tent shops which sold everything except decent food, past the post office and on to the bar. He manoeuvred around a few lone drinkers, paid for a new jug and retraced his steps.

He passed the jug to the new man then waited till it completed the circle and came back to him, when he filled his mug and poured the liquor down his throat. Even though men sat around him talking and joking Joseph felt alone. He thought of Millie and when the jug came round again he refilled his mug. He knew he should be going back to his tent but it would be cold and lonely and right now the liquid was warming the ache in his heart. His eyes felt heavy and his body was sore all over. How he longed for Millie's gentle caress.

A hand shook his shoulder. He patted it dreaming of his wife but it was a deep male voice that broke into his dream. "Time to go home, Baker."

Joseph peered at the man who was a farmer from the country near Quorn, an older man whose tent they were drinking near. Joseph blinked and rubbed at his eyes. There was no-one else at the campfire. He dragged himself up from the ground where he'd slumped against a rock pile and looked around. The fire had burned low and it was a moonless night. He stumbled.

"Will you be able to get home?" The farmer looked at him closely, his face lost in the grey of the night.

"Of course." Joseph straightened but his head spun and his stomach roiled. He took a deep breath of cold night air and tried to focus, aware the farmer was watching with one arm stretched towards Joseph as if ready to support him.

Why had he stayed? He turned away from the concerned eyes and began to weave his way back to his tent. He made it to a rough track that lead away from the goldfields and followed it to the edge of the diggings closest to his claim. There was still the occasional flicker from a candle or a fire but most men, exhausted from work or drink or both, were asleep. Even so, there were still the sounds so many men made even in sleep. The muffled sleep talkers, the snores and night-time noises of thousands of men followed him as he stumbled his way home. Particularly loud snores reverberated from the last tent where he turned to leave the track and make his way back to his claim.

Joseph paused at the sound of another boot besides his connecting with a rock. He stood still and tried to listen but his liquor-fired brain wouldn't oblige. He took one more step and then crumpled as something hard hit his head.

The sound of liquid splashing penetrated Joseph's throbbing head. The stringent smell of urine brought bile to his throat. He squinted and groaned as the rays of the early sun pained his eyes.

"Jesus, Mary and Joseph," a deep Irish voice exclaimed. "What are you doing sleeping there?"

Once more Joseph groaned. He could only see from his right eye. The left refused to open and that side of his face ached. He felt like he'd been trampled by a team of bullocks. Why wasn't he in his swag bed inside his tent?

A hand gently shook his shoulder. "What's happened to you? You've got a lump on the side of your head, so you have."

Joseph squinted at the kindly face leaning over him. What had happened? He'd been walking home and then … Once more he groaned and rolled over. He dragged himself to a sitting position with the help of the Irishman, then twisted sideways and spat foul-tasting liquid from his mouth.

He winced as the movement made his head throb. His one good eye focused on a dark object a few feet in front of him. Joseph frowned and tried to concentrate through the dull pain in his head. The object was familiar. He put one hand to his top pocket, then patted his jacket and his trousers. They were empty.

"My gold," he croaked and reached for the leather pouch.

"Is it robbed you've been?" The Irishmen retrieved the pouch. "Not a thing in there," he said as he handed it over.

Joseph took the empty pouch, anger surging through him mingled with sadness. His gold was gone but so was his lucky charm. A part of him didn't believe in such things and yet he'd found it in the place where Binda had saved his life.

"Lucky it was only your gold they took. To be sure it could have been your life."

The Irishman held out his hand to assist but Joseph brushed it away. "I'm all right." He glared at the man who backed away. Joseph felt a pang of guilt. The Irishman had been trying to help but Joseph felt he was beyond help. He'd lost the small amount of gold he'd managed to find and his lucky rock.

He glanced down then blinked as the rising sun sparkled off something on the ground near his feet. He bent to pick up the smooth, shiny rock that had been with him for so long and a small wave of hope glimmered as he rolled it in his hand, and rubbed his fingers over its familiar ridges and fissures. It was worthless but had been with him so long.

By the time Joseph staggered back to his camp he knew there was nothing for it but to get back to work. He'd found some gold and lost it. He'd survived to be given a second chance. There was no way he could return home with nothing to show for his absence. There'd be no more drinking for him. He'd keep digging and sifting until he found enough gold to take home.

Without even stopping to boil his billy or eat anything he set to work. By mid-morning the sun was beating down on his pounding head. The side of his jaw throbbed from whatever had hit him. His stomach roiled and his head pounded. He gripped the hilt of his knife tight and closed his eyes.

"Are you praying the gold to the surface?"

Joseph's eyes opened and he released a breath of relief. There, coming along the cutaway towards him, was Hegarty, with a grin on his big wide face. He was leading a horse loaded up to the hilt and behind him came another man also leading a loaded horse.

They came to a stop in the middle of Joseph's claim. He stood up and went to the edge of the drop. The only time he'd be taller than Hegarty.

They gripped hands.

Joseph pumped Hegarty's hand enthusiastically. "It's good to see you."

Hegarty twisted his face into a wry grin. "You're looking a bit worse for wear."

"Fell over last night." Joseph pushed his hat tighter on his head. "What brought you back?"

"Put some money in the bank, bought myself a good horse and provisions and decided to have another go. Brought my friend Peterson with me."

Where Hegarty was big like a bullock, his friend Peterson was more the build of a draught horse, still built well but not as round and beefy and with a face that looked like it might have seen a fight or two.

Joseph held out his hand to Peterson. "Welcome."

"This is the right kind of country you've picked." Hegarty cast a look around. He paused briefly in Jones's direction then looked back at Peterson. "I like the look of it." He waved his hand towards Joseph's table. "What's this you were praying over?"

"It's a long way to cart water from the dam to here. I have trouble enough keeping fresh water for drinking and cooking."

Joseph pointed to the barrel he kept by his tent. "A lot of men were using a table to spread out the dirt and sift through it so that's what I've taken to doing. It works well enough." Joseph gave a snort. "Providing there's gold in the dirt."

"Any likelihood of that?" Hegarty studied him closely.

"Some."

Hegarty pressed his lips together and held Joseph's gaze a moment longer, then he slapped his leg and turned back to Peterson. "Reckon we'll set up next to Baker here." He smiled at Joseph. "We can all help each other out if need be."

Joseph's spirits rose. He hadn't realised how lonely he'd been until the face of a man he'd only met briefly had made his day so much better.

"You get back to your prayers." Hegarty grinned and gave him a gentle poke in the chest. "It'll take Peterson and me the rest of the day to check this claim and stake it. Once we're set up we'll have a meal together. Peterson here's a dab hand with food."

"Reckon that's the only reason he brought me." Peterson's craggy face lit up in a smile.

"Wasn't for your good looks, that's for certain."

Hegarty's big body shuddered as he laughed. Peterson just shook his head.

Joseph went back to his table but he couldn't concentrate on his work with the two of them busy next door to him. He regularly stood, stretched and went to the edge of his claim to see what they were doing.

Hegarty said he was happy with the look of the soil and staked his claim while Peterson put up tents and set up their camp. He'd brought some bricks which he set down and before long he had used some precious water to make mud and had built a good semblance of a decent fire. By evening the delicious smell coming from that fire had Joseph's stomach rumbling.

"Have you finished for the day?"

Joseph sat back at Hegarty's call, lifted his hat from his head and dragged his fingers though his filthy hair. "I reckon I've found enough of nothing to call it quits."

"Come and join us." Hegarty waved at the fire.

Joseph went to the small bowl he used for washing and did his best to clean the dirt from his hands. The sun was low in an orange sky and without its heat the air chilled his damp body. He dragged the drying cloth from his hands to his neck and shoulders then shrugged on his coat. He took the last jar of his mother's preserved peaches from his provisions box and his one chair and crossed the several feet of his claim to Hegarty's where he offered the jar to Peterson. "These taste good with cream but even without it I can recommend them."

Peterson nodded, accepted the jar and went back to his cooking. Hegarty perched on a bench seat he'd put together with a plank and rocks on the other side of the fire. He lifted a mug towards Joseph. "Care for a drop?"

Joseph reached out his hand then hesitated. Only this morning he'd sworn off liquor.

"It's good whiskey. Not the belly-burning liquid they make here."

Joseph accepted the mug and placed his battered chair next to Hegarty. He'd just have one drink to be sociable.

They both took a gulp from their mugs. Joseph enjoyed the smooth warmth of the spirit as it slipped down his throat. "You're right." He wiped the back of his hand across his mouth. "This is good stuff." He glanced at Peterson who was busy stirring whatever the delicious-smelling concoction was he had in the pot over the fire.

"Peterson doesn't drink." Hegarty took another sip. "Made him silly in his younger days. Doesn't touch a drop now."

Even though Peterson was barely two feet away from them he ignored Hegarty and kept stirring. He was obviously a quiet one.

"Good at keeping his own counsel too," Hegarty said. "Which is one of the things I like about him. That and his cooking."

Hegarty laughed and Joseph found himself joining in.

"So." Hegarty leaned in closer, his large bulk testing the strength of the plank. "How have you done here, Baker? Not struck it rich yet I'm assuming?"

Joseph looked around for listening ears, which was quite useless. The sun had well and truly left the sky and there was no moon. Apart from the flicker of campfires and lanterns there was nothing to be seen. Closer to his tent he could see the glow of Jones's candle.

He kept his voice low. "I've had slim pickings but enough to keep me interested." He paused. Drained the last of the whiskey and set the mug firmly on the ground at his feet. "I'd found a small amount but ..." He clenched his fists. "I was robbed last night. It's all gone."

"Full of liquor?"

Joseph could feel Hegarty's gaze on him. He lifted his head to meet the man's look and gave a sharp nod.

Hegarty emptied his mug and put it down like Joseph had. "I stick to my own good stuff and only once a week. The rest of the time is for working. You're not the first man to lose his gold to the drink and you won't be the last."

Joseph was grateful Hegarty had offered neither sympathy nor a lecture.

"I like your table idea. There's plenty of water with the dam but like you say it's a distance from here." Hegarty looked away to where the fire threw some light over the cutaway. "These channels are more likely to have gold than anywhere else."

Joseph nodded. He hoped his friend was right. "It's filthy work but if you're careful it's easy enough to see the gold if it's there."

Hegarty cracked his knuckles and stared off into the darkness. "It's there."

Once more Joseph's spirits rose at the confident tone.

Peterson reached over their shoulders handing them each a tin plate covered with a brown stew. Joseph was quick to rest the hot plate on the thick moleskin of his trousers. He could see chunks of carrot, turnip and potato in the gravy as well as hunks of meat. Saliva filled his mouth. It had been days since he'd eaten a decent meal and longer since he'd had something as good as this stew looked.

Peterson joined Hegarty on the bench which sunk lower to the ground.

"Nice bit of beef stew even if I do say so myself," he said.

"Beef?" Joseph looked from one man to the other.

Hegarty's eyes sparkled in the firelight. "Don't ask any questions." His hearty laugh made the seat bounce and they all tucked in to the delicious food, Joseph feeling better than he had in weeks.

Forty

1888

Pain shot up Millie's arms as her hoe once more jarred against the hard earth. She had set herself some hard physical work as a distraction. This morning she'd felt melancholy, missing Joseph and thinking about the babies they hadn't had. Joseph's sister Ellen was with child again and Millie was envious. She had not wished for children of her own until Joseph was gone. They had made love so often and yet no child grew within her. She thought there must be something wrong with her but Jundala had reassured her that babies arrive when the time is right. All the same Millie was sad she had not yet given Joseph another child.

At the sound of a horse, Millie looked up from where she was attempting to dig the vegetable garden. Each time she heard hoof beats she hoped it would be Joseph. He'd been gone over a year and all she had was his letters and his assurance of his love. She pursed her lips. The horse was black and although she couldn't see the rider clearly she could tell by his seat it was Jack Aldridge.

She leaned the hoe against the paling fence and brushed her hands down her dress. Only a month ago they'd had a week of unbearable weather that had ended with the worst dust-storm any-one could remember. It was already April and they'd had no rain since last year. The only reason she was bothering to try to prepare a vegetable patch in the baked soil was to keep herself busy and her mind away from thoughts of the husband she missed so badly.

In spite of her loneliness the approaching rider was not a welcome sight. Jack had come to visit several times in Joseph's absence. Lizzie had invited him for Christmas and he'd come by each month since then. At first Millie had enjoyed his company. Jack was charming and funny, equally comfortable playing with the children or chatting with Thomas.

Millie hadn't said anything but last time he'd visited she felt as if he'd been making advances to her. When she looked back on it there was nothing in it and yet she'd felt uncomfortable. They were silly things, only minor, like the brush of his hand over hers as they'd both reached for a dish, squeezing close to her as he left the table, insisting she come and see him off. He was no doubt lonely and just being friendly but she had been glad when he'd left last time. That had been less than three weeks ago and now he was back and she was alone.

Thomas had taken Lizzie and the three younger children to Port Augusta to visit Ellen and her two children. They weren't due back for a few more days. Binda had left this morning to take Mary to Hawker. She was taking on a job there, looking after the growing family of one of the publicans. Timothy, Eliza and their children were taking a turn in the hill country tending the few remaining sheep.

She looked up towards the shearing shed. She knew William was there somewhere working on something, but he was only a boy in spite of the way he tried to take Joseph's place as the head of the family in his absence. Besides, when he got started on one of his projects, hours could go by before she would see him.

She turned back as Jack rode closer. She could see his dark eyes surveying the yard. He rode up to the fence, his lips turned up in a smile. She'd once thought it charming but now it seemed more of a leer.

"Good morning, Millie." He swept the hat from his head and bowed low on his horse. Millie shuddered internally at the sing-song sound of his voice.

"Mr Aldridge."

He slid from his saddle, tethered his horse to the fence and rested his forearms on the paling, staring at her with his deep brown eyes. "No need to be formal. We're close neighbours after all."

"It's still a long ride." Millie lifted her chin. "Is there something you need?"

His grin widened. "I thought perhaps you might be lonely with the senior Bakers away. I recall they said they'd be gone for a couple of weeks when I was here last."

"I expect them any day now."

"Is that so?" He walked around the fence to the gate and let himself in. "I met Binda and his family down at the creek boundary this morning. They were on their way to Hawker. He seemed to think the Bakers would be away for quite a while and he tells me your husband hasn't yet returned from the goldfields." He glanced back over his shoulder. "Although I see your new house continues to grow."

"William has been working on it in his father's absence." Millie couldn't help the pride in her voice. William had become a man overnight when his father had left. He was only thirteen but he took his responsibilities to his family seriously.

"He must miss his father."

Jack crossed the rough ground where she'd been trying to make some impressions with her hoe and stopped just in front of her. She felt trapped by his gaze, unable to speak or move.

"No doubt you are very lonely without your husband."

He reached for her hand but she snatched it away and side-stepped him back to the path.

Her heart skipped as she saw the brief flicker of anger cross his face. She needed to play for time and think about how she was going to handle this.

"Would you like a seat in the shade in our outdoor room?" Millie gave Jack the slightest of smiles. She didn't want to encourage him but neither did she want to alienate him. "I was thinking it was time for a pot of tea."

He took two strides and was right beside her, towering over her. Fear flowed through Millie but she stood her ground, trying not to show it.

"I'd prefer to sit inside." His smile frightened her as much as his anger. "Your house keeps so cool." He reached a hand towards her face.

They both flinched as a shot rang out. Jack's horse whinnied and pulled at his lead. Jack spun and Millie peered around him. William was walking towards them from the direction of the new house, a rifle slung over the crook of his elbow.

"Hello, Mr Aldridge." William's usually serious face was split in a grin.

"What are you firing at?" Jack's voice held a note of anger.

William frowned. "I didn't fire in this direction, Mr Aldridge. My father taught me how to use guns safely. We've had a wild dog hanging around our chickens. I thought I saw him that's all."

Relief flooded through Millie. There'd been no talk of wild dogs close to the house recently. She suspected William had been firing at nothing.

"Did you get him?" Jack folded his arms and glanced in the direction of the chicken house.

Millie took the opportunity to take a step towards the back door.

"No." William stayed where he was, his feet firmly planted, the gun lowered but still pointing in Jack's direction. "He's wily but if I'm patient I'll get him. We can't afford to lose any more chickens, can we Millie?"

"No." Millie smiled at the boy who was more like a brother than a son to her. "We've only got six left."

"Do you have any trouble with the wild dogs, Mr Aldridge?" William asked.

"Some but I've built a yard with wire and rocks. It has deterred predators."

"Would you tell me how?"

Millie heard a click of Jack's tongue. "I could but—"

"Why don't you two go round to the outdoor room and chat?" Millie cut Jack off and hoped William's presence was enough to deter him from following her. "I will make us a pot of tea."

She watched Jack's shoulders rise as he took a deep breath.

"Thanks, Mr Aldridge." William stepped back from the gate as if expecting Jack to follow him.

Jack's hand clenched at his side. He turned back to Millie, his jaw set, his dark eyes narrowed. He studied her a moment then his charming grin returned. He gave Millie a slight nod. "We shall look forward to your company."

Millie let out the breath she'd been holding and hurried inside. Her hands shook as she moved the kettle over the fire and added more wood. Usually there was someone else nearby. This was the first time she'd felt truly frightened since Joseph had left. How she wished he would give up trying to find gold and come home.

She laid out a tray with three cups and the tea things. There were some pikelets left from the breakfast she'd cooked that morning. She added them to the tray with a small pot of jam and carried it through the house and out across the verandah.

William sat a little way from Jack, the gun propped beside him. Millie's heart went out to the boy. She recognised the rifle as one Joseph kept at the quarters. William rarely carried a gun but he did know how to use it. Jack was quickly on his feet and hurrying towards her as if he'd been watching for her. He placed his big hands over hers and leaned closer.

"Let me take that for you," he murmured.

Millie tried to extract her hands but she couldn't. They were trapped underneath Jack's and if she struggled the tray would tip. He smiled and eased his grip so she could pull away.

He fell into step beside her and placed the tray on the outside table.

"Mr Aldridge has some good ideas for keeping the hens safe." William maintained his seat slightly apart from Millie and Jack.

"That's good." Millie poured the tea. A breeze had sprung up from the gully disturbing the branches that cast some shade over them.

Jack remained standing even after she had passed him his tea and offered the plate of pikelets. There was an awkward silence and finally Millie sat. Jack lowered himself to the seat next to her. She wished he would leave. It was worrying, him being here and William seated with the gun close by. To her it was obvious he was on guard but she wondered if Jack realised that's what he was doing.

"It's so good to taste a woman's cooking." Jack licked the jam from his fingers slowly, watching Millie as he did.

"Someone's coming." William leapt to his feet.

Millie heard Jack mutter under his breath as they both turned to look in the direction William was pointing. It was the track that led in the direction of Hawker.

"It's a cart." William climbed a little way up the trunk of the tree. "It's Grandpa."

Millie felt a flood of relief wash over her.

"They're back early." William jumped from the tree and came to stand beside Millie.

"They weren't absolutely sure how long they'd be." Millie gave Jack a self-assured look now that she knew help was on its way.

As the wagon drew closer they could see the younger children waving. There was no sign of Lizzie. It wouldn't surprise Millie if she'd stayed on in Port Augusta to be with Ellen.

"Hello, hello." Esther's voice was loud above the others.

Thomas gave them a brief wave and drove the cart right to the front steps of the house.

Millie hurried towards him. She could tell by the look on his face something was wrong. A hacking cough echoed from the cart and Lizzie's head appeared as she struggled to sit up, one hand clasped to her mouth.

"Lizzie's sick again." Thomas climbed down from the cart and William helped his sisters and brother down from the other side.

"Don't fuss, Thomas." Lizzie's voice was a weak rasp.

Millie went straight to the back of the cart to open the end. Her mother-in-law was prone to coughs and had been laid low several times already this year.

"I wanted her to stay in Port Augusta and go to the doctor but she insisted I bring her home."

"It was too much, all of us in Ellen's house." Lizzie's words were followed by another bout of coughing.

Millie and Thomas helped her to the edge of the cart. Jack came to join them. "Let me carry you inside, Mrs Baker."

He slid his arms beneath her before she could protest. Millie hated to see Lizzie in his arms but Thomas looked exhausted and Jack was a strong man.

"I'll take care of the horses, Grandpa." William took the reins and once everyone was clear led the horses and cart away.

Millie hugged the younger children. Violet seemed to have filled out since they'd been away. She was eleven and such a sensible, helpful girl.

"There are pikelets on a plate in the kitchen." Millie smiled at the three young faces looking at her with such trust. She had grown to love Joseph's children as if they were her own. She knew they felt the same way about her. "Violet, can you get some for everyone while I help your grandmother?" Millie gave the young girl's shoulder a quick squeeze then led the way up the steps and into the front bedroom where Jack had laid Lizzie carefully on the bed.

"Thank you, Jack." Lizzie smiled briefly.

"I came over to see how everyone was." Jack patted Lizzie's hand. "It must be difficult with your son away."

"You're very kind, Jack."

Millie clenched her teeth together. Now that she observed him through clearer eyes she could see how easily he charmed people.

"Thank you for your help." Millie propelled him firmly to the door and he let her, encasing her hand, clasping her elbow with his. Once more he gave her a bold grin. She pulled her arm away and shut the door firmly between them. Lizzie's terrible cough drew Millie's attention and she immediately dismissed Jack Aldridge from her thoughts as she rushed to her mother-in-law's side.

Millie couldn't help but be concerned at the dark shadows under Lizzie's eyes and the sheen of perspiration on her pale forehead.

"How long have you been like this?"

Lizzie flapped a hand. "Several days." Her hand flopped back to the bed as if even that had been too hard. She tried to smile. "Now that I'm home I'll be better in two shakes of a lamb's—" Once more the coughing brought a pained expression to her face.

Millie didn't like the sound of her cough. She thought about some of the remedies she had learned in her childhood. The smoking leaves had assisted Lizzie in the past but she might need something more this time. Millie smiled to herself. If only her father knew. Yardu had badly wanted her to know her own culture better. He thought she was completely alienated from it but there was still so much she remembered and understood about her native upbringing.

Thomas came into the room and sat on the other side of the bed. He took Lizzie's hand and kissed it. Millie's heart melted at the love and concern that mingled in his look.

"You're home now, my dear Lizzie. Rest and get better."

"I will, Thomas." Lizzie's eyes closed. A smile played on her lips.

Millie took a step back. "I'm going to make some special medicine."

Lizzie groaned but she didn't open her eyes. "Not that foul-smelling leaf again."

"You said it helped last time." Thomas patted her hand then looked up at Millie. "Jack is waiting in the front room. He wanted to say goodbye."

Millie pressed her fingers into her palms. She'd forgotten about Jack. "I won't be long." Millie would send Jack on his way and set off to collect the leaves and branches she needed for her smoke and medicine. "Perhaps Mother Baker should get out of those clothes and under the covers."

Lizzie groaned again.

"Millie's right." Thomas slid an arm under Lizzie to sit her up. "I'll help you."

Millie watched as Lizzie's grey face creased in pain. The older woman looked so thin in her husband's arms. Lizzie had had coughs before but this time she appeared much worse. Thomas looked so worried. If only Joseph was here. Millie felt the burden of his family's dependence on her. She longed for his touch, for the gaze of love like she'd just witnessed between Lizzie and Thomas.

She took a deep breath, let herself out of the bedroom and closed the door softly. To her annoyance Jack sat in Joseph's comfortable chair as casually as if he belonged in it. He was playing knuckles with Robert and Esther.

Millie moved to the middle of the room and steeled herself. "Thank you for your assistance, Mr Aldridge, but we all have jobs to do now. Robert, you must bring me in some more wood and Esther, you can help Violet unpack the trunk." She was aware she sounded abrupt but she didn't care. There was much to do and she wanted to be rid of the man who made her feel so uneasy.

Esther opened her mouth to complain. Millie clapped her hands.

"Now children, quickly. Your grandmother is unwell and we all need to do our bit to help her get better." Millie surprised herself by her sharp tone. She rarely spoke that way to anyone let alone the little ones.

"Goodbye, Mr Aldridge." Dear little Robert was quick to do as she bid but Esther gave her a sulky look before turning on her heel and marching from the room.

Jack unfurled himself from the chair but stayed where he was, studying her with his brash gaze. "Are you sure there's nothing more I can do to help?"

"No."

He took a step towards her.

"Good day, Mr Aldridge." Millie crossed the room to the kitchen door and turned back. He still watched her then he gave a smirk and a nod, collected his hat and left by the front door. Millie stared at the back of the wooden door he'd closed behind him. From the bedroom the sound of coughing reminded her she had work to do. Once more she dismissed Jack Aldridge from her mind and set off in search of the leaves she needed to boil for Lizzie's medicine.

Forty-one

Henry strode through the Smith's Ridge house, opening doors and peering into corners. Jack's bedding was pulled up and the rest of the place was relatively tidy even though covered in dust. Jack was obviously still managing without a housekeeper. With only a small amount of furniture and a couple of cupboards there were few places for Henry to examine in search of anything that might give him some leverage over Jack. It rankled that after all this time he could still find no chink in his half-brother's facade that would give some insight into the man.

Henry shut the bedroom door and went back to the kitchen. He poked at the fire. It was stone cold. Jack must have been gone a while. Perhaps to see Brand who lived in the hilly country at the back of Smith's Ridge with their remaining stock.

Jack seemed to think they were in relatively good condition. Henry wondered how much he would get for those last few sheep. His finances were stretched in every direction and he had made up his mind to quit Smith's Ridge. The last person he wanted to take it over was Jack but as no way had shown itself to be rid of his half-brother, Henry had little choice.

Now that he was an elected councillor on the newly formed Hawker District Council his good name and reputation were paramount. Jack was a liability whom Henry needed to distance himself from but with great care. Henry had been so sure he'd find a way to rid himself of Jack but no plan had shown itself and Jack had settled well to life at Smith's Ridge.

There was a small pile of kindling in the wood box by the fireplace. Henry set a new fire and struck a match, watching until the larger sticks caught. He set the kettle over it and he went out to begin unloading the supplies he'd brought with him.

Outside the April day was warm in spite of the large clouds that blotted out the sun and gave the day a grey appearance. After the first two trips he took off his jacket and hung it on the hook in the kitchen before going back for the next load. Damn Jack's absence. Henry would very much like to leave the supplies and go again but he needed to have a talk with Jack so he would have to await his return.

Henry stacked everything just inside the back door. Jack could put it away. Finally the wagon was unloaded and Henry sat at the large table with a mug of tea and a slice of Flora's egg-and-bacon pie. The delectable Flora had made an extra one for his journey.

Her wage was another drain on his dwindling finances but he couldn't be without Flora to take to bed when Catherine was always so lacking interest in that department. His wife was in Adelaide having a holiday with her family. She had recently lost another baby, the fourth since Charles. Catherine was so fragile these days he wondered how she'd managed to produce their strapping, healthy son, who at six years of age was the image of Henry.

He was so proud of his son. Charles was a quick learner and already showing a keen interest in the business. He hadn't wanted to go with his mother to Adelaide but Henry had insisted. He was happy for his son to learn the more genteel manners and sensibilities his wife's family could offer and he knew Harriet would be pleased to see her grandson.

The sun came out from behind the clouds, lighting the gloomy day. Henry looked past the ragged curtains through the windows that hadn't been cleaned in some time. It was nothing in comparison to the home he'd built in Hawker but this house had seemed much grander when he'd taken over the property. Word was that the arrogant Joseph Baker had fallen on such hard times he'd left his family at Wildu Creek in search of gold, and hadn't returned.

Henry thought those who chased silver and gold were often fools with little to show for their efforts but the increased traffic through Hawker had been of benefit to his shop. Hawker continued to go ahead in spite of the poor seasons and the lack of rain. The governor had finally allowed them to form a council and Henry was proud to be one of those appointed.

Now that he was a councillor they would have to do more entertaining, another reason he needed Flora Nixon's services. Catherine would never cope alone with cooking dinner for a large party.

He took another mouthful of the pie and glanced at a newspaper open on the table. It was an old copy of the *Port Augusta Dispatch* where there were several reports regarding the business of the new Hawker District Council, the names of the councillors including his, and reports of their latest meeting. Henry cast a look over it while he ate. He had hoped to keep his new position from Jack but there was no chance of that.

Once more he glanced out the window and this time he saw a rider heading towards the house. The horse and man were idling along in no great hurry. It was Jack. Henry stood and peered closer as the horse went past the front of the house. Jack was well dressed for someone who should be out working.

Henry collected his plate and mug and carried them back to the kitchen and let himself out the back door. Jack had stopped his horse beside Henry's cart and turned when he heard the door.

"Well, well, well, a visitor." Jack slid from his horse and tethered it near the gate. "What brings you all the way to Smith's Ridge, dear brother?"

Henry winced at the words but reassured himself there was no-one out here to hear them. "Supplies." He jerked his thumb over his shoulder. "I've been waiting a while so I've unloaded them." He took in Jack's good white shirt under a chocolate-brown jacket and his clean moleskin trousers. "Where have you been?"

Jack was approaching him along the stony path. "Keeping busy." He gave Henry a laconic smile and walked past him to the door. "I hope you've got something good to eat amongst those supplies."

"I think you'll be pleased." Henry followed Jack inside. While he looked like a man who'd been in the saddle a while he didn't look like a man who'd been working. "How are the remaining sheep?"

"As well as can be expected, I assume." Jack lathered his hands with soap then splashed water on his face and patted it dry with a cloth. "I haven't been to see Brand for a few weeks. Now that you've come I can go and check on him and take him some supplies."

Henry watched Jack sweep his thick black hair back from his forehead. He was a good-looking man in spite of his dark skin. It was a wonder he had no woman of his own. Still that was the last thing Henry needed to worry about. There were more pressing concerns.

"I think we should sell the remaining sheep. Destock the place completely until it rains."

Jack glared at him. "That would be short-sighted. Brand is camped near permanent water. He's keeping some breeding stock alive."

"You said you hadn't seen him for weeks."

"That's because I have to maintain the rest of the property alone. There are fences and buildings that need work and even though we have no stock on the lower country there are still native animals that get caught in fences or in the mud at the last of the waterholes. Brand does his job and I do mine."

"You look very clean for someone who's been doing all that."

Jack tossed the cloth aside and stared hard at Henry. "What's brought this on? It's my job to manage Smith's Ridge and I've been doing it."

"Well, I can't afford you any longer. If you want to keep Smith's Ridge you'll have to take over the lease and Brand's wage."

Jack's hand flashed out and grabbed Henry by the throat before he had the chance to back away. Jack shoved him hard against the warm tin of the back wall and pinned him there. Henry panicked at the tight grip around his throat and pushed at Jack but he had little effect.

Jack leaned in. Henry could smell his sweat and the odour of horse.

"You have to afford me." Jack pressed him harder. "Unless of course you want your friends at Hawker to know that Councillor Wiltshire has a brother with black blood."

Henry tried to suck in a breath through his nose. Jack's grip on his throat was like a vice. His brother glared at him, his dark eyes glittering with malice.

"I heard about your fancy dinner celebration." Jack pulled a sad face. "No invitation for me."

Jack's grip tightened. Henry put a hand up and pushed against the toffee-coloured face only inches from his.

"Sell off one of your other properties or dismiss one of your employees, whatever it takes." Jack hissed. "We're in this together for the time being – brother." Then as quickly as he'd grasped Henry, he let him go.

Henry sagged against the wall sucking in deep breaths of air. He heard Jack walk away, the sound of the kitchen fire opening, the scrape of a plate. Henry put tentative fingers to his neck. No doubt there would be bruises by tomorrow. He heard Jack's boots echo across the wooden floor in the direction of the front room. Henry stuck his head into the kitchen. The room was empty. He retrieved his coat and made for his cart. Physically he wasn't a match for Jack but he now knew what he had to do. He had to find someone who could discreetly rid him of Jack Aldridge – permanently.

Jack watched Henry leave from the front-room window where he sat with his egg-and-bacon pie. He had wanted to laugh in Henry's face, humiliate him like Jack had been humiliated over the years, but he sensed a deep resentment in his brother, one that it was best not to stir too hard for the moment. Jack still relied on Henry for money. He was close to being able to take over Smith's Ridge completely but he would milk every last penny out of Henry first. Once Smith's Ridge was his he didn't care what happened to his brother other than he would experience disgrace, Jack would make sure of that. And Harriet, such an arrogant woman, she'd pay the price for looking down her nose at Jack Aldridge.

He shovelled a large piece of pie into his mouth. It was damn good and reminded him of more pressing issues. He needed a woman, not just to warm his bed but one who could cook and clean. There was a woman in Hawker he visited a few times who'd been happy for a romp but she wasn't a suitable wife.

Of course he had harboured a hope that the delectable Millie might be a dalliance while her husband was away. Wildu

Creek was closer than Hawker and there was something about a black woman dressed as a white that excited his senses. He was a man trapped between two worlds. He loved the black skin of his mother's people but wanted the more comfortable life his father's people led. Millie was living that life and he found her enticing. She had always welcomed him with a ready smile and a warm laugh but something had changed this last visit. When he'd found out she was all but alone at Wildu Creek he'd seized the chance. He was so sure she would have come readily into his arms. It was something to do with the boy.

William was a smart-mouthed pup, arrogant like his father. There had been no dingo, Jack was sure of that. William had fired a warning shot, clear and simple. The boy was protecting Millie. It had been laughable. Jack could easily have disarmed him, turned the gun on William, but he knew that would have been the end of his chance with Millie. He had sensed her fear and it had aroused him. He had been so sure he could have charmed her to come to him willingly. While they had been sipping tea he had been working on a way of getting William away so that he could take Millie, make her his, but the rest of the blasted family had turned up.

Jack sat back, his belly full for the first time in several days. It was all very well to have a neighbour who was a useful dalliance but he needed a wife, one with white skin who would bring him respectability. So far he'd found no-one suitable in Hawker. Somehow he'd have to look further afield.

Jack drained his mug and pushed back from the table. He had to pack up some supplies to take to Brand. The man was like a hermit, happily living in his tent in the hills. He had little intelligence but was very good with animals and knew how to take care of the sheep. That was all that mattered to Jack.

Forty-two

Joseph drank in his first view of Wildu Creek. Exhaustion from riding for days, only resting in the darkest hours and swapping between his two horses, was replaced by the brief exhilaration of seeing his home for the first time in eighteen months. The rays of the morning sun were turning the ridges beyond the buildings pink. The huge gums that dotted the creek were alive with the chatter of birds but not a breath of air disturbed their leaves. The houses and sheds were still in shadow but showing signs of life with puffs of smoke emanating from the chimneys.

He shifted his aching bones in the saddle and let the horse take the lead. Both man and horse were happy to be home, but only Joseph carried the lump of regret and worry inside. His mother was gravely ill. He only hoped in the several days since he'd received that telegram that perhaps she'd turned a corner and was on the road to recovery.

Hegarty had come across him slumped over his table with the telegram crumpled in his hand.

"Praying again, mate," Hegarty had joked but he'd galvanised into action as soon as he realised Joseph's distress. He'd helped

Joseph pack his horses, Peterson had prepared food for the journey and they'd both promised to watch his lease.

Now finally, he was here, home. Joseph turned the horse up the slope towards the back of his parents' house, just as a figure reached the gate from the other direction. His heart leapt as she lifted her head and recognition lit up the face of his beloved Millie. He slithered from his horse as she put down the bucket she had been carrying and raced to his arms.

"Joseph." Her face was pressed to his chest and her arms encircled him. "You're home."

He pressed his lips to the top of her head and felt dizzy with the sweet smell of her and the soft feel of her body against his.

She lifted her head and he kissed her, softly and then more urgently. How he'd missed her. Finally they pulled apart and he held her at arm's length.

"How's Mother?"

"I'm sorry." Tears pooled in her big brown eyes.

Joseph shook his head. "She's … she can't …"

"She's gone, Joseph." Millie reached a hand up and laid it gently on his cheek. "We all did our best to save her. Even Dr Bruehl came from Hawker but there was nothing we could do. He said it was pneumonia."

"But Mother was so strong."

"Her chest was weak. She succumbed to coughs easily and this last one was too much for her. She tried so hard to fight it. We sent the telegram to you and Ellen when we realised how sick she was. Ellen made it here before she died but only just. She went quickly in the end."

Joseph let himself slump against Millie, drawing from her strength. On the long, lonely journey home he hadn't dared think his mother wouldn't be here when he returned but she was gone. The dear woman who had loved him, made him laugh when all seemed dark, cared for his children when Clara died and welcomed his new wife with open arms had left them.

"It's been so warm and we weren't sure when you would return. We couldn't wait for you to hold the funeral."

Joseph felt Millie's tears through his shirt. He had to be strong for her, for his children, for all of them.

"How is Father?"

"We've hardly seen him since the funeral." Millie turned to look towards the ridge behind the house. "He spends nearly all day sitting up there by her grave. Sometimes one of us sits with him. Esther's the only one who can get him to come back to the house. I've been trying to coax him to eat but he's hardly had any food since your mother took sick. Ellen was a big help but she went home yesterday." Millie hugged him again. "I'm so glad you're here, Joseph. You of all people understand his grief the most."

Joseph swallowed the lump in his throat. His union with Clara had been much shorter than his father and mother's long happy marriage but he knew exactly how his father would be feeling. Joseph had been consumed by the same overwhelming sadness when Clara had died. It had been Thomas who had helped him then, now it was Joseph's turn to offer kindness and strength to a broken heart.

"He'll be up there now. I saw him go past when I was milking the cow."

Millie looked up at Joseph with such compassion it was nearly his undoing. He pulled her close and took comfort from the hug she gave him in return.

"I should go and see him."

"Come inside first. Let me make you some food." Once more she reached a gentle hand to his face and brushed his cheek with her fingers. "You look so tired. Thomas won't be going anywhere and the children need to see you. There're also some decisions to be made about stock. Timothy will appreciate your help. Thomas has no interest now."

Millie took his hand and walked beside him with the horses following behind.

"I'll see to the horses and come inside."

"I'll boil some water so you can wash and bring you some fresh clothes."

Joseph managed a grin. "I guess I don't smell so good."

"A wash will make you feel and look better."

Joseph bent and kissed her. "Such a diplomatic answer, my love."

He was pleased to see her beautiful smile open up her face.

"We don't want to frighten the children." Millie turned on her heel, picked up the bucket of milk and hurried through the gate.

Joseph found himself grinning. In spite of the sad reason for his return it was good to be home. He took the horses to the yard, removed the saddle and his bags and made sure they had plenty to eat and drink. He slung the bags over his shoulder. One had the little bottle of gold chips he'd been accumulating since Hegarty's arrival. He'd had no chance to exchange the gold for cash, not that he was ready to yet. They had just found a very promising vein of gold running along their adjoining leases. Joseph had to go back before too long. He wouldn't think about it now. Hegarty had told him to take his time and Joseph trusted his friend, as much as you could trust anyone in a goldfield.

His quick gaze across the land behind the house brought him up sharp. The new house that he'd left with little more than a few layers of rock up the walls had grown to take on the shape of a real house. It was grand in stature just like he'd imagined it and was ready to receive windows he hadn't been able to afford. He could see retaining walls against the side of the hill, which had been almost non-existent when he left, and the entrance to the cellar had been dug out.

"I hope you like it, Father."

Joseph spun to take in his oldest son. He was much taller, more solid and with no trace of his boyish looks. Joseph struggled to remember the date. William would be fourteen now.

Joseph took a couple of steps to his son and wrapped him in his arms. William gave him a faint pat on the back in return. Joseph let him go. He was a young man, no doubt too old for hugs now. He looked back at the growing house.

"It's certainly coming along well. Your doing I suppose?"

Joseph saw the flicker of a smile and the look of pride on William's face as he moved towards the construction.

"I wanted to do something to help."

Joseph followed his son and gripped his shoulder. "Millie's letters have told me many of the things you've helped with but she didn't mention this."

"I asked her not to."

Joseph looked again at the house taking shape in front of him. The gold he was finding would enable them to finish it off and buy more stock if it ever rained. "It's a wonderful surprise."

"Father."

Joseph looked down at his son's serious face. Up close he could see dark shadows under the boy's eyes.

"I'm sorry about Grandmother."

"Me too." Once more Joseph squeezed William's shoulder, then before the tears could overflow in his own eyes Joseph pulled William into a quick hug. Once more the boy was stiff in his arms. Joseph held him a moment then let him go.

"It's good to see you Father." William's nose wrinkled. "But you smell rather bad."

Joseph grinned. "Do I now? I seem to remember a young boy who didn't like washing much at all."

William stood tall. "We have to share the water for a bath but at least we wash once a week."

"I think Millie is boiling me some water now."

They fell into step and walked towards the house.

"Have you seen Grandfather?"

"Not yet."

"He's probably up the hill by now."

"Millie said he was."

"We're all sad, Father, but …" William stopped at the gate. "Well, it's like you were when Mother died but much worse. He doesn't even hear us when we talk to him."

"Grief can devastate a man, son. We all bear the unbearable in different ways. Grandfather will be all right. He needs time and care."

There was a cry from behind them. Joseph turned to see his three younger children running towards him from the direction of the hut. Like William they'd grown taller and Robert more nuggety. He was nearly knocked over as they all launched themselves at him. There was babble of voices, hugs and kisses and finally Esther's voice above the rest.

"Phew, Father, you smell."

Joseph scooped her into his arms and they made a ruckus all the way to the back door where Millie was waiting.

"There's a consensus, my love," he called above the noise. "I smell."

William sat at the table at his father's right hand. In Joseph's absence William had taken to sitting at the end of the table opposite his grandfather but this morning Thomas was already up the hill keeping vigil with Grandmother, who would no longer be taking her place at the family table.

William had often wished they'd been able to bring the big table from Smith's Ridge. It was a squeeze to fit them all in around the smaller table at Wildu Creek but with Joseph away and now Grandmother gone and Grandfather hardly eating, there were less of them to fit.

He listened as Esther and Robert plied their father with questions. Like him, Violet didn't say much. She had been very close to her grandmother and had hardly stopped crying for days after her death. Now Violet's face was pale and her eyes red but there were no tears. She'd told William only last night she had none left.

"Have you found lots of gold, Father?" Robert asked the question William had longed to ask but hadn't felt able to.

Joseph put down the spoon he'd been using to eat his porridge. He gripped his hands in front of him as if he was going to say his prayers and looked at each of them in turn.

"I know I've been gone a long time and I'm very sorry."

"Is it fun at the goldfields?" Esther bounced up and down on her seat. "Is there lots of gold?"

"No, not lots, but there are many men trying to search for it."

Joseph reached into the pocket of the clean shirt Millie had found for him and pulled out a small glass bottle. He handed it to William.

William held the top in his fingers and peered closely. There were tiny chips of rock and grains that sparkled in the light now streaming through the window.

"Where are the big rocks?" Robert's face creased in a frown.

"I haven't found any nuggets." Joseph grimaced. "I had to sort a lot of dirt and rocks to find this much."

"Let me see." Esther leaned forward.

Joseph put out a restraining arm to stop her climbing right onto the table. "William will pass it around."

"It doesn't seem very much, Father." William couldn't help but feel disappointed. Like Robert he had imagined large rocks of glittering gold, or at least a pouch full. The little bottle didn't seem much for his father to bring home after all this time away.

"Are you staying here with us now?" This time it was Esther who asked the question they all wanted to know the answer to.

William saw the concerned look his father gave Millie and his heart sank.

"I will stay home for a while." Joseph looked at each of the children and his gaze stopped at William. "I have to go back."

The other children groaned and cried out, even Violet. Millie put an arm around her shoulders and cuddled her close.

Joseph reached out a hand to Esther who was sitting on his other side. "I know it's been a difficult time for you all but I need you to continue to be strong. I'm working with friends and they are minding my lease." He directed his words to Millie who studied him gravely. "Just before I left we found a vein of rock with some larger chips of gold in it. If I find some more like that we will have enough money to help us get back on our feet once the drought is over."

"Will it ever be over, Father?" Violet's eyes were round with worry.

"Of course, sweetheart."

William wondered at his father's reply. They had had little rain for so long he found it hard to remember a time when water flowed freely in Wildu Creek and there was thick grass and thousands of sheep.

"We will have money to finish the new house." Joseph smiled at Millie.

Her lips turned up but William could see it was not her usual smile that made her eyes sparkle.

"Why do we need a new house, Father?" Esther put her elbows on the table and rested her chin in her hands.

"It will be a place of our own. A special house just for us."

"But Grandfather would be all alone." Violet's eyes remained dry but her chin wobbled.

"Perhaps he'd like to live in the new house," Joseph said. "There will be lots of room."

"We don't need to worry for now." Millie let Violet go and gave her back a gentle rub. "It will take a long time to finish the house. Your grandfather might feel much better by then."

"Shall I go and fetch him for breakfast?" Esther jumped to her feet, bumping the table.

"No." Joseph stood and lifted his filthy old hat from the back of his chair. "I will go." He gripped Millie's hand and the look between them was full of love. William was relieved. He'd wondered with his father being away so long if he might have somehow forgotten about Millie. William had seen how that Jack Aldridge came calling more and more often and how he tried to be alone with Millie. They hadn't spoken about it but she'd been worried last time. William knew if he'd gone with Uncle Timothy to inspect the fences that day she would have been all alone. He should warn his father but what would he say? Jack hadn't really done anything wrong except be neighbourly.

"William." Joseph turned back. "Can you let Timothy know that I'm back? I should talk to him about the state of the property once I've spoken with my father. I expect you will be there too, son."

A sense of pride swept through William. "Yes, Father."

Forty-three

Thomas sat perfectly still. He didn't see the contrasting colours of the vivid green bush sprouting from the red and brown of the rocks that spread down the ridge and onto the plain. The tall gums that followed the meandering trail of Wildu Creek were a stark contrast to the faded colours of dry grass and dirt on the plain, but his gaze was on the freshly turned earth with its covering of rocks.

With the sun now higher in the sky the birds were not so noisy although two young magpies hopped back and forth, their beaks spearing the ground for some delicious morsel. One hopped close, tipped its head and looked his way with one bright eye. Thomas smiled. The black-and-white birds had been amongst his first friends all those years ago when he'd come to the country alone after arriving in Adelaide as a green young Englishman.

There was a soft rustle of movement in a bush nearby and the chirrups of the grasshoppers that were in plague proportions on the plains, but apart from that it was only him on the hill with his girls. In his hand he held a bunch of wattle sprigs. Lizzie had always favoured the small, round yellow flowers. She rarely had them in the house, their perfume was so strong, but they reminded her of their wedding. Each year she picked some and asked Thomas to dance with her to mark their anniversary.

He shook his head. That had been almost forty years ago.

"Where did the time go Lizzie?" he murmured. "So much has happened since you made me the happiest man alive by becoming my wife and now you've left me."

He glanced at the rough pine cross he'd made years ago, now painted white with his firstborn's name, Annie, carved into it. Then there was another little grave for the baby girl who had come too early and they hadn't named. They'd lost two little girls and now, lying in the earth beside them, was their mother.

The ache that burned constantly inside his chest since his wife had become gravely ill gnawed deeper as his gaze swept over the fresh grave and came to rest on the cross. *Lizzie Baker* had been painted neatly in black letters by Violet who was so clever with fine jobs like that.

Thomas reached out and laid the brightly coloured twigs of wattle at the base of the cross.

"I wasn't ready for you to leave me, my love."

A rock skittered nearby accompanied by a footfall. Thomas looked around to see Joseph climbing the hill towards him. It warmed Thomas's heart to see his son and also that he carried some sprigs of wattle he would have collected on his way up the hill. Thomas smiled at the cross. "Your boy has come home, Lizzie." He stood and waited for their son to arrive.

Joseph came to a stop at the base of the grave. He removed his hat and gripped it tightly in his hands with the wattle, staring at the mound of dirt and rocks as if he could see right through it. He lifted his gaze to his father. Thomas could see the raw grief on his face.

"It's good to see you, son."

"I am so sorry, Father."

Thomas nodded and watched Joseph's mouth twist and his jaw harden as he struggled with his emotions. He waited a moment then took the few short steps between them and opened his arms. The two of them hugged, drawing on each other for strength. Thomas clapped his son's back firmly then stepped back, his hands resting on Joseph's shoulders.

Joseph wiped his eyes with his sleeve. "I wish I was here before … to see her."

"She knew you were coming but she had grown so weak. It was too hard for her to wait."

Joseph bent and placed the wattle next to the branches already lying there.

"Was there nothing that could be done?"

Thomas returned to the rock beside the graves he used as a seat. "Everyone tried. Millie was wonderful. She hardly left your mother's side and she brewed some native remedies but the disease had already taken a hold. Dr Bruehl said your mother's chest was weak and there was nothing else that could have been done."

"How do you go on, Father?"

Thomas looked at the sorrow etched in his son's face and blocked his own feelings. "That's something I'm grateful to your mother for. When your older sister Annie died I sunk into despair. I wanted Lizzie to go back to her parents while I built up Wildu Creek but she would have none of it. She said we had to keep going or we were dishonouring Annie. We had to work for the children and grandchildren we hadn't had yet. Now look at our family." Thomas turned his eyes to the vista in front of him. "When we buried Annie your mother made me look at this." He swept his arm out in a wide arc. "Look up, Thomas, she said. And I cast my gaze across the land. You must look up too, Joseph. Wildu Creek is our home. Where else would we go, what else would we do?"

Thomas watched his son take in the view that was partly obscured by trees but allowed glimpses of the valley and plains below, the tree-lined creek and the distant mountains. Then Joseph's lips turned up in a grin.

"Remember when I thought Wildu Creek was the name you'd made up –'will do'? I thought you'd meant this will do."

"*Wildu* is eagle in Gulda's language but 'this will do' is correct as well. Where else would we live, Joseph? This is our home."

Joseph sucked in a deep breath and found himself a place to sit on the other side of Lizzie's grave. He pushed his hat back on his head, if you could still call it a hat. It was dark with grime and had several holes in the crown.

"You've lost weight, Joseph. How has it been at the goldfields?"

"I am managing."

"You've been away a long time."

"I had planned to come home earlier."

"It must have been worth staying." Thomas was careful with his words. He could tell Joseph was burdened by guilt at not being home with his family.

Joseph glanced at Lizzie's cross again.

Thomas gave him an encouraging smile. "Your mother would want to hear all about it. You know what she was like." He could see her in his mind's eye. Sitting Joseph down to a big meal and firing several questions at a time, barely waiting for the answers before she asked more.

Joseph rested his hands on his knees. "It's been hell."

Thomas frowned. "But your letters? Millie read them to us. They were full of hope."

"If I'd written the truth Millie and mother would have come and demanded I return home."

Thomas raised his eyebrows and nodded. "So why didn't you come back? You know we would have welcomed you with open arms."

"I know but I have actually been finding gold. It's the conditions and the life I don't enjoy."

"You're used to hardship. We don't exactly live a high life here."

Joseph dug the heel of his boot into the dry ground. "Wildu Creek is a kingdom in comparison to life at Teetulpa."

"So you're not going back? Millie and the children will be—"

"I have to go back."

Once more Thomas raised his eyebrows.

"I did something stupid, Father." Joseph kept worrying at the hole with his heel. "I had some gold and I lost it."

Thomas didn't speak. Instead he allowed his son time. It was never easy to admit your mistakes.

Joseph looked up. "There are men from all walks of life on the goldfields. I found a group that were like me, all from the land, good men but desperate for gold to save their properties. We would meet up most nights and have a few drinks around one of the campfires." Joseph shook his head slowly. "There's little else to do. I had found some gold before last Christmas and had planned to come home with gifts and money lining my pockets. One night I was feeling sorry for myself. I missed you all, I longed for Millie and I drank too much. Someone knocked me out and stole my gold."

Thomas kept his eyes on the bright gold balls of wattle. *Do you hear that Lizzie? You were always worried about Joseph's drinking.*

"I had to stay then." Joseph went on, relief in his voice as if he'd wanted to tell someone. "I had to find more gold. I couldn't come home empty-handed."

Strong-willed like you too, Lizzie. Thomas maintained the conversation with his dead wife in his head but remained outwardly silent.

"A man I met when I first travelled to Teetulpa has come back and staked his claim beside mine. He's found gold before and he thinks we have a good vein running through our claims. It was just starting to show some promise when I got the telegram about ..." Joseph glanced at the grave. "About Mother."

Thomas waited until the silence had stretched out between them before he spoke. "You must do what you think is best, Joseph. Your family are safe here and I appreciate their looking after me." Thomas leaned forward and waited until Joseph lifted his gaze to meet his. "I was deceived by Henry Wiltshire's father when I first came to South Australia and I let it eat away at me but your mother was so wise. We mustn't look back, she said. She was so brave."

A frown crossed Joseph's brow. "You're the bravest man I know, Father. Look at all that's happened and all that you've achieved."

Once more the pain deepened in Thomas's chest and tears that he'd thought had all been shed brimmed in his eyes. His gaze swept Lizzie's grave. "She made me brave." Thomas gasped as the sadness threatened to engulf him again like it had on the first days after Lizzie's death. He had to be strong, for his family, for Lizzie's memory.

Hands gripped his shoulders. Joseph had come to stand behind him. His son understood the pain of losing the person you loved more than life itself.

"She will always be with us, Father, making us laugh, making us behave and making us brave."

Thomas reached up a hand and gripped that of his son. He nodded, a quick stiff movement of his head and focused on the wattle. *He's a good man our son, dear Lizzie, a good man.*

Joseph made his way back down the hill alone. His father said he would be back later. Joseph allowed him his time. He knew how it felt to lose the love of his life. The pain of Clara's loss had faded. He was so lucky to have Millie but he also had the beautiful children Clara had borne. She would always live on in them and the happy memories they'd shared.

William and Timothy were waiting for him when he got back to the house.

Timothy shook his hand. "I'm so sorry for your loss."

"She was special to all of us."

Timothy nodded. "That she was."

They went inside, where Millie had set out fresh mugs of tea. Joseph's eyes widened at the sight of a cake adorning the middle of the table. In spite of the big breakfast he'd not long finished, his mouth watered. He kissed the top of Millie's head and squeezed her hand as she passed him ushering the younger children out. How he longed to be alone with her but there were other priorities that needed his attention.

Joseph sat himself at the table and cut a slice of the cake. The delicious lemon flavour was enough to make him want to shovel the whole piece into his mouth at once but he returned the rest of it to his plate and looked from William to Timothy.

"How are things here?"

"Not good. Binda has less than three hundred sheep in the hills."

Joseph swallowed his mouthful of cake. "Any of them my breeding stock?"

"A few but it makes no difference now, we've had to let them wander. Jundala and Joe are with Binda and I spend as much time as I can there but it's hard to keep the wild dogs from taking what they will. There's little left for the sheep to eat, they're competing with rabbits now."

"I should have come back sooner."

"Only if you had the power to bring rain with you. We've enough bodies to maintain the property. William is a hard worker along with my boy but hard work doesn't change the weather." Timothy clasped his hands around his mug and looked steadily at Joseph. "I'm sorry to say it when we've had such sadness but I can't see how the last of the stock will survive the summer."

Joseph sat back in his chair, the cake forgotten. He had hoped things wouldn't be so bad here even though he'd seen for himself the devastation on the plains as he'd returned home.

"We've still got sheep agisted." William's serious voice cut through his thoughts.

"Yes, of course." Joseph couldn't believe he'd forgotten them. "We sent a thousand head south before I went to Teetulpa."

"We've no money to pay for that agistment." Timothy's expression was grim.

"Yes we do." Joseph reached into his pocket and showed Timothy his bottle of gold.

Timothy nodded. "If that means money it would be most welcome."

"When was the last time you were paid?"

"I'm not worried about that. We are surviving here and I'm grateful to have a place to live and something to do."

Joseph stood and walked to the window. Outside the August sky was clear except for some high wispy cloud. "The rain has to come eventually."

"Always the optimist, just like your mother."

They all looked around at the sound of Thomas's voice.

He studied them all a moment then gave a short nod. "All we have to do is hang on." He came to the table and sat.

William poured another mug of tea and Millie appeared with some damper and cheese.

Joseph felt a lump rise in his throat. He was so grateful to his family for their care of his father. He owed it to them to find more gold and make their life easier while they waited for the rain. He had to go back to Teetulpa.

Forty-four

Jack slammed the door of the hotel hard against the wall. Several pairs of eyes watched him but he had enough drink in him not to care. The devil of a publican had refused him any more drink, said he was upsetting patrons. Curse the man, he'd pay for asking Jack to leave.

Outside the early evening light and the dust that hung in the air gave Hawker an ethereal look. It was late November and the sprinkle of rain they'd had earlier that month had had little effect on the dry conditions.

Jack spat into the dirt and hung onto a verandah post willing his eyes to focus. He'd drunk far more than he'd intended, all because of a whore. The lusty young woman who'd been a willing companion on his visits to town had left. He'd arrived midmorning ready to spend the day in bed with her. The frustration and disappointment had gone with him to the hotel where he'd found himself a corner and drunk the day away.

He let go of the post and stood on the edge of wooden verandah. He wobbled forward, stepped carefully off into the dirt of the road and turned left. He would have to find himself a place for the night. Several people gave him a wide berth. Jack glared at them. Light shone from a shop window where a group of people were saying goodnight. The next shop was in darkness, a thin young man standing on its verandah looked up and down the street. Jack recognised Henry's assistant and then realised it was Henry's shop he was approaching.

Henry lived a fine life in town while Jack slaved out in the hills. He could find Jack a comfortable bed for the night. Councillor Wiltshire was a man of the town these days, perhaps he even had a woman tucked away who'd be an obliging bed companion.

Jack straightened his jacket, pressed his hat low on his head and approached the assistant who was turning back to the door.

"I've come to see, Mr Wiltshire."

The young man turned his quick gaze on Jack who planted his feet slightly apart to stop the swaying.

"Did you have an appointment, Mr …?"

"I don't need an appointment to see my … Mr Wiltshire and I are very close."

"I'm sorry, sir." The man's look seemed genuinely concerned. "Mr Wiltshire is out of town. We don't expect him back for several days."

Jack clenched his fingers into his palms. Damn, he was to be thwarted at every turn.

"Perhaps Mrs Wiltshire can help. She's just left for the day but she will be back in the shop tomorrow."

A vision of Catherine's sweet smile sent the blood pounding through Jack. Henry's wife was a pretty thing with plump breasts. He'd always been able to charm women to do his bidding, maybe with Henry away … He shook his head, a bad move. He reached out for the horse rail as everything spun.

"Are you all right, sir?"

The assistant took a step towards him. Jack pushed out one palm to stop the man.

"I have been unwell. Thank you for your concern. I shall visit Mr Wiltshire when next I am in Hawker."

Jack turned and walked back past the shop that still had lights on and the sound of someone whistling from within. He kept going until there was a gap between buildings then he turned into it. He paused a moment then followed the alley to the lane at the back of the shops. The early evening light was failing fast and the air behind the shops particularly foul. He strode along the lane, watching where he put his feet, and turned up the road that led to Henry's house. On the corner, hanging over a fence, was the scrawny bough of a young lemon tree. He pulled off a leaf and chewed until the bitter taste filled his mouth then he spat it out.

He hurried on, only slowing when he saw a figure walking ahead of him, a woman. From her outline he guessed it was Catherine and she was carrying what appeared to be a heavy bag. He crossed to the middle of the road and hastened his footsteps to appear as if he had come from another direction.

"Mrs Wiltshire?"

She gasped and almost dropped her bag.

"Please don't be alarmed. It is I, Jack Aldridge." He reached for the bag. "Let me help you with that."

"Oh, Mr Aldridge." There was relief in her voice and she allowed him to take it. "What are you doing here? Don't tell me you've got yourself into trouble with cards again."

Jack swallowed the words he had been going to say. He was surprised by Catherine's almost cheeky response. He responded with his charming smile. "Ahh Mrs Wiltshire, you know what a fool I was. I have been far more careful since." He gave her a small bow and pushed open the creaking front gate. "Tonight I was simply taking in some air."

"Not a good idea tonight." Catherine gave a small giggle. "Your lungs will be full of dust."

"The air is particularly thick. Those farmers on the plains must have little dirt left in their paddocks."

Jack followed Catherine to her front verandah. She wore a soft white shirt that tucked into a navy skirt. The fabric draped and flowed softly around her, a tantalising curtain covering the delights that hid beneath. The house behind her was in darkness. She took out her key and looked back to him. Once more she favoured him with an enchanting smile.

"Thank you, Mr Aldridge. Please leave the potatoes there. I will fetch them in later. My housekeeper must still be away. There was a concert at the school this evening and she was taking the children. I should have gone but I felt rather weary after we closed the shop. It will no doubt go late."

Jack smiled. Everything was falling into place. All he had to do was get himself inside and he was sure he could charm Catherine into his arms.

"I will wait here until you've lit the lamps. It's not right you should be alone."

"Oh, kind Mr Aldridge, thank you. I must admit I do not enjoy this big house by myself."

Jack found it hard to remain still. The woman was practically throwing herself at him. He looked around as she went inside. There were lights glowing at other windows. On this side of the road there was an empty block on one side and a small cottage on the other. No-one stirred in either direction

Once he saw the glow of a lamp at the other end of the long hall he picked up the bag, carried it inside and shut the door firmly behind him. He reached the end of the hall as Catherine came through the door carrying a candle.

"Oh!" Her pretty pink lips made a circle. "You startled me."

"Where would you like these?" Jack lifted the bag of potatoes.

"Oh," she said again. Her cheeks glowed in the soft light. "In the kitchen, thank you. I have just added some kindling to the fire."

She spun on her heel. He followed close behind. She had lit the lamp in here. It was a large room with a solid wooden table at its centre. There was a double fireplace, one side showing the flicker of flames, and a scullery under the side window. Very impressive. His gaze drifted back to Catherine who stood beside the table, the candelabra still clutched in her hand. It was three pronged, full of candles, but she'd only lit one.

Jack put down the bag and stepped closer. "Don't worry about lighting more lamps for me." Jack bent and gently blew out the candle. His face now level with hers, he took in the tiny freckles on her nose and the dark brown of her eyelashes.

Catherine backed away. "Can I offer you a drink, Mr Aldridge? I am in dire need of a cup of tea myself." She moved to the fire where the kettle was beginning to steam.

Jack drew in a breath. She was drawing out the game but that would make it all the more tantalising. "Thank you."

"Please sit down." Catherine took two cups from the cupboard beside the fire and put tea in the teapot.

Jack drew out a chair, watching her every move before he sat.

"Are you hungry? I have some cold potato pie and some slices of mutton."

"That would be most kind. I haven't had time to eat today." Jack thought perhaps food would be a good thing. His head had cleared but his stomach churned with the liquor he'd consumed.

The cup wobbled on the saucer as Catherine placed his tea in front of him. He glanced up but she had already turned away, busy with the food. Jack sat back in his chair. Something had put her on edge. He needed to distract her.

"You have a lovely home."

"Thank you." She placed slices of meat on two plates. "It's very large. I am grateful for my housekeeper." She glanced around. "Mrs Nixon and the children should be home soon."

He raised his eyebrows. "I thought you said they would be late."

"One never knows how long these things will take." She placed a plate of food in front of him. Hers was across the table.

"Shouldn't we eat in the dining room?" Jack felt a sudden flash of annoyance. He was not some servant to be fed in the kitchen. Besides he'd seen their dining room through the window one night and he had a fancy to sit at the grand table.

"If you wish." She took down a wooden tray from its hook on the wall, placed the plates and utensils on it then added the cups of tea.

Jack picked up the tray. Catherine lit the candles, all three this time, and led the way along the passage to the top room. She crossed the room to light the lamp.

"Don't bother with that." He set the tray on the highly polished table. "Candlelight will do well enough."

Catherine came back to the table and set the candelabra close to Jack. He put his plate at the head where he'd seen Henry sit and indicated the chair beside him. She glanced towards the door. Her eyes sparkled in the candlelight, indecision flickering on her face, then she took her place. Catherine was a desirable woman. Jack wondered how well Henry looked after her. There were things Jack had learned about pleasing women he was sure his straitlaced brother wouldn't know about.

He shifted uncomfortably in his seat as he hardened with desire. If only Henry could see him now. Not only was Jack sitting at his table with his wife but Jack was going to take that same wife to bed, hopefully Henry's bed. Jack was sure it would be big and soft, perfect for what he planned to do with Henry's wife and there was nothing Henry could do about it. He was full of tough talk but Jack was sure one hint of violence would send his brother cowering away.

"Where do you live, Mr Aldridge?" Catherine's question drew his gaze back to her. She sat perfectly still, her hands in her lap.

"In the hills to the east."

"That's where my husband has property."

"Yes." Jack started on the food. Hunger gnawed in his stomach. "We are close."

"Oh. I didn't realise you knew my husband."

Jack wagged a finger towards her plate. "Please eat, Catherine. I hope you don't mind me using your first name but since we are sharing a meal I would prefer it, and you must call me Jack."

A lock of hair fell forward on her face. He reached across and swept it back gently, his fingers brushing her cheek. Her eyes widened. His fingers trailed down her neck.

Catherine gasped. The sound excited Jack more. Damn the food, he would take her now. He knew how to make her more than gasp, she'd be squirming with delight at his touch.

A thud and a thump sounded from somewhere in the house.

Catherine jerked away from his hand. He could see the terror in her eyes, no doubt at the interruption.

"Mother." A boy's voice called in the distance.

Jack scowled. Damn, it sounded like the blasted housekeeper had returned with Catherine's child.

Catherine stood. "You're most welcome to finish your meal, Mr Aldridge, but I would prefer Mrs Nixon and my son didn't know you were here."

"Mother!" The call was more urgent now.

She crossed to the door. "I will meet them in the kitchen. I expect you will be gone soon. Good night, Mr Aldridge."

Open-mouthed, Jack watched as she left, shutting the door behind her.

Catherine moved down the hall on shaking legs. She patted her hair with trembling fingers and bit back the sob that threatened to burst from her mouth. Thank the dear Lord for Mrs Nixon's return or who knows what Jack Aldridge might have done next.

"Mother?" Charles appeared, silhouetted in the kitchen door.

"Yes, my darling, I'm coming."

He puffed out his chest. "I was one of the best singers."

"The concert went well then?" Catherine ushered her son back to the kitchen, her mind a whirl of terrified thoughts. What had she been thinking, all alone and letting a stranger into her house?

Flora looked up, the pie Catherine had left out in her hands. "It went very well. The children performed wonderfully. Mr Harry has done a fine job with them."

"You should have been there, Mother." Charles's tone was accusatory.

"I'm sorry, my darling." Catherine ruffled his hair, her fingers still trembling. "I will be next time, I'm sure."

"Have you eaten supper?" Flora cut a piece of pie for Charles.

"Yes. I was tired and hungry when I returned from the shop."

Flora moved closer and patted her arm. "You do look pale. Do you have a headache? Can I get you something?"

Flora's kindness was nearly Catherine's undoing. They'd become such good friends and she badly wanted to tell someone about Jack Aldridge's terrifying visit but Flora would most likely insist they tell Henry. He'd been so touchy of late she didn't want to burden him. She had managed to extricate herself from Jack's clutches and she would never let him in the house again.

A door banged from the front of the house.

Catherine's hand went to her chest. Her heart beat rapidly beneath her shirt.

"What was that?" Flora looked towards the hall.

"The wind must have caught a door."

Flora's gaze locked with Catherine's. She studied her mistress with a puzzled expression then turned back to the bench. They both knew the night was still, not a breath of air moved outside.

Catherine closed her eyes and sent a silent prayer that the bang had been Jack letting himself out the front door. She would be checking the locks on every door and window after Flora went home and tonight she would need a large dose of her regular tonic to calm her nerves and help her sleep.

Forty-five

William shadowed Millie and Eliza along the main street of Hawker. They had made stops at nearly every business except the hotels, and it wouldn't surprise him if they even called in there. For two women with little money to spend they had done a lot of shopping. There were all the usual supplies already stashed in the wagon and several extras. They were all looking forward to his father being home for Christmas.

The road was busy with carts and wagons, several loaded with bales of wool. A herd of emaciated cattle were moving about forlornly in a holding yard near the railway station. The sky was grey with a thin layer of cloud but the sun-bleached earth radiated heat. Everywhere he looked dust was thick in the air.

William watched as a camel train passed heading north. There were twelve camels each loaded with timber, no doubt bound for the silver mine in the north.

"My goodness it's hot." Millie came out of the saddlers shop, yet another brown paper parcel in her hands, closely followed by Eliza. She smiled at William and handed over her package.

"I think it's time for lemonade." Eliza gave William the slightly smaller parcel she carried.

"Good morning, Mrs Baker, Mrs Castles, William."

They smiled and nodded at Dr Bruehl as he lifted his hat and continued on his way. William was grateful to the doctor who always made the effort to make people feel at ease, unlike some of the locals who still looked down their nose at Millie. Both women had passed Mr Wiltshire's shop without so much as a sideways glance. The Bakers never shopped there.

"Can you bring the wagon, please William?" Millie gave him one of her brilliant smiles. "Eliza and I will walk over to the hotel and have some refreshments in the side room. I'm sure you'd enjoy a cool drink too."

William nodded. "I have some gifts to buy first. I will join you later."

Millie smiled and put her dark hand to his cheek. "You're such a thoughtful young man, William. Don't spend all your hard-earned money."

"I won't."

He watched the two women walk away. They were an odd pair. Millie short, petite and dark, Eliza tall and broad and fair.

William carried the two parcels he'd been given to the wagon. He found a place for their shopping but wondered how all three of them were to fit on the journey home. He was pondering this as he stepped backwards to the verandah and didn't notice someone coming the other way.

"Goodness, watch where you're going." The tone was authoritarian, the voice familiar. He looked into the pale green eyes of Georgina Prosser and a lump formed in his throat.

"I'm sorry." His voice squeaked. It hadn't done that for some time. He cleared his throat.

"William?"

Her mouth turned up in a smile and his heart gave a thump.

"It is you, William Baker?"

He swallowed. "Yes. Hello, Georgina." In the time since he'd last seen her she'd become a young woman.

"I've not long arrived back in Hawker. I came on the train." She brushed her hands down her skirt. "What a tedious journey that is. I'd much rather ride a horse. At least I can from here to Prosser's Run. Father has bought me a new horse for Christmas." She put a hand on William's arm. "Would you like to meet him? The horse that is, not Father." She grinned and the dull day seemed brighter.

He never thought about clothes much but next to Georgina he felt plain in his rough shirt and patched pants. He'd grown so much these last few months the pants only came to his ankles. She on the other hand was wearing a vivid green skirt that reflected the colour of her eyes. Her shirt was crisp white with ruffles of lace running down the centre either side of the buttons. Perched on her thick red curls was a hat that matched her skirt. Her clothes fitted her perfectly and she was the prettiest girl William had ever seen.

"Are you going to stand there catching flies or come with me?"

William blinked. He had to move the wagon but it would be all right where it was for now and his shopping could wait. "I'd like to see your horse," he said.

They walked side by side along the shop verandahs until they came to the last one where Georgina turned right towards some stables. All the while she talked about Adelaide and how she hated school there. William loved the sound of her voice, and the way she chattered brightly reminded him of his grandma.

Just before they reached the stables she stopped abruptly, forcing William to do the same.

"What's that smell?" Her dainty nose scrunched up and her lips turned down.

William looked around. There was a trough full of water beside them. "It's the water." He'd noticed the terrible stench when he'd tried to water the horses as soon as they'd arrived in Hawker. "The horses won't drink it."

Georgina fanned her face. "Didn't they build a new reservoir?"

"Yes but I've heard the water lies in the pipes too long and by the time it comes out it smells rotten."

"Oh. I do hope Father has found something for my new horse to drink."

"Of course I have Georgina." Ellis Prosser strode out of the stables. "Where have you been? I've been waiting."

"Sorry, Father." Georgina's smile slipped. "Mother wanted me to go with her to the dress shop."

Ellis Prosser shook his head. Then he noticed William. "And what are you doing with a stable boy?"

William felt his cheeks burn. He drew back his shoulders but before he could speak Georgina did.

"He's not a stable boy, Father. This is our old neighbour, William Baker."

Ellis Prosser's eyes widened and he looked William up and down. "I never would have recognised you, boy."

Now William didn't feel simply plain, he felt shabby. Mr Prosser had a way of looking that made him feel as if he was nothing more than a piece of horse dung.

"Good morning, Mr Prosser." He thrust out his hand. Prosser either didn't notice or he ignored it.

"Come along, Georgina. We have to check this saddle is right. I want to set off for home as soon as we've eaten our midday meal." He strode back towards the stables.

Georgina gave William one of her brilliant smiles. "It was nice seeing you again, William. I will be home for two months over summer. Perhaps we will meet up again."

He smiled and nodded, once more struck speechless.

She turned to follow her father. Her skirt flashed with a hint of brighter green in spite of the dull day and then she was gone, swallowed up by the shadows inside the stables.

William turned and made his way back towards the wagon. How could someone as nice as Georgina be the daughter of such a pompous prig as Ellis Prosser? Now he had a better understanding of why his father didn't like the man. Mr Wiltshire was similar, looking down his nose at the Bakers. William paused beside a shop. He looked up and realised he was outside the very same Mr Wiltshire's shop.

The money in his pocket was there to be spent. William had worked hard to get it. He'd had to strip the wool from the poor sheep that hadn't been strong enough to survive the terrible conditions. Money was money and Mr Wiltshire would have to accept William's the same as anyone else's. He went to the window. A large tree decorated with red bows almost filled the space beyond the glass but William could see the young man behind the counter was not Mr Wiltshire. He pushed open the door and went inside.

There were other customers in the shop and William had to wait his turn to be served but now he was feeling much happier. He bought sweets for each of his siblings along with some marbles for Robert and some chalk for his sisters' slates. For Grandpa, Father and Millie he picked out a fine cotton handkerchief, each with their first initial embroidered in the corner. That was nearly all his money gone. He wandered around the shop looking for something he might buy for himself. A whole set of new clothes that fitted would be good but he didn't have the money for that. A flash of emerald green caught his eye. It was a wide ribbon that shone in the reflection of the shop lamps. Immediately he thought of Georgina. He decided he would buy a length. He didn't know when but one day he would give it to her.

*

"The wagon is still where we left it." Eliza turned to Millie. "William said he wanted to shop."

"He shouldn't take this long." Millie looked up and down the street. Several people walked along the road or along the shop verandahs but none of them were William. She told herself he would be here somewhere but ever since Jack's last visit she was edgy when people weren't where they were supposed to be. She felt the weight of responsibility for Joseph's children, even more so now their grandmother was dead. "You wait with the wagon. I'll look in the shops."

Millie hurried down the street, peering in the windows as she went. Finally she saw him, and it was such a relief she didn't stop to see which shop she'd arrived at. She opened the door. A bell rang over her head and the man behind the counter looked up from the woman he was serving. He was young with his dark hair oiled flat on his head. Millie saw his expression change straight away. Just as she realised where she was, the door from the back opened and Henry Wiltshire stepped up to the counter. He peered at Millie and she saw the shock register on his face. He glanced at the customers who all appeared busy.

Millie looked in William's direction. He was picking through a pile of belts and hadn't noticed her arrival. She kept her back straight and walked steadily across the room in his direction. She'd been looked down on by better people than Henry Wiltshire. She cared little for him but she did care about William. Before she could reach him Henry stepped in front of her.

"What are you doing in my shop?" he hissed.

William came to stand beside her.

"Shopping," he said.

Henry glowered from Millie to William. "You can't afford to shop in my establishment."

"I already have."

Millie could see the other customers had noticed them and were all watching with interest. She was astounded to see William almost strut across the room, nod at the assistant and pick up some parcels from the counter.

"I believe my money is as good as anyone else's." He offered Millie his arm which she took. "Good day to you, Mr Wiltshire."

Millie bit back the giggle at the astounded look on Henry's face.

"You young—"

"And merry Christmas." William cut off Wiltshire and escorted Millie outside.

The door shut firmly behind them and Millie could hold in her mirth no longer. "Oh, William." She giggled. "Mr Wiltshire turned as red as the bows on his Christmas tree."

"Silly man." William laughed too as they walked back towards Eliza and the wagon. "I see why Father doesn't like him."

"They're probably as stubborn as each other if the truth be known."

"You found him." Eliza looked from one to the other as they approached.

"Just as you said, Eliza." Millie put a hand on William's shoulder. "He was shopping."

William tucked his parcels under the canvas then helped Eliza and Millie up onto the seat of the wagon before he clambered up next to them. It was a tight squeeze as he set the horses for home. Later they would have to take turns at finding a place in the back but for now Millie was happy to be bunched up between Eliza and William.

She felt light-headed with relief and joy and perhaps it also had something to do with the new life she knew was growing inside her. She hadn't told anyone about that yet. It would be her Christmas surprise when Joseph was home and they were all together. For now Millie was content to keep the news to herself. There was a lot to be done between now and Christmas.

Forty-six

Jack approached the homestead at Wildu Creek with caution. He'd tethered his horse back in the last bit of bush before the bigger trees that marked the edge of the house area. There was a half moon, enough to guide his way up the hill to the rough wooden hut where he knew Millie slept. He'd been watching the place since late afternoon. There was no sign of the couple that worked for Baker, nor of William, only old man Baker, Millie and the three young children.

Jack paused by a large gum and slipped his flask from his pocket. He took a swig of the whiskey he'd been continuing to drink daily since his return from Hawker. He'd felt angry and frustrated at letting Catherine slip from his grasp. He'd ridden home and drunk so much he'd hardly left the house for days. Finally he'd decided to come for Millie. He'd be happy to take her willingly but if she wasn't going to accept his advances he was past caring. Tonight he would bed her, one way or another.

He stuffed the flask back in his pocket and scratched at his chin. He'd washed before he left Smith's Ridge but he'd been a day in the saddle. Still, Baker was never much for appearances, so maybe Millie liked her men rough and rugged.

He looked at the houses. There was no sign of light or life from either of them. He assumed the overseer and his wife were away and that Thomas Baker had retired for the night. Millie and the children slept up in the crude hut. He wondered about that. Now that Mrs Baker senior had died the main house was all but empty. Still it was better for his purpose if Millie slept in the hut away from the other houses. He had easier access there since her bedroom opened onto the verandah.

A glimmer of light shone from the gap around her door and that of the youngest boy's room. Jack took another swig from his flask. He was getting tired of waiting and he was desperate for a woman. Millie Baker was going to fix that need.

Millie sat up and listened. She'd heard Robert's bedroom door open a little while ago. She'd thought perhaps he'd gone to relieve himself but he'd been gone a long time. Robert wasn't a good sleeper since his father had been away. Sometimes he wandered. It bothered her. Not that she thought he'd come to much harm but he was young and if he strayed too far from the house yards he could get lost in the dark.

She slipped from her bed and took up the lantern she'd placed on the cupboard. The days were hot but the hills often cooled in the late evening. She only wore a cotton nightdress so she pulled a woollen shawl around her bare shoulders and let herself out the door.

She stood on the verandah, the lamp at her feet, waiting for her eyes to adjust to the darkness. Then she saw it, a glow of light from a window gap in the side wall of the new house. The partly completed cellar was one of Robert's favourite places. Millie left her own lantern on the verandah and picked her way down the slope. Her feet were used to shoes now and in her bare feet she hobbled over the occasional rock, slowing her down.

When she reached the gap in the walls that was to be the front door she stopped. The night was very quiet, almost too quiet. She shivered and drew her shawl tightly around her. Robert's lamp was on the ground in the middle of the house. She peered in each room as she went but she couldn't see him.

"Robert," she called softly. "Where are you?"

"Millie?" His gruff young voice answered from further in. No doubt he was in the cellar. She was about to step in that direction when she thought she heard something. She turned and stared into the darkness beyond the lamp but she could see nothing. Once more she shivered.

"I can see you." Robert's whisper drew her back to him. She went to the mouth of the cellar and peered in. Once her eyes adjusted she could see his silhouette, a darker shape a few feet in, waving to her.

She went and sat beside him. "What are you doing here in the dark?"

"I like it here."

Millie gazed out of the cellar opening. Something moved beyond the lamp in what was to be the great hall. She put a hand to her mouth. There was someone out there and from the stance it looked a lot like Jack Aldridge.

"What's wrong, Millie?" Robert was still whispering.

She put a finger to her lips and glanced around. She knew Jack wouldn't be able to see her. When she'd been on the other side of the lantern its light had stopped her seeing into the darkness beyond. He must have seen her come into the house though. Why was he here? She imagined his searching eyes and a shiver ran through her. She was barely dressed and all alone except for Robert.

She bent down and whispered in Robert's ear. "I need you to show me how quiet you can be. I want you to wake Grandfather and tell him Jack is here."

"Why is Jack here?"

"I'll tell you later but you need to go now, very quietly in the dark. Do you think you can do that for me?"

Robert's head nodded up and down.

"Good boy."

They got to their knees and shuffled to the cellar entrance. Once more Millie put a finger to her lips and then pointed to the side passage of the house that would lead to the kitchen one day. If Robert could get out that way, Jack wouldn't see him. The young boy had barely left when Jack stepped into the ring of light around the lantern.

"Hello, Millie." His voice was low.

Millie knew he wouldn't be able to see her. Perhaps she could hide in the cellar long enough for Robert to get Thomas.

There was a thud and a clunk in the direction Robert had gone. Millie bit her lip. Had she heard a whimper? Jack picked up the lantern and started in that direction. Millie had to distract him and give Robert time to get help.

"I'm here." She spoke softly and shuffled back into the cellar. She sat back and curled her shoulders over her knees, trying to cover as much of the pale nightdress with the dark shawl as she could.

She heard his footfall, it was a soft sound in the dirt but he was coming closer.

"This is a good game, Millie." His voice was teasing. "Makes me desire you even more."

Millie bit down on her lip and clasped her hand over her mouth to stop herself from crying out. She could feel her heart pounding in her chest. Please hurry, Thomas.

Thomas paused. He had taken to walking some nights when sleep eluded him. He fell asleep easily enough but sometimes he'd wake only a short time later and his grief for Lizzie threatened to overwhelm him. Walking helped him clear his head and tire his body. The creek was his favourite spot and he'd been following it for some distance when he thought he heard the nicker of a horse. He was too far from the horse yards for it to be his horses and he wasn't expecting anyone to be riding around out here at this time of night.

The snort of a horse carried down the slope. Thomas left the creek and made his way towards a thick clump of bush and trees. There was plenty of moonlight and his eyes had long since adjusted to it. He made out the shape of a horse. Perhaps someone lost had camped for the night. There were people about, drifting and looking for work, but it was rare to get them out here. Thomas moved carefully closer. The horse was tethered and there was no sign of its rider.

It pulled its head back at his approach, snorting and pawing the ground.

"Easy." Thomas extended a hand to its neck and gave it a firm pat at the same time gripping the reins just in case it broke free.

The horse settled at his touch. It was a tall animal, all black. Thomas pondered it a moment. He'd seen a similar horse. Then he remembered Jack Aldridge. He'd been a regular visitor until Lizzie's death. He'd been at her funeral and then Thomas couldn't remember seeing him since. Thomas hadn't given it any thought until now but he was relieved. On Jack's last few visits the man had paid a lot of attention to Millie who did nothing to warrant it but be her usual cheerful self.

Thomas looked around. Why would Jack leave his horse here? Something niggled in Thomas's chest, a different feeling to the pain of his grief which was a permanent ache. This was more like unease. There was a firearm in a holder attached to the saddle. Thomas slipped it out and took it with him.

He made his way carefully towards his house. On the way he passed the original little cottage that Timothy and his family lived in. There was no-one home. They'd gone to help Binda with the last remaining sheep. William was camped out overnight as well, checking fences.

Thomas let himself back in his front door. The gun he only ever used to shoot animals stood behind the bedroom door against the wardrobe. He hoped he was jumping at shadows and would have no need for it but it made him feel better to have it just in case. He replaced Jack's gun with his own and crossed the passage to the spare bedroom. Inside he could see the forms of Violet and Esther sleeping peacefully. He closed the door on them. Funny little things, some nights they slept in his house and some nights up at the quarters. He was glad to know they were safe as he made his way to his back door.

He looked out towards the quarters. A lamp glowed from the front verandah. That was odd. He made his way along the path to the back gate and set off across the yard. The jagged outline of the partly completed new house rose into the air, a dark shadow against the pale night sky. The sound of a voice made him stop and turn in that direction. It was male, speaking low. Thomas raised the gun and took careful steps forward. A woman's voice said something. Was it Millie he could hear? Then a low laugh. It was definitely Jack.

"Get out!" Millie's voice was raised this time.

"Who's going to make me?" Jack's voice was taunting. "All you have to protect you are children and an old man."

Thomas stepped past the last wall and into the space in the middle of the house. Jack had his back to him and beyond him Thomas could see a movement of fabric, he assumed Millie. He lifted the barrel.

"An old man with a gun."

Jack turned slowly. Thomas could see his shirt was untucked and he bore red streaks down his cheek. Dear God, if he had hurt Millie Thomas wouldn't be able to bear it.

"Millie?" he called.

"I'm all right, Thomas."

Jack snorted and put a hand to his cheek. "That she is."

Millie skirted around Jack beyond his reach. Thomas caught a glimpse of a torn nightgown and bare feet. What had he interrupted? He hoped he'd come in time. Millie came to stand beside Thomas. He felt her clutch at his jacket.

"Get off my land." Thomas tweaked his finger a little tighter on the trigger.

Jack held up two hands, the palms to Thomas, and shook his head. "I'm done here."

"You certainly are."

Thomas and Millie backed up as Jack walked towards them and out of the house.

Jack stopped and turned to face them, then looked beyond Thomas, put his finger to his lips and winked.

Millie let out a gasp. Thomas watched until Jack disappeared into the darkness. He felt Millie shivering beside him. He leaned the gun against the wall, took off his jacket and slid it around her shoulders. Then he picked up his gun, gave another glance around and put his arm around her.

"Let's go inside. I'll make you a cup of tea."

Thomas sat Millie on a kitchen chair, replaced the jacket with a blanket and stirred the fire to life. He lit a lantern for more light. Millie sat shuddering on the chair, her hands on her stomach, her eyes brimming with tears she was trying hard not to shed.

Thomas didn't know what to say. How did he ask her if Jack had ...? He glanced up. How he wished his Lizzie was here right now.

Millie looked around. "Where's Robert?"

"Sleeping I assume."

Millie frowned. "Here?"

Thomas paused part-way through putting the kettle on the fire. "He's in the quarters isn't he?"

"No." Millie jumped up. The rug began to slip and Thomas noticed a graze on her neck.

"Do you think Jack …?"

"No." Millie shook her head. "He didn't see Robert. He was with me all the time."

Once more Thomas noticed the shudder that ran through her body.

"I sent Robert to find you."

"I wasn't in the house."

Millie wrapped herself in the rug and looked around wildly. "He must be here."

They went from room to room. He was nowhere in the house.

Millie stopped by the back door, her hand on the handle. "How did you know to come and find me?"

"I was out walking and came across Jack's horse. I thought it was odd so I removed his gun and came back for mine. I checked on the girls then but there was no sign of Robert when I looked outside. I heard Jack's voice."

Millie wrenched open the door. "Robert." Her voice echoed in the still night. "Robert!"

Thomas came to stand behind her. "Perhaps he went back to the quarters. There's a lantern on up there."

Millie turned back. Fear filled her face. "I left it there. Robert wasn't in his bed. I could see a light from the new house so I left mine on the verandah and went to find him. When I heard Jack coming I was frightened and I sent Robert to find you." She ran along the path, her hair trailing wildly behind her.

"Wait, Millie. Let me bring some lanterns." Thomas lit a second wick and carried both outside. He gave one to Millie.

"Robert." Once more her voice echoed back and Thomas added his calls to the still night.

"Was the new house the last place you saw him?"

Millie nodded. "He must be so frightened. Maybe he's hiding."

"Let's go there first, then we'll check the quarters and the sheds."

Millie halted at the huge opening in the front wall of the new building.

"I'll check inside."

Thomas moved from room to room, holding the lantern up to throw light into every corner. In the cellar he found Millie's shawl and an extinguished lantern. He picked them both up and stepped out of the cellar just as Millie cried out.

"I've found him."

Thomas could see the glow of her light beyond the far left wall. He picked his way towards it. There was another gap in the outer wall where the kitchen would be. As he reached it Millie cried out again.

Thomas stepped outside to see his grandson stretched out on his side on the ground. Millie was bending over him, saying his name over and over. The light from her lantern illuminated the blood on Robert's head. Thomas bent closer. Robert's eyes were closed.

Thomas sank to his knees beside Millie. She gently shook the little boy's shoulders.

"Robert."

"Careful, Millie. It looks like he's had a blow to the head."

"He must have climbed over the wall instead of going round." Millie's voice came out in a whisper.

Thomas could see Robert's threadbare pyjamas were ripped and he had grazes on his arms and legs. One leg was splayed out at a funny angle. Stones from the partly completed wall littered the ground around him and the one near his head was smeared with blood.

Thomas picked up Robert's small hand in his. It was warm. He squeezed it gently. "Robert?"

The little boy's lips moved and he groaned.

"Oh thank goodness." Millie bent over the child as his eyes fluttered.

Thomas sat back. "We should take him to Dr Bruehl. It won't be a pleasant journey for the poor young lad; I suspect his leg is broken."

Millie looked up. Her usually carefree face was lined with worry. "It would be quicker and easier for Robert if I got help from my family."

"You should be resting too, Millie. You've had a shock."

"I'm all right." Her eyes flashed with determination.

"Are you sure?"

"Yes, Thomas. Jack frightened me, that's all. He grabbed me but I fought back." She put her hand to her throat where the bruise was deepening. "He had his hand around my neck but I got my fingernails into his cheek." Her hand dropped to her stomach. "I'm thankful you came when you did. He was angry."

Thomas breathed a sigh of relief. It appeared he'd arrived before anything worse could happen. "Joseph should know about this. He must come home."

Robert moaned and they both looked down at him.

"We need to straighten that leg before he wakes." Thomas ran a hand down his grandson's body.

"I'll get a blanket." Millie stood up. "We can use it to carry him inside. Then I'll go and get help." She reached out and put a hand on Thomas's arm. "Please don't tell Joseph. There's nothing that can be done now."

"We must report Jack's attack."

"No-one will listen, Thomas." She squeezed his arm. "I am not badly hurt. Joseph will only be upset and angry and then who knows what he might do. I will tell him when the time is right."

"Are you sure?"

"Yes, Thomas, please. I don't want any more trouble." Her big round eyes looked at him beseechingly.

"If Jack Aldridge ever comes this way again …"

"Then we will deal with him." Her face set with purpose.

"Very well."

She gave him a tremulous smile and let go of his arm.

Thomas watched as she ran to the house. What a strong woman she was. He glanced up at the night sky. You were right Lizzie, he thought. Millie is a fine mother and companion. I only hope that my silence is the right thing.

Forty-seven

"Damn it Ellis, the ratepayers are a lot of weak-hearted simpletons." Henry strutted up and down in his sitting room, one hand behind his back and the other clutching a mug of whiskey. He came to a stop in front of the fireplace which was filled with pine cones and adorned with a large red bow. There was no need for a fire in the heat of mid-December. "They are petitioning the governor to have the council taken off the list of councils."

Prosser harrumphed. "It hasn't even served a full year."

"It's preposterous." Henry spluttered into his drink. "Mr Jones went as far as to resign from his position as chairman."

"I heard there was some kind of petition."

"There was." Henry thumped the back of one of Catherine's good chairs. "A group of so-called ratepayers say they can't even procure themselves the base necessities of life let alone find any money for rates, no matter how low we make them." Once more Henry thumped the chair. "I've had to sell off my land both at Cradock and at Wilson and consolidate my losses. These jolly farmers, common riff-raff some of them, they need to get their priorities right."

"Pay the council rates before they feed their families?" Prosser pursed his lips in a silly pout.

Henry glared at him. "Well no, that's not what I mean but they do have to be accountable. They are complaining it's the poor seasons that are the reason for their losses, or the grasshoppers or the rabbits or the wild dogs. They're always blaming something. Never think it could be their poor farming practices that are to blame."

"I've always said they shouldn't be using the land in these parts for growing crops." Prosser inclined his mug towards Henry to show it was empty.

"So you have, Ellis." Henry refilled his friend's mug and topped up his own. "I am hopeful tomorrow night's council meeting will sort it all out."

"Enough of this doom-and-gloom news." Prosser took a large gulp of Henry's good whiskey. "You were hopeful your trip to Adelaide would bring good news regarding moving that man your wife's family feel beholden to off Smith's Ridge."

Henry slumped into the chair next to Prosser. He regretted his boastful moment, saying he would find a way to move Jack Aldridge on. The less Prosser knew about that business the better. Henry had gone in search of someone who would do the job for him. Even though Harriet had put up a pretty purse he'd had no luck. "It may take a little longer than I expected."

"I think it's a bit much. Just because we live so far from Adelaide doesn't mean our standards have to slip. Are you sure he's of Indian descent? People are saying he's of native blood. The man has shown he can manage the place but I won't abide blacks."

"I will take care of it, Ellis."

"You'd better. Especially if you want my vote and that of my friends to sort out this debacle with the council."

"You know I'm always grateful for your help." Henry took a sip of his whiskey. Prosser could be a pompous man, full of self-importance, but Henry needed him on-side.

There was a knock at the door and Catherine came in. She wore a pale blue dress that flowed softly around her as she walked.

"Catherine, my dear." Prosser leapt to his feet and took Catherine's hand.

Her cheeks flushed a pretty pink and she lowered her eyelashes. "Hello, Ellis."

Henry was so pleased Catherine still kept her pretty looks. She carried more weight these days but she was still a beautiful woman. Prosser's wife had been looking rather haggard the last time she'd come into Henry's shop. Still, she was quite a lot older than Catherine and she did have to live with Prosser. No doubt the loss of two sons weighed heavily as well.

"How is Johanna?"

"Well thank you, my dear." Prosser patted Catherine's hand.

She smiled and withdrew it. "And Georgina? You must be pleased to have her home again."

"She's wilful as ever but ..." Prosser leaned in closer to Catherine. "I don't know what we'd do without her. She's determined to fill her brothers' boots."

"You must bring her in for a visit after Christmas."

"I'm sure she'd be delighted."

Catherine inclined her head. "I've just come in to say supper is ready. Will you be joining us, Ellis?"

"No, no, thank you Catherine, I must be away." Prosser turned and nodded in Henry's direction. "Good evening to you, Wiltshire. I will call on you when next I am in Hawker."

Henry allowed Catherine to see Prosser out. He put a hand to his head. He'd had to sell off his land to keep enough money to pay Jack and then there was all this business with the council. He felt as if he was going crazy trying to keep up with it all.

"Are you ready to dine, Henry?" Catherine had returned and was watching him from the door. She fiddled with the locket around her neck. She was much more jumpy of late. He wondered about that.

"Of course." He crossed the room and took his wife's arm. "What delights has Mrs Nixon prepared for us this evening?"

"I have prepared our meal." Catherine's tone was huffy. "I gave Mrs Nixon the afternoon off. Her daughter is sick."

Henry paused. He much preferred Flora's meals to Catherine's but he could hardly say as much. He placed a kiss on his wife's cheek.

"How delightful, my dear."

He led Catherine to their dining room. The large table was covered in a white damask cloth and set for the two of them.

"Charles has eaten. He's playing with his trains." Catherine crossed to the dresser to pour the wine. "He is enjoying the *Treasure Island* book you brought him from Adelaide. He would very much appreciate you sharing another chapter before he goes to bed."

"Of course." Henry was very proud of Charles and his achievements. He had worried perhaps the local school wouldn't be good enough but Mr Harry had written Charles a glowing report card. The only minor concern was something about bossing other children but Henry saw that as meaning Charles could stand up for himself.

He waited as Catherine brought his wine. "Are you not joining me, my dear?"

"Not tonight, Henry." Catherine gave him a quick glance. Her movements were jerky. She placed a goblet of red wine on the cloth in front of his place and gasped as it wobbled. They both tried to save it but the goblet toppled and the red wine spread across the white cloth.

"Oh dear." Catherine reached for her locket.

"Be calm, Catherine. It was an accident."

She waved a hand over the pool of red and stood the goblet up again. "That will stain. I must remove the cloth and soak it at once."

Henry sucked in a breath. "Very well."

Catherine rolled the fabric from the other end. He lifted the goblet and the utensils and she swept the cloth from underneath.

"I'll bring a fresh one and our supper." She bustled out of the room, the large cloth gathered together in her arms.

Henry poured himself a fresh goblet of wine and sat in his chair. He ran a hand over the finely polished wood. He was glad they had acquired some fine pieces of furniture before their fortunes reached this current downturn. It was easier to keep up appearances when one had a grand house and good furniture. The sale of the land at Cradock and Wilson was barely enough to cover Jack's wages for much longer. Ellis was right, Henry did need to rid himself of the man.

He took a sip of wine and nearly spat it back all over himself. He gulped it down and leaned forward. There on the lip of the table someone had carved something. Who would do such a thing? He ran his finger over the crude letters etched into his mahogany table then he leaned forward to look closer. JA. He bent even closer and anger surged through him. Who was JA? None of Henry's guests had those initials and none would have the bad manners to do such a thing.

He pushed back in his chair and leapt to his feet almost knocking over his new goblet of wine. Jack Aldridge. He was the only person Henry knew with those initials but how on earth would he have access to Henry's dining table? Had the vile man come creeping in at night while they slept?

Catherine bustled back through the door. She carried the tray to the table, spread serviettes over their places and set out their plates and utensils. "This will do instead of a new cloth. The meal is only mutton and cheese but we have some of Flora's delicious pickles." She looked back at him. "What is it Henry?"

He flicked his serviette back from the table. It flopped over his plate.

"Henry?"

"Someone has carved their initials in my table."

"Oh, surely not in the mahogany. Charles wouldn't do such a thing."

Henry glared at her. "I don't believe our son did this."

"Where is it?"

He waved his hand at the exposed lip of the table.

Catherine bent down to peer closer. "Oh, it looks like a J and an A." She straightened and looked back at Henry, her expression puzzled.

"The only JA I know is a man called Jack Aldridge."

The colour left Catherine's face and she wobbled sideways. Henry caught her and lowered her to her chair. He passed her a cup of water and helped her sip it.

"You remember Jack Aldridge?"

She looked at him, fear in her big round eyes.

Henry placed a hand on her shoulder and squeezed it gently. "Tell me, Catherine. Has Jack Aldridge been inside my house?"

She sucked her lips into her mouth and nodded.

It was only his deference to good manners that kept back the profanities he wanted to blurt out. "When?"

"While you were in Adelaide." Her voice was a whisper. She reached for her cup and took another sip of water. Her hands trembled.

"You invited him into our house and you were alone? Catherine, what were you thinking?"

"I didn't exactly invite him. He came in. He carried the bag of potatoes for me. He was very charming and the next thing I knew we were having dinner."

Henry put his hands to his head and took in a deep breath. He lowered his hands and spoke very slowly. "A stranger and a man with black blood sat at my table?"

"Well not exactly a stranger. He was the man who played ball with Charles that time and he's not very dark of skin."

Henry thumped the table in front of her. Catherine jumped along with the utensils.

"He was very polite." Once more her voice was a whisper. "He said he knew you."

"What else did he say?" If Jack had told Catherine about their connection Henry would kill the man himself.

"Nothing really, small talk. He was very charming at first and then ... well then ..." Catherine's hand went to her locket.

"He didn't ... harm you?"

"No. I did begin to feel uncomfortable. Then Flora and Charles came home and I asked him to leave."

Henry's eyes widened. "Our son and housekeeper saw you with another man in the house?"

Catherine shook her head and looked down at her lap. "I left him here in the dining room. He let himself out." She put a hand to her mouth and looked back at Henry with tears in her eyes. "I'm sorry, Henry. I should have told but you weren't home and then I put the whole awful incident from my mind."

Henry wrapped her in his arms and drew her to his chest.

"There, there, my dear. Don't upset yourself any more."

She sobbed against his shirt a moment then he gently pushed her upright.

"Promise me you'll tell me if you ever see him again."

She nodded.

"I mean it, Catherine. Jack Aldridge is a dangerous man."

"Why Henry, surely you don't associate with him?"

"Not for much longer." Henry sat back in his chair. "Let's not talk about him any more. We have your lovely supper to eat."

"I'm not hungry, Henry."

Catherine wobbled to her feet. He rose to help her.

"I think I will retire early."

"Very well, my dear." He pecked her on the cheek. "I will look in on Charles once I've eaten."

She gave him a weak smile and left.

Henry flopped back in his chair, snatched up his fork and stabbed at the slice of mutton on his plate. Anger surged inside him. Here he was at his own table with Jack's ugly initials gouged right before his eyes. He took a mouthful then slammed down his fork. Jack Aldridge had to go.

Forty-eight

"You're only leaving a week earlier than we'd planned." Hegarty's big voice was gentle. "You've been away from your family long enough, Joseph. They need you even more now. Go home."

Home. That word rattled around in Joseph's head. He should have stayed there and then perhaps his youngest son wouldn't have been injured. He ached inside. Joseph felt a failure. He'd let his family down with his pursuit of gold. Millie had been right. They needed each other, not things. At least this time he would return with a wad of money in his pocket.

Automatically his hand reached for the gold bottle.

"I've got the rest of your gold, remember." Hegarty patted his shoulder with the look of someone talking to a child. "I'll bring your money once I've traded the gold in Adelaide."

Joseph looked at his screening table, his knife and empty gold bottle lay there along with the pouch. He reached for it.

"You know that's an unusual rock you've got in there," Hegarty said. "Why don't you let me take that with your gold to Adelaide? See what the dealer thinks it is."

Joseph's hand hovered over the pouch. He gave a snort. "Might as well. I used to think it was lucky but now I think I've used up all that luck."

He turned back to his tent and began tugging at the ropes that had held it upright for almost two years.

"We'll sort it out, man." Once more Hegarty's hand was on his shoulder. "You go."

"There's nothing here I want." Joseph waved his hand at the tent. "Give it away." Joseph wished poor old Jones was still around. He could have done with Joseph's tent.

Joseph shook Peterson's hand then Hegarty's before he mounted his horse. He gave them one final look, then he turned his horses for home.

"Go well, Joseph." Hegarty's voice called after him. "We'll find you in the new year and bring your money."

Joseph sat with his father by the creek. They were silent, both staring into the darkness alone with their thoughts. It had been a long day. Everyone else was in bed but them. Christmas at Wildu Creek had been a quiet affair. Lizzie's absence had been keenly felt at a time when she would have been in her element, cleaning, cooking, singing, infecting them with her happiness.

Instead small gifts were exchanged with little fanfare and they had eaten delicious but simple meals. Robert had been irritable with his leg bound up. He had not been content sitting in a chair watching the others play nor did he want to be with the adults. His head ached, he said. Joseph worried about his recovery. Millie said the child suffered less from pains in both his head and leg but Joseph was still troubled. Since his return both his wife and youngest son had been distant.

"I'm glad you're back to stay, Joseph." Thomas's words drew him back to the present.

"I wish I hadn't gone."

"You can't undo what's done."

Joseph shook his head. They hadn't spoken much since his return. He'd ridden with William to see Binda and the last of their sheep in the hills and then Christmas day had arrived. Eliza had prepared most of the food. Millie spent a lot of time fussing over Robert. He was sure his wife and youngest son blamed him for not being home when Robert had his accident and he couldn't fault them for that. He felt the same.

"I shouldn't have left."

Once more they lapsed into silence. The evening breeze ruffled the leaves above their heads.

"How is Millie?"

Joseph took a moment to respond to his father's question.

"I don't really know. She's ... distant. I'm worried I've let her down so badly she won't be able to forgive me. I should have been here to protect my wife and son."

"I understand. I keep going over it myself. I think Millie blames herself for Robert's accident."

Joseph turned to his father in surprise. "Why would she do that?"

Thomas shook his head. "We all felt we should have done better to prevent it."

"I don't understand, Father, what was Robert doing out at the house in the dark?"

"Have you talked about it with Millie?"

"Yes. She said he got restless some nights but she didn't elaborate and I don't like to press her."

"She hasn't said anything else about that night?"

"No." Joseph leaned towards his father. "Did something else happen?"

"She didn't want me to say anything." Thomas continued to stare into the night. "But I'm worried about her."

Joseph's stomach squirmed. He reached out to touch his father's arm. "Please, if there's something more tell me. I need to know what happened."

Thomas turned weary eyes to his son. "Jack Aldridge was here that night."

"Jack? What for?"

Thomas drew in a deep breath then slowly let it out. "I can only tell you what I know. The rest you'll have to ask Millie."

Joseph's stomach churned more. What did that mean? Millie and Jack. Joseph felt cold. He had been away a long time.

"Before you go jumping to any conclusions, your wife loves you. Remember that. Jack Aldridge was not here that night at her bidding." Once more Thomas looked off into the darkness. "We had all retired for the night. The girls were in my spare room, Millie and Robert up at the quarters and everyone else away. Like Robert I sometimes don't sleep well. I took a walk along the creek and I came across Jack's horse, tethered in the bushes a way back from the house. It seemed odd. I took his gun and went to find my own. I discovered Jack in the new house with ... I believe he was going to ... well anyway my arrival stopped him from hurting Millie any more."

Joseph leapt to his feet. "He hurt Millie?"

"Not badly but there had obviously been a fight. He had scratches down his cheek and ... Millie had a scrape on her neck."

Joseph shook his head. "She didn't tell me."

"Jack left and then we realised Robert was missing. Millie had sent him to fetch me when she saw Jack coming but he never found me. For some reason he climbed over one of the walls. The top layer dislodged and he fell ..." Thomas's shoulders sagged. "Like you I wish I'd been there and I know Millie wishes she hadn't sent Robert to find me but we can't undo what's done."

"What should I do?"

"Give her time." Thomas stood. "I'm going to bed. You should too."

"Good night, Father." Joseph put his head back and stared up at the stars. The night sky glittered like thousands of diamonds. He felt so useless and small. His wife needed him yet wouldn't let him get close. He stood and picked up a stone from the small pile Robert had used to make his marble tracks. Joseph threw the stone into the darkness and turned for his hut.

The days continued to slip by and 1889 began with little acknowledgment from those at Wildu Creek. Like the months before, the gruelling weather continued into January. Even the cooler nighttime breeze from the gully had deserted them. Everyone was listless from the heat. Dust seeped through the gaps of the quarters into every corner and flies made their lives a misery.

It was late afternoon, grey clouds were building on the horizon and the heat was oppressive. Joseph had taken it upon himself to improve their living conditions in the quarters. He was hammering some small pieces of wood over the larger gaps around the doors to each room in an attempt to keep them a little more dust free.

"Please stop." Millie was at the door of their bedroom. She held a hand to her head.

"I'm sorry." Joseph put down his hammer. "I thought everyone was down at the house."

"I was … I just needed some sleep." She swayed in the doorway.

Joseph reached out and put an arm around her shoulders. She had hardly let him touch her since he'd come home and now he could feel the bones of her arms through her shirt. She'd grown so thin in his absence. She spent most of her waking hours looking after Robert. He guided her back inside and sat her on the bed. Her eyes were round and full of sadness.

Joseph opened his mouth then closed it again. How was he to make up for all that he'd put her through alone? He didn't want to alienate her more but he needed some answers. He sat himself on the bed beside her leaving a gap between them but taking her hand in his.

"Father told me Jack Aldridge was here the night Robert was injured." He felt her hand stiffen. "Father is worried about you, like I am Millie. I have to know." He put his large hand to her chin and gently turned her face to him. He saw more than sadness in her eyes, there was fear there as well. "Did Jack ..." How was he to ask this question? "Did he hurt you?"

Millie's lip trembled and large tears rolled silently down her cheeks. She shook her head. "He frightened me. I fought him off but he was so strong. Your father came just in time."

A pain as sharp as a knife stabbed through Joseph but he kept outwardly calm.

"What did he—"

"Nothing more than some bruises."

Joseph tried to pull her close but she pushed him away, her eyes focused on something on the wall beside them.

"I was down at the new house looking for Robert. I saw Jack coming and I was frightened. He thought I was playing a game with him and I knew that look in his eye." She gripped Joseph's hand tighter. "I told Robert to find your father." She turned her anguished face to Joseph. "If I hadn't sent him he wouldn't have been injured."

"You weren't to know Robert would climb the wall instead of going round."

Millie's mouth crumpled. "I heard him whimper." She gasped. "I thought he must have bumped himself and then Jack was there, he grabbed hold of me. He had his hand at my throat. I pushed him and scratched his cheek. He reeked of liquor and became angry. He was so strong I knew I wouldn't survive if I tried to fight him ..." Her voice trailed off.

Joseph closed his eyes as black dots of anger clouded his vision. That bastard.

"If it had just been me I would have."

Millie's voice forced his eyes open. "What do you mean?"

She put a hand to her stomach. "I was with child, Joseph. Our baby. I didn't care about me but the baby ... I was terrified if I fought him I would lose the baby."

Joseph reached for her and this time she fell into his arms. Great racking sobs shuddered through her body. He held her close, stroking her hair, kissing her cheek until finally she was silent in his arms. Then he recalled her words. Was with child. She'd said 'was'. His heart felt as if it would truly break.

Millie took a long deep breath and sat up. She put both hands against her skirt and he saw what he hadn't noticed before. There was a small bulge even though the rest of her was so thin. "The baby still grows inside me."

Joseph leapt to his feet then knelt in front of her taking her hands in his. He looked up into her tear-stained face. "Something good, Millie. We have to hang onto something good."

She nodded. "I didn't want to tell you because I thought you would be so angry you might do something silly, like go after Jack."

"We must tell the constable."

"No." Millie's tone was sharp and she shook her head. "What would I say? And what could the constable do? It's my word against his and I can't bear any more, Joseph."

"We can't let him get away with it. He threatened you."

"Your father sent Jack away. I don't think he'll come back again."

"But he might hurt someone else."

Once more Millie shook her head and the tears pooled in her eyes. "I'm sorry Joseph but I can't face it."

He pulled her into his arms. "All right. Shhh." He stroked her back and rocked her gently.

His thoughts turned to Jack and it was as if fire ran through his veins. Joseph would say nothing more to Millie but he knew what he had to do. There was only one way to atone for Robert's injuries and for what Jack had done to Millie. Joseph had to kill Jack Aldridge.

In the gloomy light of the room next door William lay on his bed keeping as still as his fury would let him. Like Millie he had been trying to get some rest out of the heat. Outside there was not a breath of air. The sun was hidden behind the thickening clouds. There was no relief from its ferocity and yet William sensed something was building. Like a festering boil there was little to see until it exploded. Not a creature stirred except his father, even the birds had gone quiet as if waiting for something to happen. Inside his room the air was so hot it was like a great weight pressing down on him. He had been just about to get up and help his father with the hammering when Millie had spoken. William had remained silent and through the thin wall he had heard most of what had been said.

He should have told his father about Jack's visit that day he'd almost bailed Millie up and William had fired a shot. Perhaps they would have dealt with their vile neighbour then and there and saved Millie and Robert from their injuries. William didn't blame Millie for the accident. It was Jack Aldridge's fault and he would have to pay for all the grief he'd caused.

Forty-nine

1889

Huge clouds rolled overhead as Henry rode up the hill to Smith's Ridge. There had been no movement of air when he'd left Hawker now the wind whipped at his coat and swirled dust in his face. Something was brewing. A low rumble reverberated behind him. Henry didn't expect anything much would come of it. For three years they'd had little more than showers of rain. A hawk wheeled overhead screeching its lonely cry into the wind.

Henry shuddered as a shiver ran down his back. He had been riding since early morning and his behind ached along with his back. The only reason he'd come by horse was to get here quickly and then be ready for a swift departure.

His anger at Jack Aldridge had deepened with every hour he drew closer to Smith's Ridge. Jack's audacity at coming into Henry's home, playing up to Catherine and then leaving a sign of his presence was beyond endurance. Jack had to go and Henry was going to convince him with the last of the money he'd been able to scrounge and the point of a gun.

With Jack gone he would be able to rid himself of the burden of Smith's Ridge. It would leave him only his shop and business was poor. To top it off he'd been ousted from the council at their last meeting. The council had survived but the number of councillors had been cut from ten to five and Henry had lost his position. He hated the thought of it but his only option would be to sell up and move back to Adelaide. He blew out a breath. At least his mother and Catherine would be pleased.

Henry halted his horse before he reached the clearing around the house. The noise of the wind covered any sounds he might make. He needed to sneak up on Jack and put himself in a position of advantage. The firearm felt comfortable in his hands now. He had stopped along the way to practise. He'd found it easy to imagine the large swirls of bark on a tree were Jack's face. Even so, Henry hoped his threats and the money would be enough to send his half-brother away for good.

The sound of hammering drew his attention towards the shearing shed. Henry smiled. Jack was up a ladder fighting with a piece of loose iron on the roof. How very convenient. Here was a way to rid himself of Jack, permanently. His death would be made to look like an accident. A wayward shot during a fall from a ladder while carrying a firearm was perfect.

William had left home before the sun had come up enough to reveal the murky sky. His family would assume he'd gone early to check fences and waterholes as he often did. The light grey clouds of morning had turned to thick dark clouds as he'd ridden towards Smith's Ridge and the wind had grown. In the distance he heard the first low rumbling of thunder. The skin on the back of his neck prickled. He peered up at the sky. The clouds were black and tumbling at speed just above the ridges. He prayed there would be rain in them.

He'd arrived by mid-afternoon and found a vantage point in the trees to the east of the house. His horse was tethered well away out of sight. Jack Aldridge's gun rested on the ground beside him. William had taken it from his grandfather's house while Thomas was sleeping. He thought about how he could use the gun to make Jack's death look like an accidental shooting. For hours he'd watched Jack come and go, feeding horses, working on a broken rail in their yard and then beginning to batten things down as the wind had grown stronger. A piece of the shearing shed roof had started to clang and Jack had made his way up there and was now on a ladder trying to fix it.

William's innards rumbled and churned as if something was clawing its way about inside him. He swallowed the saliva that pooled in his mouth and picked up the gun. The branches over his head tossed harder and somewhere more iron clanged. He took a deep breath. If he was going to do this he had to do it now. A movement caught his eye beyond the shed. He peered out from his tree. It was a man taking careful steps. William couldn't make out who it was but he could see that the man carried a gun.

Joseph had made good time to reach Smith's Ridge by late afternoon. He had followed the ridge top at the back of the sheds. This property had been his and he knew it better than anyone. From his vantage point beyond the shearing shed he had a clear view of everything.

He hadn't been able to leave too early this morning. Not after Millie's outpouring yesterday and then their tender lovemaking last night. She'd been so hesitant to even let him touch her. It had broken his heart that his happy, loving Millie had been so frightened by Jack's attack. He loved her so much he only hoped that love could bring back the woman he knew. It would take some healing but she had accepted his love and gently offered it back.

Last night had been the beginning. Now he was here to avenge her and his son's injuries. Jack Aldridge was going to pay.

The weather was getting wilder. The clouds overhead were almost black and he could see lightning in the distance and thunder echoed across the hills. How ironic if they finally got some decent rain. Jack's death would bring new life.

Joseph tethered his horse and settled to watch. The clanging of iron drew his attention, and Aldridge's. Joseph watched as the bastard of a man took a ladder and moved to the shed. He disappeared from Joseph's sight then reappeared on the roof. Joseph raised his firearm. It would be the perfect shot but Jack was too far away.

A clap of thunder sounded closer and a few drops of rain began to fall. Joseph pushed his hat firmly on his head and started down the ridge.

Jack was hammering the last nail into the iron when a loud clap of thunder overhead made him jump and he almost lost his footing. The wind whipped at him and large drops of rain clattered over the iron. The air quivered around him. He'd done enough. It was time to go inside and wait out the storm. The ladder wobbled precariously below him as he moved down a step.

"Stay there."

Jack looked down in surprise at the figure standing below him. It was Henry and he was pointing a firearm at him. Stupid fool.

Henry shook the ladder and Jack slipped down one rung.

"What are you doing, Henry?" He slid down one more rung as Henry was startled by a flash of lightning.

"You're going to have an accident, Jack." Henry's face was split in a malicious grin. He wobbled the ladder again.

Jack hung on tighter, assessing the distance between himself and the ground. "What's the matter, Henry," he called calmly. "Has something upset you?"

"You living and breathing." Henry shouted over the rumble of thunder. "That's what upsets me, Jack."

Jack judged he was close enough to jump. The next time Henry shook the ladder Jack sent his weight to one side. The ladder toppled sideways and Jack jumped to the ground, knocking Henry over as he went. Jack spied the iron bar he used to dig holes leaning against the shed, scooped it up and spun to face his brother. Henry was still sprawled on the ground trying to reach his firearm. Jack got to it first. He used the butt of it to hit Henry across the forehead. His brother fell back groaning.

"What were you planning to do with this, Henry?" he yelled into the wind.

"Shoot you, I think."

Jack spun. William was crossing the yard, the firearm in his hands raised.

"So you took my gun." Jack laughed. "You've come a long way to shoot wild dogs, boy."

William raised the firearm to his eye and looked down the barrel. "I have one in my sights right now."

Jack stopped laughing. The stupid boy was probably a good shot. He'd better be careful. He dropped the gun but not the bar. He flicked a look from William to Henry who was still moaning on the ground, then another movement caught his eye. Joseph Baker was coming from beside the shearing shed, only feet away. Jack saw surprise on William's face. He swung the iron bar and connected with the boy's shoulder. William let out a yell and fell to the ground clutching his arm.

"William!"

Jack spun, swinging wildly with the bar, as Joseph called out. He missed the man but knocked the firearm from his hands. Joseph reeled back but Jack brought the bar around knocking his feet from under him.

"Stupid fools." Jack bellowed.

"Why didn't you shoot him, Baker?" Henry was struggling to sit up.

Jack kept an eye on Joseph and shoved out his boot to push Henry back.

"Now, now, brother. None of you are a match for Jack Aldridge. It's about time you realised that."

Joseph shook his head and dragged himself to his feet. "This bastard is your brother?"

Jack sneered at him through the rain that was falling more heavily now. "You got that right. I'm not only his bastard brother but a black one." He looked back at Henry. "That's what you hate more than anything else, isn't it Henry? Not that you're supporting me to live here and that the lease is to be mine. It's the colour of my skin that matters most."

"You're nothing but a black bastard, Jack." Henry shouted the words. "Nothing will change that."

"I don't know. With you out of the way that delightful wife of yours would need a good man to warm her bed."

Henry flailed his arm weakly in the air. Jack bellowed with laughter.

Joseph came at him again, but Jack swung the bar, knocking him back to the ground. Joseph lay back, clutching at his chest, gasping for breath. Jack had had enough of this. He'd have to kill the lot of them or they'd do him in. Self-defence it would be. He stood over Joseph and raised the iron bar.

"Your pretty wife tell you how much I enjoyed her?"

Joseph kicked out with his legs but Jack jumped out of reach.

"Father!"

Jack cast a sideways glance at William. Somehow the boy had managed to get on to his feet and the gun was back in his hands. One of his shoulders was lower than the other but he was aiming the gun at Jack again. This time he was too far away for Jack to disarm.

"Don't do it, William." Joseph's voice was firm.

Jack grinned back at the boy. "Better listen to your father."

The weather was wild around them, drowning out the sound of their voices. Lightening flashed and crackled with thunderclaps so loud they hurt Joseph's ears. He took small breaths and managed to get some air into his lungs. The blow from the bar had winded him and his chest was agony. He looked frantically from Jack to William. He saw the hesitation on his son's face and knew Jack had seen it too. Joseph struggled to his feet but Jack kicked out before he could reach William and knocked the gun from the boy's hands. Jack let out a rage-filled roar. The air crackled and fizzed. Joseph's skin prickled and the hairs on his arms stood up. Jack spun, raising the iron bar as he went to swing at Joseph.

A huge bang shook the ground around them accompanied by a flash of light so bright it illuminated the yard, forcing Joseph to put up his arm to shield his eyes. There was a scream. Joseph dropped his arm. William and Henry were staring down in horror at the lifeless form of Jack Aldridge. William cried out and put a hand to his mouth. Jack's hands and arms were blackened, his hair smouldering and one boot had been flung from his foot. The terrible smell of burned flesh reached them.

Another clap of thunder and crash of lightening broke their stupor. Joseph was the first to inspect Jack. He bent down and looked closer at the body sprawled on the ground.

"He's dead."

The words spurred Henry into action. "We should get inside out of this storm before anyone else gets hurt."

Joseph glanced at Henry. His face was grotesque, covered in blood and mingled with the rain it was turning his white collar pink.

"Are you all right?" Joseph reached out a hand.

Henry nodded and let Joseph help him up. Joseph drew the silent William under his other arm and together the three of them stumbled down the slope to the house, with the wind roaring in their ears and whipping at their clothes.

Once inside Joseph forced the back door shut and it was suddenly calm. He sat William in a chair and checked his arm.

"I don't think it's broken but the shoulder is dislocated." He patted William's good shoulder. "I can fix it. A quick pain and you'll feel better."

Joseph turned to Henry. "Then we'd better see to that cut."

Henry put a hand to his head then looked at his fingers. Joseph saw his eyes roll. He pushed a chair beneath Henry's legs as they buckled. Henry groaned but remained conscious.

"It's only a cut." Joseph looked around for something to put on it. There was a drying cloth hanging on a hook. It didn't look too clean but would have to do. "Hold this against it." He shoved the cloth at Henry and turned his attention back to William's shoulder. He helped his son to lie flat on the ground, then took him by the elbow, gripped hard and pulled.

William let out a yelp.

"All done." Joseph helped William back to his chair. "Rest now." He gave William a nod and turned his attention to the fire. "We could all do with getting out of these wet things."

Henry glanced around. "Perhaps some hot tea?"

"Tea be damned." Joseph opened the grate and piled more wood into the fire. "Jack would have some whiskey here somewhere. I think we could all do with a drop of that. Even William."

Another loud rumble of thunder shook the house, light flashed at the window and rain pelted down on the roof overhead.

Joseph poked at the fire some more. "We won't be going anywhere tonight."

"Shouldn't we ..." William's voice trailed off. "Shouldn't we move the ... Jack."

"Nothing's going to change the fact that he's dead." Joseph studied his son. William's eyes were bright, no doubt a mixture of pain and shock. He put a gentle hand on his son's good shoulder. "Perhaps later, when the rain eases, we can put him in the shed."

"What will we tell people?" Henry's voice wavered. "How will we explain we were all here and Jack is dead?"

"We didn't kill him." Joseph began opening cupboards looking for whiskey and something to eat. "It was an act of nature."

"How do we explain our injuries?" Henry was getting worked up now.

"What injuries?" Joseph nodded at Henry. "You're the only one with anything to show. You fell and hit your head in the shock of finding Jack."

"So I am to be the one who reports to the constable?" Henry's eyes narrowed.

"It makes sense. People know you're away and it sounds like Smith's Ridge is actually in your name, although not for much longer."

"What do you mean?"

Joseph lifted his chin. "The Bakers have the money to take it back. Once things have settled down you'll be signing the lease over to us."

They glared at each other.

"Grandfather always said this place was cursed." William's words broke the silence between the two men.

"You surely don't believe that, William. Bad things happen no matter where we are. Grandpa buried two children and his wife at Wildu Creek. It's no more cursed than Smith's Ridge. It's just life."

William slumped in his chair.

"It's all right, son. We won't live here. We'll hire an overseer or, who knows, Timothy and Eliza might like to take it on. The house could certainly use a woman's touch again." Joseph looked back at Henry. "What do you say Wiltshire? I'm sure you'll be glad to see the back of this place. It hasn't been lucky for you either."

Henry drew in a breath. "I still have sheep."

Joseph snorted. "If there are any left after this we'll buy them from you. And we'll keep the shepherd you've got with them. I hear he's a good man." Joseph knew he would have to draw deeply on the money he'd brought with him from Teetulpa but Hegarty should arrive soon with the rest which should be far greater than what Joseph had already.

"Very well." Henry held out his hand. "Smith's Ridge is yours."

Fifty

Henry stepped out his shop door, stopped on the verandah and clasped the lapels of his jacket.

"Good morning, Mr Wiltshire."

"And the same to you, Mrs Taylor." He raised his gaze to the blue sky dotted with puffs of white cloud. "Another lovely day."

"Just glorious for the first day of May."

"Indeed." Henry rocked up onto the balls of his feet.

"I'll be back later to look at the new fabrics Catherine told me about over morning tea yesterday."

"We shall look forward to it."

Henry looked up and down the street. In every direction there was movement, horses, wagons and people going about their business. Everyone had found their optimism since the huge downpour in January and the follow-up rains since. Grass sprouted everywhere, the few young trees had taken on a brighter green hue and some ladies, including Catherine, were growing flowers in their gardens.

Even the farmers of the region were happy since help had been found to buy seed for them to plant. The government hadn't been forthcoming so it had been left to benefactors and of course he'd been able to extract some money from Harriet so that he had been able to extend credit to a couple of farmers. He was quite sure he would once again build up his landholdings and own more than the local shop.

Catherine was once more with child. This time Dr Bruehl had insisted she keep to her bed and do very little. He had also discreetly indicated to Henry that she should avoid her wifely duties for the duration of her confinement. Henry smiled at the thought. These days he preferred Flora Nixon's firm body to his wife's lumpy one anyway. It had been a good day that had brought Flora to him looking for work. Not only was she their housekeeper and careful carer of her mistress but she looked after her master's needs as well.

A wagon drawn by two horses rolled to a stop in front. Henry's smile slipped when he saw Baker and his very pregnant black wife seated beside him. The lad, William, was dangling his long legs over the back. He jumped off and strode away without a glance at Henry as soon as the wagon stopped.

"Mr Wiltshire." Baker nodded.

Henry nodded back.

"Taking in the sunshine?"

"Indeed." Henry looked up and down the street in case someone was watching. He and Baker had managed to agree on the terms of the handover of Smith's Ridge but that was as far as it went. The arrogant man was still married to a native woman and could never redeem himself in Henry's eyes. It also rankled that the women Baker married could also produce children so easily.

"Don't worry." Joseph chuckled. "We're not stopping. We've a load of supplies to collect, new clothes to buy along with items for the baby but we won't put you out. Mr Garrat next door is always pleased to take our money." Joseph lifted his hat and flicked the reins to move his wagon forward.

Henry shook with rage as Baker's cheeky wife waved at him with a huge smile. He turned on his heel and strode back into his shop.

Millie gave Joseph's leg a playful pat. "You are bad to goad him."

"But it's so enjoyable." Joseph reined the horses in beside Mr Garrat's shop.

"You made it sound as if we have lots of money to spend."

Joseph turned to Millie and took her hands. "It will be tight until our first wool cheque, then we should be able to do more around the house."

"That's not necessary, Joseph. We all fit quite well in your father's house. There's little that needs doing and William seems happy enough in the quarters."

"Speaking of whom where did he disappear to?"

"Something caught his eye back along the road I suspect."

Joseph twisted in his seat but there was no sign of his son. He jumped down from the wagon and helped Millie to the ground. "Will you manage while I go to the post office?"

Millie chuckled and placed a hand over her swollen stomach. "I'm with child, not injured."

He watched her move slowly to the shop door. No matter what she said he would worry until she was safely delivered and they held their new baby in their arms. How he wished he had the rest of the money he'd earned from Teetulpa – but he assumed that was long gone. It wouldn't have guaranteed her life, but at least it would have made things more comfortable. It would be a tight squeeze in his father's house once the baby arrived.

Joseph moved off towards the post office. A young native woman pushed a large perambulator over the rough road with a child holding on each side.

"Hello, Mr Joe."

"Mary, hello. I didn't recognise you at first. You're … taller."

Mary gave him one of her shy smiles. "Thinner you mean. I don't eat so much these days and chasing after the publican's children keeps me busier than Esther ever did."

"I hope they're treating you well, Mary."

"Very well. I like it here in Hawker. I still see my mother and father, and sounds like Joe's enjoying the work at Smith's Ridge."

"He is. Binda's flat out between watching him there and William at Wildu Creek. Reckons they both need lots more learning yet."

Mary lowered her eyes. "How is Robert?"

"Making good progress. He's almost running again and no more headaches."

The children at Mary's legs began poking each other.

"I better keep going, Mr Joe."

"Nice to see you, Mary. You know you're always welcome at Wildu Creek."

She nodded and moved off.

Joseph kept walking. There were several new buildings since he'd last been to Hawker. The big rain they'd had and follow-up rains since had inspired confidence. Evidently the whole state had benefited from the heavens opening up.

Joseph pushed open the post office door and waited his turn at the counter. He was sending a telegram to the farmer agisting the last of his stock to let him know he was coming to shift them home and he would pay his outstanding accounts when he arrived. It would be a very lean year from now until their wool cheque came.

The postmaster took down the details and Joseph handed over his money. It was extravagant but a letter might not reach them before he did. As he turned to leave the postmaster called him back.

"Did your friend find you, Mr Baker?"

Joseph frowned. "My friend?"

"Big man, dark hair, bushy beard, easy laugh."

Joseph's spirits leapt. It sounded like Hegarty but it had been nearly five months since Joseph had left him his gold, surely he was long gone with the money.

"Which way did he go?"

"East, I sent him."

Joseph spun on his heel and grabbed the door.

"I didn't know you were in town," the postmaster called after him. "I gave him directions to Wildu Creek."

William paused in the doorway of the stables and looked around. There was movement at the other end of the low stone building. He moved towards the young woman patting the neck of a horse. Her red curls were pulled back from her face and caught in a bun at the back of her head, the rest of her hair flowed over her shoulders, complementing the tan jacket she wore, far better than any brooch or flower.

"I thought I saw you come in here."

Georgina looked around and smiled with her lips but not her eyes. "Hello, William." She went on patting the horse. "Saying my goodbyes to Dusty. I'm on my way back to school for another term."

"Time goes quickly. You'll be back soon enough." William could see she was sad to leave her horse. He wasn't sure how to help her feel better.

"Time certainly does. I hear your family is back at Smith's Ridge."

"We've taken back the lease."

"Good on you." Her hand was soft and warm on his arm. "I only ever met Mr Aldridge once but I didn't take to him. Not that I should speak ill of the dead."

"Georgina!"

She jumped away from William at her father's bellow. "I must go. It was very nice to see you again, William."

"And you."

She smiled and her pretty face lit up. Then she turned and hurried away. She was silhouetted a moment in the door frame and then she was gone.

William put a hand to his arm where Georgina's had rested. His insides had gone to mush at her touch. Then he remembered the ribbon in his pocket. He pulled out the crumpled paper bag and looked inside at the neatly folded emerald green satin. Each time he came to Hawker he slipped it in his pocket in the hope of meeting Georgina and the one time he did he forgot all about it. He folded the bag and slid it safely back in his pocket. The day seemed a little less bright as he stepped outside and headed back to the main street.

He found Millie by the wagon outside Mr Garrat's shop.

"Have you seen your father?" She asked as soon as he reached her.

"No." William shook his head, his thoughts still with Georgina.

"Millie, William." They both looked around at Joseph hurrying towards them, beckoning wildly. "Leave the cart. We'll come back for it later." He slipped one arm through Millie's. "There's someone I want you both to meet."

"Who is it?" Millie asked.

"You will see." Joseph patted her hand and gave William a wild grin.

They were headed towards the hotel. Even though he had seen little evidence of it since his father had returned from the goldfields, William wondered if his father had been drinking.

Joseph led them through the front door and along a hall to the rooms at the back. He stopped in front of one of the doors and knocked. A huge man opened the door. He looked from Joseph to

Millie and then to William. His eyes twinkled as his face opened wide in a grin. "Come in." He stepped back from the door. The room was narrow and cell-like. William couldn't see how the three of them would fit with the large occupant already taking up so much space.

His father led Millie to the little iron bed and patted a place for her to sit. William squeezed past the big man who closed the door behind him. There was a washbasin on a stand and a small cupboard by the bed but that was all there was in the way of furnishings which was just as well.

Joseph spoke up. "Millie, William, this is my very good friend, Hegarty."

The big man took Millie's small hand in his. "It's wonderful to meet you at last. And you William." Hegarty let go of Millie's hand and shook William's with a firm grip. "I've heard a lot about you."

"And we about you, Mr Hegarty." Millie gave him one of her big smiles

"I'm sorry it's taken so long. I've just explained to Joseph that my partner, Peterson, got sidetracked to Sydney. He's found a woman and good luck to him. I spent some time there and then took sick, ended up weak as a baby." He turned to Joseph. "You must have all but given up on me."

"You're here now." Joseph's grin hadn't left his face. He looked from Millie to William. "Hegarty's brought my share of the gold money. It's far more than I imagined." He pulled Millie to her feet and hugged her. "You can buy whatever you like."

Millie looked up at him. "I have everything I need, Joseph."

"There's something else." Hegarty reached into his pocket and pulled out a familiar pouch.

"My lucky rock." Joseph extended his hand and Hegarty dropped the pouch into it.

"A very lucky rock as it turns out. It's a diamond."

That night they made camp at the first creek as they often did. Joseph was tired but he knew his thoughts wouldn't let him sleep easily. William had already retired to his swag under the wagon. Joseph watched Millie put some wood on the fire. She had made a bed for them in some softer soil on the other side of the fire. She turned, silhouetted against the light from the flames, and he could see the huge bulge that was their baby. He took two steps, wrapped his arms around her and drew her close, her back against his stomach, his hands cradling their child. He felt Millie draw in a deep breath.

"It's a beautiful night."

Joseph looked up. There were no clouds and the vastness of the starry night spread out above him like a velvet blanket covered in tiny twinkling candles. In his arms was the woman he loved and there would be a new child soon.

"This is where we were camped when I told you I loved you." He bent down and kissed her cheek. "I am the luckiest man alive."

"I am glad you think so, Joseph."

He smiled as he felt the baby move beneath his hands.

Millie placed her hands over his and leaned her head against his neck. "This is a busy baby. Thank goodness I will have Esther and Violet to help me look after it."

"In that case I hope it's two babies or those two will tear it apart fighting over who's to hold it next."

Millie's soft laugh mingled with the crackle of the fire. A spray of sparks shot into the air in a small fire show and were gone.

"Mr Hegarty has been a good friend."

"I'm glad you like him, especially since he's going to work with us for a while."

"It sounds like he's lonely without his friend Mr Peterson."

"They've worked together a long time."

Millie reached her hand over her shoulder and patted his pocket. "And he brought your lucky rock back."

"All this time I've been carrying a diamond around in my pocket." Joseph chuckled. "Well, a rock with diamond in it anyway."

"It's the one you found when you met my brother isn't it?"

"Yes. I found it on the edge of that permanent waterhole high in the hills beyond Smith's Ridge."

"My family's country."

Joseph recalled the day he found the rock, the day he thought was his last. The rugged country at the back of Smith's Ridge held much beauty and many secrets. He was glad he had control over what happened there. Yardu may not like him but better to have his son-in-law managing the land he camped on rather than a man like Ellis Prosser.

Millie twisted her bulky frame in his arms and looked up at him with her big dark eyes. "Will you tell anyone else about the diamond?"

"No, my love. Like you say we have everything we need."

William knew about the diamond and Hegarty and Millie and he would tell his father of course but he would tell no-one else. Life on the goldfields had been enough to show him the craziness of men when they thought they could be rich. He didn't want that madness to spoil their land and their lives. The gold he had found would set them up for a brighter future. He would leave the diamonds alone and perhaps Yardu and his people could continue in peace in the rugged hills. He hoped so. It was the best he could do for his native family.

Millie stretched up and kissed him. Her eyes shone. With her stomach pressed to his he could feel the push and kick of their baby. He pulled her close and looked up at the vast spread of stars twinkling overhead. One flashed, a green streak. It shot across the sky and was lost on the horizon.

Joseph smiled. He had all the luck he needed right here in his arms.

Author's Note

Most of the people and places in this story are fictitious, however I have included real places, for example the town of Hawker, and some of the well-documented people who lived there such as the local doctor and head teacher.

This is a work of fiction so the historians amongst you may find I've been a little flexible with dates and elaborated on real events. It's all in the name of creating a work of fiction and having the plot make sense.

Whilst I have researched widely on the life and times I have discovered there are often conflicting reports on some major events and activities. I have, I hope, used this to my advantage to bring the period to life with a little manipulation on my part and yet with authenticity. Thus any mistakes are my own.

Acknowledgements

The acknowledgements are sometimes the hardest words to write. So many people support me in my writing journey and I appreciate that kindness no matter how small.

I will begin with a huge thank you to the dedicated and savvy team at Harlequin Australia. Michelle Laforest, Cristina Lee and Sue Brockhoff thank you for championing my books. To Jo Mackay and Annabel Blay, the dynamic duo, what would I do without you? Your support and feedback is invaluable and an extra big thank you to Annabel for your editorial work. The entire team at Harlequin are very kind and gracious, from the proofer Laurie Ormond – didn't I make her work – to the sales team and all in between. I am indebted to the effort that is put in to come up with the covers. Romina Panetta and the design crew do a wonderful job. Adam Van Rooijen, thank you and your team for great marketing ideas. So many hands at Harlequin have brought this book forth. You are all fabulous. Thank you.

To fellow writers across this land and over the seas who have understood my highs and lows and encouraged over the air waves, my grateful thanks. It's so good to know such a wonderful cross section of talented people who are so willing to share.

I am very lucky to have a local bookshop. Thank you to all at Meg's Bookshop and in particular Margie Arnold for such wonderful encouragement and support with getting my books out to readers. I also want to thank the many other bookshops around the country who've kindly hosted my signings and promoted my books. If you are fortunate enough to have a local bookshop please support them.

Then there are the libraries, what fantastic people work in them bringing authors and their books to readers. It's also amazing how each one is so unique and adaptive to the needs of their communities. Libraries are also a great place to research and in particular my thanks to Janet Johnstone at Moonta Community Library and Rosie Luckcraft at Hawker Community Library for helping me find some of those tricky titles I needed.

Little writing would get done without the support of friends and family. Thanks and love to you all but specially to my grown up children and their partners for help which comes in all kinds of ways from beta reading to a smiley face from afar when I need one. I am so very blessed.

To my husband, Daryl, who keeps everything running, I am forever grateful that you are my number one. My love always.

Finally to all of you wonderful readers who enjoy my books. Thanks for coming along to events to say hello or dropping me a line. I am very appreciative of your warmth and for every cheery smile and message. It makes the often lonely writer's desk a brighter place. My grateful thanks to you all … and yes, I'm still writing.